W9-ACS-767

Black Beauty

~

Black Beauty

~

Anna Sewell

Illustrated by
**Cecil Aldin
and Glenn Steward**

Sebastian Kelly

This edition published by
Sebastian Kelly

Produced by Anness Publishing Limited
Hermes House, 88-89 Blackfriars Road, London SE1 8HA

ISBN 1 84081 353 9

Printed and bound in the E.C

Contents

1	My Early Home	9
2	The Hunt	13
3	My Breaking In	17
4	Birtwick Park	21
5	A Fair Start	25
6	Liberty	29
7	Ginger	31
8	Ginger's Story Continued	35
9	Merrylegs	39
10	A Talk in the Orchard	43
11	Plain Speaking	49
12	A Stormy Day	53
13	The Devil's Trade-mark	57
14	James Howard	61
15	The Old Ostler	65
16	The Fire	69
17	John Manly's Talk	73
18	Going for the Doctor	77
19	Only Ignorance	81
20	Joe Green	85
21	The Parting	89
22	Earlshall	93
23	A Strike for Liberty	97
24	The Lady Anne	101
25	Reuben Smith	107
26	How it Ended	111
27	Ruined, and Going Downhill	115
28	A Job Horse and his Drivers	119
29	Cockneys	123
30	A Thief	129
31	A Humbug	133
32	A Horse Fair	137
33	A London Cab Horse	141
34	An Old War Horse	145
35	Jerry Barker	151
36	The Sunday Cab	157

37 The Golden Rule   163

38 Dolly and a Real Gentleman   167

39 Seedy Sam   171

40 Poor Ginger   175

41 The Butcher   177

42 The Election   181

43 A Friend in Need   183

44 Old Captain and his Successor   187

45 Jerry's New Year   191

46 Jakes and the Lady   197

47 Hard Times   201

48 Farmer Thoroughgood and Grandson Willie   205

49 My Last Home   209

Colour
Illustrations

"The new bit was very painful, and I reared up suddenly."
  (Chapter Seven.)

Then the boy got off and gave him a hard thrashing.
  (Chapter Thirteen.)

"I saw James coming through the smoke, leading Ginger."
  (Chapter Sixteen.)

The wheels stuck fast in the stiff mud of some deep ruts.
  (Chapter Twenty.)

York promptly set himself flat on her head to prevent her
  struggling. (Chapter Twenty-Three.)

A horse fair . . . "There was a great deal of bargaining,
  running up and beating down." (Chapter Thirty-Two.)

"Without a master or friend, I was alone on that great
  slaughter ground." (Chapter Thirty-Four.)

"I was driven every day for a week or so." (Chapter
  Forty-Nine.)

CHAPTER ONE

MY EARLY HOME

~

The first place that I can well remember was a large pleasant meadow with a pond of clear water in it. Some shady trees leaned over it, and rushes and waterlilies grew at the deep end. Over the hedge one one side we looked into a ploughed field, and on the other we looked over a gate at our master's house, which stood by the roadside; at the top of the meadow was a plantation of fir trees, and at the bottom a running brook overhung by a steep bank.

Whilst I was young I lived upon my mother's milk, as I could not eat grass. In the daytime I ran by her side, and at night I lay down close by her. When it was hot, we used to stand by the pond in the shade of the trees, and when it was cold, we had a nice warm shed near the plantation.

As soon as I was old enough to eat grass, my mother used to go out to work in the daytime, and came back in the evening.

There were six young colts in the meadow besides me; they were older than I was; some were nearly as large as grown-up horses. I used to run with

them, and had great fun; we used to gallop all together round and round
the field, as hard as we could go. Sometimes we had rather rough play, for
they would frequently bite and kick as well as gallop.

One day, when there was a good deal of kicking, my mother whinnied
to me to come to her, and then she said:

"I wish you to pay attention to what I am going to say to you. The colts
who live here are very good colts, but they are cart-horse colts, and, of
course, they have not learned manners. You have been well bred and well
born; your father has a great name in these parts, and your grandfather won
the cup two years at the Newmarket races; your grandmother had the
sweetest temper of any horse I ever knew, and I think you have never seen
me kick or bite. I hope you will grow up gentle and good, and never learn
bad ways; do your work with a good will, lift your feet up well when you
trot, and never bite or kick, even in play."

I have never forgotten my mother's advice; I knew she was a wise old
horse, and our master thought a great deal of her. Her name was Duchess,
but he often called her Pet.

Our master was a good, kind man. He gave us good food, good lodging,
and kind words; he spoke as kindly to us as he did to his little children. We
were all fond of him, and my mother loved him very much. When she saw
him at the gate she would neigh with joy, and trot up to him. He would
pat and stroke her, and say, "Well, old Pet, and how is your little Darkie?"
I was a dull black so he called me Darkie; then he would give me a piece of
bread, which was very good, and sometimes he brought a carrot for my
mother. All the horses would come to him, but I think we were his
favourites. My mother always took him to the town on a market day in a
light gig.

There was a ploughboy, Dick, who sometimes came into our field to
pluck blackberries from the hedge. When he had eaten all he wanted, he
would have what he called fun with the colts, throwing stones and sticks at
them to make them gallop. We did not much mind him, for we could
gallop off; but sometimes a stone would hit and hurt us.

One day he was at this game, and did not know that the master was in
the next field; but he was there, watching what was going on: over the
hedge he jumped in a snap, and catching Dick by the arm, he gave him
such a box on the ear as made him roar with the pain and surprise. As soon

as we saw the master, we trotted up nearer to see what went on.

"Bad boy!" he said, "bad boy! to chase the colts. This is not the first time, nor the second, but it shall be the last; there – take your money and go home, I shall not want you on my farm again." So we never saw Dick any more. Old Daniel, the man who looked after the horses, was just as gentle as our master, so we were well off.

CHAPTER TWO

THE HUNT

~

Before I was two years old, a circumstance happened which I have never forgotten. It was early in the spring; there had been a little frost in the night, and a light mist still hung over the plantations and meadows. I and the other colts were feeding at the lower part of the field when we heard, quite in the distance, what sounded like the cry of dogs. The oldest of the colts raised his head, pricked his ears, and said, "There are the hounds!" and immediately cantered off followed by the rest of us to the upper part of the field, where we could look over the hedge and see several fields beyond. My mother and an old riding horse of our master's were also standing near, and seemed to know all about it.

"They have found a hare," said my mother, "and if they come this way we shall see the hunt."

And soon the dogs were all tearing down the field of young wheat next to ours. I never heard such a noise as they made. They did not bark, nor howl, nor whine, but kept on a "yo! yo, o, o! yo, o, o!" at the top of their voices. After them came a number of men on horseback, some of them in green coats, all galloping as fast as they could. The old horse snorted and looked eagerly after them, and we young colts wanted to be galloping with them, but they were soon away into the fields lower down; here it seemed as if they had come to a stand; the dogs left off barking, and ran about every way with their noses to the ground.

"They have lost the scent," said the old horse; "perhaps the hare will get off."

"What hare?" I said.

"Oh; I don't know *what* hare; likely enough it may be one of our own hares out of the plantation; any hare they can find will do for the dogs and men to run after"; and before long the dogs began their "yo! yo, o, o!" again, and back they came all together at full speed, making straight for our meadow at the part where the high bank and hedge overhang the brook.

"Now we shall see the hare," said my mother; and just then a hare, wild with fright, rushed by and made for the plantation. On came the dogs; they burst over the bank, leapt the stream, and came dashing across the field, followed by the huntsmen. Six or eight men leaped their horses clean over, close upon the dogs. The hare tried to get through the fence; it was too thick, and she turned sharp round to make for the road, but it was too late; the dogs were upon her with their wild cries; we heard one shriek, and that was the end of her. One of the huntsmen rode up and whipped off the dogs, who would soon have torn her to pieces. He held her up by the leg, torn and bleeding, and all the gentlemen seemed well pleased.

As for me, I was so astonished that I did not at first see what was going on by the brook; but when I did look, there was a sad sight; two fine horses were down, one was struggling in the stream, and the other was groaning on the grass. One of the riders was getting out of the water covered with mud, the other lay quite still.

"His neck is broken," said my mother.

"And serve him right too," said one of the colts.

I thought the same, but my mother did not join with us.

"Well, no," she said, "you must not say that; but though I am an old horse, and have seen and heard a great deal, I never yet could make out why men are so fond of this sport; they often hurt themselves, often spoil good horses, and tear up the fields, and all for a hare or a fox, or a stag, that they could get more easily some other way; but we are only horses, and don't know."

Whilst my mother was saying this we stood and looked on. Many of the riders had gone to the young man; but my master, who had been watching what was going on, was the first to raise him. His head fell back and his arms hung down, and every one looked very serious. There was no noise now; even the dogs were quiet, and seemed to know that something was wrong. They carried him to our master's house. I heard afterwards that it was young George Gordon, the Squire's only son, a fine, tall young man, and the pride of his family.

There was now riding off in all directions to the doctor's, to the farrier's, and, no doubt, to Squire Gordon's, to let him know about his son. When Mr. Bond, the farrier, came to look at the black horse that lay groaning on the grass, he felt him all over, and shook his head; one of his legs was broken. Then someone ran to our master's house and came back with a gun; presently there was a loud bang and a dreadful shriek, and then all was still; the black horse moved no more.

My mother seemed much troubled; she said she had known that horse for years, and that his name was "Rob Roy"; he was a good bold horse, and there was no vice in him. She never would go to that part of the field afterwards.

Not many days after we heard the church bell tolling for a long time; and looking over the gate we saw a long strange black coach that was covered with black cloth and was drawn by black horses; after that came another and another and another, and all were black, while the bell kept tolling, tolling. They were carrying young Gordon to the churchyard to bury him. He would never ride again. What they did with Rob Roy I never knew; but 'twas all for one little hare.

CHAPTER THREE

MY BREAKING IN

~

I was now beginning to grow handsome; my coat had grown fine and soft, and was bright black. I had one white foot, and a pretty white star on my forehead. I was thought very handsome; my master would not sell me till I was four years old; he said lads ought not to work like men, and colts ought not to work like horses till they were quite grown up.

When I was four years old, Squire Gordon came to look at me. He examined my eyes, my mouth, and my legs; he felt them all down; and then I had to walk and trot and gallop before him; he seemed to like me, and said, "When he has been well broken in, he will do very well." My master said he would break me in himself, as he should not like me to be frightened or hurt, and he lost no time about it, for the next day he began.

Every one may not know what breaking in is, therefore I will describe it. It means to teach a horse to wear a saddle and bridle and to carry on his back a man, woman, or child; to go just the way they wish, and to go quietly. Besides this, he has to learn to wear a collar, a crupper, and a breeching, and to stand still whilst they are put on; then to have a cart or a chaise fixed behind him, so that he cannot walk or trot without dragging it after him: and he must go fast or slow, just as the driver wishes. He must never start at what he sees, nor speak to other horses, nor bite, nor kick, nor have any will of his own; but always do his master's will, even though he may be very tired or hungry; but the worst of all is, when his harness is once on, he may neither jump for joy nor lie down for weariness. So you see this breaking in is a great thing.

I had, of course, long been used to a halter and a headstall, and to be led about in the field and lanes quietly, but now I was to have a bit and a bridle; my master gave me some oats as usual, and after a good deal of coaxing, he got the bit into my mouth, and the bridle fixed, but it was a nasty thing! Those who have never had a bit in their mouths cannot think how bad it feels; a great piece of cold, hard steel as thick as a man's finger to be pushed into one's mouth, between one's teeth and over one's tongue, with the ends coming out at the corner of your mouth, and held fast there by straps over your head, under your throat, round your nose, and under your chin; so that no way in the world can you get rid of the nasty, hard thing; it is very bad! yes, very bad! at least I thought so, but I knew my mother always wore one when she went out, and all horses did when they were grown up; and so, what with the nice oats, and what with my master's pats, kind words, and gentle ways, I got to wear my bit and bridle.

Next came the saddle, but that was not half so bad; my master put it on my back very gently, whilst old Daniel held my head; he then made the girths fast under my body, patting and talking to me all the time; then I had a few oats, then a little leading about, and this he did every day till I began to look for the oats and the saddle. At length, one morning my master got on my back and rode me round the meadow on the soft grass. It certainly did feel queer; but I must say I felt rather proud to carry my master, and as he continued to ride me a little every day, I soon became accustomed to it.

The next unpleasant business was putting on the iron shoes; that too was very hard at first. My master went with me to the smith's forge, to see that I was not hurt or got any fright. The blacksmith took my feet in his hand one after the other and cut away some of the hoof. It did not pain me, so I stood still on three legs till he had done them all. Then he took a piece of iron the shape of my foot and clapped it on, and drove some nails through the shoe quite into my hoof so that the shoe was firmly on. My feet felt very stiff and heavy, but in time I got used to it.

And now having got so far, my master went on to break me to harness; there were more new things to wear. First, a stiff heavy collar just on my neck, and a bridle with great sidepieces against my eyes, called blinkers, and blinkers indeed they were, for I could not see on either side, but only straight in front of me; next there was a small saddle with a nasty stiff strap that went right under my tail; that was the crupper. I hated the crupper – to have my long tail doubled up and poked through that strap was almost as bad as the bit. I never felt more like kicking, but of course I could not kick such a good master, and so in time I got used to everything, and could do my work as well as my mother.

I must not forget to mention one part of my training, which I have always considered a very great advantage. My master sent me for a fortnight to a neighbouring farmer's, who had a meadow which was skirted on one side by the railway. Here were some sheep and cows, and I was turned in amongst them.

I shall never forget the first train that ran by. I was feeding quietly near the pales which separated the meadow from the railway when I heard a strange sound at a distance, and before I knew whence it came – with a rush and a clatter, and a puffing out of smoke – a long black train of something flew by, and was gone almost before I could draw my breath. I turned and galloped to the farther side of the meadow as fast as I could go, and there I stood snorting with astonishment and fear. In the course of the day many other trains went by, and sometimes made an awful shriek and groan before they stopped. I thought it very dreadful, but the cows went on eating very quietly, and hardly raised their heads as the black frightful thing came puffing and grinding past.

For the first few days I could not feed in peace; but as I found that this terrible creature never came into the field, or did me any harm, I began to disregard it, and very soon I cared as little about the passing of a train as the cows and sheep did.

Since then I have seen many horses much alarmed and restive at the sight or sound of a steam-engine; but thanks to my good master's care, I am as fearless at railway stations as in my own stable.

Now if any one wants to break in a young horse well, that is the way.

My master often drove me in double harness with my mother because she was steady, and could teach me how to go better than a strange horse. She told me the better I behaved the better I should be treated, and that it was wisest always to do my best to please my master; "but," said she, "there are a great many kinds of men: there are good, thoughtful men like our master that any horse may be proud to serve; but there are bad, cruel men who never ought to have a horse or dog to call their own. Beside, there are a great many foolish men, vain, ignorant, and careless, who never trouble themselves to think; these spoil more horses than all, just for want of sense; they don't mean it, but they do it for all that. I hope you will fall into good hands; but a horse never knows who may buy him, or who may drive him; it is all a chance for us, but still I say, do your best, wherever it is, and keep up your good name."

CHAPTER FOUR

BIRTWICK PARK

~

At this time I used to stand in the stable, and my coat was brushed every day till it shone like a rook's wing. It was early in May when there came a man from Squire Gordon's, who took me away to the Hall. My master said, "Good-bye, Darkie; be a good horse, and always do your best." I could not say "good-bye", so I put my nose into his hand; he patted me kindly, and I left my first home. As I lived some years with Squire Gordon, I may as well tell something about the place.

Squire Gordon's Park skirted the village of Birtwick. It was entered by a large iron gate, at which stood the first lodge, and then you trotted along on a smooth road between clumps of large old trees; then another lodge and another gate which brought you to the house and the gardens. Beyond this lay the home paddock, the old orchard, and the stables. There was accommodation for many horses and carriages; but I need only describe the stable into which I was taken; this was very roomy, with four good stalls; a large swinging window opened into the yard, which made it pleasant and airy.

The first stall was a large square one, shut in behind with a wooden gate; the others were common stalls, good stalls, but not nearly so large; it had a low rack for hay and a low manger for corn; it was called a loose box, because the horse that was put into it was not tied up, but left loose to do as he liked. It is a great thing to have a loose box.

Into this fine box the groom put me; it was clean, sweet, and airy. I never was in a better box than that, and the sides were not so high but that I could see all that went on through the iron rails that were at the top.

He gave me some very nice oats, he patted me, spoke kindly, and then went away.

When I had eaten my corn I looked round. In the stall next to mine stood a little fat grey pony, with a thick mane and tail, a very pretty head, and a pert little nose.

I put my head up to the iron rails at the top of my box, and said, "How do you do? What is your name?"

He turned round as far as his halter would allow, held up his head, and said, "My name is Merrylegs; I am very handsome. I carry the young ladies on my back, and sometimes I take our mistress out in the low chair. They think a great deal of me, and so does James. Are you going to live next door to me in the box?"

I said "Yes."

"Well, then," he said, "I hope you are good-tempered; I do not like any one next door who bites."

Just then a horse's head looked over from the stall beyond; the ears were laid back, and the eye looked rather ill-tempered. This was a tall chestnut mare, with a long handsome neck; she looked across to me, and said:

"So it is you who have turned me out of my box; it is a very strange thing for a colt like you to come and turn a lady out of her own home."

"I beg your pardon," I said, "I have turned no one out; the man who brought me put me here, and I had nothing to do with it; and as to my being a colt, I am turned four years old, and am a grown-up horse; I never had words yet with horse or mare, and it is my wish to live at peace."

"Well," she said, "we shall see; of course I do not want to have words with a young thing like you." I said no more.

In the afternoon when she went out, Merrylegs told me all about it.

"The thing is this," said Merrylegs, "Ginger has a bad habit of biting and snapping; that is why they call her Ginger, and when she was in the loose box she used to snap very much. One day she bit James in the arm and made it bleed, and so Miss Flora and Miss Jessie, who are very fond of me, were afraid to come into the stable. They used to bring me nice things to eat – an apple or a carrot, or a piece of bread, but after Ginger stood in that box they dare not come, and I missed them very much. I hope they will now come again, if you do not bite or snap."

I told him I never bit anything but grass, hay, and corn, and could not think what pleasure Ginger found in it.

"Well, I don't think she does find pleasure," said Merrylegs; "it is just a bad habit; she says no one was ever kind to her, and why should she not bite? Of course it is a very bad habit; but I am sure, if all she says be true, she must have been very ill-used before she came here. John does all he can to please her, and James does all he can, and our master never uses a whip if a horse acts right; so I think she might be good-tempered here; you see," he said, with a wise look, "I am twelve years old; I know a great deal, and I can tell you there is not a better place for a horse all round the country than this. John is the best groom that ever was – he has been here fourteen years; and you never saw such a kind boy as James is, so that it is all Ginger's own fault that she did not stay in that box."

CHAPTER FIVE

A FAIR START

~

The name of the coachman was John Manly; he had a wife and one little child, and they lived in the coachman's cottage, very near the stables.

The next morning he took me into the yard and gave me a good grooming, and just as I was going into my box with my coat soft and bright, the Squire came in to look at me, and seemed pleased. "John," he said, "I meant to have tried the new horse this morning, but I have other business. You may as well take him a round after breakfast; go by the common and the Highwood, and back by the watermill and the river; that will show his paces."

"I will, sir," said John. After breakfast he came and fitted me with a bridle. He was very particular in letting out and taking in the straps, to fit my head comfortably; then he brought a saddle, but it was not broad enough for my back; he saw it in a minute and went for another, which fitted nicely. He rode me first slowly, then a trot, then a canter, and when we were on the common he gave me a light touch with his whip, and we had a splendid gallop.

"Ho, ho! my boy," he said as he pulled me up, "you would like to follow the hounds, I think."

As we came back through the Park we met the Squire and Mrs. Gordon walking; they stopped, and John jumped off.

"Well, John, how does he go?"

"First-rate, sir," answered John; "he is as fleet as a deer, and has a fine spirit, too; but the lightest touch of the rein will guide him. Down at the end of the common we met one of those travelling carts hung all over with baskets, rugs, and such like; you know, sir, many horses will not pass those carts quietly; he just took a good look at it, and then went on as quiet and pleasant as could be. They were shooting rabbits near the Highwood, and a gun went off close by; he pulled up a little and looked, but did not stir a step to right or left. I just held the rein steady and did not hurry him, and it's my opinion he has not been frightened or ill-used while he was young."

"That's well," said the Squire; "I will try him myself to-morrow."

The next day I was brought up for my master. I remembered my mother's counsel and my good old master's, and I tried to do exactly what he wanted me to do. I found he was a very good rider, and thoughtful for his horse too. When we came home the lady was at the hall door as he rode up.

"Well, my dear," she said, "how do you like him?"

"He is exactly what John said," he replied; "a pleasanter creature I never wished to mount. What shall we call him?"

"Would you like Ebony?" said she; "he is as black as ebony."

"No, not Ebony."

"Will you call him Blackbird, like your uncle's old horse?"

"No; he is far handsomer than old Blackbird ever was."

"Yes," she said, "he is really quite a beauty, and he has such a sweet good-tempered face and such a fine intelligent eye – what do you say to calling him Black Beauty?"

"Black Beauty – why, yes, I think that is a very good name. If you like, it shall be his name," and so it was.

When John went into the stable he told James that master and mistress had chosen a good sensible English name for me that meant something, not like Marengo, or Pegasus, or Abdullah. They both laughed, and James said, "If it was not for bringing back the past, I should have named him Rob Roy, for I never saw two horses more alike."

"That's no wonder," said John, "didn't you know that Farmer Grey's old Duchess was the mother of them both?"

I had never heard that before. And so poor Rob Roy who was killed at that hunt was my brother! I did not wonder that my mother was so troubled. It seems that horses have no relations; at least, they never know each other after they are sold.

John seemed very proud of me: he used to make my mane and tail almost as smooth as a lady's hair, and he would talk to me a great deal; of course I did not understand all he said, but I learned more and more to know what he *meant*, and what he wanted me to do. I grew very fond of him, he was so gentle and kind, he seemed to know just how a horse feels, and when he cleaned me he knew the tender places, and the ticklish places; when he brushed my head he went as carefully over my eyes as if they were his own, and never stirred up any ill temper.

James Howard, the stable boy, was just as gentle and pleasant in his way, so I thought myself well off. There was another man who helped in the yard, but he had very little to do with Ginger and me.

A few days after this I had to go out with Ginger in the carriage. I wondered how we should get on together; but, except for laying her ears back when I was led up to her, she behaved very well. She did her work honestly, and did her full share, and I never wish to have a better partner in double harness. When we came to a hill, instead of slackening her pace, she would throw her weight right into the collar, and pull away straight up. We had both the same sort of courage at our work, and John had oftener to hold us in than to urge us forward; he never had to use the whip with either of us; then our paces were much the same, and I found it very easy to keep step with her when trotting, which made it pleasant; and master always liked it when we kept step well, and so did John. After we had been out two or three times together we grew quite friendly and sociable, which made me feel very much at home.

As for Merrylegs, he and I soon became great friends; he was such a cheerful, plucky, good-tempered little fellow that he was a favourite with every one, and especially with Miss Jessie and Flora, who used to ride him about in the orchard, and have fine games with him and their little dog Frisky.

Our master had two other horses that stood in another stable. One was Justice, a roan cob, used for riding, or for the luggage cart; the other was an old brown hunter, named Sir Oliver; he was past work now, but was a great favourite with the master, who gave him the run of the Park; he sometimes did a little light carting on the estate, or carried one of the young ladies when they rode out with their father; for he was very gentle, and could be trusted with a child as well as Merrylegs. The cob was a strong, well-made, good-tempered horse, and we sometimes had a little chat in the paddock, but of course I could not be so intimate with him as with Ginger, who stood in the same stable.

CHAPTER SIX

LIBERTY

~

I was quite happy in my new place, and if there was one thing that I missed it must not be thought I was discontented; all who had to do with me were good, and I had a light airy stable and the best of food. What more could I want? Why, liberty! For three years and a half of my life I had had all the liberty I could wish for, but now, week after week, month after month, and no doubt year after year, I must stand up in a stable night and day except when I am wanted, and then I must be just as steady and quiet as any old horse who has worked twenty years. Straps here and straps there, a bit in my mouth, and blinkers over my eyes. Now I am not complaining, for I know it must be so. I only mean to say that for a young horse full of strength and spirits who has been used to some large field or plain, where he can fling up his head, and toss up his tail and gallop away at full speed, then round and back again with a snort to his companions — I say it is hard never to have a bit more liberty to do as you like. Sometimes, when I have had less exercise than usual, I have felt so full of life and spring that when John has taken me out to exercise I really could not keep quiet; do what I would, it seemed as if I must jump, or dance, or prance, and many a good shake I know I must have given him, specially at the first; but he was always good and patient.

"Steady, steady, my boy," he would say; "wait a bit, and we'll have a good swing, and soon get the tickle out of your feet." Then, as soon as we were out of the village, he would give me a few miles at a spanking trot, and then bring me back as fresh as before, only clear of the fidgets, as he called them. Spirited horses, when not enough exercised, are often called skittish when it is only play; and some grooms will punish them, but our John did not; he knew it was only high spirits. Still, he had his own ways of making me understand by the tone of his voice or the touch of the rein. If he was very serious and quite determined, I always knew it by his voice, and that had more power with me than anything else, for I was very fond of him.

I ought to say that sometimes we had our liberty for a few hours; this used to be on fine Sundays in the summer-time. The carriage never went out on Sundays, because the church was not far off.

It was a great treat to us to be turned out into the home paddock or the old orchard. The grass was so cool and soft to our feet; the air so sweet, and the freedom to do as we liked was so pleasant – to gallop, to lie down and roll over on our backs, or to nibble the sweet grass. Then it was a very good time for talking as we stood together under the shade of the large chestnut tree.

CHAPTER SEVEN

GINGER

~

One day when Ginger and I were standing alone in the shade we had a great deal of talk; she wanted to know all about my bringing up and breaking in, and I told her.

"Well," said she, "if I had had your bringing up I might have had as good a temper as you, but now I don't believe I ever shall."

"Why not?" I said.

"Because it has been all so different with me," she replied. "I never had any one, horse or man, that was kind to me, or that I cared to please; for, in the first place, I was taken from my mother as soon as I was weaned, and put with a lot of other young colts: none of them cared for me, and I cared for none of them. There was no kind master like yours to look after me, and talk to me, and bring me nice things to eat. The man that had the care of us never gave me a kind word in my life. I do not mean that he ill-used me, but that he did not care for us one bit further than to see that we had plenty to eat and shelter in the winter.

"A footpath ran through our field, and very often the great boys passing through would fling stones to make us gallop. I was never hit, but one fine young colt was badly cut in the face, and I should think it would be a scar for life. We did not care for them, but, of course, it made us more wild, and we settled it in our minds that boys were our enemies.

"We had very good fun in the free meadows, galloping up and down and chasing each other round and round the field, then standing still under the shade of the trees. But when it came to breaking in, that was a bad time for me; several men came to catch me, and when at last they closed me in at one corner of the field, one caught me by the forelock, another caught me by the nose, and held it so tight I could hardly draw my breath; then another took my under jaw in his hard hand and wrenched my mouth open, and so by force they got on the halter and the bar into my mouth; then one dragged me along by the halter, another flogging behind, and this was the first experience I had of men's kindness. It was all force; they did not give me a chance to know what they wanted. I was high bred and had a great deal of spirit, and was very wild, no doubt, and gave them, I dare say, plenty of trouble, but then it was dreadful to be shut up in a stall day after day instead of having my liberty, and I fretted and pined and wanted to get loose. You know yourself it's bad enough when you have a kind master and plenty of coaxing, but there was nothing of that sort for me.

"There was one – the old master, Mr. Ryder, who, I think, could soon have brought me round, and could have done anything with me, but he had given up all the hard part of the trade to his son and to another experienced man, and he only came at times to oversee. His son was a strong, tall, bold man; they called him Samson, and he used to boast that he had never found a horse that could throw him. There was no gentleness in him as there was in his father, but only hardness – a hard voice, a hard eye, a hard hand; and I felt from the first that what he wanted was to wear all the spirit out of me, and just make me into a quiet, humble, obedient piece of horse-flesh. 'Horse-flesh!' Yes, that is all that he thought about," and Ginger stamped her foot as if the very thought of him made her angry.

She went on: "If I did not do exactly what he wanted he would get put out, and make me run round with that long rein in the training field till he had tired me out. I think he drank a good deal, and I am quite sure that the oftener he drank the worse it was for me. One day he had worked me hard in every way he could, and when I laid down I was tired and miserable and angry; it all seemed so hard. The next morning he came for me early, and ran me round again for a long time. I had scarcely had an hour's rest when he came again for me with a saddle and bridle and a new kind of bit. I could never quite tell how it came about; he had only just mounted me on the training ground when something I did put him out of temper and he chucked me hard with the rein. The new bit was very painful, and I reared up suddenly, which angered him still more, and he began to flog me. I felt my whole spirit set against him, and I began to kick, and plunge, and rear as I had never done before, and we had a regular fight. For a long time he stuck to the saddle and punished me cruelly with his whip and spurs, but my blood was thoroughly up, and I cared for nothing he could do if only I could get him off. At last, after a terrible struggle, I threw him off backwards. I heard him fall heavily on the turf, and without looking behind me I galloped off to the other end of the field; there I turned round and saw my persecutor slowly rising from the ground and going into the stable. I stood under an oak tree and watched, but no one came to catch me. The time went on, the sun was very hot, the flies swarmed round me, and settled on my bleeding flanks where the spurs had dug in. I felt hungry, for I had not eaten since the early morning, but there was not enough grass in that meadow for a goose to live on. I wanted to lie down and rest, but with the saddle strapped tightly on there was no comfort, and there was not a drop of water to drink. The afternoon wore on, and the sun got low. I saw the other colts led in, and I knew they were having a good feed.

"At last, just as the sun went down, I saw the old master come out with a sieve in his hand. He was a very fine old gentleman with quite white hair, but his voice was what I should know him by amongst a thousand. It was not high, nor yet low, but full, and clear, and kind, and when he gave orders it was so steady and decided that every one knew, both horses and men, that he expected to be obeyed. He came quietly along, now and then shaking the oats about that he had in the sieve, and speaking cheerfully and gently to me, 'Come along, lassie, come along, lassie; come along, come along.' I stood still and let him come up; he held the oats to me and I began to eat without fear; his voice took all my fear away. He stood by, patting and stroking me whilst I was eating, and seeing the clots of blood on my side, he seemed very vexed; 'Poor lassie! it was a bad business, a bad business!'

then he quietly took the rein and led me to the stable. Just at the door stood Samson. I laid my ears back and snapped at him. 'Stand back,' said the master, 'and keep out of her way; you've done a bad day's work for this filly.' He growled out something about a vicious brute. 'Hark ye,' said the father, 'a bad-tempered man will never make a good-tempered horse. You've not learned your trade yet, Samson.' Then he led me into my box, took off the saddle and bridle with his own hands, and tied me up; then he called for a pail of warm water and a sponge, took off his coat, and while the stableman held the pail, he sponged my sides a good while so tenderly that I was sure he knew how sore and bruised they were. 'Whoa! my pretty one,' he said; 'stand still, stand still.' His very voice did me good, and the bathing was very comfortable. The skin was so broken at the corners of my mouth that I could not eat the hay – the stalks hurt me. He looked closely at it, shook his head, and told the man to fetch a good bran mash and put some meal into it. How good that mash was, and so soft and healing to my mouth! He stood by all the time I was eating, stroking me and talking to the man. 'If a high-mettled creature like this,' said he, 'can't be broken in by fair means, she will never be good for anything.'

"After that he often came to see me, and when my mouth was healed, the other breaker, Job they called him, went on training me. He was steady and thoughtful, and I soon learned what he wanted."

CHAPTER EIGHT

GINGER'S STORY CONTINUED

~

The next time that Ginger and I were together in the paddock she told me about her first place. "After my breaking in," she said, "I was bought by a dealer to match another chestnut horse. For some weeks he drove us together, and then we were sold to a fashionable gentleman, and were sent up to London. I had been driven with a bearing rein by the dealer, and I hated it worse than anything else; but in this place we were reined far tighter; the coachman and his master thinking we looked more stylish so. We were often driven about in the Park and other fashionable places. You who never had a bearing rein on don't know what it is, but I can tell you it is dreadful.

"I like to toss my head about, and hold it as high as any horse; but fancy now yourself, if you tossed your head up high and were obliged to hold it there, and that for hours together, not able to move it at all, except with a jerk still higher, your neck aching till you did not know how to bear it. Beside that, to have two bits instead of one; and mine was a sharp one; it hurt my tongue and my jaw, and the blood from my tongue coloured the froth that kept flying from my lips, as I chafed and fretted at the bits and rein; it was worse when we had to stand by the hour waiting for our mistress at some grand party or entertainment; and if I fretted or stamped with impatience the whip was laid on. It was enough to drive one mad."

"Did not your master take any thought for you?" I said.

"No," said she, "he only cared to have a stylish turnout, as they call it; I think he knew very little about horses; he left that to his coachman, who told him I had an irritable temper; that I had not been well broken to the bearing rein, but I should soon get used to it; but *he* was not the man to do it, for when I was in the stable, miserable and angry, instead of being soothed and quieted by kindness, I got only a surly word or a blow. If he had been civil I would have tried to bear it. I was willing to work, and ready to work hard too; but to be tormented for nothing but their fancies angered me. What right had they to make me suffer like that? Besides the soreness in my mouth and the pain in my neck, it always made my windpipe feel bad, and if I had stopped there long I know it would have spoiled my breathing; but I grew more and more restless and irritable – I could not help it – and I began to snap and kick when anyone came to harness me. For this the groom beat me, and one day as they had just buckled us into the carriage, and were straining my head up with that rein, I began to plunge and kick with all my might. I soon broke a lot of harness, and kicked myself clear; so that was an end of that place.

"After this I was sent to Tattersalls to be sold. Of course I could not be warranted free from vice, so nothing was said about that. My handsome appearance and good paces soon brought a gentleman to bid for me, and I was bought by another dealer; he tried me in all kinds of ways and with different bits, and soon found out what I could bear. At last he drove me quite without a bearing rein, and then sold me as a perfectly quiet horse to a gentleman in the country; he was a good master, and I was getting on very well, but his old groom left him and a new one came. This man was as hard-tempered and hard-handed as Samson; he always spoke in a rough, impatient voice, and if I did not move in the stall the moment he wanted me, he would hit me above the hocks with his stable broom or the fork, whichever he might have in his hand. Everything he did was rough, and I began to hate him; he wanted to make me afraid of him, but I was too high-mettled for that; and one day when he had aggravated me more than usual I bit him, which of course put him in a great rage, and he began to hit me about the head with a riding whip. After that he never dared to come into my stall again, either my heels or my teeth were ready for him, and he knew it. I was quite quiet with my master, but, of course, he listened to what the man said, and so I was sold again.

"The same dealer heard of me, and said he thought he knew one place where I should do well. ''Twas a pity,' he said, 'that such a fine horse should go to the bad for want of a real good chance,' and the end of it was that I came here not long before you did; but I had then made up my mind that men were my natural enemies, and that I must defend myself. Of course it is very different here, but who knows how long it will last? I wish I could think about things as you do; but I can't after all I have gone through."

"Well," I said, "I think it would be a real shame if you were to bite or kick John or James."

"I don't mean to," she said, "while they are good to me. I did bite James once, pretty sharp, but John said, 'Try her with kindness,' and instead of punishing me as I expected, James came to me with his arm bound up, and brought me a bran mash and stroked me; and I have never snapped at him since, and I won't either."

I was sorry for Ginger, but, of course, I knew very little then, and I thought most likely she made the worst of it; however, I found that as the weeks went on, she grew much more gentle and cheerful, and had lost the watchful, defiant look that she used to turn on any strange person who came near her; and one day James said, "I do believe that mare is getting fond of me; she quite whinnied after me this morning when I had been rubbing her forehead."

"Aye, aye, Jim, 'tis the Birtwick balls," said John; "she'll be as good as Black Beauty by and by; kindness is all the physic she wants, poor thing!" Master noticed the change too, and one day when he got out of the carriage and came to speak to us as he often did, he stroked her beautiful neck, "Well, my pretty one, well, how do things go with you now? You are a good bit happier than when you came to us, I think."

She put her nose up to him in a friendly, trustful way while he rubbed it gently.

"We shall make a cure of her, John," he said.

"Yes, sir; she's wonderfully improved; she's not the same creature that she was. It's the Birtwick balls, sir," said John, laughing.

This was a little joke of John's. He used to say that a regular course of the Birtwick horse-balls would cure almost any vicious horse. These balls, he said, were made up of patience and gentleness, firmness and petting, one pound of each to be mixed up with half a pint of common sense and given to the horse every day.

CHAPTER NINE

MERRYLEGS

~

M r. Blomefield, the Vicar, had a large family of boys and girls; sometimes they used to come and play with Miss Jessie and Flora. One of the girls was as old as Miss Jessie; two of the boys were older, and there were several little ones. When they came there was plenty of work for Merrylegs, for nothing pleased them so much as getting on him by turns and riding him all about the orchard and the home paddock, and this they would do by the hour together.

One afternoon he had been out with them a long time, and when James brought him in and put on his halter, he said:

"There, you rogue, mind how you behave yourself, or we shall get into trouble."

"What have you been doing, Merrylegs?" I asked.

"Oh!" said he, tossing his little head, "I have only been giving those young people a lesson; they did not know when they had had enough, nor when I had had enough, so I just pitched them off backwards. That was the only thing they could understand."

"What?" said I, "you threw the children off? I thought you did know better than that! Did you throw Miss Jessie or Miss Flora?"

He looked very much offended, and said:

"Of course not; I would not do such a thing for the best oats that ever came into the stable. Why, I am as careful of our young ladies as the master could be, and as for the little ones, it is I who teach them to ride. When they seem frightened or a little unsteady on my back, I go as smooth and quiet as old pussy when she is after a bird; and when they are all right, I go on again faster, you see, just to use them to it; so don't you trouble yourself preaching to me; I am the best friend and the best riding master those children have. It is not them; it is the boys. Boys," said he, shaking his mane, "are quite different; they must be broken in, as we were broken in when we were colts, and just be taught what's what. The other children had ridden me about for nearly two hours, and then the boys thought it was their turn; and so it was, and I was quite agreeable. They rode me by turns, and I galloped them about up and down the fields and all about the orchard for a good hour. They had each cut a great hazel stick for a riding whip, and laid it on a little too hard; but I took it in good part, till at last I thought we had had enough, so I stopped two or three times by way of a hint. Boys, you see, think a horse or pony is like a steam-engine or a thrashing machine, and can go on as long and as fast as they please; they never think that a pony can get tired, or have any feelings; so as the one who was whipping me could not understand, I just rose up on my hind legs and let him slip off behind – that was all; he mounted me again, and I did the same. Then the other boy got up, and as soon as he began to use his stock I laid him on the grass, and so on, till they were able to understand, that was all. They are not bad boys; they don't wish to be cruel. I like them very well; but, you see, I had to give them a lesson. When they brought me to James and told him, I think he was very angry to see such big sticks. He said they were only fit for drovers or gipsies, and not for young gentlemen."

"If I had been you," said Ginger, "I would have given those boys a good kick, and that would have given them a lesson."

"No doubt you would," said Merrylegs, "but then I am not quite such a fool (begging your pardon) as to anger our master or make James ashamed of me; besides, those children are under my charge when they are riding; I tell you they are entrusted to me. Why, only the other day I heard our master say to Mrs. Blomefield, 'My dear madam, you need not be anxious about the children, my old Merrylegs will take as much care of them as you or I could. I assure you I would not sell that pony for any money, he is so perfectly good-tempered and trustworthy.' And do you think I am such an ungrateful brute as to forget all the kind treatment I have had here for five years, and all the trust they place in me, and turn vicious because a couple of ignorant boys used me badly? No! no! You never had a good place where they were kind to you, and so you don't know, and I'm sorry for you, but I can tell you good places make good horses. I wouldn't vex our people for anything; I love them, I do," said Merrylegs, and he gave a low "ho, ho, ho" through his nose, as he used to do in the morning when he heard James's footstep at the door.

"Besides," he went on, "if I took to kicking, where should I be? Why, sold off in a jiffy, and no character, and I might find myself slaved about under a butcher's boy, or worked to death at some seaside place where no one cared for me, except to find out how fast I could go, or be flogged along in some cart with three or four great men in it going out for a Sunday spree, as I have often seen in the place I lived in before I came here. No," said he, shaking his head, "I hope I shall never come to that."

CHAPTER TEN

A TALK IN THE ORCHARD

~

Ginger and I were not of the regular tall carriage horse breed; we had more of the racing blood in us. We stood about fifteen and a half hands high; we were therefore just as good for riding as we were for driving, and our master used to say that he disliked either horse or man that could do but one thing; and as he did not want to show off in London parks, he preferred a more active and useful kind of horse. As for us, our greatest pleasure was when we were saddled for a riding party; the master on Ginger, the mistress on me, and the young ladies on Sir Oliver and Merrylegs. It was so cheerful to be trotting and cantering all together that it always put us in high spirits. I had the best of it, for I always carried the mistress; her weight was little, her voice was sweet, and her hand was so light on the rein that I was guided almost without feeling it.

Oh! if people knew what a comfort to horses a light hand is, and how it keeps a good mouth and a good temper, they surely would not chuck, and drag, and pull at the rein as they often do. Our mouths are so tender that

43

where they have not been spoiled or hardened with bad or ignorant treatment, they feel the slightest movement of the driver's hand, and we know in an instant what is required of us. My mouth had never been spoiled, and I believe that was why the mistress preferred me to Ginger, although her paces were certainly quite as good. She used often to envy me, and said it was all the fault of breaking in, and the gag bit in London, that her mouth was not so perfect as mine; and then old Sir Oliver would say, "There, there! don't vex yourself; you have the greatest honour; a mare that can carry a tall man of our master's weight, with all your spring and sprightly action, does not need to hold her head down because she does not carry the lady. We horses must take things as they come, and always be contented and willing so long as we are kindly used."

I had often wondered how it was that Sir Oliver had such a very short tail; it really was only six or seven inches long, with a tassel of hair hanging from it; and on one of our holidays in the orchard I ventured to ask him by what accident it was that he had lost his tail. "Accident!" he snorted, with a fierce look; "it was no accident! It was a cruel, shameful, cold-blooded act! When I was young I was taken to a place where these cruel things were done; I was tied up, and made fast so that I could not stir, and they then came and cut off my long beautiful tail, through the flesh, and through the bone, and took it away."

"How dreadful!" I exclaimed.

"Dreadful! Ah! it was dreadful. But it was not only the pain, though that was terrible, and lasted a long time; it was not only the indignity of having my best ornament taken from me, though that was bad; but it was this, how could I ever brush the flies off my sides and my hind legs any more? You who have tails just whisk the flies off without thinking about it, and you can't tell what a torment it is to have them settle upon you and sting and sting, and have nothing in the world to lash them off with. I tell you it is a lifelong wrong, and a lifelong loss; but, thank Heaven, they don't do it now."

"What did they do it for then?" said Ginger.

"For fashion!" said the old horse with a stamp of his foot. "For fashion! if you know what that means; there was not a well-bred young horse in my time that had not his tail docked in that shameful way, just as if the good God that made us did not know what we wanted and what looked best."

"I suppose it is fashion that makes them strap our heads up with those horrid bits that I was tortured with in London," said Ginger.

"Of course it is," said he. "To my mind, fashion is one of the wickedest things in the world. Now look, for instance, at the way they serve dogs, cutting off their tails to make them look plucky, and shearing up their pretty little ears to a point to make them look sharp, forsooth! I had a dear friend once, a brown terrier – 'Skye', they called her. She was so fond of me that she never would sleep out of my stall; she made her bed under the manger, and there she had a litter of five as pretty little puppies as need be; none were drowned, for they were a valuable kind, and how pleased she was with them! And when they got their eyes open and crawled about it was a real pretty sight; but one day the man came and took them all away; I thought he might be afraid I should tread on them. But it was not so. In the evening poor Skye brought them back again, one by one in her mouth; not the happy little things that they were, but bleeding and crying pitifully; they had all had a piece of their tails cut off, and the soft flap of their pretty little ears was cut quite off. How their mother licked them, and how troubled she was, poor thing! I never forgot it. They healed in time, and they forgot the pain, but the nice soft flap that of course was intended to protect the delicate part of their ears from dust and injury was gone for ever. Why don't they cut their own children's ears into points to make them look sharp? Why don't they cut the end off their noses to make them look plucky? One would be just as sensible as the other. What right have they to torment and disfigure God's creatures?"

Sir Oliver, though he was so gentle, was a fiery old fellow, and what he said was all so new to me and so dreadful that I found a bitter feeling toward men rise up in my mind that I had never had before. Of course Ginger was much excited; she flung up her head with flashing eyes and distended nostrils, declaring that men were both brutes and blockheads.

"Who talks about blockheads?" said Merrylegs, who just came up from the old apple tree, where he had been rubbing himself against the low branch; "who talks about blockheads? I believe that is a bad word."

"Bad words were made for bad things," said Ginger, and she told him what Sir Oliver had said. "It is all true," said Merrylegs sadly, "and I've seen that about the dogs over and over again where I lived first; but we won't talk about it here. You know that master, and John, and James are always good to us, and talking against men in such a place as this doesn't seem fair or grateful, and you know there are good masters and good grooms besides ours, though, of course, ours are the best." This wise speech of good little Merrylegs, which we knew was quite true, cooled us all down, especially Sir Oliver, who was dearly fond of his master; and to turn the subject I said, "Can any one tell me the use of blinkers?"

"No!" said Sir Oliver shortly, "because they are no use."

"They are supposed," said Justice in his calm way, "to prevent horses from shying and starting and getting so frightened as to cause accidents."

"Then what is the reason they do not put them on riding horses; especially on ladies' horses?" said I.

"There is no reason at all," said he quietly, "except the fashion; they say that a horse would be so frightened to see the wheels of his own cart or carriage coming behind him that he would be sure to run away, although, of course, when he is ridden, he sees them all about him if the streets are crowded. I admit they do sometimes come too close to be pleasant, but we don't run away; we are used to it, and understand it, and if we never had blinkers put on we should never want them; we should see what was there, and know what was what, and be much less frightened than by only seeing bits of things that we can't understand."

Of course there may be some nervous horses who have been hurt or frightened when they were young, and may be the better for them, but as I never was nervous, I can't judge.

"I consider," said Sir Oliver, "that blinkers are dangerous things in the night; we horses can see much better in the dark than man can, and many an accident would never have happened if horses might have had the full use of their eyes. Some years ago, I remember, there was a hearse with two horses returning one dark night, and just by Farmer Sparrow's house, where the pond is close to the road, the wheels went too near the edge, and the hearse was overturned into the water; both of the horses were drowned, and the driver hardly escaped. Of course, after this accident a stout white rail was put up that might be easily seen, but if those horses had not been partly blinded they would of themselves have kept farther from the edge, and no accident would have happened. When our master's carriage was over-turned, before you came here, it was said that if the lamp on the left side had not gone out John would have seen the great hole that the roadmakers had left; and so he might, but if old Colin had not had blinkers on, he would have seen it, lamp or no lamp, for he was far too knowing an old horse to run into danger. As it was, he was very much hurt, the carriage was broken, and how John escaped nobody knew."

"I should say," said Ginger, curling her nostril, "that these men, who are so wise, had better give orders that in future all foals should be born with their eyes set just in the middle of their foreheads instead of on the side; they always think they can improve upon Nature and mend what God has made."

Things were getting rather sore again, when Merrylegs held up his knowing little face, and said, "I'll tell you a secret; I believe John does not approve of blinkers; I heard him talking with master about it one day. The master said that 'if horses had been used to them, it might be dangerous in some cases to leave them off', and John said he thought it would be a good thing if all colts were broken in without blinkers, as was the case in some foreign countries; so let us cheer up, and have a run to the other end of the orchard; I believe the wind has blown down some apples, and we might just as well eat them as the slugs."

Merrylegs could not be resisted, so we broke off our long conversation, and got up our spirits by munching some very sweet apples which lay scattered on the grass.

PLAIN SPEAKING

~

The longer I lived at Birtwick, the more proud and happy I felt at having such a place. Our master and mistress were respected and loved by all who knew them; they were good and kind to everybody and everything; not only men and women, but horses and donkeys, dogs and cats, cattle and birds; there was no oppressed or ill-used creature that had not a friend in them, and their servants took the same tone. If any of the village children were known to treat any creature cruelly, they soon heard about it from the Hall.

The Squire and Farmer Grey had worked together, as they said, for more than twenty years, to get bearing reins on the cart horses done away with, and in our parts you seldom saw them; but sometimes if mistress met a heavily-laden horse, with his head strained up, she would stop the carriage and get out, and reason with the driver in her sweet serious voice, and try to show him how foolish and cruel it was.

I don't think any man could withstand our mistress. I wish all ladies

49

were like her. Our master, too, used to come down very heavy sometimes. I remember he was riding me towards home one morning when we saw a powerful man driving towards us in a light pony chaise, with a beautiful little bay pony with slender legs and a high-bred sensitive head and face. Just as we came to the Park gates, the little thing turned towards them; the man, without word or warning, wrenched the creature's head round with such a force and suddenness that he nearly threw it on its haunches; recovering itself, it was going on when he began to lash it furiously; the pony plunged forward, but the strong, heavy hand held the pretty creature back with force almost enough to break its jaw, whilst the whip still cut into him. It was a dreadful sight to me, for I knew what fearful plain it gave that delicate little mouth; but master gave me the word, and we were up with him in a second.

"Sawyer," he cried in a stern voice, "is that pony made of flesh and blood?"

"Flesh and blood and temper," he said; "he's too fond of his own will, and that won't suit me." He spoke as if he was in a strong passion; he was a builder who had often been to the Park on business.

"And do you think," said master sternly, "that treatment like this will make him fond of your will?"

"He had no business to make that turn: his road was straight on!" said the man roughly.

"You have often driven that pony up to my place," said master; "it only shows the creature's memory and intelligence; how did he know that you were not going there again? But that has little to do with it. I must say, Mr. Sawyer, that more unmanly, brutal treatment of a little pony it was never my painful lot to witness; and by giving way to such passions you injure your own character as much, nay more, than you injure your horse, and remember, we shall all have to be judged according to our works, whether they be towards man or towards beast."

Master rode me home slowly, and I could tell by his voice how the thing had grieved him. He was just as free to speak to gentlemen of his own rank as to those below him; for another day, when we were out, we met a Captain Langley, a friend of our master's; he was driving a splendid pair of greys in a kind of brake. After a little conversation the Captain said:

"What do you think of my new team, Mr. Gordon? You know you are the judge of horses in these parts, and I should like your opinion."

The master backed me a little, so as to get a good view of them. "They are an uncommonly handsome pair," he said, "and if they are as good as they look, I am sure you need not wish for anything better; but I see you got hold of that pet scheme of yours for worrying your horses and lessening their power."

"What do you mean," said the other, "the bearing reins? Oh, ah! I know that's a hobby of yours; well, the fact is I like to see my horses hold their heads up."

"So do I," said master, "as well as any man, but I don't like to see them *held up*; that takes all the shine out of it. Now, you are a military man, Langley, and no doubt like to see your regiment look well on parade, 'Heads up', and all that; but you would not take much credit for your drill if all your men had their heads tied to a backboard! It might not be much harm on parade, except to worry and fatigue them, but how would it be in a bayonet charge against the enemy, when they want the free use of every muscle, and all their strength thrown forward? I would not give much for their chance of victory, and it is just the same with horses; you fret and worry their tempers and decrease their power; you will not let them throw their weight against their work, and so they have to do too much with their joints and muscles, and, of course, it wears them up faster. You may depend upon it, horses were intended to have their heads free, as free as men's are; and if we could act a little more according to common sense, and a good deal less according to fashion, we should find many things work easier; besides, you know as well as I, that if a horse makes a false step, he has much less chance of recovering himself if his head and neck are fastened back. And now," said the master, laughing, "I have given my hobby a good trot out, can't you make up your mind to mount him too, Captain? Your example would go a long way."

"I believe you are right in theory," said the other, "and that's rather a hard hit about the soldiers, but – well – I'll think about it," and so they parted.

CHAPTER TWELVE

A STORMY DAY

~

One day late in the autumn my master had a long journey to go on business. I was put into the dogcart, and John went with his master. I always liked to go in the dogcart, it was so light, and the high wheels ran along so pleasantly. There had been a great deal of rain, and now the wind was very high, and blew the dry leaves across the road in a shower. We went along merrily till we came to the toll-bar, and the low wooden bridge. The river banks were rather high, and the bridge, instead of rising, went across just level, so that in the middle, if the river was full, the water would be nearly up to the woodwork and planks; but as there were good substantial rails on each side, people did not mind it.

The man at the gate said the river was rising fast, and he feared it would be a bad night. Many of the meadows were under water, and in one low part of the road the water was half-way up to my knees; the bottom was good, and master drove gently, so it was no matter.

When we got to the town, of course, I had a good wait, but as the master's business engaged him a long time, we did not start for home till rather late in the afternoon. The wind was then much higher, and I heard the master say to John he had never been out in such a storm; and so I thought, as we went along the skirts of a wood, where the great branches were swaying about like twigs, and the rushing sound was terrible.

"I wish we were well out of this wood," said my master.

"Yes, sir," said John; "it would be rather awkward if one of these branches came down upon us."

The words were scarcely out of his mouth when there was a groan, a crack, and a splitting sound, and tearing, crashing down amongst the other trees came an oak, torn up by the roots, and it fell right across the road just before us. I will never say I was not frightened, for I was. I stopped still, and I believe I trembled; of course I did not turn round or run away; I was not brought up to that. John jumped out and was in a moment at my head.

"That was a very near touch," said my master. "What's to be done now?"

"Well, sir, we can't drive over that tree nor get round it; there will be nothing for it but to go back to the four crossways, and that will be a good six miles before we get round to the wooden bridge again; it will make us late, but the horse is fresh."

So back we went, and round by the crossroads; but by the time we got to the bridge it was very nearly dark, we could just see that the water was over the middle of it; but as that happened sometimes when the floods were out, master did not stop. We were going along at a good pace, but the moment my feet touched the first part of the bridge I felt sure there was something wrong. I dare not go forward, and I made a dead stop. "Go on, Beauty," said my master, and he gave me a touch with the whip. But I dare not stir; he gave me a sharp cut; I jumped, but I dare not go forward.

"There's something wrong, sir," said John, and he sprang out of the dogcart and come to my head and looked all about. He tried to lead me forward, "Come on, Beauty, what's the matter?" Of course I could not tell him, but I knew very well that the bridge was not safe.

Just then the man at the toll-gate on the other side ran out of the house, tossing a torch about like one mad. "Hoy, hoy, hoy, halloo, stop!" he cried.

"What's the matter?" shouted my master.

"The bridge is broken in the middle and part of it is carried away; if you come on you'll be into the river."

"Thank God!" said my master.

"You Beauty!" said John, and took the bridle and gently turned me round to the right-hand road by the river side.

The sun had set some time, the wind seemed to have lulled off after that furious blast which tore up the tree. It grew darker and darker, stiller and stiller. I trotted quietly along, the wheels hardly making a sound on the soft road. For a good while neither master nor John spoke, and then master began in a serious voice. I could not understand much of what they said, but I found they thought if I had gone on, as the master wanted me, most likely the bridge would have given way under us, and horse, chaise, master, and man would have fallen into the river; and as the current was flowing very strongly, and there was no light and no help at hand, it was more than likely we should all have been drowned. Master said God had given men reason by which they could find out things for themselves, but He had given animals knowledge which did not depend on reason, and which was much more prompt and perfect in its way, and by which they had often saved the lives of men. John had many stories to tell of dogs and horses, and the wonderful things they had done; he thought people did not value their animals half enough, nor make friends of them as they ought to do. I am sure he makes friends of them if ever a man did.

At last we came to the Park gates, and found the gardener looking out for us. He said that mistress had been in a dreadful way ever since dark, fearing some accident had happened, and that she had sent James off on Justice, the roan cob, towards the wooden bridge to make inquiry after us.

We saw a light at the hall door and at the upper windows, and as we came up, mistress ran out, saying, "Are you really safe, my dear? Oh! I have been so anxious, fancying all sorts of things. Have you had an accident?"

"No, my dear; but if your Black Beauty had not been wiser than we were, we should all have been carried down the river at the wooden bridge." I heard no more, as they went into the house, and John took me to the stable. Oh! what a good supper he gave me that night, a good bran mash and some crushed beans with my oats, and such a thick bed of straw, and I was glad of it, for I was tired.

CHAPTER THIRTEEN

THE DEVIL'S TRADE-MARK

~

One day when John and I had been out on some business of our master's, and were returning gently on a long straight road, at some distance we saw a boy trying to leap a pony over a gate; the pony would not take the leap, and the boy cut him with the whip, but he only turned off on one side; he whipped him again, but the pony turned off on the other side. Then the boy got off and gave him a hard thrashing, and knocked him about the head; then he got up again and tried to make him leap the gate, kicking him all the time shamefully, but still the pony refused. When we were nearly at the spot, the pony put down his head and threw up his heels and sent the boy neatly over into a broad quickset hedge, and with the rein dangling from his head he set off home at a full gallop. John laughed out quite loud. "Served him right," he said.

"Oh! oh! oh!" cried the boy as he struggled about amongst the thorns; "I say, come and help me out."

"Thank ye," said John, "I think you are quite in the right place, and maybe a little scratching will teach you not to leap a pony over a gate that is too high for him," and so with that John rode off. "It may be," said he to himself, "that young fellow is a liar as well as a cruel one; we'll just go home by Farmer Bushby's, Beauty, and then if anybody wants to know, you and I can tell 'em, ye see"; so we turned off to the right, and soon came up to the stackyard and within sight of the house. The farmer was hurrying out into the road, and his wife was standing at the gate, looking very frightened.

"Have you seen my boy?" said Mr. Bushby as we came up. "He went out an hour ago on my black pony, and the creature is just come back without a rider."

"I should think, sir," said John, "he had better be without a rider, unless he can be ridden properly."

"What do you mean?" said the farmer.

"Well, sir, I saw your son whipping, and kicking, and knocking that good little pony about shamefully because he would not leap a gate that was too high for him. The pony behaved well, sir, and showed no vice; but at last he just threw up his heels, and tipped the young gentleman into the thorn hedge; he wanted me to help him out; but I hope you will excuse me, sir, I did not feel inclined to do so. There's no bones broken, sir; he'll only get a few scratches. I love horses, and it roiles me to see them badly used; it is a bad plan to aggravate an animal till he uses his heels; the first time is not always the last."

During this time the mother began to cry, "Oh! my poor Bill, I must go and meet him, he must be hurt."

"You had better go into the house, wife," said the farmer; "Bill wants a lesson about this, and I must see that he gets it; this is not the first time nor the second that he has ill-treated that pony, and I shall stop it. I am much obliged to you, Manly. Good evening."

So we went on, John chuckling all the way home, then he told James about it, who laughed, and said, "Serve him right. I knew that boy at school; he took great airs on himself because he was a farmer's son; he used to swagger about and bully the little boys; of course, we elder ones would not have any of that nonsense, and let him know that in the school and the playground farmers' sons and labourers' sons were all alike. I well remember one day just before afternoon school, I found him at the large window catching flies and pulling off their wings. He did not see me, and I gave him a box on the ears that laid him sprawling on the floor. Well, angry as I was, I was almost frightened, he roared and bellowed in such a style. The boys rushed in from the playground, and the master ran in from the road to see who was being murdered. Of course I said fair and square at once what I had done, and why; then I showed the master the poor flies, some crushed and some crawling about helpless, and I showed him the wings on the window-sill. I never saw him so angry before; but as Bill was still howling and whining, like the coward that he was, he did not give him any more punishment of that kind, but set him up on a stool for the rest of the afternoon, and said that he should not go out to play for that week. Then he talked to all the boys very seriously about cruelty, and said how hard-hearted and cowardly it was to hurt the weak and the helpless; but what stuck in my mind was this, he said that cruelty was the devil's own trade-mark, and if we saw any one who took pleasure in cruelty, we might know who he belonged to, for the devil was a murderer from the beginning, and a tormentor to the end. On the other hand, where we saw people who loved their neighbours, and were kind to man and beast, we might know that was God's mark, for 'God is Love'."

"Your master never taught you a truer thing," said John; "there is no religion without love, and people may talk as much as they like about their religion, but if it does not teach them to be good and kind to man and beast, it is all a sham — all a sham, James, and it won't stand when things come to be turned inside out and put down for what they are."

JAMES HOWARD

~

One morning early in December John had just led me into my box after my daily exercise, and was strapping my cloth on, and James was coming in from the corn chamber with some oats, when the master came into the stable; he looked rather serious, and held an open letter in his hand. John fastened the door of my box, touched his cap, and waited for orders.

"Good morning, John," said the master; "I want to know if you have any complaint to make of James?"

"Complaint, sir? No, sir."

"Is he industrious at his work and respectful to you?"

"Yes, sir; always."

"You never find he slights his work when your back is turned?"

"Never, sir."

"That's well; but I must put another question; have you any reason to suspect that when he goes out with the horses to exercise them, or to take a message, he stops about talking to his acquaintances, or goes into houses where he has no business, leaving the horses outside?"

"No, sir, certainly not, and if anybody has been saying that about James, I don't believe it, and I don't mean to believe it unless I have it fairly proved before witnesses; it's not for me to say who has been trying to take away James's character, but I will say this, sir, that a steadier, pleasanter, honester, smarter fellow I never had in this stable. I can trust his word and I can trust his work; he is gentle and clever with the horses, and I would rather have them in his charge than in that of half the young fellows I know in laced hats and liveries; and whoever wants a character of James Howard," said John, with a decided jerk of his head, "let them come to John Manly."

The master stood all this time grave and attentive, but as John finished his speech a broad smile spread over his face, and looking kindly across at James, who all this time had stood still at the door, he said: "James, my lad, set down the oats and come here; I am very glad to find that John's opinion of your character agrees so exactly with my own. John is a cautious man," he said, with a droll smile, "and it is not always easy to get his opinion about people, so I thought if I beat the bush on this side, the birds would fly out, and I should learn what I wanted to know quickly; so now we will come to business. I have a letter from my brother-in-law, Sir Clifford Williams, of Clifford Hall; he wants me to find him a trustworthy young groom, about twenty or twenty-one, who knows his business. His old coachman, who has lived with him twenty years, is getting feeble, and he wants a man to work with him and get into his ways, who would be able, when the old man was pensioned off, to step into his place. He would have eighteen shillings a week at first, a stable suit, a driving suit, a bedroom over the coach-house, and a boy under him. Sir Clifford is a good master, and if you could get the place, it would be a good start for you. I don't want to part with you, and if you left us I know John would lose his right hand."

"That I should, sir," said John; "but I would not stand in his light for the world."

"How old are you James?" said master.

"Nineteen next May, sir."

"That's young. What do you think, John?"

"Well, sir, it is young; but he is as steady as a man, and is strong and well grown, and though he has not had much experience in driving, he has a light, firm hand, and a quick eye, and he is very careful, and I am quite sure no horse of his will be ruined for want of having his feet and shoes looked after."

"Your word will go the farthest, John," said the master, "for Sir Clifford adds in a postscript, 'If I could find a man trained by your John, I should like him better than any other'; so James, lad, think it over, talk to your mother at dinner-time, and then let me know what you wish."

In a few days after this conversation it was fully settled that James should go to Clifford Hall in a month or six weeks, as it suited his master, and in the meantime he was to get all the practice in driving that could be given to him. I never knew the carriage go out so often before: when the mistress did not go out, the master drove himself in the two-wheeled chaise; but now, whether it was master or the young ladies, or only an errand, Ginger and I were put into the carriage and James drove us. At the first, John rode with him on the box, telling him this and that, and after that James drove alone.

Then it was wonderful what a number of places the master would go to in the city on Saturday, and what queer streets we were driven through. He was sure to go to the railway station just as the train was coming in, and cabs and carriages, carts and omnibuses were all trying to get over the bridge together; that bridge wanted good horses and good drivers when the railway bell was ringing, for it was narrow, and there was a very sharp turn up to the station, where it would not have been at all difficult for people to run into each other if they did not look sharp and keep their wits about them.

CHAPTER FIFTEEN

THE OLD OSTLER

~

After this it was decided by my master and mistress to pay a visit to some friends who lived about forty-six miles from our home, and James was to drive them. The first day we travelled thirty-two miles; there were some long, heavy hills, but James drove so carefully and thoughtfully that we were not at all harassed. He never forgot to put on the drag as we went downhill, nor to take it off at the right place. He kept our feet on the smoothest part of the road, and if the uphill was very long, he set the carriage wheels a little across the road, so as not to run back, and gave us a breathing. All these little things help a horse very much, particularly if he gets kind words into the bargain.

We stopped once or twice on the road, and just as the sun was going down, we reached the town where we were to spend the night. We stopped at the principal hotel, which was in the market-place; it was a very large one; we drove under an archway into a long yard, at the farther end of which were the stables and coach-houses. Two ostlers came to take us out. The head ostler was a pleasant, active little man, with a crooked leg, and a yellow-striped waistcoat. I never saw a man unbuckle harness so quickly as he did, and with a pat and a good word he led me to a long stable, with six or eight stalls in it, and two or three horses. The other man brought Ginger; James stood by whilst we were rubbed down and cleaned.

I was never cleaned so lightly and quickly as by that little old man. When he had done, James stepped up and felt me over, as if he thought I could not be thoroughly done, but he found my coat as clean and smooth as silk.

"Well," he said, "I thought I was pretty quick, and our John quicker still, but you do beat all I ever saw for being quick and thorough at the same time."

"Practice makes perfect," said the crooked little ostler, "and 'twould be a pity if it didn't; forty years' practice, and not perfect! ha, ha! that would be a pity; and as to being quick, why, bless you! that is only a matter of habit; if you get into the habit of being quick, it is just as easy as being slow; easier, I should say; in fact, it don't agree with my health to be hulking about over a job twice as long as it need take. Bless you! I couldn't whistle if I crawled over my work as some folks do! You see, I have been about horses ever since I was twelve years old, in hunting stables and racing stables; and being small, ye see, I was jockey for several years; but at the Goodwood, ye see, the turf was very slippery and my poor Larkspur got a fall, and I broke my knee, and so, of course, I was of no more use there; but I could not live without horses, of course I couldn't, so I took to the hotels, and I can tell ye it is a downright pleasure to handle an animal like this, well bred, well mannered, well cared for; bless ye! I can tell how a horse is treated. Give me the handling of a horse for twenty minutes, and I'll tell you what sort of groom he has had; look at this one, pleasant, quiet, turns about just as you want him, holds up his feet to be cleaned out, or anything else you please to wish; then you'll find another, fidgety, fretty, won't move the right way, or starts across the stall, tosses up his head as soon as you come near him, lays his ears, and seems afraid of you; or else squares about at you with his heels. Poor things! I know what sort of treatment they have had. If they are timid, it makes them start or shy; if they are high-mettled, it makes them vicious or dangerous; their tempers are mostly made when they are young. Bless you! they are like children: train 'em up in the way they should go, as the good Book says, and when they are old they will not depart from it − if they have a chance, that is."

"I like to hear your talk," said James; "that's the way we lay it down at home, at our master's."

"Who is your master, young man? if it be a proper question. I should judge he is a good one from what I see."

"He is Squire Gordon, of Birtwick Park, the other side the Beacon hills," said James.

"Ah! so, so, I have heard tell of him; fine judge of horses, ain't he? The best rider in the county?"

"I believe he is," said James, "but he rides very little now since the poor young master was killed."

"Ah! poor gentleman; I read all about it in the paper at the time; a fine horse killed too, wasn't there?"

"Yes," said James, "he was a splendid creature, brother to this one, and just like him."

"Pity! pity!" said the old man, "'twas a bad place to leap, if I remember; a thin fence at top, a steep bank down to the stream, wasn't it? no chance for a horse to see where he is going. Now, I am for bold riding as much as any man, but still there are some leaps that only a very knowing old huntsman has any right to take; a man's life and a horse's life are worth more than a fox's tail; at least I should say they ought to be."

During this time the other man had finished Ginger and had brought our corn, and James and the old man left the stable together.

CHAPTER SIXTEEN

THE FIRE

~

Later on in the evening a traveller's horse was brought in by the second ostler, and whilst he was cleaning him a young man with a pipe in his mouth lounged into the stable to gossip.

"I say, Towler," said the ostler, "just run up the ladder into the loft and put some hay down into this horse's rack, will you? Only lay down your pipe."

"All right," said the other, and went up through the trapdoor; and I heard him step across the floor overhead and put down the hay. James came in to look at us the last thing, and then the door was locked.

I cannot say how long I had slept, nor what time in the night it was, but I woke up very uncomfortable, though I hardly knew why. I got up, the air seemed all thick and choking. I heard Ginger coughing, and one of the other horses moved about restlessly; it was quite dark and I could see nothing, but the stable was very full of smoke, and I hardly knew how to breathe.

69

The trapdoor had been left open, and I thought that was the place it came through. I listened and heard a soft rushing sort of noise, and a low crackling and snapping. I did not know what it was, but there was something in the sound so strange that it made me tremble all over. The other horses were now all awake; some were pulling at their halters, others were stamping.

At last I heard steps outside, and the ostler who had put up the traveller's horse burst into the stable with a lantern, and began to untie the horses, and try to lead them out; but he seemed in such a hurry, and so frightened himself that he frightened me still more. The first horse would not go with him; he tried the second and third — they too would not stir. He came to my next and tried to drag me out of the stall by force; of course that was no use. He tried us all by turns and then left the stable.

No doubt we were very foolish, but danger seemed to be all round, and there was nobody we knew to trust in, and all was strange and uncertain. The fresh air that had come in through the open door made it easier to breathe, but the rushing sound overhead grew louder, and as I looked upward, through the bars of my empty rack, I saw a red light flickering on the wall. Then I heard a cry of "Fire" outside, and the old ostler quietly and quickly came in; he got one horse out, and went to another, but the flames were playing round the trapdoor, and the roaring overhead was dreadful.

The next thing I heard was James's voice, quiet and cheery, as it always was.

"Come, my beauties, it is time for us to be off, so wake up and come along." I stood nearest the door, so he came to me first, patting me as he came in.

"Come, Beauty, on with your bridle, my boy; we'll soon be out of this smother." It was on in no time; then he took the scarf off his neck and tied it lightly over my eyes, and patting and coaxing he led me out of the stable. Safe in the yard, he slipped the scarf off my eyes, and shouted, "Here, somebody! take this horse while I go back for the other."

A tall broad man stepped forward and took me, and James darted back into the stable. I set up a shrill whinny as I saw him go. Ginger told me afterwards that whinny was the best thing I could have done for her, for had she not heard me outside, she would never have had courage to come out.

There was much confusion in the yard; the horses being got out of other stables, and the carriages and gigs being pulled out of houses and sheds, lest the flames should spread farther. On the other side the yard, windows were thrown up, and people were shouting all sorts of things; but I kept my eye fixed on the stable door, were the smoke poured thicker than ever, and I could see flashes of red light; presently I heard above all the stir and din a loud clear voice which I knew was master's:

"James Howard! James Howard! are you there?"

There was no answer, but I heard a crash of something falling in the stable, and the next moment I gave a loud joyful neigh, for I saw James coming through the smoke leading Ginger with him; she was coughing violently and he was not able to speak.

"My brave lad!" said master, laying his hand on his shoulder, "are you hurt?"

James shook his head, for he could not yet speak.

"Aye," said the big man who held me, "he is a brave lad, and no mistake."

"And now," said master, "when you have got your breath, James, we'll get out of this place as quickly as we can," and we were moving towards the entry, when from the market-place there came a sound of galloping feet and loud rumbling wheels.

"'Tis the fire engine! the fire engine!" shouted two or three voices, "stand back, make way!" and clattering and thundering over the stones two horses dashed into the yard with the heavy engine behind them. The firemen leaped to the ground; there was no need to ask where the fire was – it was torching up in a great blaze from the roof.

We got out as fast as we could into the broad, quiet market-place; the stars were shining, and except the noise behind us, all was still. Master led the way to a large hotel on the other side, and as soon as the ostler came he said, "James, I must now hasten to your mistress; I trust the horses entirely to you, order whatever you think is needed," and with that he was gone. The master did not run, but I never saw mortal man walk so fast as he did that night.

There was a dreadful sound before we got into our stalls; the shrieks of those poor horses that were left burning to death in the stable – it was very terrible, and made both Ginger and me feel very bad! We, however, were taken in and well done by.

The next morning the master came to see how we were and to speak to James. I did not hear much, for the ostler was rubbing me down, but I could see that James looked very happy, and I thought the master was proud of him. Our mistress had been so much alarmed in the night, that the journey was put off till the afternoon, so James had the morning on hand, and went first to the inn to see about our harness and the carriage, and then to hear more about the fire. When he came back we heard him tell the ostler about it. At first no one could guess how the fire had been caused, but at last a man said he saw Dick Towler go into the stable with a pipe in his mouth, and when he came out he had not one, and went to the tap for another. Then the under ostler said he had asked Dick to go up the ladder to put down some hay, but told him to lay down his pipe first. Dick denied taking the pipe with him, but no one believed him. I remember our John Manly's rule, never to allow a pipe in the stable, and thought it ought to be the rule everywhere.

James said the roof and floor had all fallen in, and that only the black walls were standing; the two poor horses that could not be got out were buried under the burnt rafters and tiles.

CHAPTER SEVENTEEN

JOHN MANLY'S TALK

~

The rest of our journey was very easy, and a little after sunset we reached the house of my master's friend. We were taken into a clean, snug stable; there was a kind coachman, who made us very comfortable, and who seemed to think a good deal of James when he heard about the fire.

"There is one thing quite clear, young man," he said; "your horses know who they can trust. It is one of the hardest things in the world to get horses out of a stable when there is either fire or flood. I don't know why they won't come out, but they won't – not one in twenty."

We stopped two or three days at this place, and then returned home. All went well on the journey; we were glad to be in our own stable again, and John was equally glad to see us.

Before he and James left us for the night, James said, "I wonder who is coming in my place?"

"Little Joe Green at the lodge," said John.

"Little Joe Green! Why, he's a child!"

"He is fourteen and a half," said John.

"But he is such a little chap."

"Yes, he is small, but he is quick, and willing, and kind-hearted too, and then he wishes very much to come, and his father would like it; and I know the master would like to give him the chance. He said, if I thought he would not do, he would look out for a bigger boy; but I said I was quite agreeable to try him for six weeks."

"Six weeks!" said James, "why, it will be six months before he can be of much use! It will make you a deal of work, John."

"Well," said John with a laugh, "work and I are very good friends; I never was afraid of work yet."

"You are a very good man," said James, "I wish I may ever be like you."

"I don't often speak of myself," said John, "but as you are going away from us out into the world, to shift for yourself, I'll just tell you how I look on these things. I was just as old as Joseph when my father and mother died of the fever, within ten days of each other, and left me and my crippled sister, Nelly, alone in the world, without a relation that we could look to for help. I was a farmer's boy, not earning enough to keep myself, much less both of us, and she must have gone to the workhouse, but for our mistress (Nelly calls her her angel, and she has good right to do so). She went and hired a room for her with old widow Mallet, and she gave her knitting and needlework when she was able to do it; and when she was ill she sent her dinners and many nice comfortable things, and was like a mother to her. Then the master, he took me into the stable under old Norman, the coachman that was then. I had my food at the house, and my bed in the loft, and a suit of clothes, and three shillings a week, so that I could help Nelly. Then there was Norman; he might have turned round and said that at his age he could not be troubled with a raw boy from the plough-tail, but he was like a father to me, and took no end of pains with me. When the old man died some years after, I stepped into his place, and now, of course, I have top wages, and can lay by for a rainy day or a sunny day as it may happen, and Nelly is as happy as a bird. So you see, James, I am not the man that should turn up his nose at a little boy and vex a good, kind master. No! no! I shall miss you very much, James, but we shall pull through, and there's nothing like doing a kindness when 'tis put in your way, and I am glad I can do it."

"Then," said James, "you don't hold with that saying, 'Everybody look after himself, and take care of number one'."

"No, indeed," said John, "where should I and Nelly have been if master and mistress and old Norman had only taken care of number one? Why — she in the workhouse and I hoeing turnips! Where would Black Beauty and Ginger have been if you had only thought of number one? Why, roasted to death! No, Jim, no! that is a selfish, heathenish saying whoever uses it, and any man who thinks he has nothing to do but take care of number one, why, it's a pity but what he had been drowned, like a puppy or a kitten, before he got his eyes open, that's what I think," said John, with a very decided jerk of his head.

James laughed at this; but there was a thickness in his voice when he said, "You have been my best friend except my mother; I hope you won't forget me."

"No, lad, no!" said John, "and if ever I can do you a good turn, I hope you won't forget me."

The next day Joe came to the stables to learn all he could before James left. He learned to sweep the stable, to bring in the straw and hay; he began to clean the harness, and helped to wash the carriage. As he was quite too short to do anything in the way of grooming Ginger and me, James taught him upon Merrylegs, for he was to have full charge of him, under John. He was a nice little bright fellow, and always came whistling to his work.

Merrylegs was a good deal put out at being "mauled about," as he said, "by a boy who knew nothing"; but towards the end of the second week he told me confidentially that he thought the boy would turn out well.

At last the day came when James had to leave us; cheerful as he always was, he looked quite down-hearted that morning.

"You see," he said to John, "I am leaving a great deal behind; my mother and Betsy, and you, and a good master and mistress, and then the horses, and my old Merrylegs. At the new place there will not be a soul that I shall know. If it were not that I shall get a higher place, and be able to help my mother better, I don't think I should have made up my mind to it. It is a real pinch, John."

"Aye, James, lad, so it is, but I should not think much of you if you could leave your home for the first time and not feel it; cheer up, you'll make friends there, and if you get on well — as I am sure you will — it will be a fine thing for your mother, and she will be proud enough that you have got into such a good place as that."

So John cheered him up, but every one was sorry to lose James; as for Merrylegs, he pined after him for several days, and went quite off his appetite. So John took him out several mornings with a leading rein, when he exercised me, and trotting and galloping by my side, got up the little fellow's spirits again, and he was soon all right.

Joe's father would often come in and give a little help, as he understood the work, and Joe took a great deal of pains to learn, and John was quite encouraged about him.

GOING FOR THE DOCTOR

~

One night, a few days after James had left, I had eaten my hay and was laid down in my straw fast asleep, when I was suddenly awoke by the stable bell ringing very loud. I heard the door of John's house open, and his feet running up to the Hall. He was back again in no time; he unlocked the stable door, and came in, calling out, "Wake up, Beauty; you must go well now, if ever you did"; and almost before I could think, he had got the saddle on my back and the bridle on my head; he just ran round for his coat, and then took me at a quick trot up to the Hall door. The Squire stood there with a lamp in his hand.

"Now, John," he said, "ride for your life; that is, for your mistress's life; there is not a moment to lose. Give this note to Doctor White; give your horse a rest at the inn, and be back as soon as you can."

John said "Yes, sir", and was on my back in a minute. The gardener who lived at the lodge had heard the bell ring, and was ready with the gate open, and away we went through the Park and through the village and down the hill till we came to the toll-gate. John called very loud and thumped upon the door: the man was soon out and flung open the gate.

"Now," said John, "do you keep your gate open for the Doctor; here's the money," and off we went again.

There was before us a long piece of level road by the river-side; John said to me, "Now, Beauty, do your best", and so I did. I wanted no whip nor spur, and for two miles I galloped as fast as I could lay my feet to the ground; I don't believe that my old grandfather who won the race at Newmarket could have gone faster. When we came to the bridge, John pulled me up a little and patted my neck. "Well done, Beauty! good old fellow," he said. He would have let me go slower, but my spirit was up, and I was off again as fast as before. The air was frosty, the moon was bright, it was very pleasant; we came through a village, then through a dark wood, then uphill, then downhill, till after an eight miles run we came to the town, through the streets and into the market-place. It was all quite still except the clatter of my feet on the stones – everybody was asleep. The church clock struck three as we drew up at Doctor White's door. John rang the bell twice, and then knocked at the door like thunder. A window was thrown up, and Doctor White, in his nightcap, put his head out and said, "What do you want?"

"Mrs. Gordon is very ill, sir; master wants you to go at once; he thinks she will die if you cannot get there – here is a note."

"Wait," he said, "I will come."

He shut the window and was soon at the door.

"The worst of it is," he said, "that my horse has been out all day and is quite done up; my son has just been sent for, and he has taken the other. What is to be done? Can I have your horse?"

"He has come at a gallop nearly all the way, sir, and I was to give him a rest here; but I think my master would not be against it if you think fit, sir."

"All right," he said, "I will soon be ready."

John stood by me and stroked my neck; I was very hot. The doctor came out with his riding whip.

"You need not take that, sir," said John; "Black Beauty will go till he drops. Take care of him, sir, if you can; I should not like any harm to come to him."

"No! no! John," said the doctor, "I hope not", and in a minute we had left John far behind.

I will not tell you about our way back; the doctor was a heavier man than John, and not so good a rider; however, I did my very best. The man at the toll-gate had it open. When we came to the hill the doctor drew me up. "Now, my good fellow," he said, "take some breath." I was glad he did, for I was nearly spent, but that breathing helped me on, and soon we were in the Park, Joe was at the lodge gate, my master was at the Hall door, for he had heard us coming. He spoke not a word; the doctor went into the house with him, and Joe led me to the stable. I was glad to get home; my legs shook under me, and I could only stand and pant. I had not a dry hair on my body, the water ran down my legs, and I steamed all over – Joe used to say, like a pot on the fire. Poor Joe! he was young and small, and as yet he knew very little, and his father, who would have helped him, had been sent to the next village; but I am sure he did the very best he knew. He rubbed my legs and my chest, but he did not put any warm cloth on me; he thought I was so hot I should not like it. Then he gave me a pail full of water to drink; it was cold and very good, and I drank it all; then he gave me some hay and some corn, and thinking he had done right, he went away. Soon I began to shake and tremble, and turned deadly cold, my legs ached, my loins ached, and my chest ached, and I felt sore all over. Oh! how I wished for my warm thick cloth as I stood and trembled. I wished for John, but he had eight miles to walk, so I lay down in my straw and tried to go to sleep. After a long while I heard John at the door. I gave a low moan, for I was in great pain. He was at my side in a moment, stooping down by me. I could not tell him how I felt, but he seemed to know it all. He covered me up with two or three warm cloths, and then ran to the house for some hot water; he made me some warm gruel, which I drank, and then I think I went to sleep.

John seemed to be very much put out. I heard him say to himself, over and over again, "Stupid boy! stupid boy! no cloth put on, and I dare say the water was cold too; boys are no good," but Joe was a good boy after all.

I was now very ill; a strong inflammation had attacked my lungs, and I could not draw my breath without pain. John nursed me night and day; he would get up two or three times in the night to come to me; my master, too, often came to see me.

"My poor Beauty," he said one day, "my good horse, you saved your mistress's life, Beauty! yes, you saved her life." I was very glad to hear that, for it seems the doctor had said if we had been a little longer it would have been too late. John told my master he never saw a horse go so fast in his life; it seemed as if the horse knew what was the matter. Of course I did, though John thought not; at least I knew as much as this, that John and I must go at the top of our speed, and that it was for the sake of the mistress.

CHAPTER NINETEEN

ONLY IGNORANCE
~

I do not know how long I was ill. Mr. Bond, the horse doctor, came every day. One day he bled me; John held a pail for the blood; I felt very faint after it, and thought I should die, and I believe they all thought so too.

Ginger and Merrylegs had been moved into the other stable, so that I might be quiet, for the fever made me very quick of hearing; any little noise seemed quite loud, and I could tell every one's footsteps going to and from the house. I knew all that was going on. One night John had to give me a draught; Thomas Green came in to help him. After I had taken it and John had made me as comfortable as he could, he said he would stay half an hour to see how the medicine settled. Thomas said he would stay with him, so they went and sat down on a bench that had been brought into Merrylegs' stall, and put down the lantern at their feet, that I might not be disturbed with the light.

For a while both men sat silent, and then Tom Green said in a low voice:

"I wish, John, you'd say a bit of a kind word to Joe; the boy is quite broken-hearted; he can't eat his meals, and he can't smile. He says he knows it was all his fault, though he is sure he did the best he knew, and he says if Beauty dies no one will ever speak to him again. It goes to my heart to hear him. I think you might give him just a word; he is not a bad boy."

After a short pause John said slowly, "You must not be too hard on me, Tom. I know he meant no harm, I never said he did; I know he is not a bad boy, but you see I am sore myself. That horse is the pride of my heart, to say nothing of his being such a favourite with the master and mistress; and to think that his life may be flung away in this manner is more than I can bear; but if you think I am hard on the boy, I will try to give him a good word to-morrow – that is, I mean, if Beauty is better."

"Well, John! thank you, I knew you did not wish to be too hard, and I am glad you see it was only ignorance."

John's voice almost startled me as he answered, "*Only* ignorance! only *ignorance*! how can you talk about *only* ignorance? Don't you know that it is the worst thing in the world, next to wickedness? – and which does the most mischief, heaven only knows. If people can say, 'Oh! I did not know, I did not mean any harm', they think it is all right. I suppose Martha Mulwash did not mean to kill that baby when she dosed it with Dalby and soothing syrups; but she did kill it, and was tried for manslaughter."

"And serve her right, too," said Tom. "A woman should not undertake to nurse a tender little child without knowing what is good and what is bad for it."

"Bill Starkey," continued John, "did not mean to frighten his brother into fits when he dressed up like a ghost, and ran after him in the moonlight; but he did; and that bright, handsome little fellow, that might have been the pride of any mother's heart, is just no better than an idiot, and never will be, if he live to be eighty years old. You were a good deal cut up yourself, Tom, two weeks ago, when those young ladies left your hot-house door open, with a frost easy wind blowing right in. You said it killed a good many of your plants."

"A good many!" said Tom; "there was not one of the tender cuttings that was not nipped off; I shall have to strike all over again, and the worst of it is that I don't know where to go to get fresh ones. I was nearly mad when I came in and saw what was done."

"And yet," said John, "I am sure the young ladies did not mean it; it was only ignorance!"

I heard no more of this conversation, for the medicine did well and sent me to sleep, and in the morning I felt much better; but I often thought of John's words when I came to know more of the world.

CHAPTER TWENTY

JOE GREEN

~

Joe Green went on very well; he learned quickly, and was so attentive and careful that John began to trust him in many things; but, as I have said, he was small for his age, and it was seldom that he was allowed to exercise either Ginger or me; but it so happened one morning that John was out with Justice in the luggage cart, and the master wanted a note to be taken immediately to a gentleman's house about three miles distant, and sent his orders for Joe to saddle me and take it; adding the caution that he was to ride carefully.

The note was delivered, and we were quietly returning till we came to the brickfield. Here we saw a cart heavily laden with bricks; the wheels had suck fast in the stiff mud of some deep ruts, and the carter was shouting and flogging the two horses unmercifully. Joe pulled up. It was a sad sight. There were the two horses straining and struggling with all their might to drag the cart out, but they could not move it; the sweat streamed from their legs and flanks, their sides heaved, and every muscle was strained, whilst the man, fiercely pulling at the head of the forehorse, swore and lashed out brutally.

"Hold hard," said Joe, "don't go on flogging the horses like that; the wheels are so stuck that they cannot move the cart." The man took no heed, but went on lashing.

"Stop! pray stop," said Joe; "I'll help you to lighten the cart; they can't move it now."

"Mind your own business, you impudent young rascal, and I'll mind mine." The man was in a towering passion and the worse for drink, and laid on the whip again. Joe turned my head, and the next moment we were going at a round gallop towards the house of the master brickmaker. I cannot say if John would have approved of our pace, but Joe and I were both of one mind, and so angry that we could not have gone slower.

The house stood close by the roadside. Joe knocked at the door and shouted, "Hulloa! is Mr. Clay at home?" The door was opened, and Mr. Clay himself came out.

"Hulloa! young man! you seem in a hurry; any orders from the Squire this morning?"

"No, Mr. Clay, but there's a fellow in your brickyard flogging two horses to death. I told him to stop, and he wouldn't; I said I'd help him lighten the cart, and he wouldn't; so I have come to tell you. Pray, sir, go." Joe's voice shook with excitement.

"Thank ye, my lad," said the man, running in for his hat; then pausing a moment: "Will you give evidence of what you saw if I should bring the fellow up before a magistrate?"

"That I will," said Joe, "and glad too." The man was gone, and we were on our way home at a smart trot.

"Why, what's the matter with you, Joe? you look angry all over," said John as the boy flung himself from the saddle.

"I am angry all over, I can tell you," said the boy, and then in hurried excited words he told all that had happened. Joe was usually such a quiet, gentle little fellow that it was wonderful to see him so roused.

"Right, Joe! you did right, my boy, whether the fellow gets a summons or not. Many folks would have ridden by and said 'twas not their business to interfere. Now, I say, that with cruelty and oppression it is everybody's business to interfere when they see it. You did right, my boy."

Joe was quite calm by this time, and proud that John approved of him, and he cleaned my feet, and rubbed me down with a firmer hand than usual.

They were just going home to dinner when the footman came down to the stable to say that Joe was wanted directly in master's private room; there was a man brought up for ill-using horses, and Joe's evidence was wanted. The boy flushed up to his forehead and his eyes sparkled. "They shall have it," said he.

"Put yourself a bit straight," said John. Joe gave a pull at his necktie and a twitch at his jacket, and was off in a moment. Our master being one of the county magistrates, cases were often brought to him to settle, or say what should be done. In the stable we heard no more for some time, as it was the men's dinner hour, but when Joe came next into the stable I saw he was in high spirits. He gave me a good-natured slap, and said, "We won't see such things done, will we, old fellow?" We heard afterwards that he had given his evidence so clearly, and the horses were in such an exhausted state, bearing marks of such brutal usage, that the carter was committed to take his trial, and might possibly be sentenced to two or three months in prison.

It was wonderful what a change had come over Joe. John laughed, and said he had grown an inch taller in that week, and I believe he had. He was just as kind and gentle as before, but there was more purpose and determination in all that he did – as if he had jumped at once from a boy into a man.

CHAPTER TWENTY-ONE

THE PARTING

~

I had now lived in this happy place three years, but sad changes were about to come over us. We heard from time to time that our mistress was ill. The doctor was often at the house, and the master looked grave and anxious. Then we heard that she must leave her home at once and go to a warm country for two or three years. The news fell upon the household like the tolling of a death-bell. Everybody was sorry; but the master began directly to make arrangements for breaking up his establishment and leaving England. We used to hear it talked about in our stable; indeed, nothing else was talked about.

John went about his work silent and sad, and Joe scarcely whistled. There was a great deal of coming and going; Ginger and I had full work.

The first of the party who went were Miss Jessie and Miss Flora with their governess. They came to bid us good-bye. They hugged poor Merrylegs like an old friend, and so indeed he was. Then we heard what had been arranged for us. Master had sold Ginger and me to his old friend, the

Earl of W——, for he thought we should have a good place there. Merrylegs he had given to the Vicar, who was wanting a pony for Mrs. Blomefield, but it was on the condition that he should never be sold, and when he was past work that he should be shot and buried.

Joe was engaged to take care of him, and to help in the house, so I thought that Merrylegs was well off. John had the offer of several good places, but he said he should wait a little and look round.

The evening before they left, the master came into the stable to give some directions and to give his horses the last pat. He seemed very low-spirited; I knew that by his voice. I believe we horses can tell more by the voice than many men can.

"Have you decided what to do, John?" he said. "I find you have not accepted any of those offers."

"No, sir; I have made up my mind that if I could get a situation with some first-rate colt-breaker and horse-trainer, that it would be the right thing for me. Many young animals are frightened and spoiled by wrong treatment which need not be, if the right man took them in hand. I always get on well with horses, and if I could help some of them to a fair start, I should feel as if I was doing some good. What do you think of it, sir?"

"I don't know a man anywhere," said master, "that I should think so suitable for it as yourself. You understand horses, and somehow they understand you, and in time you might set up for yourself; I think you could not do better. If in any way I can help, write to me; I shall speak to my agent in London, and leave your character with him."

Master gave John the name and address, and then he thanked him for his long and faithful service; but that was too much for John. "Pray don't, sir; I can't bear it. You and my dear mistress have done so much for me that I could never repay it; but we shall never forget you, sir, and please God we may some day see mistress back again like herself; we must keep up hope, sir." Master gave John his hand, but he did not speak, and they both left the stable.

The last sad day had come; the footman and the heavy luggage had gone off the day before, and there was only master and mistress and her maid. Ginger and I brought the carriage up to the Hall door for the last time. The servants brought out cushions and rugs and many other things, and when all were arranged, master came down the steps carrying the mistress in his arms (I was on the side next the house and could see all that went on); he placed her carefully in the carriage, while the house servants stood round crying.

"Good-bye again," he said; "we shall not forget any of you," and he got in. "Drive on, John."

Joe jumped up, and we trotted slowly through the Park, and through the village, where the people was standing at their doors to have a last look and to say "God bless them".

When we reached the railway station, I think mistress walked from the carriage to the waiting-room. I heard her say in her own sweet voice, "Good-bye, John; God bless you." I felt the rein twitch, but John made no answer, perhaps he could not speak. As soon as Joe had taken the things out of the carriage, John called him to stand by the horses, while he went on the platform. Poor Joe! he stood close up to our heads to hide his tears. Very soon the train came puffing up into the station; then two or three minutes, and the doors were slammed to; the guard whistled and the train glided away, leaving behind it only clouds of white smoke, and some very heavy hearts.

When it was quite out of sight, John came back.

"We shall never see her again," he said, "never." He took the reins, mounted the box, and with Joe drove slowly home; but it was not our home now.

EARLSHALL

~

The next morning after breakfast Joe put Merrylegs into the mistress's low chaise to take him to the vicarage; he came first and said good-bye to us, and Merrylegs neighed to us from the yard. Then John put the saddle on Ginger and the leading rein on me, and rode us across the country about fifteen miles to Earlshall Park, where the Earl of W— lived. There was a very fine house, and a great deal of stabling; we went into the yard through a stone gateway, and John asked for Mr. York. It was some time before he came. He was a fine-looking, middle-aged man, and his voice said at once that he expected to be obeyed. He was very friendly and polite to John, and after giving us a slight look, he called a groom to take us to our boxes, and invited John to take some refreshment.

We were taken to a light, airy stable, and placed in boxes adjoining each other, where we were rubbed down and fed. In about half an hour John and Mr. York, who was to be our new coachman, came in to see us.

"Now, Mr. Manly," he said, after carefully looking at us both, "I can see no fault in these horses, but we all know that horses have their peculiarities as well as men, and that sometimes they need different treatment; I should like to know if there is anything particular in either of these that you would like to mention."

"Well," said John, "I don't believe there is a better pair of horses in the country, and right grieved I am to part with them, but they are not alike. The black one is the most perfect temper I ever knew; I suppose he has never known a hard word or a blow since he was foaled, and all his pleasure seems to be to do what you wish; but the chestnut, I fancy, must have had bad treatment; we heard as much from the dealer. She came to us snappish and suspicious, but when she found what sort of place ours was it all went off by degrees; for three years I have never seen the smallest sign of temper, and if she is well treated there is not a better, more willing animal than she is; but she is naturally a more irritable constitution than the black horse; flies tease her more; anything wrong in the harness frets her more; and if she were ill-used or unfairly treated she would not be unlikely to give tit for tat; you know that many high-mettled horses will do so."

"Of course," said York, "I quite understand, but you know it is not easy in stables like these to have all the grooms just what they should be; I do my best, and there I must leave it. I'll remember what you have said about the mare."

They were going out of the stable, when John stopped and said, "I had better mention that we have never used the bearing rein with either of them; the black horse never had one on, and the dealer said it was the gag-bit that spoiled the other's temper."

"Well," said York, "if they come here they must wear the bearing rein. I prefer a loose rein myself, and his lordship is always very reasonable about horses; but my lady – that's another thing, she will have style; and if her carriage horses are not reined up tight she wouldn't look at them. I always stand out against the gag-bit, and shall do so, but it must be tight up when my lady rides!"

"I am sorry for it, very sorry," said John; "but I must go now or I shall lose my train."

He came round to each of us to pat and speak to us for the last time; his voice sounded very sad.

I held my face close to him, that was all I could do to say good-bye; and then he was gone, and I have never seen him since.

The next day Lord W— came to look at us; he seemed pleased with our appearance.

"I have great confidence in these horses," he said, "from the character my friend, Mr. Gordon, has given me of them. Of course, they are not a match in colour, but my idea is that they will do very well for the carriage whilst we are in the country. Before we go to London I must try to match Baron; the black horse, I believe, is perfect for riding."

York then told him what John had said about us.

"Well," said he, "you must keep an eye to the mare, and put the bearing rein easy; I dare say they will do very well with a little humouring at first. I'll mention it to her ladyship."

In the afternoon we were harnessed and put in the carriage, and as the stable clock struck three we were led round to the front of the house. It was all very grand, and three or four times as large as the old house at Birtwick, but not half so pleasant, if a horse may have an opinion. Two footmen were standing ready, dressed in drab livery, with scarlet breeches and white stockings. Presently we heard the rustling sound of silk as my lady came down the flight of stone steps. She stepped round to look at us; she was a tall, proud-looking woman, and did not seem pleased about something, but she said nothing, and got into the carriage. This was the first time of wearing a bearing rein, and I must say, though it certainly was a nuisance not to be able to get my head down now and then, it did not pull my head higher than I was accustomed to carry it. I felt anxious about Ginger, but she seemed to be quiet and content.

The next day at three o'clock we were again at the door, and the footmen as before; we heard the silk dress rustle, and the lady came down the steps, and in an imperious voice she said, "York, you must put those horses' heads higher, they are not fit to be seen."

York got down and said very respectfully, "I beg your pardon, my lady, but these horses have not been reined up for three years, and my lord said it would be safer to bring them to it by degrees; but if your ladyship pleases, I can take them up a little more."

"Do so," she said.

York came round to our heads and shortened the rein himself, one hole,

I think; every little makes a difference, be it for better or worse, and that day we had a steep hill to go up. Then I began to understand what I had heard of. Of course I wanted to put my head forward and take the carriage up with a will, as we had been used to do; but no, I had to pull with my head up now, and that took all the spirit out of me, and the strain came on my back and legs. When we came in, Ginger said, "Now you see what it is like, but this is not bad, and if it does not get much worse than this I shall say nothing about it, for we are very well treated here; but if they strain me up tight, why, let 'em look out! I can't bear it, and I won't."

Day by day, hole by hole, our bearing reins were shortened, and instead of looking forward with pleasure to having my harness put on as I used to do, I began to dread it. Ginger, too, seemed restless, though she said very little. At last I thought the worst was over; for several days there was no more shortening, and I determined to make the best of it and do my duty, though it was now a constant harass instead of a pleasure; but the worst was not come.

*"The new bit was very painful, and I reared up
suddenly." (Chapter Seven.)*

Then the boy got off and gave him a hard thrashing.
(Chapter Thirteen.)

"I saw James coming through the smoke, leading Ginger." (Chapter Sixteen.)

The wheels stuck fast in the stiff mud of some deep ruts. (Chapter Twenty.)

CHAPTER TWENTY-THREE

A STRIKE FOR LIBERTY

~

One day my lady came down later than usual, and the silk rustled more than ever.

"Drive to the Duchess of B—'s," she said, and then, after a pause, "Are you never going to get those horses' heads up, York? Raise them at once, and let us have no more of this humouring and nonsense."

York came to me first, whilst the groom stood at Ginger's head. He drew my head back and fixed the rein so tight that it was almost intolerable; then he went to Ginger, who was impatiently jerking her head up and down against the bit, as was her way now. She had a good idea of what was coming, and the moment York took the rein off the terret in order to shorten it, she took her opportunity, and reared up so suddenly that York had his nose roughly hit, and his hat knocked off; the groom was nearly thrown off his legs. At once they both flew to her head, but she was a match for them, and went on plunging, rearing, and kicking in a most desperate manner; at last she kicked right over the carriage pole and fell down, after giving me a severe blow on my near quarter. There is no knowing what further mischief she might have done had not York promptly sat himself down flat on her head, to prevent her struggling, at the same time calling out, "Unbuckle the black horse! Run for the winch and unscrew the carriage pole; cut the trace here, somebody, if you can't unhitch it." One of the footmen ran for the winch, and another brought a knife from the house. The groom soon set me free from Ginger and the carriage, and led me to my box. He just turned me in as I was, and ran back to York. I was much excited by what had happened, and if I had ever been used to kick or rear, I am sure I should have done it then; but I never had, and there I stood angry, sore in my leg, my head still strained up to the terret on the saddle, and no power to get it down. I was very miserable, and felt much inclined to kick the first person who came near me.

Before long, however, Ginger was led in by two grooms, a good deal knocked about and bruised. York came with her and gave his orders, and then came to look at me. In a moment he let down my head.

"Confound these bearing reins!" he said to himself. "I thought we should have some mischief soon – master will be sorely vexed; but there – if a woman's husband can't rule her, of course a servant can't; so I wash my hands of it, and if she can't get to the duchess's garden party I can't help it.'

York did not say this before the men; he always spoke respectfully when they were by. Now he felt me all over, and soon found the place above my hock where I had been kicked. It was swelled and painful; he ordered it to be sponged with hot water, and then some lotion was put on.

Lord W— was much put out when he learned what had happened; he blamed York for giving way to the mistress, to which he replied that in future he would much prefer to receive his orders only from his lordship; but I think nothing came of it, for things went on the same as before. I thought York might have stood up better for his horses; but perhaps I am no judge.

Ginger was never put into the carriage again, but when she was well of her bruises, one of Lord W—'s younger sons said he should like to have her; he was sure she would make a good hunter. As for me, I was obliged still to go in the carriage, and had a fresh partner called Max; he had always been used to the tight rein. I asked him how it was he bore it.

"Well," he said, "I bear it because I must, but it is shortening my life, and it will shorten·yours too, if you have to stick to it."

"Do you think," I said, "that our masters know how bad it is for us?"

"I can't say," he replied; "but the dealers and the horse doctors know it very well. I was at a dealer's once, who was training me and another horse to go as a pair; he was getting our heads up, as he said, a little higher and a little higher every day. A gentleman who was there asked him why he did so. 'Because,' said he, 'people won't buy them unless we do. The London people always want their horses to carry their heads high, and to step high; of course it is very bad for the horses, but then it is good for trade. The horses soon wear up, or get diseased, and they come for another pair.' That," said Max, "is what he said in my hearing, and you can judge for yourself."

What I suffered with that rein for four long months in my lady's carriage it would be hard to describe; but I am quite sure that, had it lasted much longer, either my health or my temper would have given way. Before that I never knew what it was to foam at the mouth, but now the action of the sharp bit on my tongue and jaw, and the constrained position of my head and throat always caused me to froth at the mouth more or less. Some people think it very fine to see this, and say, "What fine, spirited creatures!" But it is just as unnatural for horses as for men to foam at the mouth: it is a sure sign of some discomfort, and should be attended to. Besides this, there was a pressure on my windpipe, which often made my breathing very uncomfortable; when I returned from my work, my neck and chest were strained and painful, my mouth and tongue tender, and I felt worn and depressed.

In my old home I always knew that John and my master were my friends; but here, although in many ways I was well treated, I had no friend. York might have known, and very likely did know, how that rein harassed me; but I suppose he took it as a matter of course that could not be helped; at any rate, nothing was done to relieve me.

CHAPTER TWENTY-FOUR

THE LADY ANNE

~

Early in the spring Lord W— and part of his family went up to London, and took York with them. I and Ginger and some other horses were left at home for use, and the head groom was left in charge.

The Lady Harriet, who remained at the Hall, was a great invalid, and never went out in the carriage, and the Lady Anne preferred riding on horseback with her brother or cousins. She was a perfect horsewoman, and as gay and gentle as she was beautiful. She chose me for her horse, and named me "Black Auster". I enjoyed these rides very much in the clear, cold air, sometimes with Ginger, sometimes with Lizzie. This Lizzie was a bright bay mare, almost thoroughbred, and a great favourite with the gentlemen on account of her fine action and lively spirit; but Ginger, who knew more of her than I did, told me she was rather nervous.

There was a gentleman of the name of Blantyre staying at the Hall; he always rode Lizzie, and praised her so much that one day Lady Anne ordered the side-saddle to be put on her, and the other saddle on me.

When we came to the door, the gentleman seemed very uneasy.

"How is this?" he said. "Are you tired of your good Black Auster?"

"Oh no, not all!" she replied, "but I am amiable enough to let you ride him for once, and I will try your charming Lizzie. You must confess that in size and appearance she is far more like a lady's horse than my own favourite."

"Do let me advise you not to mount her," he said. "She is a charming creature, but she is too nervous for a lady. I assure you she is not perfectly safe; let me beg you to have the saddles changed."

"My dear cousin," said Lady Anne, laughing, "pray do not trouble your good careful head about me; I have been a horsewoman ever since I was a baby, and I have followed the hounds a great many times, though I know you do not approve of ladies hunting; but still that is the fact, and I intend to try this Lizzie that you gentlemen are all so fond of; so please help me to mount like a good friend, as you are."

There was no more to be said; he placed her carefully on the saddle, looked to the bit and curb, gave the reins gently into her hand, and then mounted me. Just as we were moving off, a footman came out with a slip of paper and message from the Lady Harriet, "Would they ask this question for her at Dr. Ashley's, and bring the answer?"

The village was about a mile off, and the doctor's house was the last in it. We went along gaily enough till we came to his gate. There was a short drive up to the house between tall evergreens. Blantyre alighted at the gate, and was going to open it for Lady Anne, but she said, "I will wait for you here, and you can hang Auster's rein on the gate."

He looked at her doubtfully. "I will not be five minutes," he said.

"Oh! do not hurry yourself; Lizzie and I shall not run away from you."

He hung my rein on one of the iron spikes and was soon hidden amongst the trees. Lizzie was standing quietly by the side of the road a few paces off with her back to me. My young mistress was sitting easily with a loose rein, humming a little song. I listened to my rider's footsteps until they reached the house, and heard him knock at the door. There was a meadow on the opposite side of the road, the gate of which stood open; just then, some cart horses and several young colts came trotting out in a very disorderly manner, whilst a boy behind was cracking a great whip. The colts were wild and frolicsome, and one of them bolted across the road and blundered up against Lizzie's hind legs; and whether it was the stupid colt, or the loud cracking of the whip, or both together, I cannot say, but she gave a violent kick, and dashed off into a headlong gallop. It was so sudden that Lady Anne was nearly unseated; but she soon recovered herself. I gave a loud shrill neigh for help: again and again I neighed, pawing the ground impatiently, and tossing my head to get the rein loose. I had not long to wait. Blantyre came running to the gate; he looked anxiously about, and just caught sight of the flying figure, now far away on the road. In an instant he sprang into the saddle. I needed no whip or spur, for I was as eager as my rider; he saw it, and giving me a free rein, and leaning a little forward, we dashed after them.

For about a mile and a half the road ran straight, and then bent to the right, after which it divided into two roads. Long before we came to the bend she was out of sight. Which way had she turned? A woman was standing at her garden gate, shading her eyes with her hand, and looking eagerly up the road. Scarcely drawing the rein, Blantyre shouted, "Which way?" "To the right," cried the woman, pointing with her hand, and away we went up the right-hand road; then for a moment we caught sight of her; another bend and she was hidden again. Several times we caught glimpses, and then lost them. We scarcely seemed to gain ground upon them at all. An old road-mender was standing near a heap of stones – his shovel dropped, and his hands raised. As we came near he made a sign to speak. Blantyre drew the rein a little. "To the common, to the common, sir; she has turned off there." I knew this common very well; it was for the most part very uneven ground, covered with heather and dark green furze bushes, with here and there a scrubby old thorn tree; there were also open spaces of fine short grass, with ant-hills and mole turns everywhere; the worst place I ever knew for a headlong gallop.

We had hardly turned on the common when we caught sight again of the green habit flying on before us. My lady's hat was gone, and her long brown hair was streaming behind her. Her head and body were thrown back, as if she were pulling with all her remaining strength, and as if that strength were nearly exhausted. It was clear that the roughness of the ground had very much lessened Lizzie's speed, and there seemed a chance that we might overtake her.

Whilst we were on the highroad, Blantyre had given me my head; but now with a light hand and a practised eye he guided me over the ground in such a masterly manner that my pace was scarcely slackened, and we were decidedly gaining on them.

About half-way across the heath there had been a wide dike recently cut, and the earth from the cutting was cast up roughly on the other side. Surely this would stop them! But no; with scarcely a pause, Lizzie took the leap, stumbled among the rough clods, and fell. Blantyre groaned. "Now, Auster, do your best!" He gave me a steady rein, I gathered myself well together, and with one determined leap cleared both dike and bank.

Motionless among the heather, with her face to the earth, lay my poor young mistress. Blantyre kneeled down and called her name – there was no sound; gently he turned her face upward, it was ghastly white, and the eyes were closed. "Annie, dear Annie, do speak!" but there was no answer. He unbuttoned her habit, loosened her collar, felt her hands and wrists, then started up and looked wildly round him for help.

At no great distance there were two men cutting turf, who, seeing Lizzie running wild without a rider, had left their work to catch her.

Blantyre's halloo soon brought them to the spot. The foremost man seemed much troubled at the sight, and asked what he could do.

"Can you ride?"

"Well, sir, I bean't much of a horseman, but I'd risk my neck for the Lady Anne; she was uncommon good to my wife in the winter."

"Then mount this horse, my friend; your neck will be quite safe, and ride to the doctor's and ask him to come instantly – then on to the Hall – tell them all that you know, and bid them send me the carriage with Lady Anne's maid and help. I shall stay here."

"All right, sir, I'll do my best, and I pray God the dear young lady may open her eyes soon." Then seeing the other man, he called out, "Here, Joe, run for some water, and tell my missis to come as quick as she can to the Lady Anne."

He then somehow scrambled into the saddle, and with a "Gee-up" and a clap on my sides with both his legs, he started on his journey, making a little circuit to avoid the dike. He had no whip, which seemed to trouble him, but my pace soon cured that diffculty, and he found the best thing he could do was to stick to the saddle and hold me in, which he did manfully. I shook him as little as I could help, but once or twice on the rough ground he called out "Steady! Woah! Steady!" On the highroad we were all right; and at the doctor's and the Hall he did his errand like a good man and true. They asked him in to take a drop of something. "No, no," he said, "I'll be back to 'em again by a short cut through the fields, and be there afore the carriage."

There was a great deal of hurry and excitement after the news became known. I was just turned into my box, and saddle and bridle were taken off, and a cloth thrown over me.

Ginger was saddled and sent off in great haste for Lord George, and I soon heard the carriage roll out of the yard.

It seemed a long time before Ginger came back and before we were left alone; and then she told me all that she had seen.

"I can't tell much," she said; "we went a gallop nearly all the way, and got there just as the doctor rode up. There was a woman sitting on the ground with the lady's head in her lap. The doctor poured something into her mouth, but all that I heard was 'she is not dead'. Then I was led off by a man to a little distance. After a while she was taken to the carriage, and we came home together. I heard my master say to a gentleman who stopped him to inquire, that he hoped no bones were broken, but that she had not spoken yet."

When Lord George took Ginger for hunting, York shook his head; he said it ought to be a steady hand to train a horse for the first season, and not a random rider like Lord George.

Ginger used to like it very much, but sometimes when she came back I could see that she had been very much strained, and now and then she gave a short cough. She had too much spirit to complain, but I could not help feeling anxious about her.

Two days after the accident Blantyre paid me a visit. He patted me and praised me very much; he told Lord George that he was sure the horse knew of Anne's danger as well as he did. "I could not have held him in if I would," said he; "she ought never to ride any other horse." I found by their conversation that my young mistress was now out of danger, and would soon be able to ride again. This was good news to me, and I looked forward to a happy life.

CHAPTER TWENTY-FIVE

REUBEN SMITH
~

I must now say a little about Reuben Smith, who was left in charge of the stables when York went to London. No one more thoroughly understood his business than he did, and when he was all right there could not be a more faithful or valuable man. He was gentle and very clever in his management of horses, and could doctor them almost as well as a farrier, for he had lived two years with a veterinary surgeon. He was a first-rate driver; he could take a four-in-hand, or a tandem, as easily as a pair. He was a handsome man, a good scholar, and had very pleasant manners. I believe everybody liked him; certainly the horses did; the only wonder was that he should be in an under situation, and not in the place of a head coachman like York; but he had one great fault, and that was the love of drink. He was not like some men, always at it; he used to keep steady for weeks or months together; and then he would break out and have a "bout" of it, as York called it, and be a disgrace to himself, a terror to his wife, and a nuisance to all that had to do with him. He was, however, so useful, that two or three times York had hushed the matter up, and kept it from the Earl's knowledge; but one night, when Reuben had to drive a party home from a ball, he was so drunk that he could not hold the reins, and a gentleman of the party had to mount the box and drive the ladies home. Of course this could not be hidden, and Reuben was at once dismissed; his poor wife and little children had to turn out of the pretty cottage by the Park gate and go where they could. Old Max told me all this, for it happened a good while ago; but shortly before Ginger and I came Smith had been taken back again. York had interceded for him with the Earl, who was very kind-hearted, and the man had promised faithfully that he would never taste another drop as long as he lived there. He had kept his promise so well that York thought he might safely be trusted to fill his place whilst he was away, and he was so clever and honest that no one else seemed so well fitted for it.

It was now early in April, and the family was expected home some time in May. The light brougham was to be freshly done up, and as Colonel Blantyre was obliged to return to his regiment, it was arranged that Smith should drive him to the town in it, and ride back. For this purpose he took the saddle with him, and I was chosen for the journey. At the station the colonel put some money into Smith's hand and bid him good-bye, saying, "Take care of your young mistress, Reuben, and don't let Black Auster be hacked about by any random young prig that wants to ride him – keep him for the lady."

We left the carriage at the maker's, and Smith rode me to the White Lion and ordered the ostler to feed me well and have me ready for him at four o'clock. A nail in one of my front shoes had started as I came along, but the ostler did not notice it till just about four o'clock. Smith did not come into the yard till five, and then he said he should not leave till six, as he had met with some old friends. The man then told him of the nail, and asked if he should have the shoe looked to.

"No," said Smith, "that will be all right till we get home."

He spoke in a very loud, off-hand way, and I thought it very unlike him not to see about loose nails in our shoes. He did not come at six, nor seven, nor eight, and it was nearly nine o'clock before he called for me, and then it was with a loud, rough voice. He seemed in a very bad temper, and abused the ostler, though I could not tell what for.

The landlord stood at the door and said, "Have a care, Mr. Smith!" but he answered angrily with an oath; and almost before he was out of the town he began to gallop, frequently giving me a sharp cut with his whip, though I was going at full speed. The moon had not yet risen, and it was very dark. The roads were stony, having been recently mended; going over them at this pace, my shoe became looser, and when we were near the turnpike gate it came off.

If Smith had been in his right senses he would have been sensible of something wrong in my pace; but he was too madly drunk to notice anything.

Beyond the turnpike was a long piece of road upon which fresh stones had just been laid; large sharp stones, over which no horse could be driven quickly without risk of danger. Over this road, with one shoe gone, I was forced to gallop at my utmost speed, my rider meanwhile cutting into me with his whip, and with wild curses urging me to go still faster. Of course my shoeless foot suffered dreadfully. The hoof was broken and split down to the very quick, and the inside was terribly cut by the sharpness of the stones.

This could not go on; no horse could keep his footing under such circumstances, the pain was too great. I stumbled, and fell with violence on both my knees. Smith was flung off by my fall, and owing to the speed I was going at, he must have fallen with great force. I soon recovered my feet and limped to the side of the road, where it was free from stones. The moon had just risen above the hedge, and by its light I could see Smith lying a few yards beyond me. He did not rise, he made one slight effort to do so, and then there was a heavy groan. I could have groaned too, for I was suffering intense pain both from my foot and knees; but horses are used to bear their pain in silence. I uttered no sound, but I stood there and listened. One more heavy groan from Smith; but though he now lay in the full moonlight, I could see no motion. I could do nothing for him nor myself, but, oh! how I listened for the sound of horse, or wheels, or footsteps. The road was not much frequented, and at this time of the night we might stay for hours before help came to us. I stood watching and listening. It was a calm sweet April night; there were no sounds but a few low notes of a nightingale, and nothing moved but the white clouds near the moon and a brown owl that flitted over the hedge. It made me think of the summer nights long ago, when I used to lie beside my mother in the green pleasant meadow at Farmer Grey's.

How it Ended

~

It must have been nearly midnight when I heard at a great distance the sound of a horse's feet. Sometimes the sound died away, then it grew clearer again and nearer. The road to Earlshall led through plantations that belonged to the Earl; the sound came in that direction, and I hoped it might be some one coming in search of us. As the sound came nearer and nearer I was almost sure I could distinguish Ginger's step; a little nearer still, and I could tell she was in the dog-cart. I neighed loudly, and was overjoyed to hear an answering neigh from Ginger, and men's voices. They came slowly over the stones, and stopped at the dark figure that lay upon the ground.

One of the men jumped out, and stooped down over it. "It is Reuben!" he said, "and he does not stir."

The other man followed and bent over him. "He's dead," he said; "feel how cold his hands are."

They raised him up, but there was no life, and his hair was soaked with blood. They laid him down again, and came and looked at me. They soon saw my cut knees.

"Why, the horse has been down and thrown him! Who would have thought the black horse would have done that? Nobody thought he could fall. Reuben must have been lying here for hours! Odd, too, that the horse has not moved from the place."

Robert then attempted to lead me forward. I made a step, but almost fell again.

"Hallo! he's bad in his foot as well as his knees; look here – his hoof is cut all to pieces, he might well come down, poor fellow! I tell you what, Ned, I'm afraid it hasn't been all right with Reuben! Just think of him riding a horse over these stones without a shoe! Why, if he had been in his right senses he would just as soon have tried to ride him over the moon. I'm afraid it has been the old thing over again. Poor Susan! she looked awfully pale when she came to my house to ask if he had not come home. She made believe she was not a bit anxious, and talked of a lot of things that might have kept him. But for all that she begged me to go and meet him – but what must we do? There's the horse to get home as well as the body – and that will be no easy matter."

Then followed a conversation between them, till it was agreed that Robert as the groom should lead me, and that Ned must take the body. It was a hard job to get it into the dogcart, for there was no one to hold Ginger; but she knew as well as I did what was going on, and stood as still as a stone. I noticed that, because, if she had a fault, it was that she was impatient in standing.

Ned started off very slowly with his sad load, and Robert came and looked at my foot again; then he took his handkerchief and bound it closely round, and so he led me home. I shall never forget that night walk; it was more than three miles. Robert led me on very slowly, and I limped and hobbled on as well as I could with great pain. I am sure he was sorry for me, for he often patted and encouraged me, talking to me in a pleasant voice.

At last I reached my own box and had some corn, and after Robert had wrapped up my knees in wet cloths, he tied up my foot in a bran poultice to draw out the heat, and cleanse it before the horse doctor saw it in the morning, and I managed to get myself down on the straw, and slept in spite of the pain.

The next day, after the farrier had examined my wounds, he said he hoped the joint was not injured, and if so, I should not be spoiled for work, but I should never lose the blemish. I believe they did their best to make a good cure, but it was a long and painful one; proud flesh, as they called it, came up in my knees, and was burnt out with caustic, and when at last it was healed, they put a blistering fluid over the front of both knees to bring all the hair off: they had some reason for this, and I suppose it was all right.

As Smith's death had been so sudden, and no one was there to see it, there was an inquest held. The landlord and ostler at the White Lion, with several other people, gave evidence that he was intoxicated when he started from the inn. The keeper of the toll-gate said he rode at a hard gallop through the gate; and my shoe was picked up amongst the stones, so that the case was quite plain to them, and I was cleared of all blame.

Everybody pitied Susan; she was nearly out of her mind: she kept saying over and over again, "Oh! he was so good – so good! It was all that cursed drink; why will they sell that cursed drink? Oh, Reuben, Reuben!" So she went on till after he was buried, and then, as she had no home or relations, she, with her six little children, were obliged once more to leave the pleasant home by the tall oak trees, and go into that great gloomy Union House.

CHAPTER TWENTY-SEVEN

RUINED, AND GOING DOWNHILL

~

As soon as my knees were sufficiently healed I was turned into a small meadow for a month or two. No other creature was there, and though I enjoyed the liberty and the sweet grass, yet I had been so long used to society that I felt very lonely. Ginger and I had become fast friends, and now I missed her company extremely. I often neighed when I heard horses' feet passing in the road, but I seldom got an answer; till one morning the gate was opened, and who should come in but dear old Ginger. The man slipped off her halter and left her there. With a joyful whinny I trotted up to her; we were both glad to meet, but I soon found that it was not for our pleasure that she was brought to be with me. Her story would be too long to tell, but the end of it was that she had been ruined by hard riding, and was now turned off to see what rest would do.

Lord George was young and would take no warning; he was a hard rider, and would hunt whenever he could get the chance, quite careless of his horse. Soon after I left the stable there was a steeplechase, and he determined to ride. Though the groom told him she was a little strained, and was not fit for the race, he did not believe it, and on the day of the race urged Ginger to keep up with the foremost riders. With her high spirit, she strained herself to the utmost; she came in with the first three horses, but her wind was touched, beside which, he was too heavy for her, and her back was strained. "And so," she said, "here we are – ruined in the prime of our youth and strength – you by a drunkard, and I by a fool; it is very hard." We both felt in ourselves that we were not what we had been. However, that did not spoil the pleasure we had in each other's company; we did not gallop about as we once did, but we used to feed, and lie down together, and stand for hours under one of the shady lime trees with our heads close to each other; and so we passed our time till the family returned from town.

One day we saw the Earl come into the meadow, and York was with him. Seeing who it was, we stood still under our lime tree, and let them come up to us. They examined us carefully. The Earl seemed much annoyed.

"There is three hundred pounds flung away for no earthly use," said he; "but what I care most for, is that these horses of my old friend, who thought they would find a good home with me, are ruined. The mare shall have a twelvemonth's run, and we shall see what that will do for her; but the black one, he must be sold; 'tis a great pity, but I could not have knees like these in my stables."

"No, my lord, of course not," said York; "but he might get a place where appearance is not of much consequence, and still be well treated. I know a man in Bath, the master of some livery stables, who often wants a good horse at a low figure; I know he looks well after his horses. The inquest cleared the horse's character, and your lordship's recommendation, or mine, would be sufficient warrant for him."

"You had better write to him, York. I should be more particular about the place than the money he would fetch."

After this they left us.

"They'll soon take you away," said Ginger, "and I shall lose the only friend I have, and most likely we shall never see each other again. 'Tis a hard world!"

About a week after this, Robert came into the field with a halter, which he slipped over my head and led me away. There was no leave-taking of Ginger; we neighed to each other as I was led off, and she trotted anxiously along by the hedge calling to me as long as she could hear the sound of my feet.

Through the recommendation of York, I was bought by the master of the livery stables. I had to go by train, which was new to me, and required a good deal of courage the first time; but as I found the puffing, rushing, whistling, and, more than all, the trembling of the horse box in which I stood, did me no real harm, I soon took it quietly.

When I reached the end of my journey I found myself in a tolerably comfortable stable and well attended to. These stables were not so airy and pleasant as those I had been used to. The stalls were laid on a slope instead of being level, and as my head was kept tied to the manger, I was obliged always to stand on the slope, which was very fatiguing. Men do not seem to know yet that horses can do more work if they can stand comfortably and can turn about; however, I was well fed and well cleaned, and, on the whole, I think our master took as much care of us as he could. He kept a good many horses and carriages of different kinds for hire. Sometimes his own men drove them; at others the horse and chaise were let to gentlemen or ladies who drove themselves.

CHAPTER TWENTY-EIGHT

A JOB HORSE
AND HIS DRIVERS

~

Hitherto I had always been driven by people who at least knew how to drive; but in this place I was to get my experience of all the different kinds of bad and ignorant driving to which we horses are subjected; for I was a "job horse", and was let out to all sorts of people who wished to hire me; and as I was good-tempered and gentle, I think I was oftener let out to the ignorant drivers than some of the other horses, because I could be depended upon. It would take a long time to tell of all the different styles in which I was driven, but I will mention a few of them.

First, there were the tight-rein drivers — men who seemed to think that all depended on holding the reins as hard as they could, never relaxing the pull on the horse's mouth, or giving him the least liberty of movement. They are always talking about "keeping the horse well in hand", and "holding a horse up", just as if a horse was not made to hold himself up.

Some poor, broken-down horses, whose mouths have been made hard and insensible by just such drivers as these, may, perhaps, find some support in it; but for a horse who can depend upon its own legs, and who has a tender mouth, and is easily guided, it is not only tormenting, but it is stupid.

Then there are the loose-rein drivers, who let the reins lie easily on our backs, and their own hand rest lazily on their knees. Of course, such gentlemen have no control over a horse if anything happens suddenly. If a horse shies, or starts, or stumbles, they are nowhere and cannot help the horse or themselves, till the mischief's done. Of course, for myself, I had no objection to it, as I was not in the habit either of starting or stumbling, and had only been used to depend on my driver for guidance and encourage-ment; still, one likes to feel the rein a little in going downhill, and likes to know that one's driver is not gone to sleep.

Besides, a slovenly way of driving gets a horse into bad and often lazy habits; and when he changes hands, he has to be whipped out of them, with more or less pain and trouble. Squire Gordon always kept us to our best places, and our best manners. He said that spoiling a horse, and letting him get into bad habits, was just as cruel as spoiling a child, and both had to suffer for it afterwards.

Besides, these drivers are often careless altogether, and will attend to anything else rather than their horses. I went out in the phaeton one day with one of them; he had a lady, and two children behind. He flopped the reins about as we started, and of course gave me several unmeaning cuts with the whip, though I was fairly off. There had been a good deal of road-mending going on, and even where the stones were not freshly laid down there were a great many loose ones about. My driver was laughing and joking with the lady and the children, and talking about the country to the right and the left; but he never thought it worth while to keep an eye on his horse, or to drive on the smoothest parts of the road; and so it easily happened that I got a stone in one of my forefeet.

Now, if Mr. Gordon, or John, or, in fact, any good driver had been there, he would have seen that something was wrong before I had gone three paces. Or even if it had been dark, a practised hand would have felt by the rein that there was something wrong in the step, and they would have got down and picked out the stone. But this man went on laughing and talking, whilst at every step the stone became more firmly wedged between my shoe and the frog of my foot. The stone was sharp on the inside and round on the outside, which, as every one knows, is the most dangerous kind that a horse can pick up; at the same time cutting his foot, and making him most liable to stumble and fall.

Whether the man was partly blind or only very careless, I can't say; but he drove me with that stone in my foot for a good half-mile before he saw anything. By that time I was going so lame with the pain that at last he saw it and called out, "Well, here's a go! Why, they have sent us out with a lame horse! What a shame!"

He then chucked the reins and flipped about with the whip saying, "Now, then, it's no use playing the old soldier with me; there's the journey to go and it's no use turning lame and lazy."

Just at this time a farmer came riding up on a brown cob; he lifted his hat and pulled up.

"I beg your pardon, sir," he said, "but I think there is something the matter with your horse, he goes very much as if he had a stone in his shoe. If you will allow me I will look at his feet; these loose scattered stones are confounded dangerous things for the horses."

"He's a hired-horse," said my driver; "I don't know what's the matter with him, but it's a great shame to send out a lame beast like this."

The farmer dismounted and, slipping his rein over his arm, at once took up my near foot.

"Bless me, there's a stone! Lame! I should think so!"

At first he tried to dislodge it with his hand, but as it was now very tightly wedged, he drew a stone-pick out of his pocket, and very carefully, and with some trouble, got it out. Then holding it up, he said, "There, that's the stone your horse had picked up; it is a wonder he did not fall down and break his knees into the bargain!"

"Well, to be sure!" said my driver, "that is a queer thing! I never knew that horses picked up stones before."

"Didn't you?" said the farmer, rather contemptuously. "But they do, though, and the best of them will do it, and can't help it sometimes on such roads as these. And if you don't want to lame your horse you must look sharp and get them out quickly. This foot is very much bruised," he said, setting it gently down and patting me. "If I might advise, sir, you had better drive him gently for a while; the foot is a good deal hurt, and the lameness will not go off directly."

Then mounting his cob and raising his hat to the lady, he trotted off.

When he was gone my driver began to flop the reins about, and whip the harness, by which I understood that I was to go on, which of course I did, glad that the stone was gone, but still in a good deal of pain.

This was the sort of experience we job horses often came in for.

CHAPTER TWENTY-NINE

COCKNEYS

~

Then there is the steam-engine style of driving. These drivers were mostly people from towns, who never had a horse of their own, and generally travelled by rail.

They always seem to think that a horse was something like a steam-engine, only smaller. At any rate, they think that if only they pay for it, a horse is bound to go just as far, and just as fast, and with just as heavy a load as they please. And be the roads heavy and muddy, or dry and good; be they stony or smooth, uphill or downhill, it is all the same — on, on, on one must go at the same pace, with no relief, and no consideration.

These people never think of getting out to walk up a steep hill. Oh no; they have paid to ride, and ride they will! The horse. Oh, he's used to it! What were horses made for if not to drag people uphill? Walk! A good joke indeed! And so the whip is plied and the rein is chucked, and often a rough scolding voice cries out, "Go along, you lazy beast!" And then another slash of the whip, when all the time we are doing our very best to get along, uncomplaining and obedient, though often sorely harassed and down-hearted.

This steam-engine style of driving wears us up faster than any other kind. I would far rather go twenty miles with a good considerate driver than I would go ten with some of these; it would take less out of me.

Another thing — they scarcely ever put on the drag, however steep the downhill may be, and thus bad accidents sometimes happen; or if they do put it on, they often forget to take it off at the bottom of the hill; and more than once I have had to pull half-way up the next hill with one of the wheels lodged fast in the drag-shoe, before my driver chose to think about it; and that is a terrible strain on a horse.

Then these Cockneys, instead of starting at an easy pace as a gentleman would do, generally get off at full speed from the very stable yard; and when they want to stop, they first whip us and then pull up so suddenly that we are nearly thrown on our haunches, and our mouths jagged with the bit; they call that pulling up with a dash! and when they turn a corner, they do it as sharply as if there were no right side or wrong side of the road.

I well remember one spring evening I and Rory had been out for the day. (Rory was the horse that mostly went with me when a pair was ordered, and a good honest fellow he was.) We had our own driver, and as he was always considerate and gentle with us, we had a very pleasant day. We were coming home at a good smart pace about twilight; our road turned sharp to the left; but as we were close to the hedge on our own side, and there was plenty of room to pass, our driver did not pull us in. As we neared the corner I heard a horse and two wheels coming rapidly down the hill towards us. The hedge was high and I could see nothing, but the next moment we were upon each other. Happily for me I was on the side next the hedge. Rory was on the right side of the pole, and had not even a shaft to protect him. The man who was driving was making straight for the corner, and when he came in sight of us he had no time to pull over to his own side. The whole shock came upon Rory. The gig shaft ran right into the chest, making him stagger back with a cry that I shall never forget. The other horse was thrown upon his haunches, and one shaft broken. It turned out that it was a horse from our own stables, with the high-wheeled gig that the young men were so fond of.

The driver was one of those random, ignorant fellows who don't even know which is their own side of the road, or if they know, don't care. And there was poor Rory with his flesh torn open and bleeding, and the blood streaming down. They said if it had been a litle more to one side it would have killed him; and a good thing for him, poor fellow, if it had.

As it was, it was a long time before the wound healed, and then he was sold for coal carting; and what that is, up and down those steep hills, only horses know. Some of the sights I saw there, where a horse had to come downhill with a heavily loaded two-wheeled cart behind him, on which no drag could be placed, make me sad even now to think of.

After Rory was disabled I often went in the carriage with a mare named Peggy, who stood in the next stall to mine. She was a strong, well-made animal, of a bright dun colour, beautifully dappled, and with a dark-brown mane and tail. There was no high breeding about her, but she was very pretty, and remarkably sweet-tempered and willing. Still, there was an anxious look about her eye, by which I knew she had some trouble. The first time we went out together I thought she had a very odd pace; she seemed to go partly in a trot, partly in a canter – three or four paces, and then to make a little jump forward.

It was very unpleasant for any horse who pulled with her, and made me quite fidgety. When we got home I asked her what made her go in that odd, awkward way.

"Ah," she said in a troubled manner, "I know my paces are very bad, but what can I do? It really is not my fault, it is just because my legs are so short. I stand nearly as high as you, but your legs are a good three inches longer about your knees than mine, and, of course, you can take a much longer step, and go much faster. You see I did not make myself; I wish I could have done so, I would have had long legs then; all my troubles come from my short legs," said Peggy in a desponding tone.

"But how is it," I said, "when you are so strong and good-tempered and willing?"

"Why, you see," said she, "men will go so fast, and if one can't keep up to other horses, it is nothing but whip, whip, whip, all the time. And so I have had to keep up as I could, and have got into this ugly, shuffling pace. It was not always so; when I lived with my first master I always went a good regular trot, but then he was not in such a hurry. He was a young clergyman in the country, and a good kind master he was. He had two churches a good way apart, and a great deal of work, but he never scolded or whipped me for not going faster. He was very fond of me. I only wish I was with him now; but he had to leave and go to a large town, and then I was sold to a farmer.

"Some farmers, you know, are capital masters; but I think this one was a low sort of man. He cared nothing about good horses, or good driving; he only cared for going fast. I went as fast as I could, but that would not do, and he was always whipping; so I got into this way of making a spring forward to keep up. On market nights he used to stay very late at the inn, and then drive home at a gallop.

"One dark night he was galloping home as usual, when all on a sudden the wheel came against some great heavy thing in the road, and turned the gig over in a minute. He was thrown out and his arm broken, and some of his ribs, I think. At any rate, it was the end of my living with him, and I was not sorry. But you see it will be the same everywhere for me, if men *must* go so fast. I wish my legs were longer!"

Poor Peggy! I was very sorry for her, and I could not comfort her, for I knew how hard it was upon slow-paced horses to be put with fast ones; all the whipping comes to their share, and they can't help it.

She was often used in the phaeton, and was very much liked by some of the ladies, because she was so gentle; and some time after this she was sold to two ladies who drove themselves, and wanted a safe good horse.

I met her several times out in the country, going a good steady pace, and looking as gay and contented as a horse could be. I was very glad to see her, for she deserved a good place.

After she left us another horse came in her stead. He was young, and had a bad name for shying and starting, by which he had lost a good place. I asked him what made him shy.

"Well, I hardly know," he said; "I was timid when I was young, and was a good deal frightened several times, and if I saw anything strange I used to turn and look at it — you see, with our blinkers one can't see or understand what a thing is unless one looks round; and then my master always gave me a whipping, which, of course, made me start on, and did not make me less afraid. I think if he would have let me just look at things quietly, and see that there was nothing to hurt me, it would have been all right, and I should have got used to them. One day an old gentleman was riding with him, and a large piece of white paper or rag blew across just on one side of me; I shied and started forward – my master as usual whipped me smartly, but the old man cried out, 'You're wrong! you're wrong! you should never whip a horse for shying; he shies because he is frightened, and you only frighten him more, and make the habit worse.' So I suppose all men don't do so. I am sure I don't want to shy for the sake of it; but how should one know what is dangerous and what is not if one is never allowed to get used to anything? I am never afraid of what I know. Now I was brought up in a park where there were deer; of course I knew them as well as I did a sheep or a cow, but they are not common, and I know many sensible horses who are frightened at them, and who kick up quite a shindy before they will pass a paddock where there are deer."

I knew what my companion said was true, and I wished that every young horse had as good a master as Farmer Grey and Squire Gordon.

Of course we sometimes came in for good driving here. I remember one morning I was put into the light gig and taken to a house in Pulteney Street. Two gentlemen came out; the taller of them came round to my head, he looked at the bit and bridle, and just shifted the collar with his hand, to see if it fitted comfortably.

"Do you consider this horse wants a curb?" he said to the ostler.

"Well," said the man, "I should say he would go just as well without; he has an uncommon good mouth, and though he has a fine spirit he has no vice; but we generally find people like the curb."

"I don't like it," said the gentleman; "be so good as to take it off, and put the rein in at the cheek; an easy mouth is a great thing on a long journey, is it not, old fellow?" he said, patting my neck.

Then he took the reins, and they both got up. I can remember now how quietly he turned me round, and then with a light feel of the rein, and drawing the whip gently across my back, we were off.

I arched my neck and set off at my best pace. I found I had some one behind me who knew how a good horse ought to be driven. It seemed like old times again, and made me feel quite gay.

This gentleman took a great liking to me, and after trying me several times with the saddle, he prevailed upon my master to sell to a friend of his who wanted a safe pleasant horse for riding. And so it came to pass that in the summer I was sold to Mr. Barry.

CHAPTER THIRTY

A THIEF

~

My new master was an unmarried man. He lived at Bath, and was much engaged in business. His doctor advised him to take horse exercise, and for this purpose he bought me. He hired a stable a short distance from his lodgings, and engaged a man named Filcher as groom. My master knew very little about horses, but he treated me well, and I should have had a good and easy place but for circumstances of which he was ignorant. He ordered the best hay with plenty of oats, crushed beans, and bran, with vetches, or rye grass, as the man might think needful. I heard the master give the order, so I knew there was plenty of good food, and I thought I was well off.

For a few days all went on well; I found that my groom understood his business. He kept the stable clean and airy, and he groomed me thoroughly; and was never otherwise than gentle. He had been an ostler in one of the great hotels in Bath. He had given that up, and now cultivated fruit and vegetables for the market; and his wife bred and fattened poultry and rabbits for sale. After a while it seemed to me that my oats came very short; I had the beans, but bran mixed with them instead of oats, of which there were very few; certainly not more than a quarter of what there should have been. In two or three weeks this began to tell upon my strength and spirits. The grass food, though very good, was not the thing to keep up my condition without corn. However, I could not complain, nor make known my wants. So it went on for about two months; and I wondered my master did not see that something was the matter. However, one afternoon he rode out into the country to see a friend of his – a gentleman farmer who lived on the road to Wells. This gentleman had a very quick eye for horses; and after he had welcomed his friend, he said, casting his eye over me:

"It seems to me, Barry, that your horse does not look so well as he did when you first had him; has he been well?"

"Yes, I believe so," said my master, "but he is not nearly so lively as he was; my groom tells me that horses are always dull and weak in the autumn, and that I must expect it."

"Autumn! fiddlesticks!" said the farmer; "why, this is only August; and with your light work and good food he ought not to go down like this, even if it was autumn. How do you feed him?"

My master told him. The other shook his head slowly, and began to feel me over.

"I can't say who eats your corn, my dear fellow, but I am much mistaken if your horse gets it. Have you ridden very fast?"

"No! very gently."

"Then just put your hand here," said he, passing his hand over my neck and shoulder; "he is as warm and damp as a horse just come up from grass. I advise you to look into your stable a little more. I hate to be suspicious, and, thank heaven, I have no cause to be, for I can trust my men, present or absent; but there are mean scoundrels wicked enough to rob a dumb beast of his food; you must look into it." And turning to his man who had come to take me: "Give this horse a right good feed of bruised oats, and don't stint him."

"Dumb beasts!" yes we are; but if I could have spoken I could have told my master where his oats went to. My groom used to come every morning about six o'clock, and with him a little boy, who always had a covered basket with him. He used to go with his father into the harness room where the corn was kept, and I could see them, when the door stood ajar, fill a little bag with oats out of the bin and then he used to be off.

Five or six mornings after this, just as the boy had left the stable, the door was pushed open and a policeman walked in, holding the child tight by the arm; another policeman followed, and locked the door on the inside, saying, "Show me the place where your father keeps his rabbits' food."

The boy looked very frightened and began to cry; but there was no escape, and he led the way to the corn-bin. Here the policeman found another empty bag like that which was found full of oats in the boy's basket.

Filcher was cleaning my feet at the time, but they soon saw him, and though he blustered a good deal, they walked him off to the "lock-up", and his boy with him. I heard afterwards that the boy was not held to be guilty, but the man was sentenced to prison for two months.

CHAPTER THIRTY-ONE

A HUMBUG

~

My master was not immediately suited, but in a few days my new groom came. He was a tall, good-looking fellow enough; but if ever there was a humbug in the shape of a groom, Alfred Smirk was the man. He was very civil to me, and never used me ill; in fact, he did a great deal of stroking and patting when his master was there to see it. He always brushed my mane and tail with water, and my hoofs with oil before he brought me to the door, to make me look smart; but as to cleaning my feet, or looking to my shoes, or grooming me thoroughly, he thought no more of that than if I had been a cow. He left my bit rusty, my saddle damp, and my crupper stiff.

Alfred Smirk considered himself very handsome; he spent a great deal of time about his hair, whiskers, and necktie before a little looking-glass in the harness room. When his master was speaking to him, it was always, "Yes sir; yes, sir"; touching his hat at every word; and every one thought he was a very nice man, and that Mr. Barry was very fortunate to meet with him. I should say he was the laziest, most conceited fellow I ever came near. Of course, it was a great thing not to be ill-used, but then a horse wants more than that. I had a loose box, and might have been very comfortable if he had not been too indolent to clean it out. He never took all the straw away, and the smell from what lay underneath was very bad; while the strong vapours that rose up made my eyes smart and inflame, and I did not feel the same appetite for my food.

One day his master came in and said, "Alfred, the stable smells rather strong; should not you give that stall a good scrub, and throw down plenty of water?"

"Well, sir," he said, touching his cap, "I'll do so if you please, sir, but it is rather dangerous, sir, throwing down water in a horse's box, they are very apt to take cold, sir. I should not like to do him an injury, but I'll do it if you please, sir."

"Well," said his master, "I should not like him to take cold, but I don't like the smell of this stable; do you think the drains are all right?"

"Well, sir, now you mention it, I think the drain does sometimes send back a smell; there may be something wrong, sir."

"Then send for the bricklayer and have it seen to," said his master.

"Yes, sir, I will."

The bricklayer came and pulled up a great many bricks, and found nothing amiss; so he put down some lime and charged the master five shillings, and the smell in my box was as bad as ever; but that was not all – standing as I did on a quantity of moist straw my feet grew unhealthy and tender, and the master used to say:

"I don't know what is the matter with this horse, he goes very fumble-footed. I am sometimes afraid he will stumble."

"Yes, sir," said Alfred, "I have noticed the same myself when I have exercised him."

Now, the fact was that he hardly ever did exercise me, and when the master was busy I often stood for days together without stretching my legs at all, and yet being fed just as high as if I were at hard work. This often disordered my health, and made me sometimes heavy and dull, but more often restless and feverish. He never even gave me a meal of green meat, or a bran mash, which would have cooled me, for he was altogether as ignorant as he was conceited; and then, instead of exercise or change of food, I had to take horse-balls and draughts; which, beside the nuisance of having them poured down my throat, used to make me feel ill and uncomfortable.

One day my feet were so tender, that trotting over some fresh stones with my master on my back, I made two such serious stumbles that as he came down Lansdown into the city, he stopped at the farrier's, and asked him to see what was the matter with me. The man took up my feet one by one and examined them; then standing up and dusting his hands one against the other, he said:

"Your horse has got the 'thrush', and badly too; his feet are very tender; it is fortunate that he has not been down. I wonder your groom has not seen to it before. This is the sort of thing we find in foul stables, where the litter is never properly cleared out. If you will send him here to-morrow, I will attend to the hoof, and I will direct your man how to apply the liniment which I will give him."

The next day I had my feet thoroughly cleansed and stuffed with tow, soaked in some strong lotion; and a very unpleasant business it was.

The farrier ordered all the litter to be taken out of my box day by day, and the floor kept very clean. Then I was to have bran mashes, a little green meat, and not so much corn, till my feet were well again. With this treatment I soon regained my spirits, but Mr. Barry was so much disgusted at being twice deceived by his grooms that he determined to give up keeping a horse, and to hire when he wanted one. I was, therefore, kept till my feet were quite sound, and was then sold again.

CHAPTER THIRTY-TWO

A HORSE FAIR

~

No doubt a horse fair is a very amusing place to those who have nothing to lose; at any rate, there is plenty to see.

Long strings of young horses out of the country, fresh from the marshes; and droves of shaggy little Welsh ponies, no higher than Merrylegs; and hundreds of cart horses of all sorts, some of them with their long tails braided up and tied with scarlet cord; and a good many like myself, handsome and high-bred, but fallen into the middle class through some accident or blemish, unsoundness of wind, or some other complaint. There were some splendid animals quite in their prime, and fit for anything; they were throwing out their legs and showing off their paces in high style, as they were trotted out with a leading rein, the groom running by the side. But round in the background there were a number of poor things, sadly broken down with hard work; with their knees knuckling over, and their hind legs swinging out at every step; and there were some very dejected-looking old horses, with the under lip hanging down, and the ears laying back heavily, as if there was no more pleasure in life, and no more hope; there were some so thin you might see all their ribs, and some with old sores on their backs and hips; these were sad sights for a horse to look upon, who knows not but he may come to the same state.

There was a great deal of bargaining; of running up and beating down, and if a horse may speak his mind so far as he understands, I should say there were more lies told, and more trickery at that horse fair than a clever man could give an account of. I was put with two or three other strong, useful-looking horses, and a good many people came to look at us. The gentlemen always turned from me when they saw my broken knees; though the man who had me swore it was only a slip in the stall.

The first thing was to pull my mouth open, then to look at my eyes, then feel all the way down my legs, and give me a hard feel of the skin and flesh, and then try my paces. It was wonderful what a difference there was in the way these things were done. Some did it in a rough, off-handed way, as if one was only a piece of wood; while others would take their hands gently over one's body, with a pat now and then, as much as to say "by your leave". Of course, I judged a good deal of the buyers by their manners to myself.

There was one man, I thought, if he would buy me, I should be happy. He was not a gentleman, nor yet one of the loud, flashy sort that called themselves so. He was rather a small man, but well made, and quick in all his motions. I knew in a moment by the way he handled me that he was used to horses; he spoke gently, and his grey eye had a kindly, cheery look in it. It may seem strange to say – but it is true all the same – that the clean, fresh smell there was about him made me take to him; no smell of old beer and tobacco, which I hated, but a fresh smell as if he had come out of a hayloft. He offered twenty-three pounds for me; but that was refused, and he walked away. I looked after him, but he was gone, and a very hard-looking, loud-voiced man came; I was dreadfully afraid he would have me; but he walked off. One or two more came who did not mean business. Then the hard-faced man came back again and offered twenty-three pounds. A very close bargain was being driven, for my salesman began to think he should not get all he asked, and must come down; but just then the grey-eyed man came back again. I could not help reaching out my head towards him. He stroked my face kindly.

"Well, old chap," he said, "I think we should suit each other. I'll give twenty-four for him."

"Say twenty-five and you shall have him."

"Twenty-four ten," said my friend, in a very decided tone, "and not another sixpence – yes or no?"

"Done," said the salesman, "and you may depend upon it there's a monstrous deal of quality in that horse, and if you want him for cab work he's a bargain."

The money was paid on the spot, and my new master took my halter and led me out of the fair to an inn, where he had a saddle and bridle ready. He gave me a good feed of oats, and stood by whilst I ate it, talking to himself, and talking to me. Half an hour after we were on our way to London, through pleasant lanes and country roads, until we came in to the great London thoroughfare, on which we travelled steadily, till in the twilight we reached the great City. The gas lamps were already lighted; there were streets to the right, and streets to the left and streets crossing each other for mile upon mile. I thought we should never come to an end of them. At last, in passing through one, we came to a long cabstand, when my rider called out in a cheery voice, "Good night, Governor!"

"Hallo!" cried a voice, "have you got a good one?"

"I think so," replied my owner.

"I wish you luck with him."

"Thank ye, Governor," and he rode on. We soon turned up one of the side streets, and about half-way up that we turned into a very narrow street, with rather poor-looking houses on one side, and what seemed to be coach-houses and stables on the other.

My owner pulled up at one of the houses and whistled. The door flew open, and a young woman, followed by a little girl and boy, ran out. There was a very lively greeting as my rider dismounted.

"Now, then, Harry, my boy, open the gates, and mother will bring us the lantern."

The next minute they were all standing round me in a small stable yard.

"Is he gentle, father?"

"Yes, Dolly, as gentle as your own kitten; come and pat him."

At once the little hand was patting about all over my shoulder without fear. How good it felt!

"Let me get him a bran mash while you rub him down," said the mother.

"Do, Polly, it's just what he wants, and I know you've got a beautiful mash ready for me."

CHAPTER THIRTY-THREE

A LONDON CAB HORSE

~

My new master's name was Jeremiah Barker, but as every one called him Jerry, I shall do the same. Polly, his wife, was just as good a match as a man could have. She was a plump, trim, tidy little woman, with smooth dark hair, dark eyes, and a merry little mouth. The boy was nearly twelve years old; a tall, frank, good-tempered lad; and litle Dorothy (Dolly they called her) was her mother over again, at eight years old. They were all wonderfully fond of each other; I never knew such a happy, merry family before or since. Jerry had a cab of his own, and two horses, which he drove and attended to himself. His other horse was a tall, white, rather large-boned animal, called Captain; he was old now, but when he was young he must have been splendid; he had still a proud way of holding his head and arching his neck; in fact, he was a high-bred, fine-mannered, noble old horse, every inch of him. He told me that in his early youth he went to the Crimean War; he belonged to an officer in the cavalry, and used to lead the regiment; I will tell more of that hereafter.

The next morning, when I was well groomed, Polly and Dolly came into the yard to see me, and make friends. Harry had been helping his father since the early morning, and had stated his opinion that I should turn out "a regular brick". Polly brought me a slice of apple, and Dolly a piece of bread, and made as much of me as if I had been the "Black Beauty" of old time. It was a great treat to be petted again, and talked to in a gentle voice, and I let them see as well as I could that I wished to be friendly. Polly thought I was very handsome, and a great deal too good for a cab, if it was not for the broken knees.

"Of course, there's no one to tell us whose fault that was," said Jerry, "and as long as I don't know I shall give him the benefit of the doubt; for a firmer neater stepper I never rode; we'll call him 'Jack', after the old one; shall we, Polly?"

"Do," she said, "for I like to keep a good name going."

Captain went out in the cab all the morning. Harry came in after school to feed me and give me water. In the afternoon I was put into the cab. Jerry took as much pains to see if the collar and bridle fitted comfortably, as if he had been John Manly over again. When the crupper was let out a hole or two, it all fitted well. There was no bearing rein – no curb – nothing but a plain ring snaffle. What a blessing that was!

After driving through the side street we came to the large cabstand where Jerry had said "Good night." On one side of this wide street were high houses with wonderful shop fronts, and on the other was an old church and churchyard surrounded by iron palisades. Alongside these iron rails a number of cabs were drawn up, waiting for passengers; bits of hay were lying about on the ground; some of the men were standing together, some were sitting on their boxes reading the newspaper, and one or two were feeding their horses with bits of hay and a drink of water. We pulled up in the rank at the back of the last cab. Two or three men came round and began to look at me and pass their remarks.

"Very good for a funeral," said one.

"Too smart-looking," said another, shaking his head in a very wise way; "you'll find out something wrong one of these fine mornings, or my name isn't Jones."

"Well," said Jerry pleasantly, "I suppose I need not find it out till it finds me out; eh? and if so, I'll keep up my spirits a little longer."

Then came up a broad-faced man, dressed in a great grey coat with great grey capes, and great white buttons, a grey hat, and a blue comforter loosely tied round his neck; his hair was grey too, but he was a jolly-looking fellow, and the other men made way for him. He looked me all over as if he had been going to buy me; and then straightening himself up with a grunt, he said, "He's the right sort for you, Jerry; I don't care what you gave for him, he'll be worth it." Thus my character was established on the stand.

This man's name was Grant, but he was called "Grey Grant", or "Governor Grant". He had been the longest on that stand of any of the men, and he took it upon himself to settle matters, and stop disputes. He was generally a good-humoured, sensible man; but if his temper was a little out, as it was sometimes when he had drunk too much, nobody liked to come too near his fist, for he could deal a very heavy blow.

The first week of my life as a cab horse was very trying; I had never been used to London, and the noise, the hurry, the crowds of horses, carts, and carriages that I had to make my way through, made me feel anxious and harassed; but I soon found that I could perfectly trust my driver, and then I made myself easy, and got used to it.

Jerry was as good a driver as I had ever known; and, what was better, he took as much thought for his horses as he did for himself. He soon found out that I was willing to work, and do my best; and he never laid the whip on me unless it was gently drawing the end of it over my back when I was to go on; but generally I knew this quite well by the way in which he took up the reins; and I believe his whip was more frequently stuck up by his side than in his hand.

In a short time I and my master understood each other as well as horse and man can do. In the stable, too, he did all that he could for our comfort. The stalls were the old-fashioned style, too much on the slope; but he had two movable bars fixed across the back of our stalls, so that at night, and when we were resting, he just took off our halters and put up the bars, and thus we could turn about and stand whichever way we pleased, which is a great comfort.

Jerry kept us very clean, and gave us as much change of food as he could, and always plenty of it; and not only that, but he always gave us plenty of clean fresh water, which he allowed to stand by us both night and day, except, of course, when we came in warm. Some people say that a horse ought not to drink all he likes; but I know if we are allowed to drink when we want it, we drink only a little at a time, and it does us a great deal more good than swallowing down half a bucketful at a time, because we have been left without till we are thirsty and miserable. Some grooms will go home to their beer and leave us for hours with our dry hay and oats and nothing to moisten them; then, of course, we gulp down too much at once, which helps to spoil our breathing and sometimes chills our stomachs. But the best thing that we had here was our Sundays for rest; we worked so hard in the week that I do not think we could have kept up to it but for that day; besides, we had then time to enjoy each other's company. It was on these days that I learned my companion's history.

CHAPTER THIRTY-FOUR

AN OLD WAR HORSE

~

Captain had been broken in and trained for an army horse; his first owner was an officer of cavalry going out to the Crimean War. He said he quite enjoyed the training with all the other horses, trotting together, turning together, to the right hand or to the left, halting at the word of command, or dashing forward at full speed at the sound of the trumpet, or signal of the officer. He was, when young, a dark, dappled iron-grey, and considered very handsome. His master, a young, high-spirited gentleman, was very fond of him, and treated him from the first with the greatest care and kindness. He told me he thought the life of an army horse was very pleasant; but when he came to being sent abroad, over the sea in a great ship, he almost changed his mind.

"That part of it," he said, "was dreadful! Of course we could not walk off the land into the ship, so they were obliged to put strong straps under our bodies, and then we were lifted off our legs in spite of our struggles, and were swung through the air over the water to the deck of the great vessel.

145

There we were placed in small close stalls, and never for a long time saw the sky, or were able to stretch our legs. The ship sometimes rolled about in high winds, and we were knocked about, and felt bad enough. However, at last it came to an end, and we were hauled up and swung over again to the land; we were very glad, and snorted, and neighed for joy when we once more felt firm ground under our feet.

"We soon found that the country we had come to was very different to our own, and that we had many hardships to endure besides the fighting; but many of the men were so fond of their horses that they did everything they could to make them comfortable, in spite of snow, wet, and all things out of order."

"But what about the fighting?" said I. "Was not that worse than anything else?"

"Well," said he, "I hardly know; we always liked to hear the trumpet sound, and to be called out, and were impatient to start off, though sometimes we had to stand for hours waiting for the word of command; and when the word was given, we used to spring forward as gaily and eagerly as if there were no cannon balls, bayonets, or bullets. I believe so long as we felt our rider firm in the saddle, and his hand steady on the bridle, not one of us gave way to fear, not even when the terrible bombshells whirled through the air and burst into a thousand pieces.

"I, with my noble master, went into many actions together without a wound; and though I saw horses shot down with bullets, pierced through with lances, and gashed with fearful sabre-cuts; though we left them dead on the field, or dying in the agony of their wounds, I don't think I feared for myself. My master's cheery voice, as he encouraged his men, made me feel as if he and I could not be killed. I had such perfect trust in him that whilst he was guiding me I was ready to charge up to the very cannon's mouth. I saw many brave men cut down, many fall mortally wounded from their saddles. I had heard the cries and groans of the dying, I had cantered over ground slippery with blood, and frequently had to turn aside to avoid trampling on wounded man or horse; but, until one dreadful day, I had never felt terror; that day I shall never forget."

Here old Captain paused for a while and drew a long breath. I waited, and he went on:

"It was one autumn morning, and, as usual, an hour before daybreak our cavalry had turned out, ready caparisoned for the day's work, whether it might be fighting or waiting. The men stood by their horses waiting, ready for orders. As the light increased there seemed to be some excitement among the officers; and before the day was well begun we heard the firing of the enemy's guns.

"Then one of the officers rode up and gave the word for the men to mount, and in a second every man was in his saddle, and every horse stood expecting the touch of the rein or the pressure of his rider's heels, all animated, all eager; but still we had been trained so well, that except by the champing of our bits, and the restive tossing of our heads from time to time, it could not be said that we stirred.

"My dear master and I were at the head of the line, and as all sat motionless and watchful, he took a little stray lock of my mane which had turned over on the wrong side, laid it over on the right, and smoothed it down with his hand; then patting my neck, he said, 'We shall have a day of it to-day, Bayard, my beauty; but we'll do our duty as we have done.' He stroked my neck that morning, more, I think, than he had ever done before; quietly on and on, as if he were thinking of something else. I loved to feel his hand on my neck, and arched my crest proudly and happily; but I stood very still, for I knew all his moods, and when he liked me to be quiet and when gay.

"I cannot tell all that happened on that day, but I will tell of the last charge that we made together: it was across a valley right in front of the enemy's cannon. By this time we were well used to the roar of heavy guns, the rattle of musket fire, and the flying of shot near us; but never had I been under such a fire as we rode through on that day. From the right, from the left, and from the front, shot and shell poured in upon us. Many a brave man went down, many a horse fell, flinging his rider to the earth; many a horse without a rider ran wildly out of the ranks; then terrified at being alone with no hand to guide him, came pressing in amongst his old companions, to gallop with them to the charge.

"Fearful as it was, no one stopped, no one turned back. Every moment the ranks were thinned, but as our comrades fell we closed in to keep them together; and instead of being shaken or staggered in our pace, our gallop became faster and faster as we neared the cannon, all clouded in white smoke, while the red fire flashed through it.

"My master, my dear master, was cheering on his comrades with his right arm raised on high, when one of the balls, whizzing close to my head, struck him. I felt him stagger with the shock, though he uttered no cry. I tried to check my speed, but the sword dropped from his right hand, the rein fell loose from the left, and sinking backward from the saddle he fell to the earth; the other riders swept past us, and by the force of their charge I was driven from the spot where he fell.

"I wanted to keep my place by his side and not leave him under the rush of horses' feet, but it was in vain; and now, without a master or a friend, I was alone on that great slaughter ground; then fear took hold on me and I trembled as I had never trembled before; and I too, as I had seen other horses do, tried to join in the ranks and gallop with them; but I was beaten off by the swords of the soldiers. Just then a soldier, whose horse had been killed under him, caught at my bridle and mounted me; and with this new master I was again going forward. But our gallant company was cruelly overpowered, and those who remained alive after the fierce fight of the guns came galloping back over the same ground. Some of the horses had been so badly wounded that they could scarcely move from the loss of blood; other noble creatures were trying on three legs to drag themselves along, and others were struggling to rise on their forefeet, when their hind legs had been shattered by shot. Their groans were piteous to hear, and the beseeching look in their eyes as those who escaped passed by, and left them to their fate, I shall never forget. After the battle the wounded men were brought in, and the dead buried."

"And what about the wounded horses?" I said. "Were they left to die?"

"No, the army farriers went over the field with their pistols and shot all that were ruined; some that had only slight wounds were brought back and attended to, but the greater part of the noble willing creatures that went out that morning never came back! In our stables there was only about one in four that returned.

"I never saw my dear master again. I believe he fell dead from the saddle. I never loved any other master so well. I went into many other engagements, but was only once wounded, and then not seriously; and when the war was over I came back again to England, as sound and strong as when I went out."

I said, "I have heard people talk about war as if it was a very fine thing."

"Ah!" said he, "I should think they never saw it. No doubt it is very fine when there is no enemy, when it is just exercise and parade, and sham-fight. Yes, it is very fine then; but when thousands of good brave men and horses are killed, or crippled for life, it has a very different look."

"Do you know what they fought about?" said I.

"No," he said, "that is more than a horse can understand, but the enemy must have been awfully wicked people if it was right to go all that way over the sea on purpose to kill them."

CHAPTER THIRTY-FIVE

JERRY BARKER

~

I never knew a better man than my new master; he was kind and good, and as strong for the right as John Manly; and so good-tempered and merry that very few people could pick a quarrel with him. He was very fond of making little songs, and singing them to himself. One he was very fond of was this:

> *Come, father and mother,*
> *And sister and brother,*
> *Come, all of you, turn to*
> *And help one another.*

And so they did. Harry was as clever at stable work as a much older boy, and always wanted to do what he could. Then Polly and Dolly used to come in the morning to help with the cab – to brush and beat the cushions, and rub the glass, while Jerry was giving us a cleaning in the yard, and Harry was rubbing the harness. There used to be a great deal of laughing and fun between them, and it put Captain and me in much better spirits than if we had heard scolding and hard words. They were always early in the morning, for Jerry would say:

> *If you in the morning*
> *Throw minutes away,*
> *You can't pick them up*
> *In the course of the day.*
> *You may hurry and scurry,*
> *And flurry and worry,*
> *You've lost them for ever,*
> *For ever and aye.*

He could not bear any careless loitering and waste of time; and nothing was so near making him angry as to find people who were always late, wanting a cab horse to be driven hard to make up for their idleness.

One day, two wild-looking young men came out of a tavern close by the stand and called Jerry:

"Here, cabby! look sharp, we are rather late; put on the steam, will you, and take us to the Victoria in time for the one o'clock train? You shall have a shilling extra."

"I will take you at the regular pace, gentlemen; shillings don't pay for putting on the steam like that."

Larry's cab was standing next to ours. He flung open the door, and said, "I'm your man, gentlemen! take my cab, my horse will get you there all right"; and as he shut them in, with a wink towards Jerry, said, "It's against his conscience to go beyond a jog-trot." Then, slashing his jaded horse, he set off as hard as he could. Jerry patted me on the neck, "No, Jack, a shilling would not pay for that sort of thing, would it, old boy?"

Although Jerry was determinedly set against hard driving to please careless people, he always went a good fair pace, and was not against putting on the steam, as he said, if only he knew *why*.

I well remember one morning, as we were on the stand waiting for a fare, that a young man, carrying a heavy portmanteau, trod on a piece of orange peel which lay on the pavement and fell down with great force.

Jerry was the first to run and lift him up. He seemed much stunned, and as they led him into a shop he walked as if he were in great pain. Jerry, of course, came back to the stand, but in about ten minutes one of the shopmen called him, so he drew up to the pavement.

"Can you take me to the South-Eastern Railway?" said the young man. "This unlucky fall has made me late, I fear; but it is of great importance that I should not lose the twelve o'clock train. I should be most thankful if you could get me there in time, and will gladly pay you an extra fare."

"I'll do my very best," said Jerry heartily, "if you think you are well enough, sir," for he looked dreadfully white and ill.

"I *must* go," he said earnestly. "Please to open the door, and let us lose no time."

The next minute Jerry was on the box; with a cheery chirrup to me, and a twitch of the rein that I well understood.

"Now then, Jack, my boy," said he, "spin along; we'll show them how we can get over the ground if we only know why."

It is always difficult to drive fast in the city in the middle of the day, when the streets are full of traffic, but we did what could be done; and when a good driver and a good horse, who understand each other, are of one mind, it is wonderful what they can do. I had a very good mouth – that is, I could be guided by the slightest touch of the rein, and that is a great thing in London, amongst carriages, omnibuses, carts, vans, trucks, cabs, and great wagons creeping along at a walking pace; some going one way, some another; some going slowly, others wanting to pass them; omnibuses stopping short every few minutes to take up a passenger, obliging the horse that is coming behind to pull up too, or to pass, and get before them. Perhaps you try to pass, but just then something else comes dashing in through the narrow opening and you have to keep in behind the omnibus again. Presently you think you see a chance, and manage to get to the front, going so near the wheels on each side that half an inch nearer and they would scrape. Well, you get along for a bit, but soon find yourself in a long train of carts and carriages all obliged to go at a walk; perhaps you come to a regular block-up, and have to stand still for minutes together, till something clears out into a side street, or the policeman interferes. You have to be ready for any chance – to dash forward if there be an opening, and be quick as a rat dog to see if there be room, and if there be time, lest you get your own wheels locked, or smashed, or the shaft of some other vehicle run into your chest or shoulder. All this is what you have to be ready for. If you want to get through London fast in the middle of the day, it wants a deal of practice.

Jerry and I were used to it, and no one could beat us at getting through when we were set upon it. I was quick and bold, and could always trust my driver; Jerry was quick, and patient at the same time, and could trust his horse, which was a great thing too. He very seldom used the whip; I knew by his voice and his "click click" when he wanted to get on fast, and by the rein where I was to go; so there was no need for whipping; but I must go back to my story.

The streets were very full that day, but we got on pretty well as far as the bottom of Cheapside, where there was a block of three or four minutes. The young man put his head out and said anxiously, "I think I had better get out and walk, I shall never get there if this goes on."

"I'll do all that can be done, sir," said Jerry. "I think we shall be in time; this block-up cannot last much longer, and your luggage is very heavy for you to carry, sir."

Just then the cart in front of us began to move on, and then we had a good turn. In and out – in and out we went, as fast as horseflesh could do it, and for a wonder had a good clear time on London Bridge, for there was a whole train of cabs and carriages, all going our way at a quick trot – perhaps wanting to catch that very train; at any rate, we whirled into the station with many more, just as the great clock pointed to eight minutes to twelve o'clock.

"Thank God! we are in time," said the young man, "and thank you too, my friend, and your good horse. You have saved me more than money can ever pay for; take this extra half-crown."

"No, sir, no; thank you all the same. So glad we hit the time, sir; but don't stay now, sir, the bell is ringing. Here, porter! take this gentleman's luggage – Dover line – twelve o'clock – that's it," and without waiting for another word, Jerry wheeled me round to make room for other cabs that were dashing up at the last minute, and drew up on one side till the crush was past.

"So glad!" he said, "'so glad!' Poor young fellow! I wonder what it was that made him so anxious!"

Jerry often talked to himself quite loud enough for me to hear, when we were not moving.

On Jerry's return to the rank there was a good deal of laughing and chaffing at him for driving hard to the train for an extra fare, as they said, all against his principles; and they wanted to know how much he had pocketed.

"A good deal more than I generally get," said he, nodding slyly. "What he gave me will keep me in little comforts for several days."

"Gammon!" said one.

"He's a humbug," said another, "preaching to us, and then doing the same himself."

"Look here, mates," said Jerry, "the gentleman offered me half a crown extra, but I didn't take it; 'twas quite pay enough for me to see how glad he was to catch that train; and if Jack and I choose to have a quick run now and then, to please ourselves, that's our business and not yours."

"Well," said Larry, "*you'll* never be a rich man."

"Most likely not," said Jerry; "but I don't know that I shall be the less happy for that. I have heard the Commandments read a great many times, and I never noticed that any of them said, 'Thou shalt be rich'; and there are a good many curious things said in the New Testament about rich men that I think would make me feel rather queer if I was one of them."

"If you ever do get rich," said Governor Grant, looking over his shoulder across the top of his cab, "you'll deserve it, Jerry, and you won't find a curse come with your wealth. As for you, Larry, you'll die poor, you spend too much on whipcord."

"Well," said Larry, "what is a fellow to do if his horse won't go without it?"

"You never take the trouble to see if he will go without it; your whip is always going as if you had the St. Vitus's dance in your arm; and if it does not wear you out, it wears your horse out; you know you are always changing horses, and why? Because you never give them any peace or encouragement."

"Well, I have not had good luck," said Larry, "that's where it is."

"And you never will," said the Governor. "Good Luck is rather particular who she rides with, and mostly prefers those who have got common sense and a good heart; at least, that is my experience."

Governor Grant turned round again to his newspaper, and the other men went to their cabs.

CHAPTER THIRTY-SIX

THE SUNDAY CAB

~

One morning, as Jerry had just put me into the shafts and was fastening the traces, a gentleman walked into the yard. "Your servant, sir," said Jerry.

"Good morning, Mr. Barker," said the gentleman. "I should be glad to make some arrangements with you for taking Mrs. Briggs regularly to church on Sunday mornings. We go to the new church now, and that is rather farther than she can walk."

"Thank you, sir," said Jerry, "but I have only taken out a six days' licence,[1] and therefore I could not take a fare on a Sunday, it would not be legal."

"Oh!" said the other, "I did not know yours was a six days' cab; but, of

---

[1] AUTHOR'S NOTE. *Six days' licence.* A few years since the annual charge for a cab licence was very much reduced, and the difference between the six and seven days' cabs was abolished.

course, it would be very easy to alter your licence. I would see that you did not lose by it; the fact is, Mrs. Briggs very much prefers you to drive her."

"I should be glad to oblige the lady, sir, but I had a seven days' licence once, and the work was too hard for me, and too hard for my horses. Year in and year out, not a day's rest, and never a Sunday with my wife and children, and never able to go to a place of worship, which I had always been used to do before I took to the driving box; so for the last five years I have only taken a six days' licence, and I find it better all the way round."

"Well, of course," replied Mr. Briggs, "it is very proper that every person should have rest, and be able to go to church on Sundays, but I should have thought you would not have minded such a short distance for the horse, and only once a day; you would have all the afternoon and evening for yourself, and we are very good customers, you know."

"Yes, sir, that is true, and I am grateful for all favours, I am sure, and anything that I could do to oblige you, or the lady, I should be proud and happy to do; but I can't give up my Sundays, sir, indeed I can't. I read that God made man, and He made horses and all the other beasts, and as soon as He had made them, He made a day of rest, and bade that all should rest one day in seven; and I think, sir, He must have known what was good for them, and I am sure it is good for me. I am stronger and healthier altogether now that I have a day of rest; the horses are fresh, too, and do not wear up nearly so fast. The six-day drivers all tell me the same, and I have laid by more money in the Savings Bank than ever I did before; and as for the wife and children, sir – why, heart alive! they would not go back to the seven days for all they could see."

"Oh, very well," said the gentleman. "Don't trouble yourself, Mr. Barker, any further; I will inquire somewhere else," and he walked away.

"Well," says Jerry to me, "we can't help it, Jack, old boy; we must have our Sundays."

"Polly!" he shouted. "Polly! come here."

She was there in a minute.

"What is it all about, Jerry?"

"Why, my dear, Mr. Briggs wants me to take Mrs. Briggs to church every Sunday morning. I say, I have only a six days' licence. He says, 'Get a seven days' licence and I'll make it worth your while'; and you know, Polly, they are very good customers to us. Mrs. Briggs often goes out shopping for hours, or making calls, and then she pays down fair and honourable like a lady; there's no beating down, or making three hours into two hours and a half, as some folks do; and it is easy work for the horses; not like tearing along to catch trains for people that are always a quarter of an hour too late; and if I don't oblige her in this matter, it is very likely we shall lose them altogether. What do you say, little woman?"

"I say, Jerry," says she, speaking very slowly, "I say, if Mrs. Briggs would give you a sovereign every Sunday morning I would not have you a seven days' cabman again. We have known what it was to have no Sundays; and now we know what it is to call them our own. Thank God, you earn enough to keep us, though it is sometimes close work to pay for all the oats and hay, the licence, and the rent besides. But Harry will soon be earning something, and I would rather struggle on harder than we do than go back to those horrid times, when you hardly had a minute to look at your own children, and we never could go to a place of worship together, or have a happy, quiet day. God forbid that we should ever turn back to those times; that's what I say, Jerry."

"And that is just what I told Mr. Briggs, my dear," said Jerry, "and what I mean to stick to; so don't go and fret yourself, Polly (for she had begun to cry); I would not go back to the old times if I earned twice as much, so that is settled, little woman. Now, cheer up, and I'll be off again to the stand."

Three weeks had passed away after this conversation, and no order had come from Mrs. Briggs; so there was nothing but taking jobs from the stand. Jerry took it to heart a good deal, for, of course, the work was harder for horse and man; but Polly would always cheer him up and say, "Never mind, father, never mind:

> *Do your best,*
> *And leave the rest,*
> *'Twill all come right*
> *Some day or night.*

It soon became known that Jerry had lost his best customer, and for what reason; most of the men said he was a fool, but two or three took his part.

159

"If working men don't stick to their Sunday," said Truman, "they'll soon have none left; it is every man's right and every beast's right. By God's law we have a day of rest, and by the law of England we have a day of rest; and I say we ought to hold to the rights these laws give us, and keep them for our children."

"All very well for you religious chaps to talk so," said Larry, "but I'll turn a shilling when I can. I don't believe in religion, for I don't see that your religious people are any better than the rest."

"If they are not better," put in Jerry, "it is because they are *not* religious. You might as well say that our country's laws are not good because some people break them. If a man gives way to his temper, and speaks evil of his neighbour, and does not pay his debts, he is *not* religious. I don't care how much he goes to church. If some men are shams and humbugs, that does not make religion untrue. Real religion is the best and the truest thing in the world, and the only thing that can make a man really happy or make the world any better."

"If religion was good for anything," said Jones, "it would prevent your religious people from making us work on Sundays as you know many of them do, and that's why I say religion is nothing but a sham — why, if it was not for the church and chapel goers it would be hardly worth while our coming out on a Sunday; but they have their privileges, as they call them, and I go without. I shall expect them to answer for my soul, if I can't get a chance of saving it."

Several of the men applauded this, till Jerry said:

"That may sound well enough, but it won't do; every man must look after his own soul; you can't lay it down at another man's door like a foundling and expect him to take care of it; and don't you see, if you are always sitting on your box waiting for a fare, they will say, 'If we don't take him, some one else will, and he does not look for any Sunday.' Of course they don't go to the bottom of it, or they would see if they never came for a cab it would be no use your standing there; but people don't always like to go to the bottom of things; it may not be convenient to do it; but if you Sunday drivers would all strike for a day of rest, the thing would be done."

"And what would all the good people do if they could not get to their favourite preachers?" said Larry.

"'Tis not for me to lay down plans for other people," said Jerry, "but if they can't walk so far, they can go to what is nearer; and if it should rain they can put on their mackintoshes as they do on a weekday. If a thing is right, it *can* be done, and if it is wrong, it *can be done without*; and a good man will find a way; and that is as true for us cabmen as it is for the churchgoers."

CHAPTER THIRTY-SEVEN

THE GOLDEN RULE

~

Two or three weeks after this, as we came into the yard rather late in the evening, Polly came running across the road with the lantern (she always brought it to him if it was not very wet).

"It has all come right, Jerry; Mrs. Briggs sent her servant this afternoon to ask you to take her out tomorrow at eleven o'clock. I said, 'Yes, I thought so, but we supposed she employed some one else now.'"

"'Well,' says he, 'the real fact is, master was put out because Mr. Barker refused to come on Sundays, and he has been trying other cabs, but there's something wrong with them all; some drive too fast, and some too slow, and the mistress says there is not one of them so nice and clean as yours, and nothing will suit her but Mr. Barker's cab again.'"

Polly was almost out of breath, and Jerry broke out into a merry laugh:

"All come right some day or night; you were right, my dear; you generally are. Run in and get the supper, and I'll have Jack's harness off and make him snug and happy in no time."

After this, Mrs. Briggs wanted Jerry's cab quite as often as before, never, however, on a Sunday; but there came a day when we had Sunday work, and this was how it happened. We had all come home on the Saturday night very tired, and very glad to think that the next day would be all rest; but so it was not to be.

On Sunday morning Jerry was cleaning me in the yard, when Polly stepped up to him, looking very full of something.

"What is it?" said Jerry.

"Well, my dear," she said, "poor Dinah Brown has just had a letter brought to say that her mother is dangerous ill, and that she must go directly if she wishes to see her alive. The place is more than ten miles away from here, out in the country, and she says if she takes the train she should still have four miles to walk; and so weak as she is, and the baby only four weeks old, of course that would be impossible; and she wants to know if you would take her in your cab, and she promises to pay you faithfully as she can get the money."

"Tut, tut, we'll see about that. It was not the money I was thinking about, but of losing our Sunday; the horses are tired, and I am tired too — that's where it pinches."

"It pinches all round, for that matter," said Polly, "for it's only half Sunday without you, but you know we should do to other people as we should like they should do to us; and I know very well what I should like if my mother was dying; and Jerry, dear, I am sure it won't break the Sabbath; for if pulling a poor beast or donkey out of a pit would not spoil it, I am quite sure taking poor Dinah would not do it."

"Why, Polly, you are as good as the minister, and so, as I've had my Sunday morning sermon early to-day, you may go and tell Dinah that I'll be ready for her as the clock strikes ten; but stop — just step round to butcher Braydon's with my compliments, and ask him if he would lend me his light trap; I know he never uses it on the Sunday, and it would make a wonderful difference to the horse."

Away she went, and soon returned, saying that he could have the trap and welcome.

"All right," said he. "Now put me up a bit of bread and cheese, and I'll be back in the afternoon as soon as I can."

"And I'll have the meat pie ready for an early tea instead of for dinner," said Polly; and away she went, whilst he made his preparations to the tune of "Polly, the woman and no mistake", of which tune he was very fond.

I was selected for the journey, and at ten o'clock we started, in a light, high-wheeled gig, which ran so easily that, after the four-wheeled cab, it seemed like nothing.

It was a fine May day, and as soon as we were out of the town, the sweet air, the smell of the fresh grass, and the soft country roads were as pleasant as they used to be in the old times, and I soon began to feel quite fresh.

Dinah's family lived in a small farmhouse up a green lane, close by a meadow with some fine shady trees: there were two cows feeding in it. A young man asked Jerry to bring his trap into the meadow, and he would tie me up in the cowshed; he wished he had a better stable to offer.

"If your cows would not be offended," said Jerry, "there is nothing my horse would like so well as to have an hour or two in your beautiful meadow; he's quiet, and it would be a rare treat for him."

"Do, and welcome," said the young man; "the best we have is at your service for your kindness to my sister. We shall be having some dinner in an hour, and I hope you'll come in, though with mother so ill we are all out of sorts in the house."

Jerry thanked him kindly, but said as he had some dinner with him there was nothing he should like so well as walking about in the meadow.

When my harness was taken off I did not know what I should do first — whether to eat the grass, or roll over on my back, or lie down and rest, or have a gallop across the meadow out of sheer spirits at being fee; and I did all by turns. Jerry seemed to be quite as happy as I was; he sat down by a bank under a shady tree and listened to the birds, then he sang himself, and read out of the little brown book he is so fond of, then wandered round the meadow and down by a little brook, where he picked the flowers and the hawthorn, and tied them up with long sprays of ivy; then he gave me a good feed of oats which he had brought with him; but the time seemed all too short — I had not been in a field since I left poor Ginger at Earlshall.

We came home gently, and Jerry's first words were as we came into the yard, "Well, Polly, I have not lost my Sunday after all, for the birds were singing hymns in every bush, and I joined in the service; and as for Jack, he was like a young colt."

When he handed Dolly the flowers she jumped about for joy.

CHAPTER THIRTY-EIGHT

DOLLY AND A REAL GENTLEMAN

~

The winter came in early, with a great deal of cold and wet. There was snow, or sleet, or rain, almost every day for weeks, changing only for keen driving winds or sharp frosts. The horses all felt it very much. When it is a dry cold, a couple of thick rugs will keep the warmth in us; but when it is soaking rain they soon get wet through and are no good. Some of the drivers had a waterproof cover to throw over, which was a fine thing; but some of the men were so poor that they could not protect either themselves or their horses, and many of them suffered very much that winter. When we horses had worked half the day we went to our dry stables, and could rest; whilst they had to sit on their boxes, sometimes staying out as late as one or two o'clock in the morning, if they had a party to wait for.

When the streets were slippery with frost or snow that was the worst of all for us horses; one mile of such travelling, with a weight to draw, and no firm footing, would take more out of us than four on a good road; every nerve and muscle of our bodies is on the strain to keep our balance; and, added to this, the fear of falling is more exhausting than anything else. If the roads are very bad indeed, our shoes are roughed, but that makes us feel nervous at first.

When the weather was very bad, many of the men would go and sit in the tavern close by, and get some one to watch for them; but they often lost a fare in that way, and could not, as Jerry said, be there without spending money. He never went to the "Rising Sun"; there was a coffee-shop near, where he now and then went — or he bought of an old man who came to our rank with tins of hot coffee and pies. It was his opinion that spirits and beer made a man colder afterwards, and that dry clothes, good food, cheerfulness, and a comfortable wife at home were the best things to keep a cabman warm. Polly always supplied him with something to eat when he could not get home, and sometimes he would see little Dolly peeping from the corner of the street, to make sure if "father" was on the stand. If she saw him, she would run off at full speed and soon come back with something in a tin or basket — some hot soup or pudding that Polly had ready. It was wonderful how such a little thing could get safely across the street, often thronged with horses and carriages; but she was a brave little maid, and felt it quite an honour to bring "father's first course," as he used to call it. She was a general favourite on the stand, and there was not a man who would not have seen her safely across the street if Jerry had not been able to do it.

One cold windy day, Dolly had brought Jerry a basin of something hot, and was standing by him whilst he ate it. He had scarcely begun, when a gentleman, walking towards us very fast, held up his umbrella. Jerry touched his hat in return, gave the basin to Dolly, and was taking off my cloth, when the gentleman, hastening up, cried out, "No, no, finish your soup, my friend; I have not much time to spare, but I can wait till you have done, and set your little girl safe on the pavement." So saying, he seated himself in the cab. Jerry thanked him kindly, and came back to Dolly.

"There, Dolly, that's a gentleman; that's a real gentleman, Dolly; he has got time and thought for the comfort of a poor cabman and a little girl."

Jerry finished his soup, set the child across, and then took his orders to drive to "Clapham Rise." Several times after that the same gentleman took our cab. I think he was very fond of dogs and horses, for whenever we took him to his own door, two or three dogs would come bounding out to meet him. Sometimes he came round and patted me, saying in his quiet, pleasant way. "This horse has got a good master, and he deserves it." It was a very rare thing for any one to notice the horse that had been working for him. I have known ladies do it now and then, and this gentleman and one or two others have given me a pat and a kind word; but ninety-nine out of a hundred would as soon think of patting the steam-engine that drew the train.

This gentleman was not young, and there was a forward stoop in his shoulders as if he was always going at something. His lips were thin, and close shut, though they had a very pleasant smile; his eye was keen, and there was something in his jaw and the motion of his head that made one think he was very determined in anything he set about. His voice was pleasant and kind; any horse would trust that voice, though it was just as decided as everything else about him.

One day he and another gentleman took our cab; they stopped at a shop in R— Street, and whilst his friend went in, he stood at the door. A little ahead of us on the other side of the street a cart with two very fine horses was standing before some wine vaults; the carter was not with them, and I cannot tell how long they had been standing, but they seemed to think they had waited long enough, and began to move off. Before they had gone many paces the carter came running out and caught them. He seemed furious at their having moved, and with whip and rein punished them brutally, even beating them about the head. Our gentleman saw it all, and stepping quickly across the street, said in a decided voice:

"If you don't stop that directly I'll have you summoned for leaving your horses, and for brutal conduct."

The man, who had clearly been drinking, poured forth some abusive language, but he left off knocking the horses about, and taking the reins, got into his cart. Meantime our friend had quietly taken a notebook from his pocket, and looking at the name and address painted on the cart, he wrote something down.

"What do you want with that?" growled the carter, as he cracked his whip and was moving off. A nod, and a grim smile, was the only answer he got.

On returning to the cab our friend was joined by his companion, who said laughingly, "I should have thought, Wright, you had enough business of your own to look after without troubling yourself about other people's horses and servants."

Our friend stood still for a moment, and throwing his head a little back said, "Do you know why this world is as bad as it is?"

"No," said the other.

"Then I'll tell you. It is because people think *only* about their own business, and won't trouble themselves to stand up for the oppressed, nor bring the wrongdoer to light. I never see a wicked thing like this without doing what I can, and many a master has thanked me for letting him know how his horses have been used."

"I wish there were more gentlemen like you, sir," said Jerry, "for they are wanted badly enough in this city."

After this we continued our journey, and as they got out of the cab our friend was saying, "My doctrine is this, that if we see cruelty or wrong that we have the power to stop, and do nothing, we make ourselves sharers in the guilt."

CHAPTER THIRTY-NINE

SEEDY SAM

~

I should say, that for a cab horse I was very well off indeed. My driver was my owner, and it was his interest to treat me well, and not overwork me, even had he not been so good a man as he was; but there were a great many horses which belonged to the large cab owners who let them out to their drivers for so much money a day. As the horses did not belong to these men, the only thing they thought of was how to get their money out of them: first, to pay the master, and then to provide for their own living, and a dreadful time some of these horses had of it.

One day, a shabby, miserable-looking driver, who went by the name of "Seedy Sam", brought in his horse looking dreadfully beat, and the Governor said:

"You and your horse look more fit for the police station than for this rank."

The man flung his tattered rug over the horse, turned full round upon the Governor, and said, in a voice that sounded almost desperate:

"If the police have any business with the matter it ought to be with the masters who charge us so much, or with the fares that are fixed so low. If a man has to pay eighteen shillings a day for the use of a cab and two horses, as many of us have to do in the season, and must make that up before we earn a penny for ourselves – I say, 'tis more than hard work; nine shillings a day to get out of each horse before you begin to get your own living; you know that's true, and if the horses don't work we must starve, and I and my children have known what that is before now. I've six of 'em, and only one earns anything; I am on the stand fourteen or sixteen hours a day, and I haven't had a Sunday these ten or twelve weeks; you know, Skinner never gives a day if he can help it, and if I don't work hard, tell me who does; I want a warm coat and a mackintosh, but with so many to feed how can a man get it? I had to pledge my clock a week ago to pay Skinner, and I shall never see it again."

Some of the other drivers stood round nodding their heads, and saying he was right. The man went on:

"You that have your own horse and cabs, or drive for good masters, have a chance of getting on, and a chance of doing right; I haven't. We can't charge more than sixpence a mile after the first, within the four-mile radius. This very morning I had to go a clear six miles and only took three shillings. I could not get a return fare and had to come all the way back; there's twelve miles for the horse and three shillings for me. After that I had a three-mile fare, and there were bags and boxes enough to have brought in a good many twopences if they had been put outside; but you know how people do; all that could be piled up inside on the front seat were put in, and three heavy boxes went on the top, that was sixpence, and the fare one and sixpence; then I got a return for a shilling; now that makes eighteen miles for the horse and six shillings for me; there's three shillings still for that horse to earn, and nine shillings for the afternoon horse before I touch a penny. Of course it is not always as bad as that, but you know it often is, and I say 'tis a mockery to tell a man that he must not overwork his horse, for when a beast is down-right tired there's nothing but the whip that will keep his legs agoing – you can't help yourself – you must put your wife and children before the horse, the masters must look to that, we can't. I don't ill-use my horse for the sake of it; none of you can say I do. There's wrong lays somewhere – never a day's rest – never a quiet hour with the wife and children. I often feel like an old man, though I'm only forty-five. You know how quick some of the gentry are to suspect us of cheating and over-charging; why, they stand with their purses in their hands, counting it over to a penny, and looking at us as if we were pickpockets. I wish some of 'em had got to sit on my box sixteen hours a day, and get a living out of it, and eighteen shillings beside, and that in all weathers; they would not be so uncommon particular never to give us sixpence over, or to cram all the luggage inside. Of course, some of 'em tip us pretty handsome now and then, or else we could not live, but you can't *depend* upon that."

The men who stood round much approved this speech and one of them said, "It is desperate hard, and if a man sometimes does what is wrong it is no wonder; and if he gets a dram too much, who's to blow him up?"

Jerry had taken no part in this conversation, but I never saw his face look so sad before. The Governor had stood with both his hands in his pockets; now he took his handkerchief out of his hat, and wiped his forehead.

"You've beaten me, Sam," he said, "for it's all true, and I won't cast it up to you any more about the police; it was the look in that horse's eye that came over me. It is hard lines for man, and it is hard lines for beast, and who's to mend it I don't know; but any way you might tell the poor beast that you were sorry to take it out of him in that way. Sometimes a kind word is all we can give 'em, poor brutes, and 'tis wonderful what they do understand."

A few mornings after this talk a new man came to the stand with Sam's cab.

"Hallo!" said one, "what's up with Seedy Sam?"

"He's ill in bed," said the man. "He was taken last night in the yard, and could scarcely crawl home. His wife sent a boy this morning to say his father was in a high fever and could not get out; so I'm here instead."

The next morning the same man came again.

"How is Sam?" inquired the Governor.

"He's gone," said the man.

"What, gone? You don't mean to say he's dead?"

"Just snuffed out," said the other; "he died at four o'clock this morning; all yesterday he was raving – raving about Skinner, and having no Sundays. 'I never had a Sunday's rest', these were his last words."

No one spoke for a while, and then the Governor said, "I tell you what, mates, this is a warning for us."

CHAPTER FORTY

POOR GINGER

~

One day, whilst our cab and many others were waiting outside one of the parks where a band was playing, a shabby old cab drove up beside ours. The horse was an old worn-out chestnut, with an ill-kept coat, and bones that showed plainly through it. The knees knuckled over and the forelegs were very unsteady. I had been eating some hay, and the wind rolled a little lock of it that way, and the poor creature put out her long, thin neck and picked it up, and then turned round and looked about for more. There was a hopeless look in the dull eye that I could not help noticing, and then, as I was thinking where I had seen that horse before, she looked full at me and said, "Black Beauty, is that you?"

It was Ginger! But how changed! The beautifully arched and glossy neck was now straight and lank, and fallen in, the clean, straight legs and delicate fetlocks were swelled; the joints were grown out of shape with hard work; the face, that was once so full of spirit and life, was now full of suffering, and I could tell by the heaving of her sides, and her frequent cough, how bad her breath was.

Our drivers were standing together a little way off, so I sidled up to her a step or two, that we might have a little quiet talk. It was a sad tale that she had to tell.

After a twelvemonth's run off at Earlshall she was considered to be fit for work again, and was sold to a gentleman. For a little while she got on very well, but after a longer gallop than usual the old strain returned, and after being rested and doctored she was again sold. In this way she changed hands several times, but always getting lower down.

"And so at last," said she, "I was bought by a man who keeps a number of cabs and horses, and lets them out. You look well off, and I am glad of it, but I could not tell you what my life has been. When they found out my weakness they said I was not worth what they gave for me, and that I must go into one of the low cabs, and just be used up; that is what they are doing, whipping and working with never one thought of what I suffer; they paid for me, and must get it out of me, they say. The man who hires me now pays a deal of money to the owner every day, and so he has to get it out of me too; and so it's all the week round and round, with never a Sunday rest."

I said, "You used to stand up for yourself if you were ill-used."

"Ah!" she said, "I did once, but it's no use; men are strongest, and if they are cruel and have no feeling there is nothing that we can do but just bear it, bear it on and on to the end. I wish the end was come. I wish I was dead. I have seen dead horses, and I am sure they do not suffer pain. I wish I may drop down dead at my work, and not be sent off to the knacker's."

I was very much troubled, and I put my nose up to hers, and I could say nothing to comfort her. I think she was pleased to see me, for she said, "You are the only friend I ever had."

Just then her driver came up, and with a tug at her mouth, backed her out of the line and drove off, leaving me very sad indeed.

A short time after this a cart with a dead horse in it passed our cabstand. The head hung out of the cart tail, the lifeless tongue was slowly dropping with blood; and the sunken eyes! but I can't speak of them, the sight was too dreadful. It was a chestnut horse with a long, thin neck. I saw a white streak down the forehead. I believe it was Ginger; I hoped it was, for then her troubles would be over. Oh! if men were more merciful they would shoot us before we came to such misery.

CHAPTER FORTY-ONE

THE BUTCHER

~

I saw a great deal of trouble amongst the horses in London, and much of it that might have been prevented by a little common sense. We horses do not mind hard work if we are treated reasonably, and I am sure there are many driven by quite poor men who have a happier life than I had when I used to go in the Countess of W——'s carriage, with my silver-mounted harness and high feeding.

It often went to my heart to see how the little ponies were used, straining along with heavy loads, or staggering under heavy blows from some low, cruel boy. Once I saw a little grey pony with a thick mane and a pretty head, and so much like Merrylegs, that if I had not been in harness I should have neighed to him. He was doing his best to pull a heavy cart, while a strong rough boy was cutting him under the belly with his whip, and chucking cruelly at his little mouth. Could it be Merrylegs? It was just like him; but then Mr. Blomefield was never to sell him, and I think he would not do it; but this might have been quite as good a little fellow, and had as happy a place when he was young.

I often noticed the great speed at which butchers' horses were made to go, though I did not know why it was so, till one day when we had to wait some time in "St. John's Wood". There was a butcher's shop next door, and as we were standing, a butcher's cart came dashing up at a great pace. The horse was hot, and much exhausted; he hung his head down, while his heaving sides and trembling legs showed how hard he had been driven. The lad jumped out of the cart and was getting the basket, when the master came out of the shop much displeased. After looking at the horse, he turned angrily to the lad: "How many times shall I tell you not to drive in this way? You ruined the last horse and broke his wind, and you are going to ruin this in the same way. If you were not my own son, I would dismiss you on the spot; it is a disgrace to have a horse brought to the shop in a condition like that. You are liable to be taken up by the police for such driving, and if you are, you need not look to me for bail, for I have spoken to you till I am tired; you must look out for yourself."

During this speech the boy had stood by, sullen and dogged, but when his father ceased, he broke out angrily. It wasn't his fault, and he wouldn't take the blame, he was only going by orders all the time.

"You always say, 'Now be quick; now look sharp!' and when I go to the houses, one wants a leg of mutton for an early dinner, and I must be back with it in a quarter of an hour. Another cook had forgotten to order the beef; I must go and fetch it and be back in no time, or the mistress will scold; and the housekeeper says they have company coming unexpectedly and must have some chops sent up directly; and the lady at No. 4, in the Crescent, *never* orders her dinner till the meat comes in for lunch, and it's nothing but hurry, hurry, all the time. If the gentry would think of what they want, and order their meat the day before, there need not be this blow up!"

"I wish to goodness they would," said the butcher; "'twould save me a wonderful deal of harass, and I could suit my customers much better if I knew beforehand – but there – what's the use of talking – who ever thinks of a butcher's convenience, or a butcher's horse? Now, then, take him in, and look to him well: mind, he does not go out again to-day, and if anything else is wanted, you must carry it yourself in the basket." With that he went in, and the horse was led away.

But all boys are not cruel. I have seen some as fond of their pony or donkey as if it had been a favourite dog, and the little creatures have worked away as cheerfully and willingly for their young drivers as I work for Jerry. It may be hard work sometimes, but a friend's hand and voice make it easy.

There was a young coster-boy who came up our street with greens and potatoes; he had an old pony, not very handsome, but the cheerfullest and pluckiest little thing I ever saw, and to see how fond those two were of each other was a treat. The pony followed his master like a dog, and when he got into his cart, would trot off without a whip or a word, and rattle down the street as merrily as if he had come out of the Queen's stables. Jerry liked the boy, and called him "Prince Charlie", for he said he would make a king of drivers some day.

There was an old man, too, who used to come up our street with a little coal cart; he wore a coal-heaver's hat, and looked rough and black. He and his old horse used to plod together along the street, like two good partners who understood each other; the horse would stop of his own accord at the doors where they took coal of him; he used to keep one ear bent towards his master. The old man's cry could be heard up the street long before he came near. I never knew what he said, but the children called him "Old Ba-a-ar Hoo", for it sounded like that. Polly took her coal of him, and was very friendly, and Jerry said it was a comfort to think how happy an old horse *might* be in a poor place.

CHAPTER FORTY-TWO

THE ELECTION

~

As we came into the yard one afternoon, Polly came out: "Jerry! I've had Mr. B— here asking about your vote, and he wants to hire your cab for the election; he will call for an answer."

"Well, Polly, you may say that my cab will be otherwise engaged; I should not like to have it pasted over with their great bills, and as to make Jack and Captain race about to the public-houses to bring up half-drunken voters, why I think 'twould be an insult to the horses. No, I shan't do it."

"I suppose you'll vote for the gentleman? He said he was of your politics."

"So he is in some things, but I shall not vote for him, Polly; you know what his trade is?"

"Yes."

"Well, a man who gets rich by that trade may be all very well in some ways, but he is blind as to what working men want: I could not in my conscience send him up to make the laws. I dare say they'll be angry, but every man must do what he thinks to be the best for his country."

On the morning before the election, Jerry was putting me into the shafts, when Dolly came into the yard sobbing and crying, with her little blue frock and white pinafore spattered all over with mud.

"Why, Dolly, what is the matter?"

"Those naughty boys," she sobbed, "have thrown the dirt all over me, and called me a little ragga – ragga—"

"They called her a little blue raggamuffin, father," said Harry, who ran in looking very angry; "but I have given it to them, they won't insult my sister again. I have given them a thrashing they will remember; a set of cowardly, rascally, orange blackguards!"

Jerry kissed the child and said, "Run in to mother, my pet, and tell her I think you had better stay at home to-day and help her."

Then turning gravely to Harry:

"My boy, I hope you will always defend your sister, and give anybody who insults her a good thrashing – that is as it should be; but mind, I won't have any election blackguarding on my premises. There are as many blue blackguards as there are orange, and as many white as there are purple or any other colour, and I won't have any of my family mixed up with it. Even women and children are ready to quarrel for the sake of a colour, and not one in ten of them knows what it is about."

"Why, father, I thought blue was for Liberty."

"My boy, Liberty does not come from colours; they only show party, and all the liberty you can get out of them is, liberty to get drunk at other people's expense, liberty to ride to the poll in a dirty old cab, liberty to abuse any one that does not wear your colour, and to shout yourself hoarse at what you only half understand – that's your liberty!"

"Oh, father, you are laughing."

"No, Harry, I am serious, and I am ashamed to see how men go on that ought to know better. An election is a very serious thing; at least it ought to be, and every man ought to vote according to his conscience, and let his neighbour do the same."

CHAPTER FORTY-THREE

A FRIEND IN NEED

~

At last came the election day; there was no lack of work for Jerry and me. First came a stout puffy gentleman with a carpet bag; he wanted to go to the Bishopsgate Station; then we were called by a party who wished to be taken to the Regent's Park; and next we were wanted in a side street where a timid, anxious old lady was waiting to be taken to the bank. There we had to stop to take her back again, and just as we had set her down, a red-faced gentleman with a handful of papers came running up out of breath, and before Jerry could get down, he had opened the door, popped himself in, and called out, "Bow Street Police Station, quick!" so off we went with him, and when after another turn or two we came back, there was no other cab on the stand. Jerry put on my nose-bag, for, as he said, "We must eat when we can on such days as these; so munch away, Jack, and make the best of your time, old boy."

I found I had a good feed of crushed oats wetted up with a little bran; this would be a treat any day, but was specially refreshing then. Jerry was so thoughtful and kind – what horse would not do his best for such a master? Then he took out one of Polly's meat pies, and standing near me, he began to eat it. The streets were very full, and the cabs with the Candidates' colours on them were dashing about through the crowd as if life and limb were of no consequence; we saw two people knocked down that day, and one was a woman. The horses were having a bad time of it, poor things! but the voters inside thought nothing of that, many of them were half drunk, hurrahing out of the cab windows if their own party came by. It was the first election I had seen, and I don't want to be in another, though I have heard things are better now.

Jerry and I had not eaten many mouthfuls before a poor young woman, carrying a heavy child, came along the street. She was looking this way and that way, and seemed quite bewildered. Presently she made her way up to Jerry, and asked if he could tell her the way to St. Thomas's Hospital, and how far it was to get there. She had come from the country that morning, she said, in a market cart; she did not know about the election, and was quite a stranger in London. She had got an order for the Hospital for her little boy. The child was crying with a feeble pining cry.

"Poor little fellow!" she said, "he suffers a deal of pain; he is four years old, and can't walk any more than a baby; but the doctor said if I could get him into the Hospital, he might get well: pray, sir, how far is it? and which way is it?"

"Why, missus," said Jerry, "you can't get there walking through crowds like this! why, it is three miles away, and that child is heavy."

"Yes, bless him, he is; but I am strong, thank God, and if I knew the way, I think I should get on somehow. Please tell me the way."

"You can't do it," said Jerry; "you might be knocked down and the child be run over. Now, look here, just get into this cab, and I'll drive you safe to the Hospital. Don't you see the rain is coming on?"

"No, sir, no, I can't do that, thank you; I have only just money enough to get back with. Please tell me the way."

"Look you here, missus," said Jerry, "I've got a wife and dear children at home, and I know a father's feelings: now get you into that cab, and I'll take you there for nothing; I'd be ashamed of myself to let a woman and a sick child run a risk like that."

"Heaven bless you!" said the woman, and burst into tears.

"There, there, cheer up, my dear, I'll soon take you there; come, let me put you inside."

As Jerry went to open the door, two men, with colours in their hats and button-holes, ran up calling out "Cab!"

"Engaged," cried Jerry; but one of the men, pushing past the woman, sprang into the cab, followed by the other. Jerry looked as stern as a policeman. "This cab is already engaged, gentlemen, by that lady."

"Lady!" said one of them; "oh! she can wait: our business is very important. Beside we were in first, it is our right, and we shall stay in."

A droll smile came over Jerry's face as he shut the door upon them. "All right, gentlemen, stay in as long as it suits you: I can wait whilst you rest yourselves"; and turning his back upon them, he walked up to the young woman, who was standing near me. "They'll soon be gone," he said, laughing; "don't trouble yourself, my dear."

And they soon were gone, for when they understood Jerry's dodge they got out, calling him all sorts of bad names, and blustering about his number and getting a summons. After this little stoppage we were soon on our way to the Hospital, going as much as possible through by-streets. Jerry rung the great bell, and helped the young woman out.

"Thank you a thousand times," she said; "I could never have got here alone."

"You're kindly welcome, and I hope the dear child will soon be better."

He watched her go in at the door, and gently he said to himself, "Inasmuch as ye have done it to one of the least of these." Then he patted my neck, which was always his way when anything pleased him.

The rain was now coming down fast, and just as we were leaving the Hospital the door opened again, and the porter called out "Cab!" We stopped, and a lady came down the steps. Jerry seemed to know her at once; she put back her veil, and said, "Barker! Jeremiah Barker! is it you? I am very glad to find you here; you are just the friend I want, for it is very difficult to get a cab in this part of London to-day."

"I shall be proud to serve you, ma'am, I am right glad I happened to be here; where may I take you to, ma'am?"

"To the Paddington Station, and then if we are in good time, as I think we shall be, you shall tell me all about Mary and the children."

We got to the station in good time, and being under shelter, the lady stood a good while talking to Jerry. I found she had been Polly's mistress, and after many inquiries about her she said:

"How do you find the cab work suit you in winter? I know Mary was rather anxious about you last year."

"Yes, ma'am, she was; I had a bad cough that followed me up quite into the warm weather, and when I am kept out late, she does worry herself a good deal. You see, ma'am, it is all hours and all weathers, and that does try a man's constitution; but I am getting on pretty well, and I should feel quite lost if I had not horses to look after. I was brought up to it, and I am afraid I should not do so well at anything else."

"Well, Barker," she said, "it would be a great pity that you should seriously risk your health in this work, not only for your own, but for Mary and the children's sake; there are many places where good drivers or good grooms are wanted; and if ever you think you ought to give up this cab work, let me know." Then sending some kind messages to Mary, she put something into his hand, saying, "There is five shillings each for the two children; Mary will know how to spend it."

Jerry thanked her and seemed much pleased, and turning out of the station, we at last reached home, and I, at least, was tired.

CHAPTER FORTY-FOUR

OLD CAPTAIN
AND HIS SUCCESSOR
~

Captain and I were great friends. He was a noble old fellow, and he was very good company. I never thought that he would have to leave his home and go down the hill, but his turn came; and this was how it happened. I was not there, but I heard all about it.

He and Jerry had taken a party to the great railway station over London Bridge, and were coming back, somewhere between the Bridge and the Monument, when Jerry saw a brewer's empty dray coming along, drawn by two powerful horses. The drayman was lashing his horses with his heavy whip; the dray was light, and they started off at a furious rate; the man had no control over them, and the street was full of traffic; one young girl was knocked down and run over, and the next moment they dashed up against our cab; both the wheels were torn off, and the cab was thrown over. Captain was dragged down, the shafts splintered, and one of them ran into his side, Jerry, too, was thrown, but was only bruised, nobody could tell how he escaped, he always said 'twas a miracle. When poor Captain was got up, he was found to be very much cut and knocked about. Jerry led him home gently, and a sad sight it was to see the blood soaking into his white coat, and dropping from his side and shoulder. The drayman was proved to be very drunk, and was fined, and the brewer had to pay damages to our master; but there was no one to pay damages to poor Captain.

The farrier and Jerry did the best they could to ease his pain, and make him comfortable. The fly had to be mended, and for several days I did not go out, and Jerry earned nothing. The first time we went to the stand after the accident, the Governor came up to hear how Captain was.

"He'll never get over it," said Jerry, "at least not for my work, so the farrier said this morning. He says he may do for carting, and that sort of work. It has put me out very much. Carting indeed! I've seen what horses come to at that work round London. I only wish all the drunkards could be put in a lunatic asylum, instead of being allowed to run foul of sober people. If they would break their *own* bones, and smash their *own* carts, and lame their *own* horses, that would be their own affair, and we might let them alone, but it seems to me that the innocent always suffer; and then they talk about compensation! You can't make compensation – there's all the trouble, and vexation, and loss of time, besides losing a good horse that's like an old friend – it's nonsense talking of compensation! If there's one devil that I should like to see in the bottomless pit more than another, it's the drink devil."

"I say, Jerry," said the Governor, "you are treading pretty hard on my toes, you know; I'm not so good as you are, more shame for me, I wish I was."

"Well," said Jerry, "why don't you cut with it, Governor. You are too good a man to be the slave of such a thing."

"I'm a great fool, Jerry; but I tried once for two days, and I thought I should have died: how did you do?"

"I had hard work at it for several weeks; you see, I never did get drunk, but I found that I was not my own master, and that when the craving came on, it was hard work to say 'no'. I saw that one of us must knock under – the drink devil, or Jerry Barker, and I said that it should not be Jerry Barker, God helping me: but it was a struggle, and I wanted all the help I could get, for till I tried to break the habit, I did not know how strong it was; but then Polly took such pains that I should have good food, and when the craving came on, I used to get a cup of coffee, or some peppermint, or read a bit in my book, and that was a help to me: sometimes I had to say over and over to myself, 'Give up the drink or lose your soul? Give up the drink or break Polly's heart?' But thanks be to God, and my dear wife, my chains were broken, and now for ten years I have not tasted a drop, and never wish for it."

"I've a great mind to try it," said Grant, "for 'tis a poor thing not to be one's own master."

"Do, Governor, you'll never repent it, and what a help it would be to some of the poor fellows in our rank if they saw you do without it. I know there's two or three would like to keep out of that tavern if they could."

At first Captain seemed to do well, but he was a very old horse, and it was only his wonderful constitution, and Jerry's care, that had kept him up at the cab-work so long; now he broke down very much. The farrier said he might mend up enough to sell for a few ponds, but Jerry said, no! A few pounds got by selling a good old servant into hard work and misery, would canker all the rest of his money, and he thought the kindest thing he could do for the fine old fellow would be to put a sure bullet through his heart, and then he would never suffer more; for he did not know where to find a kind master for the rest of his days.

The day after this was decided, Harry took me to the forge for some new shoes; when I returned, Captain was gone. I and the family all felt it very much.

Jerry had now to look out for another horse, and he soon heard of one through an acquaintance who was under-groom in a nobleman's stables. He was a valuable young horse, but he had run away, smashed into another carriage, flung his lordship out, and so cut and blemished himself that he was no longer fit for a gentleman's stables, and the coachman had orders to look round, and sell him as well as he could.

"I can do with high spirits," said Jerry, "if a horse is not vicious or hard-mouthed."

"There is not a bit of vice in him," said the man, "his mouth is very tender, and I think myself that was the cause of the accident; you see he had just been clipped, and the weather was bad, and he had not had exercise enough, and when he did go out, he was as full of spring as a balloon. Our governor (the coachman, I mean) had him harnessed in as tight and strong as he could, with the martingale, and the bearing rein, a very sharp curb, and the reins put in at the bottom bar; it is my belief that it made the horse mad, being tender in the mouth and so full of spirit."

"Likely enough; I'll come and see him," said Jerry.

The next day, Hotspur – that was his name – came home; he was a fine brown horse, without a white hair on him, as tall as Captain, with a very handsome head, and only five years old. I gave him a friendly greeting by way of good fellowship, but did not ask him any questions. The first night he was very restless; instead of lying down, he kept jerking his halter rope up and down through the ring, and knocking the block about against the manger so that I could not sleep. However, the next day, after five or six hours in the cab, he came in quiet and sensible. Jerry patted and talked to him a good deal, and very soon they understood each other, and Jerry said that with an easy bit, and plenty of work, he would be as gentle as a lamb; and that it was an ill wind that blew nobody good, for if his lordship had lost a hundred-guinea favourite, the cabman had gained a good horse with all his strength in him.

Hotspur thought it a great comedown to be a cab horse, and was disgusted at standing in the rank, but he confessed to me at the end of the week, that an easy mouth, and a free hand, made up for a great deal, and after all, the work was not so degrading as having one's head and tail fastened to each other at the saddle. In fact, he settled in well, and Jerry liked him very much.

CHAPTER FORTY-FIVE

JERRY'S NEW YEAR

~

Christmas and the New Year are very merry times for some people; but for cabmen and cabmen's horses it is no holiday, though it may be a harvest. There are so many parties, balls, and places of amusement open, that the work is hard and often late. Sometimes driver and horse have to wait for hours in the rain or frost, shivering with cold, whilst the merry people within are dancing away to the music. I wonder if the beautiful ladies ever think of the weary cabman waiting on his box, and his patient beast standing till his legs get stiff with cold.

I had now most of the evening work, as I was well accustomed to standing, and Jerry was also more afraid of Hotspur taking cold. We had a great deal of late work in the Christmas week, and Jerry's cough was bad; but however late we were, Polly sat up for him, and came out with the lantern to meet him, looking anxious and troubled.

On the evening of the New Year we had to take two gentlemen to a house in one of the West End squares. We set them down at nine o'clock and were told to come again at eleven. "But," said one of them, "as it is a card party you may have to wait a few minutes, but don't be late."

As the clock struck eleven we were at the door, for Jerry was always punctual. The clock chimed the quarters – one, two, three, and then struck twelve, but the door did not open.

The wind had been very changeable, with squalls of rain during the day, but now it came on a sharp, driving sleet, which seemed to come all the way round; it was very cold, and there was no shelter. Jerry got off his box and came and pulled one of my cloths a little more over my neck; then he took a turn or two up and down, stamping his feet; then he began to beat his arms, but that set him off coughing; so he opened the cab door and sat at the bottom with his feet on the pavement, and was a little sheltered. Still the clock chimed the quarters and no one came. At half-past twelve, he rang the bell and asked the servant if he would be wanted that night.

"Oh, yes! you'll be wanted safe enough," said the man, "you must not go, it will soon be over," and again Jerry sat down, but his voice was so hoarse I could hardly hear him.

At a quarter past one the door opened, and the two gentlemen came out; they got into the cab without a word, and told Jerry where to drive, that was nearly two miles. My legs were numb with cold, and I thought I should have stumbled. When the men got out, they never said they were sorry to have kept us waiting so long, but were angry at the charge: however, as Jerry never charged more than was his due, so he never took less, and they had to pay for the two hours and a quarter waiting; but it was hard-earned money to Jerry.

At last we got home; he could hardly speak, and his cough was dreadful. Polly asked no questions, but opened the door and held the lantern for him.

"Can't I do something?" she said.

"Yes; get Jack something warm, and then boil me some gruel."

This was said in a hoarse whisper. He could hardly get his breath, but he gave me a rub down as usual, and even went up into the hayloft for an extra bundle of straw for my bed. Polly brought me a warm mash that made me comfortable, and then they locked the door.

It was late the next morning before any one came, and then it was only Harry. He cleaned us and fed us, and swept out the stalls, then he put the straw back again as if it was Sunday. He was very still, and neither whistled

York promptly set himself flat on her head to prevent her struggling. (Chapter Twenty-Three.)

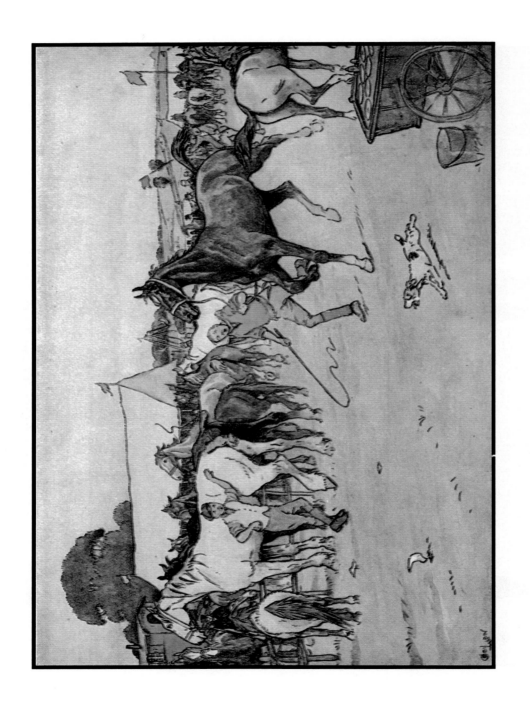

A horse fair . . . "There was a great deal of bargaining, running up and beating down." (Chapter Thirty-Two.)

"Without a master or friend, I was alone on that great slaughter ground." (Chapter Thirty-Four.)

"I was driven every day for a week or so." (Chapter Forty-Nine.)

nor sang. At noon he came again, and gave us our food and water: this time Dolly came with him; she was crying and I could gather from what they said that Jerry was dangerously ill, and the doctor said it was a bad case. So two days passed, and there was great trouble indoors. We only saw Harry, and sometimes Dolly. I think she came for company, for Polly was always with Jerry, and he had to be kept very quiet.

On the third day, whilst Harry was in the stable, a tap came at the door, and Governor Grant came in.

"I wouldn't go to the house, my boy," he said, "but I want to know how your father is."

"He is very bad," said Harry. "He can't be much worse; they call it 'bronchitis'; the doctor thinks it will turn one way or another to-night."

"That's bad, very bad!" said Grant, shaking his head; "I know two men who died of that last week; it takes 'em off in no time; but whilst there's life there's hope, so you must keep up your spirits."

"Yes," said Harry quickly, "and the doctor said that father had a better chance than most men, because he didn't drink. He said yesterday the fever was so high that if father had been a drinking man it would have burnt him up like a piece of paper; but I believe he thinks he will get over it; don't you think he will, Mr. Grant?"

The Governor looked puzzled.

"If there's any rule that good men should get over these things, I am sure he will, my boy; he's the best man I know. I'll look in early to-morrow."

Early next morning he was there.

"Well?" said he.

"Father is better," said Harry. "Mother hopes he will get over it."

"Thank God!" said the Governor, "and now you must keep him warm, and keep his mind easy, and that brings me to the horses; you see, Jack will be all the better for the rest of a week or two in a warm stable, and you can easily take him a turn up and down the street to stretch his legs; but this young one, if he does not get work, he will soon be all up on end, as you may say, and will be rather too much for you; and when he does go out, there'll be an accident."

"It is like that now," said Harry. "I have kept him short of corn; but he's so full of spirit I don't know what to do with him."

"Just so," said Grant. "Now look here, will you tell your mother that if

193

she is agreeable, I will come for him every day till something is arranged, and take him for a good spell of work, and whatever he earns I'll bring your mother half of it, and that will help with the horses' feed. Your father is in a good club, I know, but that won't keep the horses, and they'll be eating their heads off all this time: I'll come at noon and hear what she says," and, without waiting for Harry's thanks, he was gone.

At noon I think he went and saw Polly, for he and Harry came to the stable together, harnessed Hotspur and took him out.

For a week or more he came for Hotspur, and when Harry thanked him or said anything about his kindness, he laughed it off, saying, it was all good luck for him, for his horses were wanting a little rest which they would not otherwise have had.

Jerry grew better steadily, but the doctor said that he must never go back to the cab work again if he wished to be an old man. The children had many consultations together about what father and mother would do, and how they could help to earn money.

One afternoon Hotspur was brought in very wet and dirty.

"The streets are nothing but slush," said the Governor. "It will give you a good warming, my boy, to get him clean and dry."

"All right, Governor," said Harry, "I shall not leave him till he is; you know I have been trained by my father."

"I wish all the boys had been trained like you" said the Governor.

While Harry was sponging off the mud from Hotspur's body and legs, Dolly came in, looking very full of something.

"Who lives at Fairstowe, Harry? Mother has got a letter from Fairstowe; she seemed so glad, and ran upstairs to father with it."

"Don't you know? Why, it is the name of Mrs. Fowler's place – mother's old mistress, you know – the lady that father met last summer, who sent you and me five shillings each."

"Oh! Mrs. Fowler; of course I know all about her. I wonder what she is writing to mother about?"

"Mother wrote to her last week," said Harry. "You know she told father if ever he gave up the cab work she would like to know. I wonder what she says; run in and see, Dolly."

Harry scrubbed away at Hotspur with a huish! huish! like any old ostler.

In a few minutes Dolly came dancing into the stable.

"Oh Harry! there never was anything so beautiful. Mrs. Fowler says we are all to go and live near her. There is a cottage now empty that will just suit us, with a garden, and a henhouse, and apple trees and everything! And her coachman is going away in the spring, and then she will want father in his place; and there are good families round, where you can get a place in the garden, or the stable, or as a page-boy; and there's a good school for me; and mother is laughing and crying by turns, and father does look *so* happy!"

"That's uncommon jolly," said Harry, "and just the right thing, I should say; it will suit father and mother both; but I don't intend to be a page-boy with tight clothes and rows of buttons. I'll be a groom or a gardener."

It was quickly settled that as soon as Jerry was well enough they should remove to the country, and that the cab and horses should be sold as soon as possible.

This was heavy news for me, for I was not young now, and could not look for any improvement in my conditions. Since I left Birtwick I had never been so happy as with my dear master, Jerry; but three years of cab work, even under the best conditions, will tell on one's strength, and I felt that I was not the horse that I had been.

Grant said at once that he would take Hotspur, and there were men on the stand who would have bought me; but Jerry said I should not go to cab work again with just anybody, and the Governor promised to find a place for me where I should be comfortable.

The day came for going away. Jerry had not been allowed to go out yet, and I never saw him after that New Year's Eve. Polly and the children came to bid me good-bye. "Poor old Jack! dear old Jack! I wish we could take you with us," she said, and then, laying her hand on my mane, she put her face close to my neck and kissed me. Dolly was crying, and kissed me too. Harry stroked me a great deal, but said nothing, only he seemed very sad, and so I was led away to my new place.

CHAPTER FORTY-SIX

JAKES AND THE LADY

~

I was sold to a corn dealer and baker whom Jerry knew, and with him he thought I should have good food and fair work. In the first he was quite right, and if my master had always been on the premises I do not think I should have been overloaded; but there was a foreman who was always hurrying and driving every one, and frequently when I had quite a full load he would order something else to be taken on. My carter, whose name was Jakes, often said it was more than I ought to take, but the other always overruled him: "'Twas no use going twice when once would do, and he chose to get business forward."

Jakes, like the other carters, always had the bearing rein up, which prevented me from drawing easily, and by the time I had been there three or four months I found the work telling very much on my strength.

One day I was loaded more than usual, and part of the road was a steep uphill. I used all my strength, but I could not get on, and was obliged continually to stop. This did not please my driver, and he laid his whip on badly. "Get on, you lazy fellow," he said, "or I'll make you."

Again I started the heavy load, and struggled on a few yards; again the whip came down, and again I struggled forward. The pain of that great cart whip was sharp, but my mind was hurt quite as much as my poor sides. To be punished and abused when I was doing my very best was so hard it took the heart out of me. A third time he was flogging me cruelling when a lady stepped quickly up to him, and said in a sweet, earnest voice:

"Oh! pray do not whip your good horse any more; I am sure he is doing all he can, and the road is very steep, I am sure he is doing his best."

"If doing his best won't get this load up, he must do something more than his best; that's all I know, ma'am," said Jakes.

"But is it not a very heavy load?" she said.

"Yes, yes, too heavy," he said; "but that's not my fault. The foreman came just as we were starting, and would have three hundredweight more put on to save him trouble, and I must get on with it as well as I can."

He was raising the whip again when the lady said:

"Pray, stop; I think I can help you if you will let me."

The man laughed.

"You see," she said, "you do not give him a fair chance; he cannot use all his power with his head held back as it is with that bearing rein; if you would take it off I am sure he would do better – *do* try it," she said persuasively; "I should be very glad if you would."

"Well, well," said Jakes, with a short laugh, "anything to please a lady, of course. How far would you wish it down, ma'am?"

"Quite down; give him his head altogether."

The rein was taken off, and in a moment I put my head down to my very knees. What a comfort it was! Then I tossed it up and down several times to get the aching stiffness out of my neck.

"Poor fellow! that is what you wanted," said she, patting and stroking me with her gentle hand; "and now if you will speak kindly to him and lead him on, I believe he will be able to do better."

Jakes took the rein, "Come on, Blackie." I put down my head, and threw my whole weight against the collar; I spared no strength. The load moved on, and I pulled it steadily up the hill, and then stopped to take breath.

The lady had walked along the footpath, and now came across into the road. She stroked and patted my neck as I had not been patted for many a long day.

"You see, he was quite willing when you gave him the chance; I am sure he is a fine-tempered creature, and I dare say has known better days. You won't put that rein on again, will you?" for he was just going to hitch it up on the old plan.

"Well, ma'am, I can't deny that having his head has helped him up the hill, and I'll remember it another time, and thank you, ma'am; but if he went without a bearing rein I should be the laughing-stock of all the carters. It is the fashion, you see."

"Is it not better," she said, "to lead a good fashion than to follow a bad one? A great many gentlemen do not use bearing reins now; our carriage horses have not worn them for fifteen years, and work with much less fatigue that those who have them; besides," she added in a very serious voice, "we have no right to distress any of God's creatures without a very good reason. We call them dumb animals, and so they are, for they cannot tell us how they feel, but they do not suffer less because they have no words. But I must not detain you now; I thank you for trying my plan with your good horse, and I am sure you will find it far better than the whip. Good day," and with another soft pat on my neck she stepped lightly across the path, and I saw her no more.

"That was a real lady, I'll be bound for it," said Jakes to himself; "she spoke just as polite as if I was a gentleman, and I'll try her plan, uphill, at any rate." And I must do him the justice to say that he let my rein out several holes, and going uphill after that he always gave me my head; but the heavy loads went on. Good feed and fair rest will keep one's strength under full work, but no horse can stand against overloading; and I was getting so thoroughly pulled down from this cause that a younger horse was bought in my place. I may as well mention here what I suffered at this time from another cause. I had heard horses speak of it, but had never myself had experience of the evil; this was a badly lighted stable; there was only one very small window at the end, and the consequence was that the stalls were almost dark.

Besides the depressing effect this had on my spirits, it very much weakened my sight, and when I was suddenly brought out of the darkness into the glare of daylight it was very painful to my eyes. Several times I stumbled over the threshold, and could scarcely see where I was going.

I believe, had I stayed there very long, I should have become purblind, and that would have been a great misfortune, for I have heard men say that a stone-blind horse was safer to drive than one which had imperfect sight, as it generally makes them very timid. However, I escaped without any permanent injury to my sight, and was sold to a large cab owner.

CHAPTER FORTY-SEVEN

HARD TIMES

~

I shall never forget my new master; he had black eyes and a hooked nose, his mouth was as full of teeth as a bulldog's, and his voice was as harsh as the grinding of cartwheels over gravel stones. His name was Nicholas Skinner, and I believe he was the same man that poor Seedy Sam drove for.

I have heard men say that seeing is believing; but I should say that *feeling* is believing; for much as I had seen before, I never knew till now the utter misery of a cab horse's life.

Skinner had a low set of cabs and a low set of drivers; he was hard on the men, and the men were hard on the horses. In his place we had no Sunday rest, and it was in the heat of summer.

Sometimes on a Sunday morning a party of fast men would hire the cab for the day; four of them inside and another with the driver, and I had to take them ten or fifteen miles out into the country, and back again: never would any of them get down to walk up a hill, let it be ever so steep, or the day ever so hot – unless indeed, when the driver was afraid I should not manage it, and sometimes I was so fevered and worn that I could hardly touch my food. How I used to long for the nice bran mash with nitre in it that Jerry used to give us on Saturday nights in hot weather, that used to cool us down and make us so comfortable. Then we had two nights and a whole day for unbroken rest, and on Monday morning we were as fresh as young horses again; but here there was no rest, and my driver was just as hard as his master. He had a cruel whip with something so sharp at the end that it sometimes drew blood, and he would even whip me under the belly, and flip the lash out at my head. Indignities like these took the heart out of me terribly, but still I did my best and never hung back; for, as poor Ginger said, it was no use; men are the strongest.

My life was now so utterly wretched that I wished I might, like Ginger drop down dead at my work, and be out of my misery; and one day my wish very nearly came to pass.

I went on the stand at eight in the morning, and had done a good share of work, when we had to take a fare to the railway. A long train was just expected in, so my driver pulled up at the back of some of the outside cabs, to take the chance of a return fare. It was a very heavy train, and as all the cabs were soon engaged, ours was called for. There was a party of four: a noisy, blustering man with a lady, a little boy and a young girl, and a great deal of luggage. The lady and the boy got into the cab, and while the man ordered about the luggage, the young girl came and looked at me.

"Papa," she said, "I am sure this poor horse cannot take us and all our luggage so far, he is so very weak and worn out; do look at him."

"Oh! he's all right, miss," said my driver; "he"s strong enough."

The porter, who was pulling about some heavy boxes, suggested to the gentleman, as there was so much, luggage, whether he would not take a second cab.

"Can your horse do it, or can't he?" said the blustering man.

"Oh! he can do it all right, sir; send up the boxes, porter; he could take more than that," and he helped to haul up a box so heavy that I could feel the springs go down.

"Papa, papa, do take a second cab," said the young girl in a beseeching tone; "I am sure we are wrong. I am sure it is very cruel."

"Nonsense, Grace; get in at once and don't make all this fuss; a pretty thing it would be if a man of business had to examine every cab horse before he hired it — the man knows his own business of course: there, get in and hold your tongue!"

My gentle friend had to obey, and box after box was dragged up and lodged on the top of the cab, or settled by the side of the driver. At last all was ready, and with his usual jerk at the rein and slash of the whip he drove out of the station.

The load was very heavy, and I had had neither food nor rest since the morning; but I did my best, as I always had done, in spite of cruelty and injustice.

I got along fairly till we came to Ludgate Hill, but there the heavy load and my own exhaustion were too much. I was struggling to keep on, goaded by constant chucks of the rein and use of the whip, when, in a single moment — I cannot tell how — my feet slipped from under me and I fell heavily to the ground on my side; the suddenness and the force with which I fell seemed to beat all the breath out of my body. I lay perfectly still; indeed I had no power to move, and I thought now I was going to die. I heard a sort of confusion round me, loud angry voices, and the getting down of the luggage, but it was all like a dream. I thought I heard that sweet, pitiful voice saying, "Oh! that poor horse! it is all our fault." Someone came and loosened the throat strap of my bridle, and undid the traces which kept the collar so tight upon me. Someone said, "He's dead; he'll never get up again." Then I could hear a policeman giving orders, but I did not even open my eyes; I could only draw a gasping breath now and then. Some cold water was thrown over my head, and some cordial was poured into my mouth, and something was covered over me. I cannot tell how long I lay there, but I found my life coming back, and a kind-voiced man, was patting me and encouraging me to rise. After some more cordial had been given me, and after one or two attempts, I staggered to my feet, and was gently led to some stables which were close by. Here I was put into a well-littered stall, and some warm gruel was brought to me, which I drank thankfully.

In the evening I was sufficiently recovered to be led back to Skinner's stable, where I think they did the best for me they could. In the morning Skinner came with a farrier to look at me. He examined me very closely, and said: "This is a case of overwork more than disease, and if you could give him a run off for six months, he would be able to work again; but now there is not an ounce of strength in him."

"Then he must just go to the dogs," said Skinner. "I have no meadows to nurse sick horses in – he might get well or he might not; that sort of thing doesn't suit my business. My plan is to work 'em as long as they'll go, and then sell 'em for what they'll fetch, at the knacker's or elsewhere."

"If he was broken-winded," said the farrier, "you had better have him killed out of hand, but he is not. There is a sale of horses coming off in about ten days; if you rest him and feed him up he may pick up, and you may get more than his skin is worth, at any rate."

Upon this advice Skinner rather unwillingly, I think, gave orders that I should be well fed and cared for, and the stable man, happily for me, carried out the orders with a much better will than his master had in giving them. Ten days of perfect rest, plenty of good oats, hay, bran mashes, with boiled linseed mixed in them, did more to get up my condition than anything else could have done; those linseed mashes were delicious, and I began to think after all, it might be better to live than go to the dogs. When the twelfth day after the accident came I was taken to the sale, a few miles out of London. I felt that any change from my present place must be an improvement, so I held up my head and hoped for the best.

CHAPTER FORTY-EIGHT

FARMER THOROUGHGOOD
AND GRANDSON WILLIE

~

At this sale, of course, I found myself in company with the old broken-down horses — some lame, some broken-winded, some old, and some that I am sure it would have been merciful to shoot.

The buyers and sellers too, many of them, looked not much better off than the poor beasts they were bargaining about. There were poor old men, trying to get a horse or pony for a few pounds, that might drag about some little wood or coal cart. There were poor men trying to sell a worn-out beast for two or three pounds, rather than have the greater loss of killing him. Some of them looked as if poverty and hard times had hardened them all over; but there were others that I would have willingly used the last of my strength in serving; poor and shabby, but kind and human, with voices that I could trust. There was one tottering old man that took a great fancy to me, and I to him, but I was not strong enough — it was an anxious time! Coming from the better part of the fair, I noticed a man who looked like a gentleman farmer, with a young boy by his side; he had a broad back and round shoulders, a kind, ruddy face, and he wore a broad-brimmed hat. When he came up to me and my companions, he stood still and gave a pitiful look round upon us. I saw his eye rest on me; I had still my good mane and tail, which did something for my appearance. I pricked my ears and looked at him.

"There's a horse, Willie, that has known better days."

"Poor old fellow!" said the boy. "Do you think, grandpapa, he was ever a carriage horse?"

"Oh, yes, my boy," said the farmer, coming closer; "he might have been anything when he was young. Look at his nostrils and his ears, the shape of his neck and shoulder; there's a deal of breeding about that horse." He put out his hand and gave me a kind pat on the neck. I put out my nose in answer to his kindness; the boy stroked my face.

"Poor old fellow! see, grandpapa, how well he understands kindness. Could not you buy him and make him young again, as you did with Ladybird?"

"My dear boy, I can't make all old horses young; besides, Ladybird was not so very old, as she was run down and badly used."

"Well, grandpapa, I don't believe that this one is old; look at his mane and tail. I wish you would look into his mouth, and then you could tell; though he is so very thin, his eyes are not sunk like some old horses."

The old gentleman laughed. "Bless the boy! He is as horsey as his old grandfather."

"But do look at his mouth, grandpapa, and ask the price. I am sure he would grow young in our meadows."

The man who had brought me for sale now put in his word.

"The young gentleman is a real knowing one, sir; now the fact is, this 'ere hoss is just pulled down with overwork in the cabs. He's not an old one, and I heerd as how the vetenary should say, that a six months' run off would set him right up, being as how his wind was not broken. I've had the tending of him these ten days past, and a gratefuller, pleasanter animal I never met with, and 'twould be worth a gentleman's while to give a five-pound note for him, and let him have a chance. I'll be bound he'd be worth twenty pounds next spring."

The old gentleman laughed, and the little boy looked up eagerly.

"Oh! grandpapa, did you not say the colt sold for five pounds more than you expected? You would not be poorer if you did buy this one."

The farmer slowly felt my legs, which were much swelled and strained; then he looked at my mouth. "Thirteen or fourteen, I should say; just trot him out, will you?"

I arched my poor thin neck, raised my tail a little, and threw out my legs as well as I could, for they were very stiff.

"What is the lowest you will take for him?" said the farmer as I came back.

"Five pounds, sir; that was the lowest price my master set."

"'Tis a speculation," said the old gentleman, shaking his head, but at the same time slowly drawing out his purse, "quite a speculation! Have you any more business here?" he said, counting the sovereigns into his hand.

"No, sir; I can take him for you to the inn, if you please."

"Do so; I am now going there."

They walked forward, and I was led behind. The boy could hardly control his delight, and the old gentleman seemed to enjoy his pleasure. I had a good feed at the inn, and was then gently ridden home by a servant of my new master's and turned into a meadow with a shed in one corner of it.

Mr. Thoroughgood, for that was the name of my benefactor, gave orders that I should have hay and oats every night and morning, and the run of the meadow during the day, and "you, Willie," said he, "must take the oversight of him; I give him in charge to you."

The boy was proud of his charge, and undertook it in all seriousness. There was not a day when he did not pay me a visit; sometimes picking me out from amongst the other horses, and giving me a bit of carrot, or something good, or sometimes standing by me whilst I ate my oats. He always came with kind words and caresses, and of course I grew very fond of him. He called me Old Crony, as I used to come to him in the field and follow him about. Sometimes he brought his grandfather, who always looked closely at my legs:

"This is our point, Willie," he would say; "but he is improving so steadily that I think we shall see a change for the better in the spring."

The perfect rest, the good food, the soft turf, and gentle exercise, soon began to tell on my condition and my spirits. I had a good constitution from my mother, and I was never strained when I was young, so that I had a better chance than many horses, who have been worked before they came to their full strength. During the winter my legs improved so much that I began to feel quite young again. The spring came round, and one day in March, Mr. Thoroughgood determined that he would try me in the phaeton. I was well pleased, and he and Willie drove me a few miles. My legs were not stiff now, and I did the work with perfect ease.

"He's growing young, Willie. We must give him a little gentle work now, and by midsummer he will be as good as Ladybird. He has a beautiful mouth, and good paces; they can't be better."

"Oh! grandpapa, how glad I am you bought him!"

"So am I, my boy, but he has to thank you more than me; we must now be looking out for a quiet, genteel place for him, where he will be valued."

CHAPTER FORTY-NINE

MY LAST HOME

~

One day during this summer, the groom cleaned and dressed me with such extraordinary care that I thought some new change must be at hand; he trimmed my fetlocks and legs, passed the tarbrush over my hoofs, and even parted my forelock. I think the harness had an extra polish. Willie seemed half anxious, half merry as he got into the chaise with his grandfather.

"If the ladies take to him," said the old gentleman, "they'll be suited and he'll be suited: we can but try."

At the distance of a mile or two from the village, we came to a pretty, low house, with a lawn and shrubbery at the front, and a drive up to the door. Willie rang the bell, and asked if Miss Blomefield, or Miss Ellen was at home. Yes, they were. So, whilst Willie stayed with me, Mr. Thoroughgood went into the house. In about ten minutes he returned, followed by three ladies; one tall, pale lady, wrapped in a white shawl, leaned on a younger lady, with dark eyes and a merry face; the other, a very stately-looking person, was Miss Blomefield. They all came and looked at me and asked questions. The younger lady – that was Miss Ellen – took to me very much; she said she was sure she would like me, I had such a good face. The tall, pale lady said that she should always be nervous in riding behind a horse that had once been down, as I might come down again, and if I did, she would never get over the fright.

"You see, ladies," said Mr. Thoroughgood, "many first-rate horses have had their knees broken through the carelessness of their drivers, without any fault of their own, and from what I see of this horse, I should say that is his case: but of course I do not wish to influence you. If you incline, you can have him on trial, and then your coachman will see what he thinks of him."

"You have always been such a good adviser to us about our horses," said the stately lady, "that your recommendation would go a long way with me, and if my sister Lavinia sees no objection, we will accept your offer of a trial with thanks."

It was then arranged that I should be sent for the next day.

In the morning a smart-looking young man came for me. At first he looked pleased, but when he saw my knees, he said in a disappointed voice:

"I didn't think, sir, you would have recommended my ladies a blemished horse like that."

"Handsome is – that handsome does," said my master; "you are only taking him on trial, and I am sure you will do fairly by him, young man, and if he is not as safe as any horse you ever drove, send him back."

I was led home, placed in a comfortable stable, fed, and left to myself. The next day, when my groom was cleaning my face, he said:

"That is just like the star that Black Beauty had, he is much the same height too. I wonder where he is now."

A little farther on, he came to the place in my neck where I was bled, and where a little knot was left in the skin. He almost started, and began to look me over carefully, talking to himself.

"White star in the forehead, one white foot on the off side, this little knot just in that place"; then looking at the middle of my back: "and as I am alive, there is that little patch of white hair that John used to call 'Beauty's threepenny bit'. It *must* be Black Beauty! Beauty! do you know me? Little Joe Green, that almost killed you?" And he began patting and patting me as if he was quite overjoyed.

I could not say that I remembered him, for now he was a fine-grown young fellow, with black whiskers and a man's voice, but I was sure he knew me, and that he was Joe Green; so I was very glad. I put my nose up to him, and tried to say that we were friends. I never saw a man so pleased.

"Give him a fair trial! I should think so indeed! I wonder who the rascal was that broke your knees, my old Beauty! You must have been badly served out somewhere. Well, well, it won't be my fault if you haven't good times of it now. I wish John Manly were here to see you."

In the afternoon I was put into a low park chair and brought to the door. Miss Ellen was going to try me, and Green went with her. I soon found that she was a good driver, and she seemed pleased with my paces. I heard Joe telling her about me, and that he was sure I was Squire Gordon's old Black Beauty.

When we returned, the other sisters came out to hear how I had behaved myself. She told them what she had just heard, and said, "I shall certainly write to Mrs. Gordon to tell her that her favourite horse has come to us. How pleased she will be!"

After this I was driven every day for a week or so and as I appeared to be quite safe, Miss Lavinia at last ventured out in the small close carriage. After this, it was quite decided to keep me and to call me by my old name of "Black Beauty."

I have now lived in this happy place a whole year. Joe is the best and kindest of grooms. My work is easy and pleasant, and I feel my strength and spirits all coming back again. Mr. Thoroughgood said to Joe the other day, "In your place he will last till he is twenty years old – perhaps more."

Willie always speaks to me when he can, and treats me as his special friend. My ladies have promised that I shall never be sold, and so I have nothing to fear; and here my story ends. My troubles are all over and I am at home; and often before I am quite awake, I fancy I am still in the orchard at Birtwick, standing with my old friends under the apple-trees.

Rebecca
of Sunnybrook Farm

~

Rebecca
of Sunnybrook Farm

~

Kate Douglas Wiggin

Illustrated by
Glenn Steward

DEDICATION

TO

CHARLES HENRY NEVILL, ESQ.,
GOOD CRITIC AND GOOD FRIEND,

OF

BRAMALL HALL, CHESHIRE,
UNDER WHOSE DEAR ENGLISH ROOF SO
MANY OF THESE CHAPTERS WERE WRITTEN

Contents

1	"We Are Seven"	221
2	Rebecca's Relations	233
3	A Difference in Hearts	239
4	Rebecca's Point of View	247
5	Wisdom's Ways	251
6	Sunshine in a Shady Place	261
7	Riverboro Secrets	267
8	Color of Rose	273
9	Ashes of Roses	279
10	Rainbow Bridges	285
11	"The Stirring of the Powers"	291
12	"See the Pale Martyr"	297
13	Snow-White: Rose-Red	307
14	Mr. Aladdin	313
15	The Banquet Lamp	319
16	Seasons of Growth	325
17	Gray Days and Gold	333
18	Rebecca Represents the Family	339
19	Deacon Israel's Successor	347
20	A Change of Heart	353
21	The Sky-line Widens	361
22	Clover Blossoms and Sunflowers	369
23	The Hill Difficulty	379
24	Aladdin Rubs His Lamp	385
25	Roses of Joy	393
26	"Over the Teacups"	403
27	"The Vision Splendid"	409
28	"Th' Inevitable Yoke"	417
29	Mother and Daughter	425
30	Good-Bye, Sunnybrook!	431
31	Aunt Miranda's Apology	437

Colour Illustrations

Miss Miranda entered, and as her eye wandered about the vacant room, it fell upon a white and tempestuous ocean of counterpane. (Chapter Three.)

Then came the 'woodsy bit,' with her feet pressing the slippery carpet of brown pine-needles. (Chapter Five.)

While crossing the bridge she was suddenly overcome by the beauty of the river. (Chapter Twelve.)

"I am the lady of the house at present," said the stranger, with a whimsical smile. (Chapter Fourteen.)

Then there was the sleigh ride, during which she found her tongue, and chattered like any magpie. (Chapter Seventeen.)

"Then I must give up all hope of ever being a writer!" sighed Rebecca. (Chapter Twenty-One.)

A haycart had been decked with green vines and bunches of long-stemmed field daisies, those gay darlings of New England meadows. (Chapter Twenty-Seven.)

"I look like a drudge," said Rebecca mysteriously, with laughing eyes, "but I really am a princess." (Chapter Twenty-Nine.)

CHAPTER ONE

"We Are Seven"

~

The old stage-coach was rumbling along the dusty road that runs from Maplewood to Riverboro. The day was as warm as midsummer, though it was only the middle of May, and Mr. Jeremiah Cobb was favoring the horses as much as possible, yet never losing sight of the fact that he carried the mail. The hills were many, and the reins lay loosely in his hands as he lolled back in his seat and extended one foot and leg luxuriously over the dashboard. His brimmed hat of worn felt was well pulled over his eyes, and he revolved a quid of tobacco in his left cheek.

There was one passenger in the coach, a small dark-haired person in a glossy buff calico dress. She was so slender and so stiffly starched that she slid from space to space on the leather cushions, though she braced herself against the middle seat with her feet, and extended her cotton-gloved hands on each side, in order to maintain some sort of balance. Whenever the wheels sank farther than usual into a rut, or jolted suddenly over a stone, she bounded involuntarily into the air, came down again, pushed back her funny little straw hat, and picked up or settled more firmly a small pink sunshade, which seemed to be her chief responsibility, unless we except a bead purse, into which she looked whenever the condition of the roads would permit, finding great apparent satisfaction in that its precious contents neither disappeared nor grew less. Mr. Cobb guessed nothing of these harassing details of travel, his business being to carry people to their destinations, not, necessarily, to make them comfortable on the way. Indeed, he had forgotten the very existence of this one unnoteworthy little passenger.

When he was about to leave the post-office in Maplewood that morning, a woman had alighted from a waggon, and coming up to him, inquired whether this were the Riverboro stage, and if he were Mr. Cobb. Being answered in the affirmative, she nodded to a child who was eagerly waiting for the answer, and who ran towards her as if she feared to be a moment too late. The child might have been ten or eleven years old, perhaps, but whatever the number of her summers, she had an air of being small for her age. Her mother helped her into the stage-coach, deposited a bundle and a bouquet of lilacs beside her, superintended the "roping on" behind of an old hair-trunk, and finally paid the fare, counting out the silver with great care.

"I want you should take her to my sisters' in Riverboro," she said. "Do you know Mirandy and Jane Sawyer? They live in the brick house."

Lord bless your soul, he knew 'em as well as if he'd made 'em!

"Well, she's going there, and they're expecting her. Will you keep an eye on her, please? If she can get out anywhere and get with folks, or get anybody in to keep her company, she'll do it. Good-bye, Rebecca; try not to get into any mischief, and sit quiet, so you'll look neat an' nice when you get there. Don't be any trouble to Mr. Cobb. You see, she's kind of excited. We came on the cars from Temperance yesterday, slept all night at my cousin's, and drove from her house – eight miles it is – this morning."

"Good-bye, mother; don't worry. You know, it isn't as if I hadn't travelled before."

The woman gave a short sardonic laugh and said in an explanatory way to Mr. Cobb: "She's been to Wareham and stayed overnight; that isn't much to be journey-proud on!'

"It *was travelling*, mother," said the child eagerly and wilfully. "It was leaving the farm, and putting up lunch in a basket, and a little riding and a little steam-cars, and we carried our nightgowns."

"Don't tell the whole village about it, if we did," said the mother, interrupting the reminiscences of this experienced voyager. "Haven't I told you before," she whispered, in a last attempt at discipline, "that you shouldn't talk about nightgowns and stockings and – things like that, in a loud tone of voice, and especially when there's men-folks round?"

"I know, mother, I know, and I won't. All I want to say is" – here Mr. Cobb gave a cluck, slapped the reins, and the horses started sedately on their daily task – "all I want to say is that it is a journey when" – the stage was really under way now, and Rebecca had to put her head out of the window over the door in order to finish her sentence – "it *is* a journey when you carry a nightgown!"

The objectionable word, uttered in a high treble, floated back to the offended ears of Mrs. Randall, who watched the stage out of sight, gathered up her packages from the bench at the store-door, and stepped into the waggon that had been standing at the hitching-post. As she turned the horse's head towards home she rose to her feet for a moment, and, shading her eyes with her hand, looked at a cloud of dust in the dim distance.

"Mirandy'll have her hands full, I guess," she said to herself; "but I shouldn't wonder if it would be the making of Rebecca."

All this had been half an hour ago, and the sun, the heat, the dust, the contemplation of errands to be done in the great metropolis of Milltown, had lulled Mr. Cobb's never active mind into complete oblivion as to his promise of keeping an eye on Rebecca.

Suddenly he heard a small voice above the rattle and rumble of the wheels and the creaking of the harness. At first he thought it was a cricket, a tree toad, or a bird, but having determined the direction from which it came, he turned his head over his shoulder and saw a small shape hanging as far out of the window as safety would allow. A long black braid of hair swung with the motion of the coach; the child held her hat in one hand and with the other made ineffectual attempts to stab the driver with her microscopic sunshade.

"Please let me speak!" she called.

Mr. Cobb drew up the horses obediently.

"Does it cost any more to ride up there with you?" she asked. "It's so slippery and shiny down here, and the stage is so much too big for me, that I rattle round in it till I'm most black and blue. And the windows are so small I can only see pieces of things, and I've 'most broken my neck stretching round to find out whether my trunk has fallen off the back. It's my mother's trunk, and she's very choice of it."

Mr. Cobb waited until this flow of conversation, or more properly speaking this flood of criticism, had ceased, and then said jocularly:

"You can come up if you want to; there ain't no extry charge to sit side o' me." Whereupon he helped her out, "boosted" her up to the front seat, and resumed his own place.

Rebecca sat down carefully, smoothing her dress under her with painstaking precision, and putting her sunshade under its extended folds between the driver and herself. This done, she pushed back her hat, pulled up her darned white cotton gloves, and said delightedly:

"Oh, this is better! This is like travelling! I am a real passenger now, and down there I felt like our setting hen when we shut her up in a coop. I hope we have a long, long ways to go?"

"Oh, we've only just started on it," Mr. Cobb responded genially; "it's more 'n two hours."

"Only two hours!" she sighed. "That will be half-past one; mother will be at Cousin Ann's, the children at home will have had their dinner, and Hannah cleared all away. I have some lunch, because mother said it would be a bad beginning to get to the brick house hungry, and have Aunt Mirandy have to get me something to eat the first thing. It's a good growing day, isn't it?"

"It is, certain; too hot, most. Why don't you put up your parasol?"

She extended her dress still farther over the article in question as she said: "Oh dear no! I never put it up when the sun shines. Pink fades awfully, you know; and I only carry it to meetin' cloudy Sundays. Sometimes the sun comes out all of a sudden, and I have a dreadful time covering it up. It's the dearest thing in life to me; but it's an awful care."

At this moment the thought gradually permeated Mr. Jeremiah Cobb's slow-moving mind that the bird perched by his side was a bird of very different feather from those to which he was accustomed in his daily drives. He put the whip back in its socket, took his foot from the dashboard, pushed his hat back, blew his quid of tobacco into the road, and, having thus cleared his mental decks for action, he took his first good look at the passenger – a look which she met with a grave, childlike stare of friendly curiosity.

The buff calico was faded, but scrupulously clean, and starched within an inch of its life. From the little standing ruffle at the neck the child's slender throat rose very brown and thin, and the head looked small to bear the weight of dark hair that hung in a thick braid to her waist. She wore an odd little visored cap of white Leghorn, which may either have been the latest thing in children's hats, or some bit of ancient finery furbished up for the occasion. It was trimmed with a twist of buff ribbon and a cluster of black and orange porcupine quills, which hung or bristled stiffly over one ear, giving her the quaintest and most unusual appearance. Her face was without colour and sharp in outline. As to features, she must have had the usual number, though Mr. Cobb's attention never proceeded so far as nose, forehead, or chin, being caught on the way and held fast by the eyes. Rebecca's eyes were like faith — "the substance of things hoped for, the evidence of things not seen." Under her delicately etched brows they glowed like two stars, their dancing lights half hidden in lustrous darkness. Their glance was eager and full of interest, yet never satisfied; their steadfast gaze was brilliant and mysterious, and had the effect of looking directly through the obvious to something beyond — in the object, in the landscape, in you. They had never been accounted for, Rebecca's eyes. The school-teacher and the minister at Temperance had tried and failed; the young artist who came for the summer to sketch the red barn, the ruined mill, and the bridge, ended by giving up all these local beauties and devoting herself to the face of a child — a small, plain face, illuminated by a pair of eyes carrying such messages, such suggestions, such hints of sleeping power and insight, that one never tired of looking into their shining depths, nor of fancying that what one saw there was the reflection of one's own thought.

Mr. Cobb made none of these generalizations; his remark to his wife that night was simply to the effect that whenever the child looked at him she knocked him galley west.

"Miss Ross, a lady that paints, gave me the sunshade," said Rebecca, when she had exchanged looks with Mr. Cobb and learned his face by heart. "Did you notice the pinked double ruffle and the white tip and handle? They're ivory. The handle is scarred, you see. That's because Fanny sucked and chewed it in meeting when I wasn't looking. I've never felt the same to Fanny since."

"Is Fanny your sister?"

"She's one of them."

"How many are there of you?"

"Seven. There's verses written about seven children:

> *'"Quick was the little maid's reply –*
> *'O master, we are seven!'"*

I learned it to speak in school, but the scholars were hateful and laughed. Hannah is the oldest; I come next, then John, then Jenny, then Mark, then Fanny, then Mira."

"Well, that *is* a big family!"

"Far too big, everybody says," replied Rebecca, with an unexpected and thoroughly grown-up candour that induced Mr. Cobb to murmur, "I swan!" and insert more tobacco in his left cheek.

"They're dear, but such a bother, and cost so much to feed, you see," she rippled on. "Hannah and I haven't done anything but put babies to bed at night and take them up in the morning for years and years. But it's finished, that's one comfort; and we'll have a lovely time when we're all grown up and the mortgage is paid off."

"All finished? Oh, you mean you've come away?"

"No; I mean they're all over and done with – our family's finished. Mother says so, and she always keeps her promises. There hasn't been any since Mira, and she's three. She was born the day father died. Aunt Miranda wanted Hannah to come to Riverboro instead of me, but mother couldn't spare her; she takes hold of housework better than I do, Hannah does. I told mother last night if there was likely to be any more children while I was away I'd have to be sent for, for when there's a baby it always takes Hannah and me both, for mother has the cooking and the farm."

"Oh, you live on a farm, do ye? Where is it? Near to where you got on?"

"Near? Why, it must be thousands of miles! We came from Temperance in the cars. Then we drove a long ways to Cousin Ann's and went to bed. Then we got up and drove ever so far to Maplewood, where the stage was. Our farm is away off from everywheres, but our school and meeting-house is at Temperance, and that's only two miles. Sitting up here with you is most as good as climbing the meeting-house steeple. I know a boy who's been up on our steeple. He said the people and cows looked like flies. We haven't met any people yet, but I'm *kind* of disappointed in the cows; they don't look so little as I hoped they would, still" – brightening – "they don't look quite as big as if we were down side of them, do they? Boys always do the nice splendid things, and girls can only do the nasty dull ones that get left over. They can't climb so high, or go so far, or stay out so late, or run so fast, or anything."

Mr. Cobb wiped his mouth on the back of his hand and gasped. He had a feeling that he was being hurried from peak to peak of a mountain range without time to take a good breath in between.

"I can't seem to locate your farm," he said, "though I've been to Temperance, and used to live up that way. What's your folks' name?"

"Randall. My mother's name is Aurelia Randall. Our names are Hannah Lucy Randall, Rebecca Rowena Randall, John Halifax Randall, Jenny Lind Randall, Marquis Randall, Fanny Ellsler Randall, and Miranda Randall. Mother named half of us and father the other half; but we didn't come out even, so they both thought it would be nice to name Mira after Aunt Miranda, in Riverboro. They hoped it might do some good; but it didn't, and now we call her Mira. We are all named after somebody in particular. Hannah is Hannah at the Window Binding Shoes, and I am taken out of 'Ivanhoe'; John Halifax was a gentleman in a book; Mark is after his uncle, Marquis de Lafayette, that died a twin. (Twins very often don't live to grow up, and triplets almost never. Did you know that, Mr. Cobb?) We don't call him Marquis, only Mark. Jenny is named for a singer and Fanny for a beautiful dancer; but mother says they're both misfits, for Jenny can't carry a tune, and Fanny's kind of stiff-leggèd. Mother would like to call them Jane and Frances and give up their middle names, but she says it wouldn't be fair to father. She says we must always stand up for father, because everything was against him, and he wouldn't have died if he hadn't had such bad luck. I think that's all there is to tell about us," she finished seriously.

"Land o' liberty! I should think it was enough," ejaculated Mr. Cobb. "There wa'n't many names left when your mother got through choosin'. You've got a powerful good memory. I guess it ain't no trouble for you to learn your lessons, is it?"

"Not much; the trouble is to get the shoes to go and learn 'em. These are spandy new I've got on, and they have to last six months. Mother always says to save my shoes. There don't seem to be any way of saving shoes but taking 'em off and going barefoot; but I can't do that in Riverboro without shaming Aunt Mirandy. I'm going to school right along now when I'm living with Aunt Mirandy, and in two years I'm going to the seminary at Wareham. Mother says it ought to be the making of me. I'm going to be a painter, like Miss Ross, when I get through school. At any rate, that's what *I* think I'm going to be. Mother thinks I'd better teach."

"Your farm 'ain't the old Hobbs' place, is it?"

"No, it's just Randall's Farm — at least, that's what mother calls it. I call it Sunnybrook Farm."

"I guess it don't make no difference what you call it so long as you know where it is," remarked Mr. Cobb sententiously.

Rebecca turned the full light of her eyes upon him reproachfully, almost severely, as she answered;

"Oh, don't say that and be like all the rest! It does make a difference what you call things. When I say Randall's Farm, do you see how it looks?"

"No, I can't say I do," responded Mr. Cobb uneasily.

"Now, when I say Sunnybrook Farm, what does it make you think of?"

Mr. Cobb felt like a fish removed from his native element and left panting on the sand. There was no evading the awful responsibility of a reply, for Rebecca's eyes were searchlights that pierced the fiction of his brain and perceived the bald spot on the back of his head.

"I s'pose there's a brook somewhere near it," he said timorously.

Rebecca looked disappointed, but not quite disheartened. "That's pretty good," she said encouragingly. "You're warm, but not hot. There's a brook, but not a common brook. It has young trees and baby bushes on each side of it, and it's a shallow, chattering little brook, with a white sandy bottom and lots of little shiny pebbles. Whenever there's a bit of sunshine the brook catches it, and it's always full of sparkles the livelong day. Don't your stomach feel hollow? Mine does. I was so 'fraid I'd miss the stage I couldn't eat any breakfast."

"You'd better have your lunch, then. I don't eat nothin' till I get to Milltown, then I get a piece o' pie and cup o' coffee."

"I wish I could see Milltown. I suppose it's bigger and grander even than Wareham — more like Paris? Miss Ross told me about Paris; she bought my pink sunshade there and my bead purse. You see how it opens with a snap. I've twenty cents in it, and it's got to last three months – for stamps and paper and ink. Mother says Aunt Mirandy won't want to buy things like those when she's feeding and clothing me and paying for my school-books."

"Paris ain't no great," said Mr. Cobb disparagingly. "It's the dullest place in the State o' Maine. I've druv there many a time."

Again Rebeccas was obliged to reprove Mr. Cobb, tacitly and quietly, but none the less surely, though the reproof was dealt with one glance, quickly sent and as quickly withdrawn.

"Paris is the capital of France, and you have to go to it on a boat," she said instructively. "It's in my geography, and it says: 'The French are a gay and polite people, fond of dancing and light wines.' I asked the teacher what light wines were, and he thought it was something like new cider, or, maybe, ginger-pop. I can see Paris as plain as day by just shutting my eyes. The beautiful ladies are always gaily dancing around, with pink sunshades and bead purses, and the grand gentlemen are politely dancing and drinking ginger-pop. But you can see Milltown most every day with your eyes wide open," Rebecca said wistfully.

"Milltown ain't no great neither," replied Mr. Cobb with the air of having visited all the cities of the earth, and found them as naught. "Now, you watch me heave this newspaper right on to Miss Brown's doorstep."

Piff! and the packet landed exactly as it was intended – on the corn-husk mat in front of the screen door.

"Oh, how splendid that was!" cried Rebecca with enthusiasm – "just like the knife-thrower Mark saw at the circus. I wish there was a long, long row of houses, each with a corn-husk mat and a screen door in the middle, and a newspaper to throw on every one!"

"I might fail on some of 'em, you know,' said Mr. Cobb, beaming with modest pride. "If your aunt Mirandy'll let you, I'll take you down to Milltown some day this summer when the stage ain't full."

A thrill of delicious excitement ran through Rebecca's frame, from her new shoes up, up to the Leghorn cap and down the black braid. She pressed Mr. Cobb's knee ardently, and said in a voice choking with tears of joy and astonishment: "Oh, it can't be true – it can't! To think I should see Milltown! It's like having a fairy godmother, who asks you your wish and then gives it to you. Did you ever read 'Cinderella,' or 'The Yellow Dwarf,' or 'The Enchanted Frog,' or 'The Fair One with Golden Locks'?"

"No," said Mr. Cobb cautiously after a moment's reflection. "I don't seem to think I ever did read jest those partic'lar ones. Where'd you get a chance at so much readin'?"

"Oh, I've read lots of books," answered Rebecca casually – "father's, and Miss Ross's, and all the dif'rent school-teachers', and all in the Sunday-school library. I've read 'The Lamplighter,' and 'Scottish Chiefs,' and 'Ivanhoe,' and 'The Heir of Redclyffe,' and 'Cora, the Doctor's Wife,' and 'David Copperfield,' and 'The Gold of Chickaree,' and Plutarch's 'Lives,' and 'Thaddeus of Warsaw,' and 'Pilgrim's Progress,' and lots more. What have you read?"

"I've never happened to read those partic'lar books; but land! I've read a sight in my time! Nowadays I'm so drove I get along with the Almanac, the *Weekly Argus*, and the *Maine State Agriculturist*. There's the river again; this is the last long hill, and when we get to the top of it we'll see the chimbleys of Riverboro in the distance. 'Tain't fur. I live 'bout half a mile beyond the brick house myself."

Rebecca's hand stirred nervously in her lap and she moved in her seat. "I didn't think I was going to be afraid," she said almost under her breath; "but I guess I am, just a little mite – when you say it's coming so near."

"Would you go back?" asked Mr. Cobb curiously.

She flashed him an intrepid look and then said proudly, "I'd never go back – I might be frightened, but I'd be ashamed to run. Going to Aunt Mirandy's is like going down cellar in the dark. There might be ogres and giants under the stairs, but, as I tell Hannah, there *might* be elves and fairies and enchanted frogs! Is there a main street to the village, like that in Wareham?"

"I s'pose you might call it main street, an' your Aunt Sawyer lives on it, but there ain't no stores nor mills, an' it's an awful one-horse village! You have to go 'cross the river an' get on to our side if you want to see anything goin' on."

"I'm almost sorry," she sighed, "because it would be so grand to drive down a real main street sitting high up like this behind two splendid horses, with my pink sunshade up, and everybody in town wondering who the bunch of lilacs and the hair-trunk belongs to. It would be just like the beautiful lady in the parade. Last summer the circus came to Temperance, and they had a procession in the morning. Mother let us all walk in and wheel Mira in the baby-carriage, because we couldn't afford to go to the circus in the afternoon. And there were lovely horses and animals in cages, and clowns on horseback; and at the very end came a little red-and-gold chariot drawn by two ponies, and in it, sitting on a velvet cushion, was the snake-charmer, all dressed in satin and spangles. She was so beautiful beyond compare, Mr. Cobb, that you had to swallow lumps in your throat when you looked at her, and little cold feelings crept up and down your back. Don't you know how I mean? Didn't you ever see anybody that made you feel like that?"

Mr. Cobb was more distinctly uncomfortable at this moment than he had been at any one time during the eventful morning, but he evaded the point dexterously by saying: "There ain't no harm, as I can see, in our makin' the grand entry in the biggest style we can. I'll take the whip out, set up straight, an' drive fast; you hold your bo'quet in your lap, an' open your little red parasol, an' we'll jest make the natives stare!"

The child's face was radiant for a moment, but the glow faded just as quickly as she said: "I forgot — mother put me inside, and maybe she'd want me to be there when I got to Aunt Mirandy's. Maybe I'd be more genteel inside, and then I wouldn't have to be jumped down and my clothes fly up, but could open the door and step down like a lady passenger. Would you please stop a minute, Mr. Cobb, and let me change?"

The stage-driver good-naturedly pulled up his horses, lifted the excited little creature down, opened the door, and helped her in, putting the lilacs and pink sunshade beside her.

"We've had a great trip," he said, "and we've got real well acquainted, haven't we? You won't forget about Milltown?"

"Never!" she exclaimed fervently; "and you're sure you won't either?"

"Never! Cross my heart!" vowed Mr. Cobb solemnly, as he remounted his perch; and as the stage rumbled down the village stret beween the green maples, those who looked from their windows saw a little brown elf in buff calico sitting primly on the back-seat holding a great bouquet tightly in one hand, and a pink parasol in the other. Had they been far-sighted enough they might have seen, when the stage turned into the side doorway of the old brick house, a calico yoke rising and falling tempestuously over the beating heart beneath, the red color coming and going in two pale cheeks, and a mist of tears swimming in two brilliant dark eyes – Rebecca's journey had ended.

"There's the stage turnin' into the Sawyer girls' dooryard," said Mrs. Perkins to her husband. "That must be the niece from up Temperance way. It seems they wrote to Aurelia and invited Hannah, the oldest, but Aurelia said she could spare Rebecca better, if 'twas all the same to Mirandy 'n' Jane; so it's Rebecca that's come. She'll be good comp'ny for our Emma Jane; but I don't believe they'll keep her three months! She looks black as an Injun, what I can see of her – black and kind of up-an'-comin'. They used to say that one o' the Randalls married a Spanish woman – somebody that was teachin' music and languages at a boardin'-school. Lorenzo was dark complected, you remember; and this child is, too. Well, I don't know as Spanish blood is any real disgrace, not if it's a good ways back and the woman was respectable."

CHAPTER TWO

REBECCA'S RELATIONS

~

They had been called the Sawyer girls when Miranda at eighteen, Jane at twelve, and Aurelia at eight, participated in the various activities of village life; and when Riverboro fell into a habit of thought or speech, it saw no reason for falling out of it – at any rate, in the same century. So, although Miranda and Jane were between fifty and sixty at the time this story opens, Riverboro still called them the Sawyer girls. They were spinsters; but Aurelia, the youngest, had made what she called a romantic marriage, and what her sisters termed a mighty poor speculation. "There's worse things than bein' old maids," they said; whether they thought so is quite another matter.

The element of romance in Aurelia's marriage existed chiefly in the fact that Mr. L. D. M. Randall had a soul above farming or trading, and was a votary of the Muses. He taught the weekly singing-school (then a feature of village life) in half a dozen neighboring towns; he played the violin, and "called off" at dances, or evoked rich harmonies from church melodeons on

Sundays. He taught certain uncouth lads, when they were of an age to enter society, the intricacies of contra dances, or the steps of the schottische and mazurka; and he was a marked figure in all social assemblies, though conspicuously absent from town meetings, and the purely masculine gatherings at the store, or tavern, or bridge.

His hair was a little longer, his hands a little whiter, his shoes a little thinner, his manner a trifle more polished, than that of his soberer mates; indeed, the only department of life in which he failed to shine was the making of sufficient money to live upon. Luckily, he had no responsibilities; his father and his twin brother had died when he was yet a boy, and his mother, whose only noteworthy achievement had been the naming of her twin sons Marquis de Lafayette and Lorenzo de Medici Randall, had supported herself and educated her child by making coats up to the very day of her death. She was wont to say plaintively: "I'm afraid the faculties was too much divided up between my twins. L. D. M. is awful talented; but I guess M. D. L. would 'a' be'n the practical one if he'd 'a' lived."

"L. D. M. was practical enough to get the richest girl in the village," replied Mrs. Robinson.

"Yes," sighed his mother; "there it is again. If the twins could 'a' married Aurelia Sawyer, 'twould 'a' been all right. L. D. M. was talented 'nough to *get* Reely's money, but M. D. L. would 'a' be'n practical 'nough to have *kep'* it."

Aurelia's share of the modest Sawyer property had been put into one thing after another by the handsome and luckless Lorenzo de Medici. He had a graceful and poetic way of making an investment for each new son and daughter that blessed their union. "A birthday present for our child, Aurelia," he would say; "a little nest-egg for the future." But Aurelia once remarked in a moment of bitterness that the hen never lived that could sit on those eggs and hatch anything out of them.

Miranda and Jane had virtually washed their hands of Aurelia when she married Lorenzo de Medici Randall. Having exhausted the resources of Riverboro and its immediate vicinity, the unfortunate couple had moved on and on in a steadily decreasing scale of prosperity until they had reached Temperance, where they had settled down and invited fate to do its worst – an invitation which was promptly accepted. The maiden sisters at home wrote to Aurelia two or three times a year, and sent modest but serviceable presents to the children at Christmas, but refused to assist L. D. M. with the regular expenses of his rapidly-growing family. His last investment – made shortly before the birth of Miranda (named in a lively hope of favours which never came) – was a small farm two miles from Temperance. Aurelia managed this herself; and so it proved a home at least, and a place for the unsuccessful Lorenzo to die and to be buried from – a duty somewhat too long deferred, many thought, which he performed on the day of Mira's birth.

It was in this happy-go-lucky household that Rebecca had grown up. It was just an ordinary family – two or three of the children were handsome and the rest plain, three of them rather clever, two industrious, and two commonplace and dull. Rebecca had her father's facility, and had been his aptest pupil. She "carried" the alto by ear, danced without being taught, played the melodeon without knowing the notes. Her love of books she inherited chiefly from her mother, who found it hard to sweep, or cook, or sew when there was a novel in the house. Fortunately, books were scarce, or the children might sometimes have gone ragged and hungry.

But other forces had been at work in Rebecca, and the traits of unknown forbears had been wrought into her fibre. Lorenzo de Medici was flabby and boneless, Rebecca was a thing of fire and spirit; he lacked energy and courage, Rebecca was plucky at two and dauntless at five. Mrs. Randall and Hannah had no sense of humour; Rebecca possessed and showed it as soon as she could walk and talk.

She had not been able, however, to borrow her parents' virtues and those of other generous ancestors, and escape all the weaknesses in the calendar. She had not her sister Hannah's patience, or her brother John's sturdy staying-power. Her will was sometimes wilfulness, and the ease with which she did most things led her to be impatient of hard tasks or long ones. But whatever else there was or was not, there was freedom at Randall's farm. The children grew, worked, fought, ate what and slept where they could; loved one another and their parents pretty well, but with no tropical passion; and educated themselves for nine months of the year, each one in his own way.

As a result of this method, Hannah, who could only have been developed by forces applied from without, was painstaking, humdrum, and limited;

while Rebecca, who apparently needed nothing but space to develop in and a knowledge of terms in which to express herself, grew and grew and grew, always from within outward. Her forces of one sort and another had seemingly been set in motion when she was born; they needed no daily spur, but moved of their own accord – towards what no one knew, least of all Rebecca herself. The field for the exhibition of her creative instinct was painfully small, and the only use she had made of it as yet was to leave eggs out of the corn bread one day and milk another to see how it would turn out; to part Fanny's hair sometimes in the middle, sometimes on the right, and sometimes on the left side; and to play all sorts of fantastic pranks with the children, occasionally bringing them to the table as fictitious or historical characters found in her favourite books. Rebecca amused her mother and her family generally, but she never was counted of serious importance; and though considered "smart" and old for her age, she was never thought superior in any way. Aurelia's experience of genius, as exemplified in the deceased Lorenzo de Medici, led her into a greater admiration of plain, everyday common-sense – a quality in which Rebecca, it must be confessed, seemed sometimes painfully deficient.

Hannah was her mother's favourite, so far as Aurelia could indulge herself in such recreations as partiality. The parent who is obliged to feed and clothe seven children on an income of fifteen dollars a month seldom has time to discriminate carefully between the various members of her brood; but Hannah at fourteen was at once companion and partner in all her mother's problems. She it was who kept the house while Aurelia busied herself in barn and field. Rebecca was capable of certain set tasks, such as keeping the small children from killing themselves and one another, feeding the poultry, picking up chips, hulling strawberries, wiping dishes; but she was thought irresponsible, and Aurelia, needing somebody to lean on (having never enjoyed that luxury with the gifted Lorenzo), leaned on Hannah. Hannah showed the result of this attitude somewhat, being a trifle careworn in face and sharp in manner. But she was a self-contained, well-behaved, dependable child, and that is the reason her aunts had invited her to Riverboro to be a member of their family and participate in all the advantages of their loftier position in the world. It was several years since Miranda and Jane had seen the children, but they remembered with pleasure that Hannah had not spoken a word during the interview, and it was for this reason that they had asked for the pleasure of her company. Rebecca, on the other hand, had dressed up the dog in John's clothes; and, being requested to get the three younger children ready for dinner, she had held them under the pump, and then proceeded to "smack" their hair flat to their heads by vigorous brushing, bringing them to the table in such a moist and hideous state of shininess that their mother was ashamed of their appearance. Rebecca's own black locks were commonly pushed smoothly off her forehead, but on this occasion she formed what I must perforce call by its only name – a spit-curl – directly in the centre of her brow; an ornament which she was allowed to wear a short time – only, in fact, till Hannah was able to call her mother's attention to it, when she was sent into the next room to remove it, and to come back looking something like a Christian. This command she interpreted somewhat too literally, perhaps, because she contrived in the space of two minutes an extremely pious style of hairdressing, fully as effective, if not as startling, as the first. These antics were solely the result of nervous irritation, a mood born of Miss Miranda Sawyer's stiff, grim, and martial attitude. The remembrance of Rebecca was so vivid that their sister Aurelia's letter was something of a shock to the quiet, elderly spinsters of the brick house; for it said that Hannah could not possibly be spared for a few years yet, but that Rebecca would come as soon as she could be made ready: that the offer was most thankfully appreciated, and that the regular schooling and church privileges, as well as the influence of the Sawyer home, would doubtless be "the making of Rebecca."

CHAPTER THREE

A DIFFERENCE IN HEARTS

~

"I don' know as I cal'lated to be the makin' of any child," Miranda had said as she folded Aurelia's letter and laid it in the light-stand drawer. "I s'posed, of course, Aurelia would send us the one we asked for, but it's just like her to palm off that wild young one on somebody else."

"You remember we said that Rebecca or even Jenny might come, in case Hannah couldn't," interposed Jane.

"I know we did, but we hadn't any notion it would turn out that way," grumbled Miranda.

"She was a mite of a thing when we saw her three years ago," ventured Jane; "she's had time to improve."

"And time to grow worse!"

"Won't it be kind of a privilege to put her on the right track?" asked Jane timidly.

"I don' know about the privilege part; it'll be considerable of a chore, I guess. If her mother hain't got her on the right track by now, she won't take to it herself all of a sudden."

This depressed and depressing frame of mind had lasted until the eventful day dawned on which Rebecca was to arrive.

"If she makes as much work after she comes as she has before, we might as well give up hope of ever gettin' any rest," sighed Miranda as she hung the dish-towels on the barberry bushes at the side-door.

"But we should have had to clean house, Rebecca or no Rebecca," urged Jane; "and I can't see why you've scrubbed and washed and baked as you have for that one child, nor why you've about bought out Watson's stock of dry goods."

"I know Aurelia, if you don't," responded Miranda. "I've seen her house, and I've seen that batch o' children, wearin' one another's clothes, and never carin' whether they had 'em on right sid' out or not; I know what they've had to live and dress on, and so do you. That child will like as not come here with a passel o' things borrowed from the rest o' the family. She'll have Hannah's shoes and John's undershirts and Mark's socks most likely. I suppose she never had a thimble on her finger in her life, but she'll know the feelin' o' one before she's ben here many days. I've bought a piece of unbleached muslin and a piece o' brown gingham for her to make up; that'll keep her busy. Of course she won't pick up anything after herself; she probably never see a duster, and she'll be as hard to train into our ways as if she was a heathen."

"She'll make a diff'rence," acknowledged Jane, "but she may turn out more biddable 'n we think."

"She'll mind when she's spoken to, biddable or not," remarked Miranda with a shake of the last towel.

Miranda Sawyer had a heart, of course, but she had never used it for any other purpose than the pumping and circulating of blood. She was just, conscientious, economical, industrious, a regular attendant at church and Sunday-school, and a member of the State Missionary and Bible societies; but in the presence of all these chilly virtues you longed for one warm little fault, or lacking that, one likable failing, something to make you sure she was thoroughly alive. She had never had any education other than that of the neighborhood district school, for her desires and ambitions had all pointed to the management of the house, the farm, and the dairy. Jane, on the other hand, had gone to an academy, and also to a boarding-school for young ladies; so had Aurelia; and after all the years that had elapsed there was still a slight difference in language and in manner between the elder and the two younger sisters.

Jane, too, had had the inestimable advantage of a sorrow; not the natural grief at the loss of her aged father and mother, for she had been content to let them go, but something far deeper. She was engaged to marry young Tom Carter, who had nothing to marry on, it is true, but who was sure to have some time or other. Then the war broke out. Tom enlisted at the first call. Up to that time Jane had loved him with a quiet, friendly sort of affection, and had given her country a mild emotion of the same sort. But the strife, the danger, the anxiety of the time, set new currents of feeling in motion. Life became something other than the three meals a day, the round of cooking, washing, sewing, and church-going. Personal gossip vanished from the village conversation. Big things took the place of trifling ones — sacred sorrows of wives and mothers, pangs of fathers and husbands, self-denials, sympathies, new desire to bear one another's burdens. Men and women grew fast in those days of the nation's trouble and danger, and Jane awoke from the vague dull dream she had hitherto called life to new hopes, new fears, new purposes. Then, after a year's anxiety, a year when one never looked in the newspaper without dread and sickness of suspense, came the telegram saying that Tom was wounded; and without so much as asking Miranda's leave, she packed her trunk and started for the South. She was in time to hold Tom's hand through hours of pain; to show him for once the heart of a prim New England girl when it is ablaze with love and grief; to put her arms about him so that he could have a home to die in, and that was all; — all, but it served.

It carried her through weary months of nursing — nursing of other soldiers for Tom's dear sake; it sent her home a better woman; and though she had never left Riverboro in all the years that lay between, and had grown into the counterfeit presentment of her sister and of all other thin, spare, New England spinsters, it was something of a counterfeit, and underneath was still the faint echo of that wild heart-beat of her girlhood. Having learned the trick of beating and loving and suffering, the poor faithful heart persisted, although it lived on memories, and carried on its sentimental operations mostly in secret.

"You're soft, Jane," said Miranda once; "you allers was soft, and you allers will be. If 't wa'n't for me keeping you stiffened up, I b'lieve you'd leak out o' the house into the dooryard."

It was already past the appointed hour for Mr. Cobb and his coach to be lumbering down the street.

"The stage ought to be here," said Miranda, glancing nervously at the tall clock for the twentieth time. "I guess everything's done. I've tacked up two thick towels back of her washstand, and put a mat under her slop-jar; but children are awful hard on furniture. I expect we shan't know this house a year from now."

Jane's frame of mind was naturally depressed and timorous, having been affected by Miranda's gloomy presages of evil to come. The only difference between the sisters in this matter was that while Miranda only wondered how they could endure Rebecca, Jane had flashes of inspiration in which she wondered how Rebecca would endure them. It was in one of these flashes that she ran up the back-stairs to put a vase of apple-blossoms and a red tomato-pincushion on Rebecca's bureau.

The stage rumbled to the side-door of the brick house, and Mr. Cobb handed Rebecca out like a real lady passenger. She alighted with great circumspection, put the bunch of faded flowers in her aunt Miranda's hand, and received her salute; it could hardly be called a kiss without injuring the fair name of that commodity.

"You needn't 'a' bothered to bring flowers,' remarked that gracious and tactful lady; "the garden's always full of 'em here when it comes time."

Jane then kissed Rebecca, giving a somewhat better imitation of the real thing than her sister.

"Put the trunk in the entry, Jeremiah, and we'll get it carried upstairs this afternoon," she said.

"I'll take it up for ye now, if ye say the word, girls."

"No, no; don't leave the horses; somebody 'll be comin' past, and we can call 'em in."

"Well, good-bye, Rebecca; good-day, Mirandy 'n' Jane. You've got a lively little girl there. I guess she'll be a first-rate company-keeper."

Miss Sawyer shuddered openly at the adjective "lively" as applied to a child, her belief being that though children might be seen, if absolutely necessary, they certainly should never be heard if she could help it. "We're not much used to noise, Jane and me," she remarked acidly.

Mr. Cobb saw that he had taken the wrong tack, but he was too unused to argument to explain himself readily, so he drove away, trying to think by what safer word than "lively" he might have described his interesting little passenger.

"I'll take you up and show you your room, Rebecca," Miss Miranda said. "Shut the mosquito-nettin' door tight behind you, so's to keep the flies out; it ain't fly-time yet, but I want you to start right. Take your passel along with ye, and then you won't have to come down for it; always make your head save your heels. Rub your feet on that braided rug; hang your hat and cape in the entry there as you go past."

"It's my best hat," said Rebecca.

"Take it upstairs, then, and put it in the clothes-press; but I shouldn't 'a' thought you'd 'a' worn your best hat on the stage."

"It's my only hat," explained Rebecca. "My everyday hat wasn't good enough to bring. Fanny's going to finish it."

"Lay your parasol in the entry closet."

"Do you mind if I keep it in my room, please? It always seems safer."

"There ain't any thieves hereabouts, and if there was, I guess they wouldn't make for your sunshade; but come along. Remember to always go up the back way; we don't use the front-stairs on account o' the carpet; take care o' the turn, and don't ketch your foot; look to your right and go in. When you've washed your face and hands and brushed your hair you can come down, and by-and-by we'll unpack your trunk and get you settled before supper. Ain't you got your dress on hind sid' foremost?"

Rebecca drew her chin down and looked at the row of smoked pearl buttons running up and down the middle of her flat little chest.

"Hind side foremost? Oh, I see! No, that's all right. If you have seven children you can't keep buttonin' and unbuttonin' 'em all the time – they have to do themselves. We're always buttoned up in front at our house. Mira's only three, but she's buttoned up in front, too."

Miranda said nothing as she closed the door, but her looks were at once equivalent to and more eloquent than words.

Rebecca stood perfectly still in the centre of the floor and looked about her. There was a square of oilcloth in front of each article of furniture and a drawn-in rug beside the single four-poster, which was covered with a fringed white dimity counterpane.

Everything was as neat as wax, but the ceilings were much higher than Rebecca was accustomed to. It was a north room, and the window, which was long and narrow, looked out on the back buildings and the barn.

It was not the room, which was far more comfortable than Rebecca's own at the farm, nor the lack of view, nor yet the long journey, for she was not conscious of weariness; it was not the fear of a strange place, for she loved new places and courted new sensations; it was because of some curious blending of uncomprehended emotions that Rebecca stood her sunshade in the corner, tore off her best hat, flung it on the bureau with the porcupine quills on the under-side, and stripping down the dimity spread, precipitated herself into the middle of the bed, and pulled the counterpane over her head.

In a moment the door opened quietly. Knocking was a refinement quite unknown in Riverboro, and if it had been heard of would never have been wasted on a child.

Miss Miranda entered, and as her eye wandered about the vacant room, it fell upon a white and tempestuous ocean of counterpane, an ocean breaking into strange movements of wave and crest and billow.

"Rebecca!"

The tone in which the word was voiced gave it all the effect of having been shouted from the housetops.

A dark ruffled head and two frightened eyes appeared above the dimity spread.

"What are you layin' on your good bed in the daytime for, messin' up the feathers, and dirtyin' the pillers with your dusty boots?"

Rebecca rose guiltily. There seemed no excuse to make. Her offence was beyond explanation or apology.

"I'm sorry, Aunt Mirandy. Something came over me; I don't know what."

"Well, if it comes over you very soon again we'll have to find out what 'tis. Spread your bed up smooth this minute, for 'Bijah Flagg's bringin' your trunk upstairs, and I wouldn't let him see such a cluttered-up room for anything; he'd tell it all over town."

When Mr. Cobb had put up his horses that night he carried a kitchen chair to the side of his wife, who was sitting on the back porch.

"I brought a little Randall girl down on the stage from Maplewood to-day, mother. She's kin to the Sawyer girls, an' is goin' to live with 'em," he said, as he sat down and began to whittle. "She's that Aurelia's child, the one that ran away with Susan Randall's son just before we come here to live."

"How old a child?"

"'Bout ten, or somewhere along there, an' small for her age. But, land! she might be a hundred to hear her talk! She kep' me jumpin' tryin' to answer her. Of all the queer children I ever come across, she's the queerest. She ain't no beauty – her face is all eyes; but if she ever grows up to them eyes an' fills out a little, she'll make folks stare. Land, mother! I wish't you could 'a' heard her talk."

"I don't see what she had to talk about, a child like that, to a stranger," replied Mrs. Cobb.

"Stranger or no stranger, 'twouldn't make no difference to her. She'd talk to a pump or a grindstun; she'd talk to herself ruther 'n keep still."

"What did she talk about?"

"Blamed if I can repeat any of it! She kep' me so surprised, I didn't have my wits about me. She had a little pink sunshade – it kind o' looked like a doll's amberill – 'n' she clung to it like a burr to a woollen stockin'. I advised her to open it up, the sun was so hot; but she said no, 'twould fade, an' she tucked it under her dress. 'It's the dearest thing in life to me,' says she; 'but it's a dreadful care.' Them's the very words, an' it's all the words I remember. 'It's the dearest thing in life to me; but it's an awful care!'" Here Mr. Cobb laughed aloud as he tipped his chair back against the side of the house. "There was another thing, but I can't get it right exactly. She was talkin' 'bout the circus parade an' the snake-charmer in a gold chariot, an' says she, 'She was so beautiful beyond compare, Mr. Cobb, that it made you have lumps in your throat to look at her.' She'll be comin' over to see you, mother, an' you can size her up for yourself. I don't know how she'll git on with Miranda Sawyer – poor little soul!"

This doubt was more or less openly expressed in Riverboro, which, however, had two opinions on the subject – one that it was a most generous thing in the Sawyer girls to take one of Aurelia's children to educate; the other that the education would be bought at a price wholly out of proportion to its intrinsic value.

Rebecca's first letters to her mother would seem to indicate that she cordially coincided with the latter view of the situation.

CHAPTER FOUR

REBECCA'S POINT OF VIEW

~

Dear Mother,
I am safely here. My dress was not much tumbled and Aunt Jane helped me press it out. I like Mr. Cobb very much. He chews but throws newspapers straight up to the doors. I rode outside a little while, but got inside before I got to Aunt Miranda's house. I did not want to, but thought you would like it better. Miranda is such a long word that I think I will say Aunt M. and Aunt J. in my Sunday letters. Aunt J. has given me a dictionary to look up all the hard words in. It takes a good deal of time and I am glad people can talk without stoping to spell. It is much eesier to talk than write and much more fun. The brick house looks just the same as you have told us. The parler is splendid and gives you creeps and chills when you look in the door. The furnature is ellergant too, and all the rooms but there are no good sitting-down places exsept in the kitchen. The same cat is here but they do not save kittens when she has them, and the cat is too old to play with. Hannah told me once you ran away with father and I can see it would

247

be nice. If Aunt M. would run away I think I should like to live with Aunt J. She does not hate me as bad as Aunt M. does. Tell Mark he can have my paint box, but I should like him to keep the red cake in case I come home again. I hope Hannah and John do not get tired doing my chores.

Your afectionate friend
Rebecca.

P.S. – please give the piece of poetry to John because he likes my poetry even when it is not very good. This piece is not very good but it is true but I hope you won't mind what is in it as you ran away.

> *This house is dark and dull and dreer*
> *No light doth shine from far or near*
> *Its like the tomb.*
>
> *And those of us who live herein*
> *Are most as dead as serrafim*
> *Though not as good.*
>
> *My guardian angel is asleep*
> *At leest he doth no vigil keep*
> *Ah! woe is me!*
>
> *Then give me back my lonely farm*
> *Where none alive did wish me harm*
> *Dear home of youth!*

P.S. again. – I made the poetry like a piece in a book but could not get it right at first. You see "tomb" and "good" do not sound well together but I wanted to say "tomb" dreadfully and as serrafim are always "good" I couldn't take that out. I have made it over now. It does not say my thoughts as well but think it is more right. Give the best one to John as he keeps them in a box with his birds' eggs. This is the best one.

SUNDAY THOUGHTS
by Rebecca Rowena Randall

> *This house is dark and dull and drear*
> *No light doth shine from far or near*
> *Nor ever could.*
> *And those of us who live herein*

Are most as dead as seraphim
Though not as good.

My guardian angel is asleep
At least he doth no vigil keep
But far doth roam.

Then give me back my lonely farm
Where none alive did wish me harm
Dear childhood home!

Dear Mother,

        I am thrilling with unhappiness this morning. I got that out of Cora The Doctor's Wife whose husband's mother was very cross and unfealing to her like Aunt M. to me. I wish Hannah had come instead of me for it was Hannah that was wanted and she is better than I am and does not answer back so quick. Are there any peaces of my buff calico. Aunt J. wants enough to make a new waste-button behind so I wont look so outlandish. The stiles are quite pretty in Riverboro and those at Meeting quite ellergant more so than in Temperance.

This town is stilish, gay and fair,
And full of wellthy riches rare,
But I would pillow on my arm
The thought of my sweet Brookside Farm.

School is pretty good. The Teacher can answer more questions than the Temperance one but not so many as I can ask. I am smarter than all the girls but one but not so smart as two boys. Emma Jane can add and subtract in her head like a streek of lightning and knows the spelling book right through but has no thoughts of any kind. She is in the Third Reader but does not like stories in books. I am in the Sixth Reader but just because I cannot say the seventh multiplication Table Miss Dearborn threttens to put me in the baby primer class with Elijah and Elisha Simpson little twins.

Sore is my heart and bent my stubborn pride,
With Lijah and with Lisha am I tied,
My soul recoyles like Cora Doctor's Wife,
Like her I feer I cannot bare this life.

I am going to try for the speling prize but fear I cannot get it. I would not care but wrong speling looks dreadful in poetry. Last Sunday when I found seraphim in the dictionary I was ashamed I had made it serrafim but seraphim is not a word you can guess at like another long one outlandish in this letter which spells itself. Miss Dearborn says use the words you *can* spell and if you cant spell seraphim make angel do but angels are not just the same as seraphims. Seraphims are brighter whiter and have bigger wings and I think are older and longer dead than angels which are just freshly dead and after a long time in heaven around the great white throne grow to be seraphims.

I sew on brown gingham dresses every afternoon when Emma Jane and the Simpsons are playing house or running on the Logs when their mothers do not know it. Their mothers are afraid they will drown and Aunt M. is afraid I will wet my clothes so will not let me either. I can play from half past four to supper and after supper a little bit and Saturday afternoons. I am glad our cow has a calf and it is spotted. It is going to be a good year for apples and hay so you and John will be glad and we can pay a little more morgage. Miss Dearborn asked us what is the object of edducation and I said the object of mine was to help pay off the morgage. She told Aunt M. and I had to sew extra for punishment because she says a morgage is disgrace like stealing or smallpox and it will be all over town that we have one on our farm. Emma Jane is not morgaged nor Richard Carter nor Dr. Winship but the Simpsons are.

> *Rise my soul, strain every nerve,*
> *Thy morgage to remove,*
> *Gain thy mother's heartfelt thanks*
> *Thy family's grateful love.*

Pronounce family *quick* or it won't sound right.

Your loving little friend

Rebecca.

Dear John,

You remember when we tide the new dog in the barn how he bit the rope and howled. I am just like him only the brick house is the barn and I can not bite Aunt M. because I must be grateful and edducation is going to be the making of me and help you pay off the morgage when we grow up.

Your loving

Becky.

CHAPTER FIVE

WISDOM'S WAYS

~

The day of Rebecca's arrival had been Friday, and on the Monday following she began her education at the school which was in Riverboro Center, about a mile distant. Miss Sawyer borrowed a neighbour's horse and waggon and drove her to the schoolhouse, interviewing the teacher, Miss Dearborn, arranging for books, and generally starting the child on the path that was to lead to boundless knowledge. Miss Dearborn, it may be said in passing, had had no special preparation in the art of teaching. It came to her naturally, so her family said; and perhaps for this reason she, like Tom Tulliver's clergyman tutor, "set about it with that uniformity of method and independence of circumstances which distinguish the actions of animals understood to be under the immediate teaching of Nature." You remember the beaver which a naturalist tells us "busied himself as earnestly in constructing a dam in a room up three pair of stairs in London as if he had been laying his foundation in a lake in Upper Canada. It was his function to build; the

251

absence of water or of possible progeny was an accident for which he was **not accountable."** In the same manner did Miss Dearborn lay what she **fondly** imagined to be foundations in the infant mind.

Rebecca walked to school after the first morning. She loved this part of **the day's** programme. When the dew was not too heavy and the weather **was fair,** there was a short-cut through the woods. She turned off the main **road,** crept through Uncle Josh Woodman's bars, waved away Mrs. Carter's **cows,** trod the short grass of the pasture, with its well-worn path running through gardens of buttercups and whiteweed, and groves of ivory leaves and sweet fern. She descended a little hill, jumped from stone to stone across a woodland brook, startling the drowsy frogs, who were always winking and blinking in the morning sun. Then came the "woodsy bit," with her feet pressing the slippery carpet of brown pine-needles; the "woodsy bit" so full of dewy morning surprises – fungous growths of brilliant orange and crimson springing up around the stumps of dead trees, beautiful things born in a single night; and now and then the miracle of a little clump of waxen Indian pipes, seen just quickly enough to be saved from her careless tread. Then she climbed a stile, went through a grassy meadow, slid under another pair of bars, and came out into the road again, having gained nearly half a mile.

How delicious it all was! Rebecca clasped her Quackenbos's Grammar and Greenleaf's Arithmetic with a joyful sense of knowing her lessons. Her dinner-pail swung from her right hand, and she had a blissful consciousness of the two soda-biscuits spread with butter and syrup, the baked cup-custard, the doughnut, and the square of hard gingerbread. Sometimes she said whatever "piece" she was going to speak on the next Friday afternoon.

> *"A soldier of the Legion lay dying in Algiers;*
> *There was lack of woman's nursing, there was dearth of woman's tears."*

How she loved the swing and the sentiment of it! How her young voice quivered whenever she came to the refrain:

> *"But we'll meet no more at Bingen, dear Bingen on the Rhine."*

It always sounded beautiful in her ears, as she sent her tearful little treble into the clear morning air. Another early favorite (for we must remember that Rebecca's only knowledge of the great world of poetry consisted of the selections in vogue in school readers) was:

> *"Woodman, spare that tree,*
> *Touch not a single bough;*
> *In youth it sheltered me,*
> *And I'll protect it now."*

When Emma Jane Perkins walked through the "short-cut" with her, the two children used to render this with appropriate dramatic action. Emma Jane always chose to be the woodman, because she had nothing to do but raise on high an imaginary axe. On the one occasion when she essayed the part of the tree's romantic protector, she represented herself as feeling "so awful foolish" that she refused to undertake it again, much to the secret delight of Rebecca, who found the woodman's rôle much too tame for her vaulting ambition. She revelled in the impassioned appeal of the poet, and implored the ruthless woodman to be as brutal as possible with the axe, so that she might properly put greater spirit into her lines. One morning, feeling more frisky than usual, she fell upon her knees and wept in the woodman's petticoat. Curiously enough, her sense of proportion rejected this as soon as it was done.

"That wasn't right; it was silly, Emma Jane; but I'll tell you where it might come in — in 'Give me Three Grains of Corn.' You be the mother, and I'll be the famishing Irish child. For pity's sake, put the axe down! You are not the woodman any longer!"

"What 'll I do with my hands, then?" asked Emma Jane.

"Whatever you like," Rebecca would answer wearily. "You're just a mother — that's all. What does your mother do with her hands? Now, here goes:

> *"'Give me three grains of corn, mother,*
> *Only three grains of corn;*
> *'Twill keep the little life I have*
> *Till the coming of the morn.'"*

This sort of thing made Emma Jane nervous and fidgety; but she was Rebecca's slave, and hugged her chains, no matter how uncomfortable they made her.

At the last pair of bars the two girls were sometimes met by a detachment of the Simpson children, who lived in a black house with a red door and a red barn behind on the Blueberry Plains road. Rebecca felt an interest in the Simpsons from the first, because there were so many of them, and they were so patched and darned, just like her own brood at the home farm.

The little schoolhouse, with its flag-pole on top and its two doors in front, one for boys and the other for girls, stood on the crest of a hill, with rolling fields and meadows on one side, a stretch of pine-woods on the other, and the river glinting and sparkling in the distance. It boasted no attractions within. All was as bare and ugly and uncomfortable as it well could be, for the villages along the river expended so much money in repairing and rebuilding bridges that they were obliged to be very economical in school privileges. The teacher's desk and chair stood on a platform in one corner; there was an uncouth stove, never blackened oftener than once a year, a map of the United States, two blackboards, a ten-quart tin pail of water and long-handled dipper on a corner shelf, and wooden desks and benches for the scholars, who only numbered twenty in Rebecca's time. The seats were higher in the back of the room, and the more advanced and longer-legged pupils sat there, the position being greatly to be envied, as they were at once nearer to the windows and farther from the teacher.

There were classes of a sort, although nobody, broadly speaking, studied the same book with anybody else, or had arrived at the same degree of proficiency in any one branch of learning. Rebecca in particular was so difficult to classify that Miss Dearborn at the end of a fortnight gave up the attempt altogether. She read with Dick Carter and Living Perkins, who were fitting for the academy; recited arithmetic with lisping little "Thuthan Thimpthon," geography with Emma Jane Perkins, and grammar after school hours to Miss Dearborn alone. Full to the brim as she was of clever thoughts and quaint fancies, she made at first but a poor hand at composition. The labour of writing and spelling, with the added difficulties of punctuation and capitals, interfered sadly with the free expression of ideas. She took history with Alice Robinson's class, which was attacking the subject of the Revolution, while Rebecca was bidden to begin with the discovery of America. In a week she had mastered the course of events up to the Revolution, and in ten days had arrived at Yorktown, where the class had apparently established summer quarters. Then, finding that extra effort would only result in her reciting with the oldest Simpson boy, she deliberately held herself back, for wisdom's ways were not those of pleasantness, nor her paths those of peace, if one were compelled to tread them in the company of Seesaw Simpson. Samuel Simpson was generally called Seesaw because of his difficulty in making up his mind. Whether it were a question of fact, of spelling, or of date, of going swimming or fishing, of choosing a book in the Sunday-school library or a stick of candy at the village store, he had no sooner determined on one plan of action than his wish fondly reverted to the opposite one. Seesaw was pale, flaxen-haired, blue-eyed, round-shouldered, and given to stammering when nervous. Perhaps because of his very weakness, Rebecca's decision of character had a fascination for him, and although she snubbed him to the verge of madness, he could never keep his eyes away from her. The force with which she tied her shoe when the lacing came undone, the flirt over shoulder she gave her black braid when she was excited or warm, her manner of studying — book on desk, arms folded, eyes fixed on the opposite wall — all had an abiding charm for Seesaw Simpson. When, having obtained permission, she walked to the water-pail in the corner and drank from the dipper, unseen forces dragged Seesaw from his seat to go and drink after her. It was not only that there was something akin to association and intimacy in drinking next, but there was the fearful joy of meeting her in transit, and receiving a cold and disdainful look from her wonderful eyes.

On a certain warm day in summer Rebecca's thirst exceeded the bounds of propriety. When she asked a third time for permission to quench it at the common fountain Miss Dearborn nodded yes, but lifted her eyebrows unpleasantly as Rebecca neared the desk. As she replaced the dipper Seesaw promptly raised his hand, and Miss Dearborn indicated a weary affirmative.

"What is the matter with you, Rebecca?" she asked.

"I had salt mackerel for breakfast," answered Rebecca.

There seemed nothing humorous about this reply, which was merely the statement of a fact, but an irrepressible titter ran through the school. Miss Dearborn did not enjoy jokes neither made nor understood by herself, and her face flushed.

"I think you had better stand by the pail for five minutes, Rebecca; it may help you to control your thirst."

Rebecca's heart fluttered. She to stand in the corner by the water-pail and be stared at by all the scholars. She unconsciously made a gesture of angry dissent and moved a step nearer her seat, but was arrested by Miss Dearborn's command in a still firmer voice.

"Stand by the pail, Rebecca! Samuel, how many times have you asked for water to-day?"

"This is the f-f-fourth."

"Don't touch the dipper, please. The school has done nothing but drink this afternoon; it has had no time whatever to study. I suppose you had something salt for breakfast, Samuel?' queried Miss Dearborn with sarcasm.

"I had m-m-mackerel, j-just like Reb-b-becca." (Irrepressible giggles by the school.)

"I judged so. Stand by the other side of the pail, Samuel."

Rebecca's head was bowed with shame and wrath. Life looked too black a thing to be endured. The punishment was bad enough, but to be coupled in correction with Seesaw Simpson was beyond human endurance.

Singing was the last exercise in the afternoon, and Minnie Smellie chose "Shall we Gather at the River?" It was a baleful choice and seemed to hold some secret and subtle association with the situation and general progress of events; or at any rate there was apparently some obscure reason for the energy and vim with which the scholars shouted the choral invitation again and again:

> *"Shall we gather at the river —*
> *The beautiful, the beautiful river?"*

Miss Dearborn stole a look at Rebecca's bent head and was frightened. The child's face was pale save for two red spots glowing on her cheeks. Tears hung on her lashes; her breath came and went quickly, and the hand that held her pocket-handkerchief trembled like a leaf.

"You may go to your seat, Rebecca," said Miss Dearborn at the end of the first song. "Samuel, stay where you are till the close of school. And let me tell you, scholars, that I asked Rebecca to stand by the pail only to break up this habit of incessant drinking, which is nothing but empty-mindedness and desire to walk to and fro over the floor. Every time Rebecca has asked for a drink to-day the whole school has gone to the pail one after another. She is really thirsty, and I dare say I ought to have punished you for following her example, not her for setting it. What shall we sing now, Alice?"

"'The Old Oaken Bucket,' please."

"Think of something dry, Alice, and change the subject. Yes, 'The Star-spangled Banner,' if you like, or anything else."

Rebecca sank into her seat and pulled the singing-book from her desk. Miss Dearborn's public explanation had shifted some of the weight from her heart, and she felt a trifle raised in her self-esteem.

Under cover of the general relaxation of singing, votive offerings of respectful sympathy began to make their appearance at her shrine. Living Perkins, who could not sing, dropped a piece of maple sugar in her lap as he passed her on his way to the blackboard to draw the map of Maine. Alice Robinson rolled a perfectly new slate pencil over the floor with her foot until it reached Rebecca's place, while her seat-mate Emma Jane, had made up a little mound of paper balls and labelled them "Bullets for you know who."

Altogether existence grew brighter, and when she was left alone with the teacher for her grammar lesson she had nearly recovered her equanimity, which was more than Miss Dearborn had. The last clattering foot had echoed through the hall, Seesaw's backward glance of penitence had been met and answered defiantly by one of cold disdain.

"Rebecca, I am afraid I punished you more than I meant," said Miss Dearborn, who was only eighteen herself, and in her year of teaching country schools had never encountered a child like Rebecca.

"I hadn't missed a question this whole day, nor whispered either," quavered the culprit; "and I don't think I ought to be shamed just for drinking."

"You started all the others, or it seemed as if you did. Whatever you do they all do, whether you laugh, or miss, or write notes, or ask to leave the room, or drink; and it must be stopped."

"Sam Simpson is a copycoat!" stormed Rebecca. "I wouldn't have minded standing in the corner alone – that is, not so very much; but I couldn't bear standing with him."

"I saw that you couldn't, and that's the reason I told you to take your seat, and left him in the corner. Remember that you are a stranger in the place, and they take more notice of what you do, so you must be careful. Now let's have our conjugations. Give me the verb 'to be,' potential mood, past perfect tense."

> *"I might have been.*   *"We might have been.*
> *Thou mightst have been.*   *You might have been.*
> *He might have been.*   *They might have been."*

"Give me an example, please."

> *"I might have been glad.*
> *Thou mightst have been glad.*
> *He, she, or it might have been glad."*

"'He' or 'she' might have been glad because they are masculine and feminine, but could '*it*' have been glad?" asked Miss Dearborn, who was very fond of splitting hairs.

"Why not?" asked Rebecca.

"Because 'it' is neuter gender."

"Couldn't we say, 'The kitten might have been glad if it had known it was not going to be drowned'?"

"Ye – es," Miss Dearborn answered hesitatingly, never very sure of herself under Rebecca's fire; "but though we often speak of a baby, a chicken, or a kitten as 'it,' they are really masculine or feminine gender, not neuter."

Rebecca reflected a long moment and then asked, "Is a hollyhock neuter?"

"Oh yes, of course it is, Rebecca."

"Well, couldn't we say, 'The hollyhock might have been glad to see the rain, but there was a weak little hollyhock bud growing out of its stalk, and it was afraid that that might be hurt by the storm; so the big hollyhock was kind of afraid, instead of being real glad'?"

Miss Dearborn looked puzzled as she answered, "Of course, Rebecca, hollyhocks could not be sorry, or glad, or afraid, really."

"We can't tell, I s'pose," replied the child; "but *I* think they are, anyway. Now what shall I say?"

"The subjunctive mood, past perfect tense of the verb 'to know.'"

"If I had known.	*"If we had known.*
If thou hadst known.	*If you had known.*
If he had known.	*If they had known.*

"Oh, it is the saddest tense!" sighed Rebecca, with a little break in her voice; "nothing but *ifs, ifs, ifs*! And it makes you feel that if they only had known, things might have been better!"

Miss Dearborn had not thought of it before, but on reflection she believed the subjunctive mood was a "sad" one, and "if" rather a sorry "part of speech."

"Give me some more examples of the subjunctive, Rebecca, and that will do for this afternoon," she said.

"If I had not loved mackerel, I should not have been thirsty," said Rebecca with an April smile, as she closed her grammar. "If thou hadst loved me truly, thou wouldst not have stood me up in the corner. If Samuel had not loved wickedness, he would not have followed me to the water-pail."

"And if Rebecca had loved the rules of the school, she would have controlled her thirst," finished Miss Dearborn with a kiss, and the two parted friends.

SUNSHINE IN A SHADY PLACE

~

The little schoolhouse on the hill had its moments of triumph as well as its scenes of tribulation, but it was fortunate that Rebecca had her books and her new acquaintances to keep her interested and occupied, or life would have gone heavily with her that first summer in Riverboro. She tried to like her aunt Miranda (the idea of loving her had been given up at the moment of meeting), but failed ignominiously in the attempt. She was a very faulty and passionately human child, with no aspirations towards being an angel of the house, but she had a sense of duty and a desire to be good – respectably, decently good. Whenever she fell below this self-imposed standard she was miserable. She did not like to be under her aunt's roof, eating bread, wearing clothes, and studying books provided by her, and dislike her so heartily all the time. She felt instinctively that this was wrong and mean, and whenever the feeling of remorse was strong within her she made a desperate effort to please her grim and difficult relative. But how could she succeed when she was never herself in her aunt Miranda's presence? The searching look of the eyes, the sharp voice, the hard knotting fingers, the thin straight lips, the long silences, the "front-piece" that didn't match her hair, the very obvious "parting" that seemed sewed in with linen thread on black net – there was not a single item that appealed to Rebecca. There are certain narrow, unimaginative, and autocratic old people who seem to call out the most mischievous, and sometimes the worst traits in children. Miss Miranda, had she lived in a populous neighborhood, would have had her doorbell pulled, her gate tied up, or "dirt traps" set in her garden paths. The Simpson twins stood in such awe of her that they could not be persuaded to come to the side-door even when Miss Jane held gingerbread cookies in her outstretched hands.

It is needles to say that Rebecca irritated her aunt with every breath she drew. She continually forgot and started up the front stairs because it was the shortest route to her bedroom; she left the dipper on the kitchen shelf instead of hanging it up over the pail; she sat in the chair the cat liked best; she was willing to go on errands, but often forgot what she was sent for; she left the screen-doors ajar, so that flies came in; her tongue was ever in motion; she sang or whistled when she was picking up chips; she was always messing with flowers – putting them in vases, pinning them on her dress, and sticking them in her hat; finally, she was an everlasting reminder of her foolish, worthless father, whose handsome face and engaging manner had so deceived Aurelia, and perhaps, if the facts were known, others besides Aurelia. The Randalls were aliens. They had not been born in Riverboro nor even in York County. Miranda would have allowed, on compulsion, that in the nature of things a large number of persons must necessarily be born outside this sacred precinct; but she had her opinion of them, and it was not a flattering one. Now, if Hannah had come – Hannah took after the other side of the house; she was "all Sawyer." (Poor Hannah! that was true.) Hannah spoke only when spoken to, instead of first, last, and all the time; Hannah at fourteen was a member of the Church; Hannah liked to knit; Hannah was, probably, or would have been, a pattern of all the smaller virtues; instead of which here was this black-haired gipsy, with eyes as big as cartwheels, installed as a member of the household.

What sunshine in a shady place was Aunt Jane to Rebecca! Aunt Jane, with her quiet voice, her understanding eyes, her ready excuses, in these first difficult weeks, when the impulsive little stranger was trying to settle down into the "brick house ways." She did learn them in part, and by degrees, and the constant fitting of herself to these new and difficult standards of conduct seemed to make her older than ever for her years.

The child took her sewing and sat beside Aunt Jane in the kitchen, while Aunt Miranda had the post of observation at the sitting-room window. Sometimes they would work on the side-porch, where the clematis and woodbine shaded them from the hot sun. To Rebecca the lengths of brown gingham were interminable. She made hard work of sewing, broke the thread, dropped her thimble into the syringa bushes, pricked her finger, wiped the perspiration from her forehead, could not match the checks, puckered the seams. She polished her needles to nothing, pushing them in and out of the emery strawberry, but they always squeaked. Still, Aunt Jane's patience held good, and some small measure of skill was creeping into Rebecca's fingers, fingers that held pencil, paint-brush, and pen so cleverly, and were so clumsy with the dainty little needle.

When the first brown gingham frock was completed, the child seized what she thought an opportune moment, and asked her aunt Miranda if she might have another colour for the next one.

"I bought a whole piece of the brown," said Miranda laconically. "That'll give you two more dresses, with plenty for new sleeves, and to patch and let down with, an' be more economical."

"I know. But Mr. Watson says he'll take back part of it, and let us have pink and blue for the same price."

"Did you ask him?"

"Yes'm."

"It was none o' your business."

"I was helping Emma Jane choose aprons, and didn't think you'd mind which colour I had. Pink keeps clean just as nice as brown, and Mr. Watson says it'll boil without fading."

"Mr. Watson's a splendid judge of washing, I guess. I don't approve of children being rigged out in fancy colours, but I'll see what your aunt Jane thinks."

'I think it would be all right to let Rebecca have one pink and one blue gingham," said Jane. "A child gets tired of sewing on one colour. It's only natural she should long for a change; besides, she'd look like a charity child always wearing the same brown with a white apron. And it's dreadful unbecoming to her!"

"'Handsome is as handsome does,' say I. Rebecca never 'll come to grief along of her beauty, that's certain, and there's no use in humoring her to think about her looks. I believe she's vain as a peacock now, without anything to be vain of."

"She's young, and attracted to bright things – that's all. I remember well enough how I felt at her age."

"You was considerable of a fool at her age, Jane."

"Yes, I was, thank the Lord! I only wish I'd known how to take a little of my foolishness along with me, as some folks do, to brighten my declining years."

There finally was a pink gingham, and when it was nicely finished, Aunt Jane gave Rebecca a delightful surprise. She showed her how to make a pretty trimming of narrow white linen tape, by folding it in pointed shapes, and sewing it down very flat with neat little stitches.

"It'll be good fancy work for you, Rebecca: for your aunt Miranda won't like to see you always reading in the long winter evenings. Now, if you think you can baste two rows of white tape round the bottom of your pink skirt, and keep it straight by the checks, I'll stitch them on for you, and trim the waist and sleeves with pointed tape-trimming, so the dress 'll be real pretty for second best."

Rebecca's joy knew no bounds. "I'll baste like a house afire!" she exclaimed. "It's a thousand yards round that skirt, as well I know, having hemmed it; but I could sew pretty trimming on if it was from here to Milltown. Oh, do you think Aunt Mirandy 'll ever let me go to Milltown with Mr. Cobb? He's asked me again, you know; but one Saturday I had to pick strawberries, and another it rained, and I don't think she really approves of my going. It's twenty-nine minutes past four, Aunt Jane, and Alice Robinson has been sitting under the currant-bushes for a long time waiting for me. Can I go and play?"

"Yes, you may go; and you'd better run as far as you can out behind the barn, so 't your noise won't distract your aunt Mirandy. I see Susan Simpson and the twins and Emma Jane Perkins hiding behind the fence."

Rebecca leaped off the porch, snatched Alice Robinson from under the currant-bushes, and, what was much more difficult, succeeded by means of a complicated system of signals in getting Emma Jane away from the Simpson party, and giving them the slip altogether. They were much too small for certain pleasurable activities planned for that afternoon, but they were not to be despised, for they had the most fascinating dooryard in the village. In it, in bewildering confusion, were old sleighs, pungs, horse-rakes, hogsheads, settees without backs, bedsteads without heads, in all stages of disability, and never the same on two consecutive days. Mrs. Simpson was seldom at home, and even when she was had little concern as to what happened on the premises. A favourite diversion was to make the house into a fort, gallantly held by a handful of American soldiers against a besieging force of the British army. Great care was used in apportioning the parts, for there was no disposition to let anybody win but the Americans. Seesaw Simpson was usually made commander-in-chief of the British army — and a limp and uncertain one he was, capable, with his contradictory orders and his fondness for the extreme rear, of leading any regiment to an inglorious death. Sometimes the long-suffering house was a log hut, and the brave settlers defeated a band of hostile Indians, or occasionally were massacred by them; but in either case the Simpson house looked, to quote a Riverboro expression, "as if the devil had been having an auction in it."

Next to this uncommonly interesting playground as a field of action came, in the children's opinion, the "secret spot." There was a velvety stretch of ground in the Sawyer pasture which was full of fascinating hollows and hillocks, as well as verdant levels, on which to build houses. A group of trees concealed it somewhat from view, and flung a grateful shade over the dwellings erected there. It had been hard, though sweet, labour to take armfuls of "stickins" and "cutrounds" from the mill to this secluded spot; and that it had been done mostly after supper in the dusk of the evenings gave it a still greater flavour. Here in soap-boxes, hidden among the trees, were stored all their treasures — wee baskets and plates and cups made of burdock balls, bits of broken china for parties, dolls — soon to be outgrown, but serving well as characters in all sorts of romances enacted there — deaths, funerals, weddings, christenings. A tall, square house of stickins was to be built round Rebecca this afternoon, and she was to be Charlotte Corday leaning against the bars of her prison.

It was a wonderful experience standing inside the building with Emma

Jane's apron wound about her hair – wonderful to feel that when she leaned her head against the bars they seemed to turn to cold iron; that her eyes were no longer Rebecca Randall's, but mirrored something of Charlotte Corday's hapless woe.

"Ain't it lovely?" sighed the humble twain, who had done most of the labour, but who generously admired the result.

"I hate to have to take it down," said Alice; "it's been such a sight of work."

"If you think you could move up some stones and just take off the top rows, I could step out over," suggested Charlotte Corday. "Then leave the stones, and you two can step down into the prison to-morrow and be the two little Princes in the Tower, and I can murder you."

"What Princes? What Tower?" asked Alice and Emma Jane in one breath. "Tell us about them."

"Not know; it's my supper-time." (Rebecca was a somewhat firm disciplinarian.)

"It would be elergant being murdered by you," said Emma Jane loyally, "though you are awful real when you murder; or we could have Elijah and Elisha for the Princes."

"They'd yell when they was murdered," objected Alice. "You know how silly they are at plays, all except Clara Belle. Besides, if we once show them this secret place, they'll play in it all the time; and perhaps they'd steal things, like their father."

"They needn't steal just because their father does," argued Rebecca; "and don't you ever talk about it before them if you want to be my secret, partic'lar friends. My mother tells me never to say hard things about people's own folks to their face. She says nobody can bear it, and it's wicked to shame them for what isn't their fault. Remember Minnie Smellie!"

Well, they had no difficulty in recalling that dramatic episode, for it had occurred only a few days before; and a version of it, that would have melted the stoniest heart, had been presented to every girl in the village by Minnie Smellie herself, who, though it was Rebecca and not she who came off victorious in the bloody battle of words, nursed her resentment, and intended to have revenge.

CHAPTER SEVEN

RIVERBORO SECRETS

~

Mr. Simpson spent little time with his family, owing to certain awkward methods of horse-trading, or the "swapping" of farm implements and vehicles of various kinds – operations in which his customers were never long suited. After every successful trade he generally passed a longer or shorter term in gaol; for when a poor man without goods or chattels has the inveterate habit of swapping, it follows naturally that he must have something to swap, and having nothing of his own, it follows still more naturally that he must swap something belonging to his neighbors.

Mr. Simpson was absent from the home circle for the moment because he had exchanged the Widow Rideout's sleigh for Joseph Goodwin's plough. Goodwin had lately moved to North Edgewood, and had never before met the urbane and persuasive Mr. Simpson. The Goodwin plough Mr. Simpson speedily bartered with a man "over Wareham way," and got in exchange for it an old horse which his owner did not need, as he was leaving town to visit his daughter for a year. Simpson fattened the aged animal, keeping him for several weeks (at early morning or after nightfall) in one neighbour's pasture after another, and then exchanged him with a Milltown man for a top buggy. It was at this juncture that the Widow Rideout missed her sleigh from the old carriage-house. She had not used it for fifteen years, and might not sit in it for another fifteen, but it was property, and she did not intend to part with it without a struggle. Such is the suspicious nature of the village mind that the moment she discovered her loss her thought at once reverted to Abner Simpson. So complicated, however, was the nature of this particular business transaction, and so tortuous the paths of its progress (partly owing to the complete disappearance of the owner of the horse, who had gone to the West and left no address), that it took the sheriff many weeks to prove Mr. Simpson's guilt to the town's and to the Widow Rideout's satisfaction. Abner himself avowed his complete innocence, and told the neighbors how a red-haired man with a hare-lip and a pepper-and-salt suit of clothes had called him up one morning about daylight, and offered to swap him a good sleigh for an old cider-press he had layin' out in the dooryard. The bargain was struck, and he, Abner, had paid the hare-lipped stranger four dollars and seventy-five cents to boot; whereupon the mysterious one set down the sleigh, took the press on his cart, and vanished up the road, never to be seen or heard from afterwards.

"If I could once ketch that consarned old thief," exclaimed Abner righteously, "I'd make him dance — workin' off a stolen sleigh on me an' takin' away my good money an' cider-press, to say nothin' o' my character!"

"You'll never ketch him, Ab," responded the sheriff. "He's cut off the same piece o' goods as that there cider-press and that there character and that there four-seventy-five o' yourn; nobody ever see any of 'em but you, and you'll never see 'em again!"

Mrs. Simpson, who was decidedly Abner's better half, took in washing and went out to do days' cleaning, and the town helped in the feeding and clothing of the children. George, a lanky boy of fourteen, did chores on neighboring farms, and the others, Samuel, Clara Belle, Susan, Elijah, and Elisha, went to school when sufficiently clothed and not otherwise more pleasantly engaged.

There were no secrets in the villages that lay along the banks of Pleasant

River. There were many hard-working people among the inhabitants, but life wore away so quietly and slowly that there was a good deal of spare time for conversation – under the trees at noon in the hayfield; hanging over the bridge at nightfall; seated about the stove in the village store of an evening. These meeting-places furnished ample ground for the discussion of current events as viewed by the masculine eye, while choir rehearsals, sewing societies, reading circles, church picnics, and the like, gave opportunity for the expression of feminine opinion. All this was taken very much for granted, as a rule, but now and then some supersensitive person made violent objections to it, as a theory of life.

Delia Weeks, for example, was a maiden lady who did dressmaking in a small way; she fell ill, and although attended by all the physicians in the neighborhood, was sinking slowly into a decline, when her cousin Cyrus asked her to come and keep house for him in Lewiston. She went, and in a year grew into a robust, hearty, cheerful woman. Returning to Riverboro on a brief visit, she was asked if she meant to end her days away from home.

"I do most certainly, if I can get any other place to stay," she responded candidly. "I was bein' worn to a shadder here, tryin' to keep my little secrets to myself, an' never succeedin'. First they had it I wanted to marry the minister, and when he took a wife in Standish I was known to be disappointed. Then for five or six years they suspicioned I was tryin' for a place to teach school, and when I gave up hope, an' took to dressmakin', they pitied me and sympathized with me for that. When father died I was bound I'd never let anybody know how I was left, for that spites 'em worse than anything else; but there's ways o' findin' out, an' they found out, hard as I fought 'em! Then there was my brother James that went to Arizona when he was sixteen. I gave good news of him for thirty years runnin', but Aunt Achsy Tarbox had a ferretin' cousin that went out to Tombstone for her health, and she wrote to a post-master, or to some kind of a town authority, and found Jim, and wrote back Aunt Achsy all about him, and just how unfortunate he'd been. They knew when I had my teeth out and a new set made; they knew when I put on a false front-piece; they knew when the fruit-pedlar asked me to be his third wife. I never told 'em, an' you can be sure *he* never did, but they don't *need* to be told in this village; they have nothin' to do but guess, an' they'll guess right every time. I was all tuckered out tryin' to mislead 'em and deceive 'em and side-track 'em, but the minute I got where I wa'n't put under a microscope by day an' a telescope by night, and had myself *to* myself, without sayin' 'By your leave,' I begun to pick up. Cousin Cyrus is an old man an' consid'able trouble, but he thinks my teeth are handsome, an' says I've got a splendid suit of hair. There ain't a person in Lewiston that knows about the minister, or father's will, or Jim's doin's, or the fruit-pedlar; an' if they should find out, they wouldn't care, an' they couldn't remember; for Lewiston's a busy place, thanks be!"

Miss Delia Weeks may have exaggerated matters somewhat, but it is easy to imagine that Rebecca, as well as all the other Riverboro children, had heard the particulars of the Widow Rideout's missing sleigh, and Abner Simpson's supposed connection with it.

There is not an excess of delicacy or chivalry in the ordinary country school, and several choice conundrums and bits of verse dealing with the Simpson affair were bandied about among the scholars, uttered always, be it said to their credit, in undertones, and when the Simpson children were not in the group.

Rebecca Randall was of precisely the same stock, and had had much the same associations as her schoolmates, so one can hardly say why she so hated mean gossip, and so instinctively held herself aloof from it.

Among the Riverboro girls of her own age was a certain excellently-named Minnie Smellie, who was anything but a general favorite. She was a ferret-eyed, blonde-haired, spindle-legged little creature, whose mind was a cross between that of a parrot and a sheep. She was suspected of copying answers from other girls' slates, although she had never been caught in the act. Rebecca and Emma Jane always knew when she had brought a tart or a triangle of layer cake with her school luncheon, because on those days she forsook the cheerful society of her mates, and sought a safe solitude in the woods, returning after a time with a jocund smile on her smug face.

After one of these private luncheons Rebecca had been tempted beyond her strength, and when Minnie took her seat among them, asked: "Is your headache better, Minnie? Let me wipe off that strawberry-jam over your mouth."

There was no jam there, as a matter of fact, but the guilty Minnie's handkerchief went to her crimson face in a flash.

Rebecca confessed to Emma Jane that same afternoon that she felt ashamed of her prank. "I do hate her ways," she exclaimed; "but I'm sorry I let her know we 'spected her, and so, to make up, I gave her that little piece of broken coral I keep in my bead purse – you know the one?"

"It don't hardly seem as if she deserved that, and her so greedy," remarked Emma Jane.

"I know it, but it makes me feel better," said Rebecca largely. "And, then, I've had it two years, and it's broken, so it wouldn't ever be any real good, beautiful as it is to look at."

The coral had partly served its purpose as a reconciling bond, when one afternoon Rebecca, who had stayed after school for her grammar lesson as usual, was returning home by way of the short-cut. Far ahead beyond the bars she espied the Simpson children just entering the woodsy bit. Seesaw was not with them, so she hastened her steps in order to secure company on her homeward walk. They were speedily lost to view, but when she had almost overtaken them she heard in the trees beyond Minnie Smellie's voice lifted high in song and the sound of a child's sobbing. Clara Belle, Susan, and the twins were running along the path, and Minnie was dancing up and down, shrieking:

> *"'What made the sleigh love Simpson so?'*
> *The eager children cried;*
> *'Why, Simpson loved the sleigh, you know,'*
> *The teacher quick replied.'*

The last glimpse of the routed Simpson tribe and the last flutter of their tattered garments disappeared in the dim distance. The fall of one small stone cast by the valiant Elijah, known as "the fighting twin," did break the stillness of the woods for a moment; but it did not come within a hundred yards of Minnie, who shouted "Goalbirds!" at the top of her lungs, and then turned, with an agreeable feeling of excitement, to meet Rebecca, standing perfectly still in the path, with a day of reckoning plainly set forth in her blazing eyes.

Minnie's face was not pleasant to see, for a coward detected at the moment of wrongdoing is not an object of delight.

"Minnie Smellie, if ever – I – catch – you – singing – that – to the

Simpsons again – do you know what I'll do?' asked Rebecca in a tone of concentrated rage.

"I don't know, and I don't care," said Minnie jauntily, though her looks belied her.

"I'll take that piece of coral away from you; and I *think* I shall slap you besides!"

"You wouldn't darst!" retorted Minnie. "If you do, I'll tell my mother and the teacher, so there!"

"I don't care if you tell your mother, my mother, and all your relations, and the President," said Rebecca, gaining courage as the noble words fell from her lips. "I don't care if you tell the town, the whole of York County, the State of Maine, and – and the nation!" she finished grandiloquently. "Now you run home, and remember what I say. If you do it again, and especially if you say 'Goal-birds!' if I think it's right, and my duty, I shall punish you somehow."

The next morning at recess Rebecca observed Minnie telling the tale with variations to Huldah Meserve. "She *threatened* me," whispered Minnie; "but I never believe a word she says."

The latter remark was spoken with the direct intention of being overheard, for Minnie had spasms of bravery when well surrounded by the machinery of law and order.

As Rebecca went back to her seat, she asked Miss Dearborn if she might pass a note to Minnie Smellie, and received permission. This was the note:

> "*Of all the girls that are so mean,*
> *There's none like Minnie Smellie.*
> *I'll take away the gift I gave,*
> *And pound her into jelly.*

"P.S. – Now do you believe me?

R. Randall."

The effect of this piece of doggerel was entirely convincing, and for days afterwards, whenever Minnie met the Simpsons, even a mile from the brick house, she shuddered and held her peace.

CHAPTER EIGHT

COLOR OF ROSE

~

On the very next Friday after this "dreadfullest fight that ever was seen," as Bunyan says in "Pilgrim's Progress," there were great doings in the little schoolhouse on the hill. Friday afternoon was always the time chosen for dialogues, songs, and recitations; but it cannot be stated that it was a gala day in any true sense of the word. Most of the children hated "speaking pieces" – hated the burden of learning them, dreaded the danger of breaking down in them. Miss Dearborn commonly went home with a headache, and never left her bed during the rest of the afternoon or evening; and the casual female parent who attended the exercises sat on a front bench, with beads of cold sweat on her forehead, listening to the all-too-familiar halts and stammers. Sometimes a bellowing infant, who had clean forgotten his verse, would cast himself bodily on the maternal bosom, and be borne out into the open air, where he was sometimes kissed and occasionally spanked; but, in any case, the failure added an extra dash of gloom and dread to the occasion. The advent of Rebecca had somehow infused a new spirit into these hitherto terrible afternoons. She had taught Elijah and Elisha Simpson, so that they recited three verses of something with such comical effect that they delighted themselves, the teacher, and the school; while Susan, who lisped, had been provided with a humorous poem, in which she impersonated a lisping child. Emma Jane and Rebecca had a dialogue, and the sense of companionship buoyed up Emma Jane and gave her self-reliance. In fact, Miss Dearborn announced on this particular Friday morning that the exercises promised to be so interesting that she had invited the doctor's wife, the minister's wife, two members of the school committee, and a few mothers. Living Perkins was asked to decorate one of the blackboards and Rebecca the other. Living, who was the star artist of the school, chose the map of North America. Rebecca liked better to draw things less realistic; and speedily, before the eyes of the enchanted multitude, there grew under her skilful fingers an American flag, done in red, white, and blue chalk, every star in its right place, every stripe fluttering in the breeze. Beside this appeared a figure of Columbia, copied from the top of the cigar-box that held the crayons.

Miss Dearborn was delighted. "I propose we give Rebecca a good hand-clapping for such a beautiful picture – one that the whole school may well be proud of."

The scholars clapped heartily, and Dick Carter, waving his hand, gave a rousing cheer.

Rebecca's heart leaped for joy, and to her confusion she felt the tears rising in her eyes. She could hardly see the way back to her seat, for in her ignorant, lonely little life she had never been singled out for applause, never lauded, nor crowned, as in this wonderful, dazzling moment. If "nobleness enkindleth nobleness," so does enthusiasm beget enthusiasm, and so do wit and talent enkindle wit and talent. Alice Robinson proposed that the school should sing "Three Cheers for the Red, White, and Blue," and when they came to the chorus all point to Rebecca's flag. Dick Carter suggested that Living Perkins and Rebecca Randall should sign their names to their pictures, so that the visitors would know who drew them. Huldah Meserve asked permission to cover the largest holes in the pastered walls with boughs and fill the water-pail with wild-flowers. Rebecca's mood was above and beyond all practical details. She sat silent, her heart so full of grateful joy that she could hardly remember the words of her dialogue. At recess she bore herself modestly, notwithstanding her great triumph; while in the general atmosphere of goodwill the Smellie-Randall hatchet was buried, and Minnie gathered maple-boughs and covered the ugly stove with them under Rebecca's direction.

Miss Dearborn dismissed the morning session at quarter to twelve, so that those who lived near enough could go home for a change of dress. Emma Jane and Rebecca ran nearly every step of the way from sheer excitement, only stopping to breathe at the stiles.

"Will your Aunt Mirandy let you wear your best, or only your buff calico?" asked Emma Jane.

"I think I'll ask Aunt Jane," Rebecca replied. "Oh, if my pink was only finished! I left Aunt Jane making the buttonholes."

"I'm going to ask my mother to let me wear her garnet ring," said Emma Jane. "It would look perfectly elergant flashing in the sun when I point to the flag. Good-bye! Don't wait for me going back; I may get a ride."

Rebecca found the side-door locked, but she knew that the key was under the step, and so, of course, did everybody else in Riverboro, for they all did about the same thing with it. She unlocked the door and went into the dining-room, to find her lunch laid on the table and a note from Aunt Jane, saying that they had gone to Moderation with Mrs. Robinson in her carryall. Rebecca swallowed a piece of bread-and-butter, and flew up the front stairs to her bedroom. On the bed lay the pink gingham dress finished by Aunt Jane's kind hands. Could she, dare she, wear it without asking? Did the occasion justify a new costume, or would her aunts think she ought to keep it for the concert?

"I'll wear it," thought Rebecca. "They're not here to ask, and maybe they wouldn't mind a bit. It's only gingham, after all, and wouldn't be so grand if it wasn't new, and hadn't tape-trimming on it, and wasn't pink."

She unbraided her two pigtails, combed out the waves of her hair and tied them back with a ribbon, changed her shoes, and then slipped on the pretty frock, managing to fasten all but the three middle buttons, which she reserved for Emma Jane.

Then her eye fell on her cherished pink sunshade, the exact match, and the girls had never seen it. It wasn't quite appropriate for school, but she needn't take it into the room; she would wrap it in a piece of paper, just show it, and carry it coming home. She glanced in the parlor looking-glass downstairs, and was electrified at the vision. It seemed almost as if beauty of apparel could go no further than that heavenly pink gingham dress! The sparkle of her eyes, glow of her cheeks, sheen of her falling hair, passed unnoticed in the all-conquering charm of the rose-coloured garment. Goodness! it was twenty minutes to one, and she would be late. She danced out the side-door, pulled a pink rose from a bush at the gate, and covered the mile between the brick house and the seat of learning in an incredibly short time, meeting Emma Jane, also breathless and resplendent, at the entrance.

"Rebecca Randall!" exclaimed Emma Jane, "you're handsome as a picture!"

"I?" laughed Rebecca. "Nonsense! it's only the pink gingham."

"You're not good-looking every day," insisted Emma Jane; "but you're different somehow. See my garnet ring; mother scrubbed it in soap and water. How on earth did your aunt Mirandy let you put on your bran' new dress?"

"They were both away, and I didn't ask," Rebecca responded anxiously. "Why? Do you think they'd have said no?"

"Miss Mirandy always says no, doesn't she?" asked Emma Jane.

"Ye – es; but this afternoon is very special – almost like a Sunday-school concert."

"Yes," assented Emma Jane, "it is, of course; with your name on the board, and our pointing to your flag, and our elergant dialogue, and all that."

The afternoon was one succession of solid triumphs for everybody concerned. There were no real failures at all, no tears, no parents ashamed of their offspring. Miss Dearborn heard many admiring remarks passed upon her ability, and wondered whether they belonged to her or partly, at least, to Rebecca. The child had no more to do than several others, but she was somehow in the foreground. It transpired afterwards at various village entertainments that Rebecca couldn't be kept in the background; it positively refused to hold her. Her worst enemy could not have called her pushing. She was ready and willing, and never shy; but she sought for no chances of display, and was, indeed, remarkably lacking in self-consciousness, as well as eager to bring others into whatever fun or entertainment there was. If wherever the MacGregor sat was the head of the table, so in the same way wherever Rebecca stood was the center of the stage. Her clear high treble soared above all the rest in the choruses, and somehow everybody watched her, took note of her gestures, her whole-souled singing, her irrepressible enthusiasm.

Finally it was all over, and it seemed to Rebecca as if she should never be cool and calm again, as she loitered on the homeward path. There would be no lessons to learn to-night, and the vision of helping with the preserves on the morrow had no terrors for her — fears could not draw breath in the radiance that flooded her soul. There were thick gathering clouds in the sky, but she took no note of them save to be glad that she could raise her sunshade. She did not tread the solid ground at all, or have any sense of belonging to the common human family, until she entered the side-yard of the brick house and saw her Aunt Miranda standing in the open doorway. Then with a rush she came back to earth.

CHAPTER NINE

ASHES OF ROSES

~

"There she is, over an hour late. A little more, an' she'd 'a' been caught in a thunder-shower; but she'd never look ahead," said Miranda to Jane. "And, added to all her other iniquities, if she ain't rigged out in that new dress, steppin' along with her father's dancin'-school steps, and swingin' her parasol for all the world as if she was play-actin'! Now, I'm the oldest, Jane, an' I intend to have my say out. If you don't like it, you can go into the kitchen till it's over. Step right in here, Rebecca; I want to talk to you. What did you put on that good new dress for on a school-day without permission?"

"I had intended to ask you at noontime; but you weren't at home, so I couldn't," began Rebecca.

"You did no such thing. You put it on because you was left alone, though you knew well enough I wouldn't have let you."

"If I'd been *certain* you wouldn't have let me, I'd never have done it," said Rebecca, trying to be truthful. "But I wasn't *certain*, and it was worth risking. I thought perhaps you might, if you knew it was almost a real exhibition at school."

"Exhibition!" exclaimed Miranda scornfully. "You are exhibition enough by yourself, I should say. Was you exhibitin' your parasol?"

"The parasol *was* silly," confessed Rebecca, hanging her head. "But it's the only time in my whole life when I had anything to match it, and it looked so beautiful with the pink dress! Emma Jane and I spoke a dialogue about a city girl and a country girl, and it came to me just the minute before I started how nice it would come in for the city girl; and it did. I haven't hurt my dress a mite, Aunt Mirandy."

"It's the craftiness and underhandedness of your actions that's the worst," said Miranda coldly. "And look at the other things you've done! It seems as if Satan possessed you! You went up the front stairs to your room, but you didn't hide your tracks, for you dropped your handkerchief on the way up. You left the screen out of your bedroom window for the flies to come in all over the house. You never cleared away your lunch nor set away a dish, *and you left the side-door unlocked* from half-past twelve to three o'clock, so 't anybody could 'a' come in and stolen what they liked!"

Rebecca sat down heavily in her chair as she heard the list of her transgressions. How could she have been so careless? The tears began to flow now as she attempted to explain sins that never could be explained or justified.

"Oh, I'm so sorry!" she faltered. "I was trimming the schoolroom and got belated, and ran all the way home. It was hard getting into my dress alone, and I hadn't time to eat but a mouthful, and just at the last minute, when I honestly – *honestly* would have thought about clearing away and locking up, I looked at the clock, and knew I could hardly get back to school in time to form in the line; and I thought how dreadful it would be to go in late, and get my first black mark on a Friday afternoon, with the minister's wife and the doctor's wife and the school committee all there."

"Don't wail and carry on now; it's no good cryin' over spilt milk," answered Miranda. "An ounce of good behaviour is worth a pound of repentance. Instead of tryin' to see how little trouble you can make in a house that ain't your own home, it seems as if you tried to see how much you could put us out. Take that rose out o' your dress, and let me see the spot it's made on your yoke, an' the rusty holes where the wet pin went in.

No, it ain't; but it's more by luck than forethought. I ain't got any patience with your flowers, and frizzled-out hair, and furbelows, an' airs an' graces, for all the world like your Miss-Nancy father.

Rebecca lifted her head in a flash. "Look here, Aunt Mirandy: I'll be as good as I know how to be. I'll mind quick when I'm spoken to, and never leave the door unlocked again; but I won't have my father called names. He was a p-perfectly l-lovely father, that's what he was; and it's *mean* to call him Miss Nancy!"

"Don't you dare answer me back that imperdent way, Rebecca, tellin' me I'm mean. Your father was a vain, foolish, shiftless man, an' you might as well hear it from me as anybody else. He spent your mother's money, and left her with seven children to provide for."

"It's s-something to leave s-seven nice children," sobbed Rebecca.

"Not when other folks have to help feed, clothe, and educate 'em," responded Miranda. "Now you step upstairs, put on your nightgown, go to bed, and stay there till to-morrow mornin'. You'll find a bowl o' crackers an' milk on your bureau, an' I don't want to hear a sound from you till breakfast-time. Jane, run an' take the dish-towels off the line, and shut the shed doors; we're goin' to have a turrible shower."

"We've had it, I should think," said Jane quietly, as she went to do her sister's bidding. "I don't often speak my mind, Mirandy; but you ought not to have said what you did about Lorenzo. He was what he was, and can't be made any different; but he was Rebecca's father, and Aurelia always says he was a good husband."

Miranda had never heard the proverbial phrase about the only "good Indian"; but her mind worked in the conventional manner when she said grimly: "Yes; I've noticed that dead husbands are usually good ones. But the truth needs an airin' now and then; and that child will never amount to a hill o' beans till she gets some of her father trounced out of her. I'm glad I said just what I did."

"I dare say you are," remarked Jane, with what might be described as one of her annual bursts of courage. "But all the same, Mirandy, it wasn't good manners, and it wasn't good religion."

The clap of thunder that shook the house just at that moment made no such peal in Miranda Sawyer's ears as Jane's remark made when it fell with a deafening roar on her conscience.

Perhaps, after all, it is just as well to speak only once a year, and then speak to the purpose.

Rebecca mounted the back stairs wearily, closed the door of her bedroom, and took off the beloved pink gingham with trembling fingers. Her cotton handkerchief was rolled into a hard ball; and in the intervals of reaching the more difficult buttons that lay between her shoulder-blades and her belt she dabbed her wet eyes carefully, so that they should not rain salt-water on the finery that had been worn at such a price. She smoothed it out carefully, pinched up the white ruffle at the neck, and laid it away in a drawer, with an extra little sob at the roughness of life. The withered pink rose fell on the floor. Rebecca looked at it, and thought to herself, "Just like my happy day!" Nothing could show more clearly the kind of child she was than the fact that she instantly perceived the symbolism of the rose, and laid it in the drawer with the dress, as if she were burying the whole episode with all its sad memories. It was a child's poetic instinct, with a drawning hint of woman's sentiment in it.

She braided her hair in the two accustomed pigtails, took off her best shoes (which had happily escaped notice), with all the while a fixed resolve growing in her mind, that of leaving the brick house and going back to the farm. She would not be received there with open arms – there was no hope of that – but she would help her mother about the house, and send Hannah to Riverboro in her place. "I hope she'll like it!" she thought in a momentary burst of vindictiveness. She sat by the window trying to make some sort of plan, watching the lightning play over the hilltop and the streams of rain chasing each other down the lightning-rod. And this was the day that had dawned so joyfully! It had been a red sunrise, and she had leaned on the window-sill studying her lesson and thinking what a lovely world it was. And what a golden morning! The changing of the bare, ugly little schoolroom into a bower of beauty: Miss Dearborn's pleasure at her success with the Simpson twins' recitation; the privilege of decorating the blackboard; the happy thought of drawing Columbia from the cigar-box; the intoxicating moment when the school clapped her. And what an afternoon! How it went on from glory to glory, beginning with Emma Jane's telling her, Rebecca Randall, that she was as "handsome as a picture."

She lived through the exercises again in memory, especially her dialogue with Emma Jane, and her inspiration of using the bough-covered stove as a mossy bank where the country girl could sit and watch her flocks. This gave Emma Jane a feeling of such ease that she never recited better; and how generous it was of her to lend the garnet ring to the city girl, fancying truly how it would flash as she furled her parasol and approached the awe-stricken shepherdess! She had thought Aunt Miranda might be pleased that the niece invited down from the farm had succeeded so well at school; but no, there was no hope of pleasing her in that or in any other way. She would go to Maplewood on the stage next day with Mr. Cobb and get home somehow from Cousin Ann's. On second throughts, her aunts might not allow it. Very well, she would slip away now, and see if she could stay all night with the Cobbs and be off next morning before breakfast.

Rebecca never stopped long to think, more's the pity, so she put on her oldest dress and hat and jacket, then wrapped her nightdress, comb, and toothbrush in a bundle and dropped it softly out of the window. Her room was in the L, and her window at no very dangerous distance from the ground, though had it been, nothing could have stopped her at that moment. Somebody who had gone on the roof to clean out the gutters had left a cleat nailed to the side of the house about half-way between the window and the top of the back porch. Rebecca heard the sound of the sewing-machine in the dining-room, and the chopping of meat in the kitchen; so knowing the whereabouts of both her aunts, she scrambled out of the window, caught hold of the lightning-rod, slid down to the helpful cleat, jumped to the porch, used the woodbine trellis for a ladder, and was flying up the road in the storm before she had time to arrange any details of her future movements.

Jeremiah Cobb sat at his lonely supper at the table by the kitchen-window. "Mother," as he, with his old-fashioned habits, was in the habit of calling his wife, was nursing a sick neighbour. Mrs. Cobb was mother only to a little headstone in the churchyard, where reposed "Sarah Ann, beloved daughter of Jeremiah and Sarah Cobb, aged seventeen months"; but the name of mother was better than nothing, and served at any rate as a reminder of her woman's crown of blessedness.

The rain still fell, and the heavens were dark, though it was scarcely five o'clock. Looking up from his "dish of tea," the old man saw at the open door a very figure of woe. Rebecca's face was so swollen with tears and so sharp with misery that for a moment he scarcely recognised her. Then, when he heard her voice asking, "Please may I come in, Mr. Cobb?" he cried, "Well I vow! it's my little lady passenger! Come to call on old Uncle Jerry and pass the time o' day, hev ye? Why, you're wet as sops. Draw up to the stove. I made a fire, hot as it was, thinkin' I wanted somethin' warm for my supper, bein' kind o' lonesome without mother. She's settin' up with Seth Strout to-night. There, we'll hang your soppy hat on the nail, put your jacket over the chair-rail, an' then you turn your back to the stove an' dry yourself good."

Uncle Jerry had never before said so many words at a time, but he had caught sight of the child's red eyes and tear-stained cheeks, and his big heart went out to her in her trouble, quite regardless of any circumstances that might have caused it.

Rebecca stood still for a moment until Uncle Jerry took his seat again at the table, and then, unable to contain herself longer, cried: "Oh, Mr. Cobb, I've run away from the brick house, and I want to go back to the farm. Will you keep me to-night and take me up to Maplewood in the stage? I haven't got any money for my fare, but I'll earn it somehow afterwards."

"Well, I guess we won't quarrel 'bout money, you and me,' said the old man; "and we've never had our ride together, anyway, though we allers meant to go down river, not up."

"I shall never see Milltown now!" sobbed Rebecca.

"Come over here side o' me an' tell me all about it," coaxed Uncle Jerry. "Jest set down on that there wooden cricket an' out with the whole story."

Rebecca leaned her aching head against Mr. Cobb's homespun knee and recounted the history of her trouble. Tragic as that history seemed to her passionate and undisciplined mind, she told it truthfully and without exaggeration.

CHAPTER TEN

RAINBOW BRIDGES

~

*U*ncle Jerry coughed and stirred in his chair a good deal during
Rebecca's recital, but he carefully concealed any undue feeling of
sympathy, just muttering, "Poor little soul! We'll see what we can do for her!"

"You will take me to Maplewood, won't you, Mr. Cobb?" begged
Rebecca piteously.

"Don't you fret a mite," he answered, with a crafty little notion at the
back of his mind; "I'll see the lady passenger through somehow. Now take
a bite o' somethin' to eat, child. Spread some o' that tomato preserve on
your bread; draw up to the table. How'd you like to set in mother's place
an' pour me out another cup o' hot tea?"

Mr. Jeremiah Cobb's mental machinery was simple, and did not move
very smoothly save when propelled by his affection or sympathy. In the
present case these were both employed to his advantage, and mourning his
stupidity and praying for some flash of inspiration to light his path, he
blundered along, trusting to Providence.

Rebecca, comforted by the old man's tone, and timidly enjoying the dignity of sitting in Mrs. Cobb's seat and lifting the blue china teapot, smiled faintly, smoothed her hair, and dried her eyes.

"I suppose your mother 'll be turrible glad to see you back again?" queried Mr. Cobb.

A tiny fear – just a baby thing – in the bottom of Rebecca's heart stirred and grew larger the moment it was touched with a question.

"She won't like it that I ran away, I s'pose, and she'll be sorry that I couldn't please Aunt Mirandy; but I'll make her understand, just as I did you."

"I s'pose she was thinkin' o' your schoolin', lettin' you come down here; but land! you can go to school in Temperance, I s'pose?"

"There's only two months' school now in Temperance, and the farm's too far from all the other schools."

"Oh well, there's other things in the world beside edjercation," responded Uncle Jerry, attacking a piece of apple-pie.

"Ye – es; though mother thought that was going to be the making of me," returned Rebecca sadly, giving a dry little sob as she tried to drink her tea.

"It'll be nice for you to be all together again at the farm – such a houseful o' children!" remarked the dear old deceiver, who longed for nothing so much as to cuddle and comfort the poor little creature.

"It's too full, that's the trouble. But I'll make Hannah come to Riverboro in my place."

"S'pose Mirandy 'n' Jane 'll have her? I should be 'most afraid they wouldn't. They'll be kind o' mad at your goin' home, you know, and you can't hardly blame 'em."

This was quite a new thought – that the brick house might be closed to Hannah, since she, Rebecca, had turned her back upon its cold hospitality.

"How is this school down here in Riverboro – pretty good?" inquired Uncle Jerry, whose brain was working with an altogether unaccustomed rapidity, so much so that it almost terrified him.

"Oh, it's a splendid school! And Miss Dearborn is a splendid teacher!"

"You like her, do you? Well, you'd better believe she returns the compliment. Mother was down to the store this afternoon buyin' liniment for Seth Strout, an' she met Miss Dearborn on the bridge. They got to talkin' 'bout school, for mother has summer-boarded a lot o' the school-marms, an' likes 'em. 'How does the little Temperance girl git along?' asks mother. 'Oh, she's the best scholar I have!' says Miss Dearborn. 'I could teach school from sun-up to sun-down if scholars was all like Rebecca Randall,' says she."

"Oh, Mr. Cobb, *did* she say that?" glowed Rebecca, her face sparkling and dimpling in an instant. "I've tried hard all the time, but I'll study the covers right off of the books now."

"You mean you would if you'd ben goin' to stay here," interposed Uncle Jerry. "Now, ain't it too bad you've jest got to give it all up on account o' your aunt Mirandy? Well, I can't hardly blame ye. She's cranky an' she's sour; I should think she'd ben nussed on bonny clabber an' green apples. She needs bearin' with; an' I guess you ain't much on patience, be ye?"

"Not very much," replied Rebecca dolefully.

"If I'd had this talk with ye yesterday," pursued Mr. Cobb, "I believe I'd have advised ye different. It's too late now, an' I don't feel to say you've ben all in the wrong; but if 'twas to do over again, I'd say, well, your aunt Mirandy gives you clothes and board and schoolin', and is goin' to send you to Wareham at a big expense. She's turrible hard to get along with, an' kind o' heaves benefits at your head same 's she would bricks. But they're benefits jest the same, an' mebbe it's your job to kind o' pay for 'em in good behaviour. Jane's a leetle bit more easy-goin' than Mirandy, ain't she? or is she jest as hard to please?"

"Oh, Aunt Jane and I get along splendidly!" exclaimed Rebecca. "She's just as good and kind as she can be, and I like her better all the time. I think she kind of likes me, too. She smoothed my hair once. I'd let her scold me all day long, for she understands. But she can't stand up for me against Aunt Mirandy; she's about as afraid of her as I am."

"Jane 'll be real sorry to-morrow to find you've gone away, I guess. But never mind, it can't be helped. If she has a kind of a dull time with Mirandy, on account o' her bein' so sharp, why, of course she'd set great store by your comp'ny. Mother was talkin' with her after prayer-meetin' the other night. 'You wouldn't know the brick house, Sarah,' says Jane. 'I'm keepin' a sewin' school, an' my scholar has made three dresses. What do you think o' that,' says she, 'for an old maid's child? I've taken a class in Sunday-school,' says Jane, 'an' think o' renewin' my youth an' goin' to the picnic with Rebecca,' says she. An' mother declares she never see her look so young 'n' happy.'"

There was a silence that could be felt in the little kitchen, a silence only broken by the ticking of the tall clock and the beating of Rebecca's heart, which, it seemed to her, almost drowned the voice of the clock. The rain ceased, a sudden rosy light filled the room, and through the window a rainbow arch could be seen spanning the heavens like a radiant bridge. Bridges took one across difficult places, thought Rebecca, and Uncle Jerry seemed to have built one over her troubles and given her strength to walk.

"The shower's over," said the old man, filling his pipe; "it's cleared the air, washed the face o' the airth nice an' clean, an' everything to-morrer will shine like a new pin — when you an' I are drivin' up river."

Rebecca pushed her cup away, rose from the table, and put on her hat and jacket quietly. "I'm not going to drive up river, Mr. Cobb," she said. "I'm going to stay here and — catch bricks; catch 'em without throwing 'em back, too. I don't know as Aunt Mirandy will take me in after I've run away; but I'm going back now while I have the courage. You wouldn't be so good as to go with me, would you, Mr. Cobb?"

"You'd better b'lieve your Uncle Jerry don't propose to leave till he gits this thing fixed up," cried the old man delightedly. "Now you've had all you can stan' to-night, poor little soul, without gettin' a fit o' sickness; an' Mirandy 'll be sore an' cross, an' in no condition for argyment; so my plan is jest this: to drive you over to the brick house in my top buggy; to have you set back in the corner, an' I git out an' go to the side-door; an' when I git your Aunt Mirandy 'n' Aunt Jane out int' the shed to plan for a load o' wood I'm goin' to have hauled there this week, you'll slip out o' the buggy and go upstairs to bed. The front-door won't be locked, will it?"

"Not this time of night," Rebecca answered; "not till Aunt Mirandy goes to bed. But oh! what if it should be?"

"Well, it won't; an', if 't is, why, we'll have to face it out; though, in my opinion, there's things that won't bear facin' out, an' had better be settled comfortable an' quiet. You see, you ain't run away yet; you've only come over here to consult me 'bout runnin' away, an' we've concluded it ain't wuth the trouble. The only real sin you've committed, as I figger it out, was in comin' here by the winder when you'd ben sent to bed. That ain't so very black, an' you can tell your aunt Jane 'bout it come Sunday, when she's chock-full o' religion, an' she can advise you when you'd better tell your

*Miss Miranda entered, and as her eye wandered about
the vacant room, it fell upon a white and tempestuous
ocean of counterpane. (Chapter Three.)*

Then came the 'woodsy bit,' with her feet pressing the
slippery carpet of brown pine-needles. (Chapter Five.)

While crossing the bridge she was suddenly overcome by
the beauty of the river. (Chapter Twelve.)

*"I am the lady of the house at present," said the
stranger, with a whimsical smile. (Chapter Fourteen.)*

aunt Mirandy. I don't believe in deceivin' folks, but if you've hed hard thoughts, you ain't obleeged to own 'em up. Take 'em to the Lord in prayer, as the hymn says, and then don't go on hevin' 'em. Now, come on. I'm all hitched up to go over to the post-office. Don't forget your bundle. 'It's always a journey, mother, when you carry a nightgown' – them's the first words your uncle Jerry ever heard you say. He didn't think you'd be bringin' your nightgown over to his house. Step in an' curl up in the corner. We ain't goin' to let folks see little runaway gals, 'cause they're goin' back to begin all over ag'in!"

When Rebecca crept upstairs, and, undressing in the dark, finally found herself in her bed that night, though she was aching and throbbing in every nerve, she felt a kind of peace stealing over her. She had been saved from foolishness and error, kept from troubling her poor mother, prevented from angering and mortifying her aunts.

Her heart was melted now, and she determined to win Aunt Miranda's approval by some desperate means, and to try and forget the one thing that rankled worst – the scornful mention of her father, of whom she thought with the greatest admiration, and whom she had not yet heard criticised, for such sorrows and disappointments as Aurelia Randall had suffered had never been communicated to her children.

It would have been some comfort to the bruised, unhappy little spirit to know that Miranda Sawyer was passing an uncomfortable night, and that she tacitly regretted her harshness, partly because Jane had taken such a lofty and virtuous position in the matter. She could not endure Jane's disapproval, although she would never have confessed to such a weakness.

As Uncle Jerry drove homeward under the stars, well content with his attempts at keeping the peace, he thought wistfully of the touch of Rebecca's head on his knee and the rain of her tears on his hand; of the sweet reasonableness of her mind when she had the matter put rightly before her; of her quick decision when she had once seen the path of duty; of the touching hunger for love and understanding that were so characteristic in her. "Lord A'mighty!" he ejaculated under his breath – "Lord A'mighty! to hector and abuse a child like that one! 'Tain't abuse exactly, I know, or 'twouldn't be to some o' your elephant-hided young ones; but to that little tender Will-o'-the-wisp a hard word's like a lash. Miranda Sawyer would be a heap better woman if she had a little gravestun to remember, same 's mother 'n' I have."

"I never see a child improve in her work as Rebecca has to-day," remarked Miranda Sawyer to Jane on Saturday evening. "That settin' down I gave her was probably just what she needed, and I dare say it'll last for a month."

"I'm glad you're pleased," returned Jane. "A cringing worm is what you want, not a bright, smiling child. Rebecca looks to me as if she'd been through the Seven Years' War. When she came downstairs this morning, it seemed to me she'd grown old in the night. If you follow my advice, which you seldom do, you'll let me take her and Emma Jane down beside the river tomorrow afternoon, and bring Emma Jane home to a good Sunday supper. Then, if you'll let her go to Milltown with the Cobbs on Wednesday, that'll hearten her up a little and coax back her appetite. Wednesday's a holiday on account of Miss Dearborn's going home to her sister's wedding, and the Cobbs and Perkinses want to go down to the agricultural fair."

CHAPTER ELEVEN

"THE STIRRING
OF THE POWERS"

~

Rebecca's visit to Milltown was all that her glowing fancy had painted it, except that recent readings about Rome and Venice disposed her to believe that those cities might have an advantage over Milltown in the matter of mere pictorial beauty. So soon does the soul outgrow its mansions, that after once seeing Milltown her fancy ran out to the future sight of Portland, for that, having islands and a harbour and two public monuments, must be far more beautiful than Milltown, which would, she felt, take its proud place among the cities of the earth, by reason of its tremendous business activity rather than by any irresistible appeal to the imagination.

It would be impossible for two children to see more, do more, walk more, talk more, eat more, or ask more questions, than Rebecca and Emma Jane did on that eventful Wednesday.

"She's the best company I ever see in all my life," said Mrs. Cobb to her husband that evening. "We ain't had a dull minute this day. She's well-mannered, too; she didn't ask for anything, and was thankful for whatever she got. Did you watch her face when we went into that tent where they was actin' out 'Uncle Tom's Cabin'? And did you take notice of the way she told us about the book when we sat down to have our ice-cream? I tell you, Harriet Beecher Stowe herself couldn't 'a' done it better justice."

"I took it all in," responded Mr. Cobb, who was pleased that "mother" agreed with him about Rebecca. "I ain't sure but she's goin' to turn out somethin' remarkable – a singer, or a writer, or a lady doctor, like that Miss Parks up to Cornish."

"Lady doctors are always home'paths, ain't they?" asked Mrs. Cobb, who, it is needless to say, was distinctly of the old school in medicine.

"Land no, mother! there ain't no home'path 'bout Miss Parks. She drives all over the country."

"I can't see Rebecca as a lady doctor, somehow," mused Mrs. Cobb. "Her gift o' gab is what's goin' to be the makin' of her. Mebbe she'll lecture, or recite pieces, like that Portland elocutionist that come out here to the harvest supper."

"I guess she'll be able to write down her own pieces," said Mr. Cobb confidently. "She could make 'em up faster 'n she could read 'em out of a book."

"It's a pity she's so plain-looking," remarked Mrs. Cobb, blowing out the candle.

"*Plain-looking*, mother!" exclaimed her husband in astonishment. "Look at the eyes of her; look at the hair of her, an' the smile, an' that there dimple! Look at Alice Robinson, that's called the prettiest child on the river, an' see how Rebecca shines her ri' down out o' sight! I hope Mirandy 'll favour her comin' over to see us real often, for she'll let off some of her steam here, an' the brick house 'll be consid'able safer for everybody concerned. We've known what it was to hev children, even if 'twas more 'n thirty years ago, an' we can make allowances."

Notwithstanding the encomiums of Mr. and Mrs. Cobb, Rebecca made a poor hand at composition writing at this time. Miss Dearborn gave her every sort of subject that she had ever been given herself: "Cloud Pictures," "Abraham Lincoln," "Nature," "Philanthropy," "Slavery," "Intemperance," "Joy and Duty," "Solitude," but with none of them did Rebecca seem to grapple satisfactorily.

"Write as you talk, Rebecca," insisted poor Miss Dearborn, who secretly knew that she could never manage a good composition herself.

"But gracious me, Miss Dearborn! I don't talk about nature and slavery. I can't write unless I have something to say, can I?"

"That is what compositions are for," returned Miss Dearborn doubtfully: "to make you have things to say. Now, in your last one, on solitude, you haven't said anything very interesting, and you've made it too common and every-day to sound well. There are too many 'yous' and 'yours' in it; you ought to say 'one' now and then, to make it seem more like good writing. 'One opens a favourite book'; 'One's thoughts are a great comfort in solitude,' and so on."

"I don't know any more about solitude this week than I did about joy and duty last week," grumbled Rebecca.

"You tried to be funny about joy and duty," said Miss Dearborn reprovingly, "so of course you didn't succeed."

"I didn't know you were going to make us read the things out loud," said Rebecca, with an embarrassed smile of recollection.

"Joy and Duty" had been the inspiring subject given to the older children for a theme to be written in five minutes.

Rebecca had wrestled, struggled, perspired in vain. When her turn came to read she was obliged to confess she had written nothing.

"You have at least two lines, Rebecca," insisted the teacher, "for I see them on your slate."

"I'd rather not read them, please; they are not good," pleaded Rebecca.

"Read what you have, good or bad, little or much; I am excusing nobody."

Rebecca rose, overcome with secret laughter, dread, and mortification; then in a low voice she read the couplet:

> *"When Joy and Duty clash*
> *Let Duty go to smash."*

Dick Carter's head disappeared under the desk, while Living Perkins choked with laughter.

Miss Dearborn laughed too; she was little more than a girl, and the training of the young idea seldom appealed to the sense of humour.

"You must stay after school and try again, Rebecca," she said, but she said it smilingly. "Your poetry hasn't a very nice idea in it for a good little girl who ought to love duty."

"It wasn't *my* idea," said Rebecca apologetically. "I had only made the first line when I saw you were going to ring the bell and say the time was up. I had 'clash' written, and I couldn't think of anything then but 'hash' or 'rash' or 'smash.' I'll change it to this:

> *"When Joy and Duty clash,*
> *'Tis Joy must go to smash."*

"That is better," Miss Dearborn answered, "though I cannot think 'going to smash' is a pretty expression for poetry."

Having been instructed in the use of the indefinite pronoun "one" as giving a refined and elegant touch to literary efforts, Rebecca painstakingly rewrote her composition on solitude, giving it all the benefit of Miss Dearborn's suggestion. It then appeared in the following form, which hardly satisfied either teacher or pupil:

"Solitude"

"It would be false to say that one could ever be alone when one has one's lovely thoughts to comfort one. One sits by one's self, it is true, but one thinks; one opens one's favorite book and reads one's favourite story; one speaks to one's aunt or one's brother, fondles one's cat, or looks at one's photograph album. There is one's work also: what a joy it is to one, if one happens to like work. All one's little household tasks keep one from being lonely. Does one ever feel bereft when one picks up one's chips to light one's fire for one's evening meal? Or when one washes one's milk-pail before milking one's cow? One would fancy not.

"R. R. R."

"It is perfectly dreadful," sighed Rebecca when she read it aloud after school. "Putting in 'one' all the time doesn't make it sound any more like a book, and it looks silly besides."

"You say such queer things," objected Miss Dearborn. "I don't see what makes you do it. Why did you put in anything so common as picking up chips?"

"Because I was talking about 'household tasks' in the sentence before, and it *is* one of my household tasks. Don't you think calling supper 'one's evening meal' is pretty? and isn't 'bereft' a nice word?"

"Yes, that part of it does very well. It is the cat, the chips, and the milk-pail that I don't like."

"All right!" sighed Rebecca. "Out they go! Does the cow go too?"

"Yes, I don't like a cow in a composition," said the difficult Miss Dearborn.

The Milltown trip had not been without its tragic consequences of a small sort; for the next week Minnie Smellie's mother told Miranda Sawyer that she'd better look after Rebecca, for she was given to "swearing and profane language"; that she had been heard saying something dreadful that very afternoon, saying it before Emma Jane and Living Perkins, who only laughed and got down on all fours and chased her.

Rebecca, on being confronted and charged with the crime, denied it indignantly, and Aunt Jane believed her.

"Search your memory, Rebecca, and try to think what Minnie overheard you say," she pleaded. "Don't be ugly and obstinate, but think real hard. When did they chase you up the road, and what were you doing?"

A sudden light broke upon Rebecca's darkness.

"Oh! I see it now," she explained. "It had rained hard all the morning, you know, and the road was full of puddles. Emma Jane, Living, and I were walking along, and I was ahead. I saw the water streaming over the road towards the ditch, and it reminded me of 'Uncle Tom's Cabin' at Milltown, when Eliza took her baby and ran across the Mississippi on the ice blocks, pursued by the bloodhounds. We couldn't keep from laughing after we came out of the tent because they were acting on such a small platform that Eliza had to run round and round, and part of the time the one dog they had pursued her, and part of the time she had to pursue the dog. I knew Living would remember, too, so I took off my waterproof and wrapped it round my books for a baby; then I shouted, '*My God! the river!*' just like that – the same as Eliza did in the play; then I leaped from puddle to puddle, and Living and Emma Jane pursued me like the bloodhounds. It's just like that stupid Minnie Smellie who doesn't know a game when she sees one. And Eliza wasn't swearing when she said, 'My God! the river!' It was more like praying."

"Well, you've got no call to be prayin', any more than swearin', in the middle of the road," said Miranda; "but I'm thankful it's no worse. You're born to trouble as the sparks fly upward, an' I'm afraid you allers will be till you learn to bridle your unruly tongue."

"I wish sometimes that I could bridle Minnie's," murmured Rebecca, as she went to set the table for supper.

"I declare she is the beatin'est child!" said Miranda, taking off her spectacles and laying down her mending. "You don't think she's a leetle mite crazy, do you, Jane?"

"I don't think she's like the rest of us," responded Jane thoughtfully and with some anxiety in her pleasant face; "but whether it's for the better or the worse I can't hardly tell till she grows up. She's got the making of 'most anything in her, Rebecca has; but I feel sometimes as if we were not fitted to cope with her."

"Stuff an' nonsense!" said Miranda. "Speak for yourself. I feel fitted to cope with any child that ever was born int' the world!"

"I know you do, Mirandy; but that don't *make* you so," returned Jane with a smile.

The habit of speaking her mind freely was certainly growing on Jane to an altogether terrifying extent.

CHAPTER TWELVE

"SEE THE PALE MARTYR"

~

It was about this time that Rebecca, who had been reading about the Spartan boy, conceived the idea of some mild form of self-punishment, to be applied on occasions when she was fully convinced in her own mind that it would be salutary. The immediate cause of the decision was a somewhat sadder accident than was common, even in a career prolific in such things.

Clad in her best, Rebecca had gone to take tea with the Cobbs; but while crossing the bridge she was suddenly overcome by the beauty of the river, and leaned over the newly-painted rail to feast her eyes on the dashing torrent of the fall. Resting her elbows on the topmost board, and inclining her little figure forward in delicious ease, she stood there dreaming.

The river above the dam was a glassy lake, with all the loveliness of blue heaven and green shore reflected in its surface. The fall was a swirling wonder of water, ever pouring itself over and over inexhaustibly in luminous golden gushes, that lost themselves in snowy depths of foam. Sparkling in the sunshine, gleaming under the summer moon, cold and gray beneath a November sky, trickling over the dam in some burning July drought, swollen with turbulent power in some April freshet – how many young eyes gazed into the mystery and majesty of the falls along that river, and how many young hearts dreamed out their futures leaning over the bridge-rail, seeing "the vision splendid" reflected there, and often, too, watching it fade into "the light of common day."

Rebecca never went across the bridge without bending over the rail to wonder and to ponder, and at this special moment she was putting the finishing touches on a poem:

> *Two maidens by a river strayed*
> *Down in the state of Maine.*
> *The one was called Rebecca,*
> *The other Emma Jane.*
> *"I would my life were like the stream,"*
> *Said her named Emma Jane,*
> *"So quiet and so very smooth,*
> *So free from every pain."*
> *"I'd rather be a little drop*
> *In the great rushing fall!*
> *I would not choose the glassy lake*
> *'Twould not suit me at all!"*
> *(It was the darker maiden spoke*
> *The words I just have stated;*
> *The maidens twain were simply friends,*
> *And not at all related.)*
> *But O! alas! we may not have*
> *The things we hope to gain;*
> *The quiet life may come to me*
> *The rush to Emma Jane!*

"I don't like 'the rush to Emma Jane,' and I can't think of anything else. Oh, what a smell of paint! Oh, it is *on* me! Oh, it's all over my best dress! Oh, what *will* Aunt Miranda say?"

With tears of self-reproach streaming from her eyes, Rebecca flew up the hill, sure of sympathy, and hoping against hope for help of some sort.

Mrs. Cobb took in the situation at a glance, and professed herself able to remove almost any stain from almost any fabric; and in this she was corroborated by Uncle Jerry, who vowed that mother could get anything out. Sometimes she took the cloth right along with the spot, but she had a sure hand, mother had.

The damaged garment was removed and partially immersed in turpentine, while Rebecca graced the festal board clad in a blue calico wrapper of Mrs. Cobb's.

"Don't let it take your appetite away," crooned Mrs. Cobb. "I've got cream biscuit and honey for you. If the turpentine don't work, I'll try French chalk, magneshy, and warm suds. If they fail, father shall run over to Strout's, and borry some of the stuff Marthy got in Milltown to take the currant-pie out of her weddin' dress."

"I ain't got to understandin' this paintin' accident yet," said Uncle Jerry jocosely, as he handed Rebecca the honey. "Bein' as how there's 'Fresh Paint' signs hung all over the breedge, so 't a blind asylum couldn't miss 'em, I can't hardly account for your gettin' int' the pesky stuff."

"I didn't notice the signs," Rebecca said dolefully. "I suppose I was looking at the falls."

"The falls has been there sence the beginnin' o' time, an' I cal'late they'll be there till the end on't; so you needn't 'a' been in sech a brash to git a sight of 'em. Children comes turrible high, mother; but I s'pose we must have 'em," he said, winking at Mrs. Cobb.

When supper was cleared away, Rebecca insisted on washing and wiping the dishes, while Mrs. Cobb worked on the dress with an energy that plainly showed the gravity of the task. Rebecca kept leaving her post at the sink to bend anxiously over the basin and watch her progress, while Uncle Jerry offered advice from time to time.

"You must 'a' laid all over the breedge, deary," said Mrs. Cobb, "for the paint's not only on your elbows and yoke and waist, but it about covers your front breadth."

As the garment began to look a little better Rebecca's spirits took an upward turn, and at length she left it to dry in the fresh air, and went into the sitting-room.

"Have you a piece of paper, please?" asked Rebecca. "I'll copy out the poetry I was making while I was lying in the paint."

Mrs. Cobb sat by her mending basket, and Uncle Jerry took down a gingham bag of strings, and occupied himself in taking the snarls out of them – a favourite evening amusement with him.

Rebecca soon had the lines copied in her round schoolgirl hand, making such improvements as occurred to her on sober second thought.

THE TWO WISHES
by
Rebecca Randall

> *Two maidens by a river strayed;*
> *'Twas in the state of Maine.*
> *Rebecca was the darker one,*
> *The fairer, Emma Jane.*
> *The fairer maiden said "I would*
> *My life were as the stream;*
> *So peaceful, and so smooth and still,*
> *So pleasant and serene."*
>
> *"I'd rather be a little drop*
> *In the great rushing fall!*
> *I'd never choose the quiet lake;*
> *'Twould not please me at all."*
> *(It was the darker maiden spoke*
> *The words we just have stated;*
> *The maidens twain were simply friends,*
> *Not sisters, or related.)*
>
> *But O! alas! we may not have*
> *The things we hope to gain.*
> *The quiet life may come to me*
> *The rush to Emma Jane!"*

She read it aloud, and the Cobbs thought it not only surpassingly beautiful, but a marvellous production.

"I guess if that writer that lived on Congress Street in Portland could 'a' heard your poetry he'd 'a' been astonished," said Mrs. Cobb. "If you ask me, I say this piece is as good as that one o' his, 'Tell me not in mournful numbers,' and consid'able clearer."

"I never could fairly make out what 'mournful numbers' was," remarked Mr. Cobb critically.

"Then I guess you never studied fractions!" flashed Rebecca. "See here, Uncle Jerry, and Aunt Sarah: would you write another verse, especially for a last one, as they usually do – one with 'thoughts' in it – to make a better ending?"

"If you can grind 'em out jest by turnin' the crank, why, I should say the more the merrier; but I don't hardly see how you could have a better endin'," observed Mr. Cobb.

"It is horrid! grumbled Rebecca. "I ought not to have put that 'me' in. I'm writing the poetry. Nobody ought to know it is me standing by the river; it ought to be 'Rebecca,' or 'the darker maiden'; and 'the rush to Emma Jane' is simply dreadful. Sometimes I think I never will try poetry, it's so hard to make it come right; and other times it just says itself. I wonder if this would be better:

> *But oh! alas! we may not gain*
> *The good for which we pray.*
> *The quiet life may come to one*
> *Who likes it rather gay.*

"I don't know whether that is worse or not. Now for a new last verse!"

In a few minutes the poetess looked up, flushed and triumphant. "It was as easy as nothing. Just hear!" And she read slowly, with her pretty, pathetic voice:

> *"Then if our lot be bright or sad,*
> *Be full of smiles or tears,*
> *The thought that God has planned it so*
> *Should help us bear the years."*

Mr. and Mrs. Cobb exchanged dumb glances of admiration; indeed, Uncle Jerry was obliged to turn his face to the window and wipe his eyes furtively with the string-bag.

"How in the world did you do it?" Mrs. Cobb exclaimed.

"Oh, it's easy," answered Rebecca; "the hymns at meeting are all like that. You see, there's a school newspaper printed at Wareham Academy once a month. Dick Carter says the editor is always a boy, of course; but he allows girls to try and write for it, and then chooses the best. Dick thinks I can be in it."

"*In* it!" exclaimed Uncle Jerry. "I shouldn't be a bit surprised if you had to write the whole paper; an' as for any boy editor, you could lick him writin', I bate ye, with one hand tied behind ye."

"Can we have a copy of the poetry to keep in the family Bible?" inquired Mrs. Cobb respectfully.

"Oh! would you like it?" asked Rebecca. "Yes indeed! I'll do a clean, nice one with violet ink and a fine pen. But I must go and look at my poor dress."

The old couple followed Rebecca into the kitchen. The frock was quite dry, and in truth it had been helped a little by Aunt Sarah's ministrations; but the colours had run in the rubbing, the pattern was blurred, and there were muddy streaks here and there. As a last resort it was carefully smoothed with a warm iron, and Rebecca was urged to attire herself, that they might see if the spots showed as much when it was on.

They did most uncompromisingly, and to the dullest eye. Rebecca gave one searching look, and then said, as she took her hat from a nail in the entry: "I think I'll be going. Good-night. If I've got to have a scolding, I want it quick and get it over."

"Poor little onlucky misfortunate thing!" sighed Uncle Jerry, as his eyes followed her down the hill. "I wish she could pay some attention to the ground under her feet; but I vow, if she was ourn I'd let her slop paint all over the house before I could scold her. Here's her poetry she's left behind. Read it out ag'in, mother. Land!" he continued, chuckling, as he lighted his cob pipe; "I can just see the last flap o' that boy-editor's shirt-tail as he legs it for the woods, while Rebecky settles down in his revolvin' cheer! I'm puzzled as to what kind of a job editin' is, exactly; but she'll find out, Rebecky will. An' she'll just edit for all she's worth!

> "*The thought that God has planned it so*
> *Should help us bear the years.*"

Land, mother! that takes right hold, kind o' like the Gospel. How do you suppose she thought that out?"

"She couldn't have thought it out at her age," said Mrs. Cobb; "she must have just guessed it was that way. We know some things without bein' told, Jeremiah."

Rebecca took her scolding (which she richly deserved) like a soldier. There was considerable of it, and Miss Miranda remarked, among other things, that so absent-minded a child was sure to grow up into a drivelling idiot. She was bidden to stay away from Alice Robinson's birthday party, and doomed to wear her dress, stained and streaked as it was, until it was worn out. Aunt Jane six months later mitigated this martyrdom by making her a ruffled dimity pinafore, artfully shaped to conceal all the spots. She was blessedly ready with these mediations between the poor little sinner and the full consequences of her sin.

When Rebecca had heard her sentence and gone to the north chamber she began to think. If there was anything she did not wish to grow into, it was an idiot of any sort, particularly a drivelling one; and she resolved to punish herself every time she incurred what she considered to be the righteous displeasure of her virtuous relative. She didn't mind staying away from Alice Robinson's. She had told Emma Jane it would be like a picnic in a graveyard, the Robinson house being as near an approach to a tomb as a house can manage to be. Children were commonly brought in at the backdoor, and requested to stand on newspapers while making their call, so that Alice was begged by her friends to "receive" in the shed or barn whenever possible. Mrs. Robinson was not only "turrible neat," but "turrible close," so that the refreshments were likely to be peppermint lozenges and glasses of well-water.

After considering the relative values, as penances, of a piece of hair-cloth worn next the skin, and a pebble in the shoe, she dismissed them both. The hair-cloth could not be found, and the pebble would attract the notice of the Argus-eyed aunt, besides being a foolish bar to the activity of a person who had to do housework and walk a mile and a half to school.

Her first experimental attempt at martyrdom had not been a distinguished success. She had stayed at home from the Sunday-school concert, a function of which, in ignorance of more alluring ones, she was extremely fond. As a result of her desertion, two infants who relied upon her to prompt them (she knew the verses of all the children better than they did themselves) broke down ignominiously. The class to which she belonged had to read a difficult chapter of Scripture in rotation, and the various members spent an arduous Sabbath afternoon counting out verses according to their seats in the pew, and practicing the ones that would inevitably fall to them. They were too ignorant to realize, when they were called upon, that Rebecca's absence would make everything come wrong, and the blow descended with crushing force when the Jebusites and Amorites, the Girgashites, Hivites, and Perizzites had to be pronounced by the persons of all others least capable of grappling with them.

Self-punishment, then to be adequate and proper, must begin, like charity, at home, and, unlike charity, should end there too. Rebecca looked about the room vaguely as she sat by the window. She must give up something, and, truth to tell, she possessed little to give, hardly anything, but — yes, that would do, the beloved pink parasol. She could not hide it in the attic, for in some moment of weakness she would be sure to take it out again. She feared she had not the moral energy to break it into bits. Her eyes moved from the parasol to the apple-trees in the side-yard, and then fell to the well-curb. That would do: she would fling her dearest possession into the depths of the water. Action followed quickly upon decision, as usual. She slipped down in the darkness, stole out the front-door, approached the place of sacrifice, lifted the cover of the well, gave one unresigned shudder, and flung the parasol downward with all her force. At the crucial instant of renunciation she was greatly helped by the reflection that she closely resembled the heathen mothers who cast their babes to the crocodiles in the Ganges.

She slept well and arose refreshed, as a consecrated spirit always should and sometimes does. But there was great difficulty in drawing water after breakfast. Rebecca, chastened and uplifted, had gone to school. Abijah Flagg was summoned, lifted the well-cover, explored, found the inciting cause of trouble, and with the help of Yankee wit succeeded in removing it. The fact was that the ivory hook of the parasol had caught in the chain gear, and when the first attempt at drawing water was made, the little offering of a contrite heart was jerked up, bent, its strong ribs jammed into the well side, and entangled with a twig root. It is needless to say that no sleight-of-hand performer, however expert, unless aided by the powers of darkness, could have accomplished this feat; but a luckless child in the pursuit of virtue had done it with a turn of the wrist.

We will draw a veil over the scene that occurred after Rebecca's return from school. You who read may be well advanced in years, you may be gifted in rhetoric, ingenious in argument; but even you might quail at the thought of explaining the tortuous mental processes that led you into throwing your beloved pink parasol into Miranda Sawyer's well. Perhaps you feel equal to discussing the efficacy of spiritual self-chastisement with a person who closes her lips into a thin line and looks at you out of blank, uncomprehending eyes! Common-sense, right, and logic were all arrayed on Miranda's side. When poor Rebecca, driven to the wall, had to avow the reasons lying behind the sacrifice of the sunshade, her aunt said, "Now, see here, Rebecca; you're too big to be whipped, and I shall never whip you; but when you think you ain't punished enough just tell me, and I'll make out to invent a little something more. I ain't so smart as some folks, but I can do that much; and whatever it is, it'll be something that won't punish the whole family, and make 'em drink ivory dust, wood chips, and pink silk rags with their water."

CHAPTER THIRTEEN

SNOW-WHITE: ROSE-RED

~

*J*ust before Thanksgiving the affairs of the Simpsons reached what might have been called a crisis even in their family, which had been born and reared in a state of adventurous poverty and perilous uncertainty.

Riverboro was doing its best to return the entire tribe of Simpsons to the land of its fathers, so to speak, thinking rightly that the town which had given them birth, rather than the town of their adoption, should feed them, and keep a roof over their heads until the children were of an age for self-support. There was little to eat in the household and less to wear, though Mrs. Simpson did, as always, her poor best. The children managed to satisfy their appetites by sitting modestly outside their neighbors' kitchen-doors when meals were about to be served. They were not exactly popular favourites, but they did receive certain undesirable morsels from the more charitable housewives.

Life was rather dull and dreary, however; and in the chill and gloom of

November weather, with the vision of other people's turkeys bursting with fat, and other people's golden pumpkins and squashes and corn being garnered into barns, the young Simpsons groped about for some inexpensive form of excitement, and settled upon the selling of soap for a premium. They had sold enough to their immediate neighbors during the earlier autumn to secure a child's handcart, which, though very weak on its pins, could be trundled over the country roads. With large business sagacity, and an executive capacity which must have been inherited from their father, they now proposed to extend their operations to a larger area, and distribute soap to contiguous villages, if these villages could be induced to buy. The Excelsior Soap Company paid a very small return of any kind to its infantile agents, who were scattered through the State, but it inflamed their imaginations by the issue of circulars with highly-colored pictures of the premiums to be awarded for the sale of a certain number of cakes. It was at this juncture that Clara Belle and Susan Simpson consulted Rebecca, who threw herself solidly and wholeheartedly into the enterprise, promising her help and that of Emma Jane Perkins. The premiums within their possible grasp were three – a bookcase, a plush reclining chair, and a banquet lamp. Of course, the Simpsons had no books, and casting aside without thought or pang the plush chair, which might have been of some use in a family of seven persons (not counting Mr. Simpson, who ordinarily sat elsewhere at the town's expense), they warmed themselves rapturously in the vision of the banquet lamp, which speedily became to them more desirable than food, drink, or clothing. Neither Emma Jane nor Rebecca perceived anything incongruous in the idea of the Simpsons striving for a banquet lamp. They looked at the picture daily, and knew that if they themselves were free agents, they would toil, suffer, ay, sweat, for the happy privilege of occupying the same room with that lamp through the coming winter evenings. It looked to be about eight feet tall in the catalogue, and Emma Jane advised Clara Belle to measure the height of the Simpson ceilings; but a note in the margin of the circular informed them that it stood two and a half feet high when set up in all its dignity and splendour on a proper table, three dollars extra. It was only of polished brass, continued the circular, though it was invariably mistaken for solid gold; and the shade that accompanied it (at least, it accompanied it if the agent sold a hundred extra cakes) was of crinkled crêpe paper, printed in a dozen delicious hues, from which the joy-dazzled agent might take his choice.

Seesaw Simpson was not in the syndicate. Clara Belle was rather a successful agent, but Susan, who could only say "thoap," never made large returns; and the twins, who were somewhat young to be thoroughly trustworthy, could be given only a half-dozen cakes at a time, and were obliged to carry with them on their business trips a brief document stating the price per cake, dozen, and box. Rebecca and Emma Jane offered to go two or three miles in some one direction, and see what they could do in the way of stirring up a popular demand for the Snow-White and Rose-Red brands, the former being devoted to laundry purposes, and the latter being intended for the toilet.

There was a great amount of hilarity in the preparation for this event, and a long council in Emma Jane's attic. They had the soap company's circular from which to arrange a proper speech, and they had, what was still better, the remembrance of a certain patent-medicine vendor's discourse at the Milltown Fair. His method, when once observed, could never be forgotten; nor his manner, nor his vocabulary. Emma Jane practiced it on Rebecca, and Rebecca on Emma Jane.

"Can I sell you a little soap this afternoon? It is called the Snow-White and Rose-Red Soap — six cakes in an ornamental box; only twenty cents for the white, twenty-five cents for the red. It is made from the purest ingredients, and if desired could be eaten by an invalid with relish and profit."

"Oh, Rebecca, don't let's say that!" interposed Emma Jane hysterically. "It makes me feel like a fool."

"It takes so little to make you feel like a fool, Emma Jane," rebuked Rebecca, "that sometimes I think that you must be one. I don't get to feeling like a fool so awfully easy; now leave out that eating part if you don't like it, and go on."

"The Snow-White is probably the most remarkable laundry soap ever manufactured. Immerse the garments in a tub, lightly rubbing the more soiled portions with the soap; leave them submerged in water from sunset to sunrise, and then the youngest baby can wash them without the slightest effort."

"*Babe*, not baby," corrected Rebecca from the circular.

"It's just the same thing," argued Emma Jane.

"Of course it's just the same *thing*; but a baby has got to be called babe or infant in a circular, the same as it is in poetry! Would you rather say infant?"

"No," grumbled Emma Jane; "infant is worse even than babe. Rebecca, do you think we'd better do as the circular says, and let Elijah or Elisha try the soap before we begin selling?"

"I can't imagine a babe doing a family wash with *any* soap," answered Rebecca; "but it must be true or they would never dare to print it, so don't let's bother. Oh, won't it be the greatest fun, Emma Jane? At some of the houses, where they can't possibly know me, I shan't be frightened, and I shall reel off the whole rigmarole, invalid, babe, and all. Perhaps I shall say even the last sentence, if I can remember it: 'We sound every chord in the great mac-ro-cosm of satisfaction.'"

This conversation took place on a Friday afternoon at Emma Jane's house, where Rebecca, to her unbounded joy, was to stay over Sunday, her aunts having gone to Portland to the funeral of an old friend. Saturday being a holiday, they were going to have the old white horse, drive to North Riverboro three miles away, eat a twelve o'clock dinner with Emma Jane's cousins, and be back at four o'clock punctually.

When the children asked Mrs. Perkins if they could call at just a few houses coming and going, and sell a little soap for the Simpsons, she at first replied decidedly in the negative. She was an indulgent parent, however, and really had little objection to Emma Jane amusing herself in this unusual way; it was only for Rebecca, as the niece of the difficult Miranda Sawyer, that she raised scruples; but when fully persuaded that the enterprise was a charitable one she acquiesced.

The girls called at Mr. Watson's store, and arranged for several large boxes of soap to be charged to Clara Belle Simpson's account. These were lifted into the back of the waggon, and a happier couple never drove along the country road than Rebecca and her companion. It was a glorious Indian summer day, which suggested nothing of Thanksgiving, near at hand as it was. It was a rustly day, a scarlet and buff, yellow and carmine, bronze and crimson day. There were still many leaves on the oaks and maples, making a goodly show of red and brown and gold. The air was like sparkling cider, and every field had its heaps of yellow and russet good things to eat, all ready for the barns, the mills, and the markets. The horse forgot his twenty years, sniffed the sweet bright air, and trotted like a colt; Nokomis Mountain looked blue and clear in the distance; Rebecca stood in the waggon, and apostrophized the landscape with sudden joy of living:

> *"Great, wide, beautiful, wonderful World,*
> *With the wonderful water round you curled,*
> *And the wonderful grass upon your breast:*
> *World, you are beautifully drest!"*

Dull Emma Jane had never seemed to Rebecca so near, so dear, so tried and true; and Rebecca, to Emma Jane's faithful heart, had never been so brilliant, so bewildering, so fascinating, as in this visit together, with its intimacy, its freedom, and the added delights of an exciting business enterprise.

A gorgeous leaf blew into the waggon.

"Does color make you sort of dizzy?" asked Rebecca.

"No," answered Emma Jane after a long pause — "no, it don't; not a mite."

"Perhaps dizzy isn't just the right word, but it's nearest. I'd like to eat colour, and drink it, and sleep in it. If you could be a tree, which one would you choose?"

Emma Jane had enjoyed considerable experience of this kind, and Rebecca had succeeded in unstopping her ears, ungluing her eyes, and loosening her tongue, so that she could "play the game" after a fashion.

"I'd rather be an apple-tree in blossom — that one that blooms pink by our pig-pen."

Rebecca laughed. There was always something unexpected in Emma Jane's replies. "I'd choose to be that scarlet maple just on the edge of the pond there" — and she pointed with the whip. "Then I could see so much more than your pink apple-tree by the pig-pen. I could look at all the rest of the woods, see my scarlet dress in my beautiful looking-glass, and watch all the yellow and brown trees growing upside down in the water. When I'm old enough to earn money, I'm going to have a dress like this leaf, all ruby colour — thin, you know, with a sweeping train and ruffly, curly edges; then I think I'll have a brown sash like the trunk of the tree, and where could I be green? Do they have green petticoats, I wonder? I'd like a green petticoat coming out now and then underneath to show what my leaves were like before I was a scarlet maple."

"I think it would be awful homely," said Emma Jane. "I'm going to have a white satin with a pink sash, pink stockings, bronze slippers, and a spangled fan."

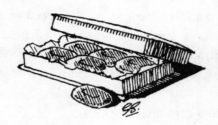

MR. ALADDIN

~

A single hour's experience of the vicissitudes incident to a business career clouded the children's spirits just the least bit. They did not accompany each other to the doors of their chosen victims, feeling sure that together they could not approach the subject seriously; but they parted at the gate of each house, the one holding the horse while the other took the soap samples, and interviewed anyone who seemed of a coming-on disposition. Emma Jane had disposed of three single cakes, Rebecca of three small boxes; for a difference in their ability to persuade the public was clearly defined at the start, though neither of them ascribed either success or defeat to anything but the imperious force of circumstances. Housewives looked at Emma Jane and desired no soap; listened to her description of its merits, and still desired none. Other stars in their courses governed Rebecca's doings. The people whom she interviewed either remembered their present need of soap, or reminded themselves that they would need it in the future; the notable point in the case being that lucky Rebecca accomplished, with almost no effort, results that poor little Emma Jane failed to attain by hard and conscientious labour.

"It's your turn, Rebecca, and I'm glad, too," said Emma Jane, drawing up to a gateway and indicating a house that was set a considerable distance from the road. "I haven't got over trembling from the last place yet." (A lady had put her head out of an upstairs window and called: "Go away, little girl. Whatever you have in your box, we don't want any.") "I don't know who lives here, and the blinds are all shut in front. If there's nobody at home you mustn't count it, but take the next house as yours."

Rebecca walked up the lane and went to the side-door. There was a porch there, and seated in a rocking-chair husking corn was a good-looking young man — or was he middle-aged? Rebecca could not make up her mind. At all events, he had an air of the city about him — well-shaven face, well-trimmed moustache, well-fitting clothes. Rebecca was a trifle shy at this unexpected encounter, but there was nothing to be done but explain her presence, so she asked: "Is the lady of the house at home?"

"I am the lady of the house at present," said the stranger, with a whimsical smile. "What can I do for you?"

"Have you ever heard of the — would you like, or, I mean — do you need any soap?" queried Rebecca.

"Do I look as if I did?" he responded unexpectedly.

Rebecca dimpled. "I didn't mean *that.* I have some soap to sell; I mean, I would like to introduce to you a very remarkable soap, the best now on the market. It is called the —"

"Oh, I must know that soap," said the gentleman genially. "Made out of pure vegetable fats, isn't it?"

"The very purest," corroborated Rebecca.

"No acid in it?"

"Not a trace."

"And yet a child could do the Monday washing with it and use no force?"

"A babe," corrected Rebecca.

"Oh, a babe, eh? That child grows younger every year, instead of older — wise child!"

This was great good fortune, to find a customer who knew all the virtues of the article in advance. Rebecca dimpled more and more, and at her new friend's invitation sat down on a stool at his side near the edge of the porch. The beauties of the ornamental box which held the Rose-Red were disclosed, and the prices of both that and the Snow-White were unfolded. Presently she forgot all about her silent partner at the gate, and was talking as if she had known this grand personage all her life.

"I'm keeping house to-day, but I don't live here," explained the delightful gentleman. "I'm just on a visit to my aunt, who has gone to Portland. I used to be here as a boy, and I am very fond of the spot."

"I don't think anything takes the place of the farm where one lived when one was a child," observed Rebecca, nearly bursting with pride at having at last successfully used the indefinite pronoun in general conversation.

The man darted a look at her, and put down his ear of corn. "So you consider your childhood a thing of the past, do you, young lady?"

"I can still remember it," answered Rebecca gravely, "though it seems a long time ago."

"I can remember mine well enough, and a particularly unpleasant one it was," said the stranger.

"So was mine," sighed Rebecca. "What was your worst trouble?"

"Lack of food and clothes principally."

"Oh!" exclaimed Rebecca sympathetically, "mine was no shoes, and too many babies, and not enough books. But you're all right and happy now, aren't you?" she asked doubtfully, for, though he looked handsome, well-fed, and prosperous, any child could see that his eyes were tired and his mouth was sad when he was not speaking.

"I'm doing pretty well, thank you," said the man, with a delightful smile. "Now tell me, how much soap ought I to buy to-day?"

"How much has your aunt on hand now?" suggested the very modest and inexperienced agent. "And how much would she need?"

"Oh, I don't know about that. Soap keeps, doesn't it?"

"I'm not certain," said Rebecca conscientiously; "but I'll look in the circular — it's sure to tell;" and she drew the document from her pocket.

"What are you going to do with the magnificent profits you get from this business?"

"We are not selling for our own benefit," said Rebecca confidentially. "My friend, who is holding the horse at the gate, is the daughter of a very rich blacksmith, and doesn't need any money. I am poor, but I live with my aunts in a brick house, and, of course, they wouldn't like me to be a pedlar. We are trying to get a premium for some friends of ours."

Rebecca had never thought of alluding to the circumstances with her previous customers, but unexpectedly she found herself describing Mr. Simpson, Mrs. Simpson, and the Simpson family, their poverty, their joyless life, and their abject need of a banquet lamp to brighten their existence.

"You needn't argue that point," laughed the man, as he stood up to get a glimpse of the "rich blacksmith's daughter" at the gate. "I can see that they ought to have it if they want it, and especially if you want them to have it. I've known what it was myself to do without a banquet lamp. Now give me the circular, and let's do some figuring. How much do the Simpsons lack at this moment?"

"If they sell two hundred more cakes this month and next they can have the lamp by Christmas," Rebecca answered; "and they can get a shade by summer-time. But I'm afraid I can't help very much after to-day, because my Aunt Miranda may not like to have me."

"I see. Well, that's all right. I'll take three hundred cakes, and that will give them shade and all."

Rebecca had been seated on a stool very near to the edge of porch, and at this remark she made a sudden movement, tipped over, and disappeared into a clump of lilac bushes. It was a very short distance, fortunately, and the amused capitalist picked her up, set her on her feet, and brushed her off. "You should never seem surprised when you have taken a large order," said he; "you ought to have replied, 'Can't you make it three hundred and fifty?' instead of capsizing in that unbusinesslike way."

"Oh, I could never say anything like that!" exclaimed Rebecca, who was blushing crimson at her awkward fall. "But it doesn't seem right for you to buy so much. Are you sure you can afford it?"

"If I can't, I'll save on something else," returned the jocose philanthropist.

"What if your aunt shouldn't like the kind of soap?" queried Rebecca nervously.

"My aunt always likes what I like," he returned.

"Mine doesn't," exclaimed Rebecca.

"Then there's something wrong with your aunt."

"Or with me," laughed Rebecca.

"What is your name, young lady?"

"Rebecca Rowena Randall, sir."

"What?" – with an amused smile. "*Both*? Your mother was generous."

"She couldn't bear to give up either of the names, she says."

"Do you want to hear my name?"

"I think I know already," answered Rebecca, with a bright glance. "I'm sure you must be Mr. Aladdin in the 'Arabian Nights.' Oh, please, can I run down and tell Emma Jane? She must be so tired waiting, and she will be so glad."

At the man's nod of assent Rebecca sped down the lane, crying irrepressibly as she neared the waggon: "Oh, Emma Jane! Emma Jane! we are sold out!"

Mr. Aladdin followed smilingly to corroborate this astonishing, unbelievable statement, lifted all their boxes from the back of the waggon, and, taking the circular, promised to write to the Excelsior Company that night concerning the premium.

"If you could contrive to keep a secret – you two little girls – it would be rather a nice surprise to have the lamp arrive at the Simpsons' on Thanksgiving Day, wouldn't it?" he asked, as he tucked the old lap-robe cosily over their feet.

They gladly assented, and broke into a chorus of excited thanks, during which tears of joy stood in Rebecca's eyes.

"Oh, don't mention it!" laughed Mr. Aladdin, lifting his hat. "I was a sort of commercial traveller myself once – years ago – and I like to see the thing well done. Good-bye, Miss Rebecca Rowena! Just let me know whenever you have anything to sell, for I'm certain beforehand I shall want it."

"Good-bye, Mr. Aladdin; I surely will!" cried Rebecca, tossing back her dark braids delightedly and waving her hand.

"Oh, Rebecca!" said Emma Jane in an awestruck whisper. "He raised his hat to us, and we not thirteen! It'll be five years before we're ladies."

"Never mind," answered Rebecca; "we are the *beginnings* of ladies, even now."

"He tucked the lap-robe round us, too," continued Emma Jane in an ecstasy of reminiscence. "Oh! isn't he perfectly elergant? And wasn't it lovely of him to buy us out? And just think of having both the lamp and the shade for one day's work! Aren't you glad you wore your pink gingham now, even if mother did make you put on flannel underneath? You do look so pretty in pink and red, Rebecca, and so homely in drab and brown!"

"I know it," sighed Rebecca. "I wish I was like you — pretty in all colors!" and Rebecca looked longingly at Emma Jane's fat, rosy cheeks; at her blue eyes, which said nothing; at her neat nose, which had no character; at her red lips, from between which no word worth listening to had ever issued.

"Never mind," said Emma Jane comfortingly. "Everybody says you're awful bright and smart, and mother thinks you'll be better looking all the time as you grow older. You wouldn't believe it, but I was a dreadful homely baby, and homely right along till just a year or two ago, when my red hair began to grow dark. What was the nice man's name?"

"I never thought to ask!" ejaculated Rebecca. "Aunt Miranda would say that was just like me, and it is. But I called him Mr. Aladdin because he gave us a lamp. You know the story of Aladdin and the wonderful lamp?"

"Oh, Rebecca! how could you call him a nickname the very first time you ever saw him?"

"Aladdin isn't a nickname exactly; anyway, he laughed and seemed to like it."

By dint of superhuman effort, and putting such a seal upon their lips as never mortals put before, the two girls succeeded in keeping their wonderful news to themselves, although it was obvious to all beholders that they were in an extraordinary and abnormal state of mind.

On Thanksgiving Day the lamp arrived in a large packing-box, and was taken out and set up by Seesaw Simpson, who suddenly began to admire and respect the business ability of his sisters. Rebecca had heard the news of its arrival, but waited until nearly dark before asking permission to go to the Simpsons', so that she might see the gorgeous trophy lighted and sending a blaze of crimson glory through its red crêpe paper shade.

CHAPTER FIFTEEN

THE BANQUET LAMP
~

There had been company at the brick house to the bountiful Thanksgiving dinner which had been provided at one o'clock — the Burnham sisters, who lived between North Riverboro and Shaker Village, and who for more than a quarter of a century had come to pass the holiday with the Sawyers every year. Rebecca sat silent with a book after the dinner dishes were washed, and when it was nearly five asked if she might go to the Simpsons'.

"What do you want to run after those Simpson children for on a Thanksgiving Day?" queried Miss Miranda. "Can't you set still for once and listen to the improvin' conversation of your elders? You never can let well enough alone, but want to be for ever on the move."

"The Simpsons have a new lamp, and Emma Jane and I promised to go up and see it lighted, and make it a kind of a party."

"What under the canopy did they want of a lamp, and where did they get the money to pay for it? If Abner was at home, I should think he'd been swappin' again," said Miss Miranda.

"The children got it as a prize for selling soap," replied Rebecca; "they've been working for a year, and you know I told you that Emma Jane and I helped them the Saturday afternoon you were in Portland."

"I didn't take notice, I s'pose, for it's the first time I ever heard the lamp mentioned. Well, you can go for an hour, and no more. Remember, it's as dark at six as it is at midnight. Would you like to take along some Baldwin apples? What have you got in the pocket of that new dress that makes it sag down so?"

"It's my nuts and raisins from dinner," replied Rebecca, who never succeeded in keeping the most innocent action a secret from her Aunt Miranda. "They're just what you gave me on my plate."

"Why didn't you eat them?"

"Because I'd had enough dinner, and I thought if I saved these it would make the Simpsons' party better," stammered Rebecca, who hated to be scolded and examined before company.

"They were your own, Rebecca," interposed Aunt Jane; "and if you chose to save them to give away, it's all right. We ought never to let this day pass without giving our neighbors something to be thankful for, instead of taking all the time to think of our own mercies."

The Burnham sisters nodded approvingly as Rebecca went out, and remarked that they had never seen a child grow and improve so fast in so short a time.

"There's plenty of room left for more improvement, as you'd know if she lived in the same house with you," answered Miranda. "She's into every namable thing in the neighborhood, an' not only into it, but generally at the head an' front of it, especially when it's mischief. Of all the foolishness I ever heard of, that lamp beats everything; it's just like those Simpsons, but I didn't suppose the children had brains enough to sell anything."

"One of them must have," said Miss Ellen Burnham, "for the girl that was selling soap at the Ladds' in North Riverboro was described by Adam Ladd as the most remarkable and winning child he ever saw."

"It must have been Clara Belle, and I should never call her remarkable," answered Miss Miranda. "Has Adam been home again?"

"Yes; he's been staying a few days with his aunt. There's no limit to the money he's making, they say; and he always brings presents for all the neighbors. This time it was a full set of furs for Mrs. Ladd; and to think we can remember the time he was a barefoot boy without two shirts to his back! It is strange he hasn't married, with all his money, and him so fond of children that he always has a pack of them at his heels."

"There's hope for him still, though," said Miss Jane smilingly; "for I don't s'pose he's more than thirty."

"He could get a wife in Riverboro if he was a hundred and thirty," remarked Miss Miranda.

"Adam's aunt says he was so taken with the little girl that sold the soap – Clara Belle, did you say her name was? – that he declared he was going to bring her a Christmas present," continued Miss Ellen.

"Well, there's no accountin' for tastes," exclaimed Miss Miranda. "Clara Belle's got cross-eyes and red hair, but I'd be the last one to grudge her a Christmas present; the more Adam Ladd gives to her the less the town 'll have to."

"Isn't there another Simpson girl?" asked Miss Lydia Burnham. "For this one couldn't have been cross-eyed; I remember Mrs. Ladd saying Adam remarked about this child's handsome eyes. He said it was her eyes that made him buy the three hundred cakes. Mrs. Ladd has it stacked up in the shed chamber."

"Three hundred cakes!" ejaculated Miranda. "Well, there's one crop that never fails in Riverboro!"

"What's that?" asked Miss Lyia politely.

"The fool crop!" responded Miranda tersely, and changed the subject, much to Jane's gratitude, for she had been nervous and ill at ease for the last fifteen minutes. What child in Riverboro could be described as remarkable and winning, save Rebecca? What child had wonderful eyes, except the same Rebecca? And, finally, was there ever a child in the world who could make a man buy soap by the hundred cakes, save Rebecca?

Meantime the "remarkable" child had flown up the road in the deepening dusk, but she had not gone far before she heard the sound of hurrying footsteps, and saw a well-known figure coming in her direction. In a moment she and Emma Jane met and exchanged a breathless embrace.

"Something awful has happened!" panted Emma Jane.

"Don't tell me it's broken!" exclaimed Rebecca.

"No, oh no, not that! It was packed in straw, and every piece came out all right. And I was there, and I never said a single thing about your selling the three hundred cakes that got the lamp, so that we could be together when you told."

"*Our* selling the three hundred cakes," corrected Rebecca. "You did as much as I."

"No, I didn't, Rebecca Randall. I just sat at the gate and held the horse."

"Yes, but *whose* horse was it that took us to North Riverboro? And besides, it just happened to be my turn. If you had gone in and found Mr. Aladdin, you would have had the wonderful lamp given to you. But what's the trouble?"

"The Simpsons have no kerosene and no wicks, I guess they thought a banquet lamp was something that lighted itself, and burned without any help. Seesaw has gone to the doctor's to try if he can borrow a wick, and mother let me have a pint of oil; but she says she won't give me any more. We never thought of the expense of keeping up the lamp, Rebecca."

"No, we didn't; but let's not worry about that till after the party. I have a handful of nuts and raisins and some apples."

"I have peppermints and maple sugar," said Emma Jane. "They had a real Thanksgiving dinner: the doctor gave them sweet potatoes and cranberries and turnips; father sent a spare-rib, and Mrs. Cobb a chicken and a jar of mince-meat."

At half-past five one might have looked in at the Simpsons' windows and seen the party at its height. Mrs. Simpson had let the kitchen fire die out, and had brought the baby to grace the festal scene. The lamp seemed to be having the party and receiving the guests. The children had taken the one small table in the house, and it was placed in the far corner of the room to serve as a pedestal. On it stood the sacred, the adored, the long-desired object, almost as beautiful and nearly half as large as the advertisement. The brass glistened like gold, and the crimson paper shade glowed like a giant ruby. In the wide splash of light that it flung upon the floor sat the Simpsons in reverent and solemn silence, Emma Jane standing behind them hand in hand with Rebecca. There seemed to be no desire for conversation; the occasion was too thrilling and serious for that. The lamp, it was tacitly felt by everybody, was dignifying the party, and providing sufficient entertainment simply by its presence, being fully as satisfactory in its way as a pianola or a string band.

"I wish father could see it," said Clara Belle loyally.

"If he onth thaw it he'd want to thwap it," murmured Susan sagaciously.

At the appointed hour Rebecca dragged herself reluctantly away from the enchanting scene.

"I'll turn the lamp out the minute I think you and Emma Jane are home," said Clara Belle. "And oh, I'm so glad you both live where you can see it shine from our windows! I wonder how long it will burn without bein' filled if I only keep it lit one hour every night."

"You needn't put it out for want o' karosene," said Seesaw, coming in from the shed, "for there's a great kag of it settin' out there. Mr. Tubbs brought it over from North Riverboro, and said somebody sent an order by mail for it."

Rebecca squeezed Emma Jane's arm, and Emma Jane gave a rapturous return squeeze. "It was Mr. Aladdin," whispered Rebecca, as they ran down the path to the gate. Seesaw followed them, and handsomely offered to see them "a piece" down the road; but Rebecca declined his escort with such decision that he did not press the matter, but went to bed to dream of her instead. In his dreams flashes of lightning proceeded from both her eyes, and she held a flaming sword in either hand.

Rebecca entered the home dining-room joyously. The Burnham sisters had gone, and the two aunts were knitting.

"It was a heavenly party!" she cried, taking off her hat and cape.

"Go back and see if you have shut the door tight, and then lock it," said Miss Miranda in her usual austere manner.

"It was a heavenly party!" reiterated Rebecca, coming in again, much too excited to be easily crushed. "And oh, Aunt Jane, Aunt Miranda, if you'll only come into the kitchen and look out of the sink window you can see the banquet lamp shining all red, just as if the Simpsons' house was on fire."

"And probably it will be before long," observed Miranda. "I've got no patience with such foolish goin's-on."

Jane accompanied Rebecca into the kitchen. Although the feeble glimmer which she was able to see from that distance did not seem to her a dazzling exhibition, she tried to be as enthusiastic as possible.

"Rebecca, who was it that sold the three hundred cakes of soap to Mr. Ladd in North Riverboro?"

"Mr. *Who?*' exclaimed Rebecca.

"Mr. Ladd, in North Riverboro."

"Is that his real name?" queried Rebecca in astonishment. "I didn't make a bad guess;" and she laughed softly to herself.

"I asked you who sold the soap to Adam Ladd?" resumed Miss Jane.

"Adam Ladd! Then he's A. Ladd, too. What fun!"

"Answer me, Rebecca!"

"Oh, excuse me, Aunt Jane; I was so busy thinking. Emma Jane and I sold the soap to Mr. Ladd."

"Did you tease him or make him buy it?"

"Now, Aunt Jane, how could I make a big grown-up man buy anything if he didn't want to? He needed the soap dreadfully as a present for his aunt. Miss Jane still looked a little unconvinced, though she only said: "I hope your aunt Miranda won't mind; but you know how particular she is, Rebecca, and I really wish you wouldn't do anything out of the ordinary without asking her first, for your actions are very queer."

"There can't be anything wrong this time," Rebecca answered confidently. "Emma Jane sold her cakes to her own relations and to Uncle Jerry Cobb, and I went first to those new tenements near the lumber-mill, and then to the Ladds'. Mr. Ladd bought all we had, and made us promise to keep the secret until the premium came; and I've been going about ever since as if the banquet lamp was inside of me all lighted up and burning for everybody to see."

Rebecca's hair was loosened and falling over her forehead in ruffled waves; her eyes were brilliant, her cheeks crimson; there was a hint of everything in the girl's face – of sensitiveness and delicacy as well as of ardour; there was the sweetness of the mayflower and the strength of the young oak, but one could easily divine that she was one of

> *"The souls by nature pitched too high,*
> *By suffering plunged too low."*

"That's just the way you look for all the world as if you did have a lamp burning inside of you," sighed aunt Jane. "Rebecca! Rebecca! I wish you could take things easier, child; I am fearful for you sometimes."

CHAPTER SIXTEEN

SEASONS OF GROWTH

~

The days flew by; as summer had melted into autumn, so autumn had given place to winter. Life in the brick house had gone on more placidly of late, for Rebecca was honestly trying to be more careful in the performance of her tasks and duties, as well as more quiet in her plays, and she was slowly learning the power of the soft answer in turning away wrath.

Miranda had not had, perhaps, quite as many opportunities in which to lose her temper, but it is only just to say that she had not fully availed herself of all that had offered themselves.

There had been one outburst of righteous wrath occasioned by Rebecca's overhospitable habits, which were later shown in a still more dramatic and unexpected fashion.

On a certain Friday afternoon she asked her aunt Miranda if she might take half her bread and milk upstairs to a friend.

"What friend have you got up there, for pity's sake?" demanded Aunt Miranda.

"The Simpson baby, come to stay over Sunday — that is, if you're willing; Mrs. Simpson says she is. Shall I bring her down and show her? She's dressed in an old dress of Emma Jane's, and she looks sweet."

"You can bring her down, but you can't show her to me! You can smuggle her out the way you smuggled her in, and take her back to her mother. Where on earth do you get your notions, borrowing a baby for Sunday?"

"You're so used to a house without a baby, you don't know how dull it is," sighed Rebecca resignedly, as she moved towards the door; "but at the farm there was always a nice fresh one to play with and cuddle. There were too many, but that's not half as bad as none at all. Well, I'll take her back. She'll be dreadfully disappointed, and so will Mrs. Simpson. She was planning to go to Milltown."

"She can un-plan then,"observed Miss Miranda.

"Perhaps I can go up there and take care of the baby?" suggested Rebecca. "I brought her home so 't I could do my Saturday work just the same."

"You've got enough to do right here, without any borrowed babies to make more steps. Now, no answering back; just give the child some supper, and carry it home where it belongs."

"You don't want me to go down the front way; hadn't I better just come through this room and let you look at her? She has yellow hair and big blue eyes! Mrs. Simpson says she takes after her father."

Miss Miranda smiled acidly as she said she couldn't take after her father, for he'd take anything there was before she got there!

Aunt Jane was in the linen-closet upstairs sorting out the clean sheets and pillow-cases for Saturday, and Rebecca sought comfort from her.

"I brought the Simpson baby home, Aunt Jane, thinking it would help us over a dull Sunday, but Aunt Miranda won't let her stay. Emma Jane has the promise of her next Sunday, and Alice Robinson the next. Mrs. Simpson wanted I should have her first because I've had so much experience in babies. Come in and look at her sitting up in my bed, Aunt Jane! Isn't she lovely! She's the fat, gurgly kind, not thin and fussy like some babies, and I thought I was going to have her to undress and dress twice each day. Oh dear! I wish I could have a printed book with everything set down in it that I *could* do, and then I wouldn't get disappointed so often."

"No book could be printed that would fit you, Rebecca," answered Aunt Jane, "for nobody could imagine beforehand the things you'd want to do. Are you going to carry that heavy child home in your arms?"

"No, I'm going to drag her in the little soap-waggon. Come, baby! Take your thumb out of your mouth, and come to ride with Becky in your go-cart." She stretched out her strong young arms to the crowing baby, sat down in a chair with the child, turned her upside down unceremoniously, took from her waistband and scornfully flung away a crooked pin, walked with her (still in a highly reversed position) to the bureau, selected a large safety-pin, and proceeded to attach her brief red flannel petticoat to a sort of shirt that she wore. Whether flat on her stomach, or head down, heels in the air, the Simpson baby knew she was in the hands of an expert, and continued gurgling placidly, while Aunt Jane regarded the pantomime with a kind of dazed awe.

"Bless my soul, Rebecca!" she ejaculated; "it beats all how handy you are with babies!"

"I ought to be; I've brought up three and a half of 'em," Rebecca responded cheerfully, pulling up the infant Simpson's stockings.

"I should think you'd be fonder of dolls than you are," said Jane.

"I do like them, but there's never any change in a doll; it's always the same everlasting old doll, and you have to make believe it's cross or sick, or it loves you, or can't bear you. Babies are more trouble, but nicer."

Miss Jane stretched out a thin hand with a slender, worn band of gold on the finger, and the baby curled her dimpled fingers round it and held it fast.

"You wear a ring on your engagement finger, don't you, Aunt Jane? Did you ever think about getting married?"

"Yes, dear, long ago."

"What happened, Aunt Jane?"

"He died — just before."

"Oh!" And Rebecca's eyes grew misty.

"He was a soldier, and he died of a gunshot wound in a hospital down South."

"Oh, Aunt Jane!" — softly. "Away from you?"

"No, I was with him."

"Was he young?"

"Yes, young and brave and handsome, Rebecca; he was Mr. Carter's brother Tom."

"Oh! I'm so glad you were with him! Wasn't he glad, Aunt Jane?"

Jane looked back across the half-forgotten years, and the vision of Tom's gladness flashed upon her: his haggard smile, the tears in his tired eyes, his outstretched arms, his weak voice saying, "Oh, Jenny! dear Jenny! I've wanted you so, Jenny!" It was too much! She had never breathed a word of it before to a human creature, for there was no one who would have understood. Now, in a shamefaced way, to hide her brimming eyes, she put her head down on the young shoulder beside her, saying, "It was hard, Rebecca!"

The Simpson baby had cuddled down sleepily in Rebecca's lap, leaning her head back and sucking her thumb contentedly. Rebecca put her cheek down until it touched her aunt's gray hair and softly patted her, as she said, "I'm sorry, Aunt Jane!"

The girl's eyes were soft and tender, and the heart within her stretched a little and grew — grew in sweetness and intuition and depth of feeling. It had looked into another heart, felt it beat, and heard it sigh; and that is how all hearts grow.

Episodes like these enlivened the quiet course of everyday existence, made more quiet by the departure of Dick Carter, Living Perkins, and Huldah Meserve for Wareham, and the small attendance at the winter school, from which the younger children of the place stayed away during the cold weather.

Life, however, could never be thoroughly dull or lacking in adventure to a child of Rebecca's temperament. Her nature was full of adaptability, fluidity, receptivity. She made friends everywhere she went, and snatched up acquaintances in every corner.

It was she who ran to the shed door to take the dish to the "meat-man" or "fish-man"; she who knew the family histories of the itinerant fruit vendors and tin pedlars; she who was asked to take supper or pass the night with children in neighboring villages — children of whose parents her aunts had never so much as heard. As to the nature of these friendships, which seemed so many to the eye of the superficial observer, they were of various kinds, and while the girl pursued them with enthusiasm and ardour, they left her unsatisfied and heart-hungry; they were never intimacies such as are so readily made by shallow natures. She loved Emma Jane, but it was a friendship born of propinquity and circumstance, not of true affinity. It was her neighbour's amiability, constancy, and devotion that she loved, and although she rated these qualities at their true value, she was always searching beyond them for intellectual treasures – searching and never finding, for although Emma Jane had the advantage in years, she was still immature. Huldah Meserve had an instinctive love of fun which appealed to Rebecca; she also had a fascinating knowledge of the world, from having visited her married sisters in Milltown and Portland; but on the other hand there was a certain sharpness and lack of sympathy in Huldah which repelled rather than attracted. With Dick Carter she could at least talk intelligently about lessons. He was a very ambitious boy, full of plans for his future, which he discussed quite freely with Rebecca, but when she broached the subject of her future his interest sensibly lessened. Into the world of the ideal Emma Jane, Huldah and Dick alike never seemed to have peeped, and the consciousness of this was always a fixed gulf between them and Rebecca.

"Uncle Jerry" and "Aunt Sarah" Cobb were dear friends of quite another sort, a very satisfying and perhaps a somewhat dangerous one. A visit from Rebecca always sent them into a twitter of delight. Her merry conversation and quaint comments on life in general fairly dazzled the old couple, who hung on her lightest word as if it had been a prophet's utterance; and Rebecca, though she had had no previous experience, owned to herself a perilous pleasure in being dazzling, even to a couple of dear, humdrum old people like Mr. and Mrs. Cobb. Aunt Sarah flew to the pantry or cellar whenever Rebecca's slim little shape first appeared on the crest of the hill, and a jelly tart or a frosted cake was sure to be forthcoming. The sight of old Uncle Jerry's spare figure in its clean white shirt-sleeves, whatever the weather, always made Rebecca's heart warm when she saw him peer longingly from the kitchen window. Before the snow came, many and many a time he had come out to sit on a pile of boards at the gate, to see if by any chance she was mounting the hill that led to their house. In the autumn Rebecca was often the old man's companion while he was digging potatoes or shelling beans, and now in the winter, when a younger man was driving the stage, she sometimes stayed with him while he did his evening milking. It is safe to say that he was the only creature in Riverboro who possessed Rebecca's entire confidence; the only being to whom she poured out her whole heart, with its wealth of hopes and dreams and vague ambitions. At the brick house she practiced scales and exercises, but at the Cobbs' cabinet organ she sang like a bird, improvising simple accompaniments that seemed to her ignorant auditors nothing short of marvellous. Here she was happy, here she was loved, here she was drawn out of herself and admired and made much of. But, she thought, if there were somebody who not only loved, but understood; who spoke her language, comprehended her desires, and responded to her mysterious longings! Perhaps in the big world of Wareham there would be people who thought and dreamed and wondered as she did.

In reality Jane did not understand her niece very much better than Miranda. The difference between the sisters was, that while Jane was puzzled, she was also attracted, and when she was quite in the dark for an explanation of some quaint or unusual action she was sympathetic as to its possible motive, and believed the best. A greater change had come over Jane than over any other person in the brick house; but it had been wrought so secretly and concealed so religiously that it scarcely appeared to the ordinary observer. Life had now a motive utterly lacking before. Breakfast was not eaten in the kitchen, because it seemed worth while, now that there were three persons, to lay the cloth in the dining-room. It was also a more bountiful meal than of yore, when there was no child to consider. The morning was made cheerful by Rebecca's start for school, the packing of the luncheon-basket, the final word about umbrella, waterproof, or rubbers; the parting admonition and the unconscious waiting at the window for the last wave of the hand. She found herself taking pride in Rebecca's improved appearance, her rounder throat and cheeks, and her better colour. She was wont to mention the length of Rebecca's hair, and add a word as to its remarkable evenness and lustre, at times when Mrs. Perkins grew too diffuse about Emma Jane's complexion. She threw herself whole-heartedly on her niece's side when it became a question between a crimson or a brown linsey-woolsey dress, and went through a memorable struggle with her sister concerning the purchase of a red bird for Rebecca's black felt hat. No one guessed the quiet pleasure that lay hidden in her heart when she watched the girl's dark head bent over her lessons at night, nor dreamed of her joy in certain quiet evenings when Miranda went to prayer-meeting;

evenings when Rebecca would read aloud "Hiawatha," or "Barbara Frietchie," "The Bugle Song," or "The Brook." Her narrow, humdrum existence bloomed under the dews that fell from this fresh spirit; her dullness brightened under the kindling touch of the younger mind, took fire from the "vital spark of heavenly flame" that seemed always to radiate from Rebecca's presence.

Rebecca's idea of being a painter like her friend Miss Ross was gradually receding, owing to the apparently insuperable difficulties in securing any instruction. Her Aunt Miranda saw no wisdom in cultivating such a talent, and could not conceive that any money could ever be earned by its exercise. "Hand-painted pictures' were held in little esteem in Riverboro, where the cheerful chromo or the dignified steel engraving were respected and valued. There was a slight, a very slight hope, that Rebecca might be allowed a few music-lessons from Miss Morton, who played the church cabinet organ; but this depended entirely upon whether Mrs. Morton would decide to accept a hayrack in return for a year's instruction from her daughter. She had the matter under advisement; but a doubt as to whether or not she would sell or rent her hayfields kept her from coming to a conclusion. Music, in common with all other accomplishments, was viewed by Miss Miranda as a trivial, useless, and foolish amusement; but she allowed Rebecca an hour a day for practice on the old piano, and a little extra time for lessons if Jane could secure them without payment of actual cash.

The news from Sunnybrook Farm was hopeful rather than otherwise. Cousin Ann's husband had died, and John, Rebecca's favourite brother, had gone to be the man of the house to the widowed cousin. He was to have good schooling in return for his care of the horse and cow and barn, and, what was still more dazzling, the use of the old doctor's medical library of two or three dozen volumes. John's whole heart was set on becoming a country doctor, with Rebecca to keep house for him, and the vision seemed now so true, so near, that he could almost imagine his horse ploughing through snowdrifts on errands of mercy, or, less dramatic, but none the less attractive, could see a physician's neat turnout trundling along the shady country roads, a medicine case between his, Dr. Randall's, feet, and Miss Rebecca Randall sitting in a black silk dress by his side.

Hannah now wore her hair in a coil and her dresses a trifle below her ankles, these concessions being due to her extreme height. Mark had broken his collar-bone, but it was healing well. Little Mira was growing very pretty. There was even a rumour that the projected railroad from Temperance to Plumville might go near the Randall Farm, in which case land would rise in value from nothing-at-all an acre to something at least resembling a price. Mrs. Randall refused to consider any improvement in their financial condition as a possibility. Content to work from sunrise to sunset to gain a mere subsistence for her children, she lived in their future, not in her own present, as a mother is wont to do when her own lot seems hard and cheerless.

CHAPTER SEVENTEEN

GRAY DAYS AND GOLD

~

When Rebecca looked back upon the year or two that followed the Simpsons' Thanksgiving party, she could only see certain milestones rising in the quiet pathway of the months.

The first milestone was Christmas Day. It was a fresh, crystal morning, with icicles hanging like dazzling pendants from the trees and a glaze of pale blue on the surface of the snow. The Simpsons' red barn stood out, a glowing mass of colour in the white landscape. Rebecca had been busy for weeks before, trying to make a present for each of the seven persons at Sunnybrook Farm, a somewhat difficult proceeding on an expenditure of fifty cents, hoarded by incredible exertion. Success had been achieved, however, and the precious packet had been sent by post two days previous. Miss Sawyer had bought her niece a nice gray squirrel muff and tippet, which was even more unbecoming, if possible, than Rebecca's other articles of wearing apparel; but Aunt Jane had made her the loveliest dress of green cashmere, a soft, soft green like that of a young leaf. It was very simply made, but the colour delighted the eye. Then there was a beautiful "tatting" collar from her mother, some scarlet mittens from Mrs. Cobb, and a handkerchief from Emma Jane.

Rebecca herself had fashioned an elaborate teacosy with a letter "M" in outline stitch, and a pretty frilled pincushion marked with a "J," for her two aunts, so that taken all together the day would have been an unequivocal success had nothing else happened; but something else did.

There was a knock at the door at breakfast-time, and Rebecca, answering it, was asked by a boy if Miss Rebecca Randall lived there. On being told that she did, he handed her a parcel bearing her name, a parcel which she took like one in a dream and bore into the dining-room.

"It's a present; it must be," she said, looking at it in a dazed sort of way; "but I can't think who it could be from."

"A good way to find out would be to open it," remarked Miss Miranda.

The parcel being untied proved to have two smaller packages within, and Rebecca opened with trembling fingers the one addressed to her. Anybody's fingers would have trembled. There was a case which, when the cover was lifted, disclosed a long chain of delicate pink coral beads – a chain ending in a cross made of coral rosebuds. A card with "Merry Christmas from Mr. Aladdin" lay under the cross.

"Of all things!" exclaimed the two old ladies, rising in their seats. "Who sent it?"

"Mr. Ladd," said Rebecca under her breath.

"Adam Ladd! Well I never! Don't you remember Ellen Burnham said he was going to send Rebecca a Christmas present? But I never supposed he'd think of it again," said Jane. "What's the other package?"

It proved to be a silver chain with a blue enamel locket on it, marked for Emma Jane. That added the last touch – to have him remember them both! There was a letter also, which ran:

"Dear Miss Rebecca Rowena,

"My idea of a Christmas present is something entirely unnecessary and useless. I have always noticed when I give this sort of thing that people love it, so I hope I have not chosen wrong for you and your friend. You must wear your chain this afternoon, please, and let me see it on your neck, for I am coming over in my new sleigh to take you both to drive. My aunt is delighted with the soap.

"Sincerely your friend,

"Adam Ladd."

"Well, well!" cried Miss Jane, "isn't that kind of him? He's very fond of children, Lyddy Burnham says. Now eat your breakfast, Rebecca, and after we've done the dishes you can run over to Emma's and give her her chain. What's the matter, child?"

Rebecca's emotions seemed always to be stored, as it were, in adjoining compartments, and to be continually getting mixed. At this moment, though her joy was too deep for words, her bread-and-butter almost choked her, and at intervals a tear stole furtively down her cheek.

Mr. Ladd called as he promised, and made the acquaintance of the aunts, understanding them both in five minutes as well as if he had known them for years. On a footstool near the open fire sat Rebecca silent and shy, so conscious of her fine apparel and the presence of Aunt Miranda that she could not utter a word. It was one of her "beauty days." Happiness, excitement, the colour of the green dress, and the touch of lovely pink in the coral necklace, had transformed the little brown wren for the time into a bird of plumage, and Adam Ladd watched her with evident satisfaction. Then there was the sleigh ride, during which she found her tongue, and chattered like any magpie; and so ended that glorious Christmas Day. And many and many a night thereafter did Rebecca go to sleep with the precious coral chain under her pillow, one hand always upon it to be certain that it was safe.

Another milestone was the departure of the Simpsons from Riverboro bag and baggage, the banquet lamp being their most conspicuous possession. It was delightful to be rid of Seesaw's hateful presence; but otherwise the loss of several playmates at one fell swoop made rather a gap in Riverboro's "younger set," and Rebecca was obliged to make friends with the Robinson baby, he being the only long-clothes child in the village that winter. The faithful Seesaw had called at the side-door of the brick house on the evening before his departure, and, when Rebecca answered his knock, stammered solemnly: "Can I k-keep comp'ny with you when you g-g-row up?"

"Certainly *not*," replied Rebecca, closing the door somewhat too speedily upon her precocious swain.

Mr. Simpson had come home in time to move his wife and children back to the town that had given them birth – a town by no means waiting with open arms to receive them. The Simpsons' moving was presided over by the village authorities, and somewhat anxiously watched by the entire neighborhood; but, in spite of all precautions, a pulpit chair, several kerosene lamps, and a small stove disappeared from the church, and were successfully swapped in the course of Mr. Simpson's driving tour from the old home to the new. It gave Rebecca and Emma Jane some hours of sorrow to learn that a certain village in the wake of Abner Simpson's line of progress had acquired, through the medium of an ambitious young minister, a magnificent lamp for its new church parlors. No money changed hands in the operation, for the minister succeeded in getting the lamp in return for an old bicycle. The only pleasant feature of the whole affair was that Mr. Simpson, wholly unable to console his offspring for the loss of the beloved object, mounted the bicycle and rode away on it, not to be seen or heard of again for many a long day.

The year was notable also as being the one in which Rebecca shot up like a young tree. She had seemingly never grown an inch since she was ten years old, but, once started, she attended to growing precisely as she did other things – with such energy that Miss Jane did nothing for months but lengthen skirts, sleeves, and waists. In spite of all the arts known to a thrifty New England woman, the limit of letting down and piecing down was reached at last, and the dresses were sent to Sunnybrook Farm to be made over for Jenny.

There was another milestone – a sad one – marking a little grave under a willow-tree at Sunnybrook Farm. Mira, the baby of the Randall family, died, and Rebecca went home for a fortnight's visit. The sight of the small still shape that had been Mira – the baby who had been her special charge ever since her birth – woke into being a host of new thoughts and wonderments, for it is sometimes the mystery of death that brings one to a consciousness of the still greater mystery of life.

It was a sorrowful home-coming for Rebecca. The death of Mira, the absence of John – who had been her special comrade – the sadness of her mother, the isolation of the little house, and the pinching economies that went on within it, all conspired to depress a child who was so sensitive to beauty and harmony as Rebecca.

Hannah seemed to have grown into a woman during Rebecca's absence. There had always been a strange, unchildlike air about Hannah, but in certain ways she now appeared older than Aunt Jane – soberer and more settled. She was pretty, though in a colorless fashion – pretty and capable.

Rebecca walked through all the old playgrounds and favourite haunts of her early childhood – all her familiar, her secret places, some of them known to John, some to herself alone. There was the spot where the Indian pipes grew; the particular bit of marshy ground where the fringed gentians used to be largest and bluest; the rock maple where she found the oriole's nest; the hedge where the field-mice lived; the moss-covered stump where the white toadstools were wont to spring up as if by magic; the hole at the root of the old pine where an ancient and honourable toad made his home – these were the landmarks of her childhood, and she looked at them as across an immeasurable distance. The dear little sunny brook – her chief companion after John – was sorry company at this season. There was no laughing water sparkling in the sunshine. In summer the merry stream had danced over white pebbles on its way to deep pools, where it could be still and think. Now, like Mira, it was cold and quiet, wrapped in its shroud of snow; but Rebecca knelt by the brink, and, putting her ear to the glaze of ice, fancied where it used to be deepest she could hear a faint tinkling sound. It was all right. Sunnybrook would sing again in the spring; perhaps Mira, too, would have her singing time somewhere – she wondered where and how. In the course of these lonely rambles she was ever thinking – thinking of one subject. Hannah had never had a chance – never been freed from the daily care and work of the farm. She (Rebecca) had enjoyed all the privileges thus far. Life at the brick house had not been by any means a path of roses, but there had been comfort and the companionship of other children, as well as chances for study and reading. Riverboro had not been the world itself, but it had been a glimpse of it through a tiny peephole that was infinitely better than nothing. Rebecca shed more than one quiet tear before she could trust herself to offer up as a sacrifice that which she so much desired for herself. Then one morning, as her visit neared its end, she plunged into the subject boldly, and said: "Hannah, after this term I'm going to stay at home and let you go away. Aunt Miranda has always wanted you, and it's only fair you should have your turn."

Hannah was darning stockings, and she threaded her needle and snipped off the yarn before she answered: "No, thank you, Becky. Mother couldn't do without me, and I hate going to school. I can read and write and cipher as well as anybody now, and that's enough for me. I'd die rather than teach school for a living. The winter 'll go fast, for Will Melville is going to lend me his mother's sewing-machine, and I'm going to make white petticoats out of the piece of muslin Aunt Jane sent, and have 'em just solid with tucks. Then there's going to be a singing-school and a social circle in Temperance after New Year's; and I shall have a real good time now I'm grown up. I'm not one to be lonesome, Becky," Hannah ended with a blush. "I love this place."

Rebecca saw that she was speaking the truth, but she did not understand the blush till a year or two later.

CHAPTER EIGHTEEN

REBECCA REPRESENTS
THE FAMILY

~

There was another milestone; it was more than that, it was an
"event" – an event that made a deep impression in several
quarters, and left a wake of smaller events in its train. This was the coming
to Riverboro of the Reverend Amos Burch and wife, returned missionaries
from Syria.

The Aid Society had called its meeting for a certain Wednesday in
March of the year in which Rebecca ended her Riverboro school-days, and
began her studies at Wareham. It was a raw, blustering day, snow on the
ground and a look in the sky of more to follow. Both Miranda and Jane had
taken cold, and decided that they could not leave the house in such weather,
and this deflection from the path of duty worried Miranda, since she was an
officer of the society. After making the breakfast-table sufficiently
uncomfortable and wishing plaintively that Jane wouldn't always insist on
being sick at the same time she was, she decided that Rebecca must go to
the meeting in their stead. "You'll be better than nobody, Rebecca," she

said flatteringly; "your Aunt Jane shall write an excuse from afternoon school for you; you can wear your rubber boots, and come home by the way of the meetin'-house. This Mr. Burch, if I remember right, used to know your grandfather Sawyer, and stayed here once when he was candidatin'. He'll mebbe look for us there, and you must just go and represent the family, an' give him our respects. Be careful how you behave. Bow your head in prayer; sing all the hymns, but not too loud and bold; ask after Mis' Strout's boy; tell everybody what awful colds we've got; if you see a good chance, take your pocket-handkerchief and wipe the dust off the melodeon before the meetin' begins, and get twenty-five cents out of the sittin'-room match-box in case there should be a collection."

Rebecca willingly assented. Anything interested her, even a village missionary meeting, and the idea of representing the family was rather intoxicating.

The service was held in the Sunday-school room, and although the Rev. Mr. Burch was on the platform when Rebecca entered, there were only a dozen persons present. Feeling a little shy and considerably too young for this assemblage, Rebecca sought the shelter of a friendly face, and seeing Mrs. Robinson in one of the side-seats near the front, she walked up the aisle and sat beside her.

"Both my aunts had bad colds," she said softly, "and sent me to represent the family."

"That's Mrs. Burch on the platform with her husband," whispered Mrs. Robinson. "She's awful tanned up, ain't she? If you're goin' to save souls seems like to hev' to part with your complexion. Eudoxy Morton ain't come yet; I hope to the land she will, or Mis' Deacon Milliken 'll pitch the tunes where we can't reach 'em with a ladder. Can't you pitch, afore she gits her breath and clears her throat?"

Mrs. Burch was a slim, frail little woman with dark hair, a broad low forehead, and patient mouth. She was dressed in a well-worn black silk, and looked so tired that Rebecca's heart went out to her.

"They're as poor as Job's turkey," whispered Mrs. Robinson; "but if you give 'em anything they'd turn right round and give it to the heathen. His congregation up to Parsonsfield clubbed together and give him that gold watch he carries; I s'pose he'd 'a' handed that over too, only heathens always tell time by the sun 'n' don't need watches. Eudoxy ain't comin'; now, for massy's sake, Rebecca, do git ahead of Mis' Deacon Milliken, and pitch real low."

The meeting began with prayer, and then the Rev. Mr. Burch announced, to the tune of Mendon:

> *"Church of our God! arise and shine,*
> *Bright with the beams of truth Divine;*
> *Then shall thy radiance stream afar,*
> *Wide as the heathen nations are.*
>
> *"Gentiles and kings thy light shall view,*
> *And shall admire and love thee too;*
> *They come, like clouds across the sky,*
> *As doves that to their windows fly."*

"Is there anyone present who will assist us at the instrument?" he asked unexpectedly.

Everybody looked at everybody else, and nobody moved; then there came a voice out of a far corner saying informally, "Rebecca, why don't you?" It was Mrs. Cobb. Rebecca could have played Mendon in the dark, so she went to the melodeon and did so without any ado, no member of her family being present to give her self-consciousness.

The talk that ensued was much the usual sort of thing. Mr. Burch made impassioned appeals for the spreading of the Gospel, and added his entreaties that all who were prevented from visiting in person the peoples who sat in darkness should contribute liberally to the support of others who could. But he did more than this. He was a pleasant, earnest speaker, and he interwove his discourse with stories of life in a foreign land — of the manners, the customs, the speech, the point of view, even giving glimpses of the daily round, the common task, of his own household, the work of his devoted helpmate, and their little group of children, all born under Syrian skies.

Rebecca sat entranced, having been given the key of another world. Riverboro had faded; the Sunday-school room, with Mrs. Robinson's red plaid shawl, and Deacon Milliken's wig, on crooked, the bare benches and torn hymn-books, the hanging texts and maps, were no longer visible, and she saw blue skies and burning stars, white turbans and gay colours; Mr.

Burch had not said so, but perhaps there were mosques and temples and minarets and date-palms. What stories they must know, those children born under Syrian skies! Then she was called upon to play "Jesus shall reign where'er the sun."

The contribution-box was passed and Mr. Burch prayed. As he opened his eyes and gave out the last hymn, he looked at the handful of people, at the scattered pennies and dimes in the contribution-box, and reflected that his mission was not only to gather funds for the building of his church, but to keep alive in all those remote and lonely neighborhoods that love for the cause which was its only hope in the years to come.

"If any of the sisters will provide entertainment" he said, "Mrs. Burch and I will remain among you to-night and to-morrow. In that event we could hold a parlour meeting. My wife and one of my children would wear the native costume, we would display some specimens of Syrian handiwork, and give an account of our educational methods with the children. These informal parlour meetings, admitting of questions or conversation, are often the means of interesting those not commonly found at church services; so, I repeat, if any member of the congregation desires it, and offers her hospitality, we will gladly stay and tell you more of the Lord's work."

A pall of silence settled over the little assembly. There was some cogent reason why every "sister" there was disinclined for company. Some had no spare room, some had a larder less well stocked than usual, some had sickness in the family, some were "unequally yoked together with unbelievers," who disliked strange ministers. Mrs. Burch's thin hands fingered her black silk nervously. Would no one speak? thought Rebecca, her heart fluttering with sympathy. Mrs. Robinson leaned over and whispered significantly: "The missionaries always used to be entertained at the brick house. Your grandfather never would let 'em sleep anywheres else when he was alive." She meant this for a stab at Miss Miranda's parsimony, remembering the four spare chambers closed from January to December; but Rebecca thought it was intended as a suggestion. If it had been a former custom, perhaps her aunts would want her to do the right thing; for what else was she representing the family? So, delighted that duty lay in so pleasant a direction, she rose from her seat, and said, in the pretty voice and with the quaint manner that so separated her from all the other young people in the village: "My aunts, Miss Miranda and Miss Jane Sawyer, would be very happy to have you visit them at the brick house, as the ministers always used to do when their father was alive. They sent their respects by me." The "respects" might have been the freedom of the city, or an equestrian statue, when presented in this way, and the aunts would have shuddered could they have foreseen the manner of delivery; but it was vastly impressive to the audience, who concluded that Mirandy Sawyer must be making her way uncommonly fast to mansions in the skies, else what meant this abrupt change of heart?

Mr. Burch bowed courteously, accepted the invitation "in the same spirit in which it was offered," and asked Brother Milliken to lead in prayer.

If the Eternal Ear could ever tire, it would have ceased long ere this to listen to Deacon Milliken, who had wafted to the Throne of Grace the same prayer, with very slight variations, for forty years. Mrs. Perkins followed. She had several petitions at her command, good sincere ones, too, but a little cut and dried, made of Scripture texts laboriously woven together. Rebecca wondered why she always ended, at the most peaceful seasons, with the form, "Do Thou be with us, God of Battles, while we strive onward, like Christian soldiers, marching as to war." But everything sounded real to her to-day. She was in a devout mood, and many things Mr. Birch had said had moved her strangely. As she lifted her head the minister looked directly at her, and said: "Will our young sister close the service by leading us in prayer?"

Every drop of blood in Rebecca's body seemed to stand still and her heart almost stopped beating. Mrs. Cobb's excited breathing could be heard distinctly in the silence. There was nothing extraordinary in Mr. Burch's request. In his journeyings among country congregations he was constantly in the habit of meeting young members who had "experienced religion," and joined the church when nine or ten years old. Rebecca was now thirteen. She had played the melodeon, led the singing, delivered her aunts' invitation with an air of great worldly wisdom, and he, concluding that she must be a youthful pillar of the church, called upon her with the utmost simplicity.

Rebecca's plight was pathetic. How could she refuse? How could she explain she was not a "member"? How could she pray before all those elderly women? John Rogers at the stake hardly suffered more than this

343

poor child for the moment as she rose to her feet, forgetting that ladies prayed sitting, while deacons stood in prayer. Her mind was a maze of pictures that the Rev. Mr. Burch had flung on the screen. She knew the conventional phraseology, of course. What New England child accustomed to Wednesday evening meetings does not? But her own secret prayers were different. However, she began slowly and tremulously:

"Our Father who art in Heaven, . . . Thou art God in Syria just the same as in Maine; . . . over there to-day are blue skies and yellow stars and burning suns . . . the great trees are waving in the warm air, while here the snow lies thick under our feet, . . . but no distance is too far for God to travel, and so He is with us here as he is with them there, . . . and our thoughts rise to Him 'as doves that to their windows fly.' . . .

"We cannot all be missionaries, teaching people to be good: . . . some of us have not learned yet how to be good ourselves; but if Thy kingdom is to come and Thy will is to be done on earth as it is in heaven, everybody must try and everybody must help . . . those who are old and tired and those who are young and strong. . . . The little children of whom we have heard, those born under Syrian skies, have strange and interesting work to do for Thee, and some of us would like to travel in far lands and do wonderful brave things for the heathen, and gently take away their idols of wood and stone. But perhaps we have to stay at home and do what is given us to do . . . sometimes even things we dislike, . . . but that must be what it means in the hymn we sang, when it talked about the sweet perfume that rises with every morning sacrifice. . . . This is the way that God teaches us to be meek and patient, and the thought that He has willed it so should rob us of our fears and help us bear the years. Amen."

Poor little ignorant, fantastic child! Her petition was simply a succession of lines from the various hymns, and images the minister had used in his sermon, but she had her own way of recombining and applying these things, even of using them in a new connection, so that they had a curious effect of belonging to her. The words of some people might generally be written with a minus sign after them, the minus meaning that the personality of the speaker subtracted from, rather than added to, their weight; but Rebecca's words might always have borne the plus sign.

The "Amen" said, she sat down, or presumed she sat down, on what she believed to be a bench, and there was a benediction. In a moment or two, when the room ceased spinning, she went up to Mrs. Burch, who kissed her affectionately and said, "My dear, how glad I am that we are going to stay with you! Will half-past five be too late for us to come? It is three now, and we have to go to the station for our valise and for our children. We left them there, being uncertain whether we should go back or stop here."

Rebecca said that half-past five was their supper hour, and then accepted an invitation to drive home with Mrs. Cobb. Her face was flushed and her lip quivered in a way that Aunt Sarah had learned to know, so the homeward drive was taken almost in silence. The bleak wind and Aunt Sarah's quieting presence brought her back to herself, however, and she entered the brick house cheerily. Being too full of news to wait in the side entry to take off her rubber boots, she carefully lifted a braided rug into the sitting-room and stood on that while she opened her budget.

"There are your shoes warming by the fire," said Aunt Jane. "Slip them right on while you talk."

CHAPTER NINETEEN

DEACON ISRAEL'S SUCCESSOR
~

"It was a very small meeting, Aunt Miranda," began Rebecca, "and the missionary and his wife are lovely people, and they are coming here to stay all night and to-morrow with you. I hope you won't mind."

"Coming here!" exclaimed Miranda, letting her knitting fall in her lap and taking her spectacles off, as she always did in moments of extreme excitement. "Did they invite themselves?"

"No," Rebecca answered. "I had to invite them for you; but I thought you'd like to have such interesting company. It was this way –"

"Stop your explainin', and tell me first when they'll be here. Right away?"

"No, not for two hours – about half-past five."

"Then you can explain, if you can, who gave you any authority to invite a passel of strangers to stop here overnight, when you know we ain't had any company for twenty years, and don't intend to have any for another twenty, or, at any rate, while I'm the head of the house."

"Don't blame her, Miranda, till you've heard her story," said Jane. "It was in my mind right along, if we went to the meeting, some such thing might happen, on account of Mr. Burch knowing father."

"The meeting was a small one," began Rebecca. "I gave all your messages, and everybody was disappointed you couldn't come, for the president wasn't there, and Mrs. Matthews took the chair, which was a pity, for the seat wasn't nearly big enough for her, and she reminded me of a line in a hymn we sang, 'Wide as the heathen nations are,' and she wore that kind of a beaver garden-hat that always gets on one side. And Mr. Burch talked beautifully about the Syrian heathen, and the singing went real well, and there looked to be about forty cents in the basket that was passed on our side. And that wouldn't save even a heathen baby, would it? Then Mr. Burch said if any sister would offer entertainment they would pass the night, and have a parlour meeting in Riverboro to-morrow, with Mrs. Burch in Syrian costume, and lovely foreign things to show. Then he waited and waited, and nobody said a word. I was so mortified I didn't know what to do. And then he repeated what he said, and explained why he wanted to stay, and you could see he thought it was his duty. Just then Mrs. Robinson whispered to me and said the missionaries always used to go to the brick house when grandfather was alive, and that he never would let them sleep anywhere else. I didn't know you had stopped having them, because no travelling ministers have been here, except just for a Sunday morning, since I came to Riverboro. So I thought I ought to invite them, as you weren't there to do it for yourself, and you told me to represent the family."

"What did you do — go up and introduce yourself as folks was goin' out?"

"No; I stood right up in meeting. I had to, for Mr. Burch's feelings were getting hurt at nobody's speaking. So I said, 'My aunts, Miss Miranda and Miss Jane Sawyer, would be happy to have you visit at the brick house, just as the missionaries always did when their father was alive, and they sent their respects by me.' Then I sat down, and Mr. Burch prayed for grandfather, and called him a man of God, and thanked our Heavenly Father that his spirit was still alive in his descendants (that was you), and that the good old house where so many of the brethren had been cheered and helped, and from which so many had gone out strengthened for the fight, was still hospitably open for the stranger and wayfarer."

Sometimes, when the heavenly bodies are in just the right conjunction, nature seems to be the most perfect art. The word or the deed coming straight from the heart, without any thought of effect, seems inspired.

A certain gateway in Miranda Sawyer's soul had been closed for years; not all at once had it been done, but gradually, and without her full knowledge. If Rebecca had plotted for days, and with the utmost cunning, she could not have effected an entrance into that forbidden country, and now, unknown to both of them, the gate swung on its stiff and rusty hinges, and the favouring wind of opportunity opened it wider and wider as time went on. All things had worked together amazingly for good. The memory of old days had been evoked, and the daily life of a pious and venerated father called to mind; the Sawyer name had been publicly dignified and praised; Rebecca had comported herself as the granddaughter of Deacon Israel Sawyer should, and showed conclusively that she was not "all Randall," as had been supposed. Miranda was rather mollified by and pleased with the turn of events, although she did not intend to show it, or give anybody any reason to expect that this expression of hospitality was to serve for a precedent on any subsequent occasion.

"Well, I see you did only what you was obliged to do, Rebecca," she said, "and you worded your invitation as nice as anybody could have done. I wish your Aunt Jane and me wasn't both so worthless with these colds; but it only shows the good of havin' a clean house, with every room in order, whether open or shut, and enough victuals cooked so 't you can't be surprised and belittled by anybody, whatever happens. There was half a dozen there that might have entertained the Burches as easy as not, if they hadn't 'a' been too mean or lazy. Why didn't your missionaries come right along with you?"

"They had to go to the station for their valise and their children."

"Are there children?" groaned Miranda.

"Yes, Aunt Miranda, all born under Syrian skies."

"Syrian grandmother!" ejaculated Miranda (and it was not a fact). "How many?"

"I didn't think to ask; but I will get two rooms ready, and if there are any over I'll take 'em into my bed," said Rebecca, secretly hoping that this would be the case. "Now, as you're both half sick, couldn't you trust me just once to get ready for the company? You can come up when I call. Will you?"

"I believe I will," sighed Miranda reluctantly. "I'll lay down side o' Jane in our bedroom and see if I can get strength to cook supper. It's half-past three — don't you let me lay a minute past five. I kep' a good fire in the kitchen stove. I don't know, I'm sure, why I should have baked a pot o' beans in the middle of the week, but they'll come in handy. Father used to say there was nothing that went right to the spot with returned missionaries like pork 'n' beans 'n' brown bread. Fix up the two south chambers, Rebecca."

Rebecca, given a free hand for the only time in her life, dashed upstairs like a whirlwind. Every room in the brick house was as neat as wax, and she had only to pull up the shades, go over the floors with a whisk broom, and dust the furniture. The aunts could hear her scurrying to and fro, beating up pillows and feather-beds, flapping towels, jingling crockery, singing meanwhile in her clear voice:

> *"In vain with lavish kindness*
> *The gifts of God are strown;*
> *The heathen in his blindness*
> *Bows down to wood and stone."*

She had grown to be a handy little creature, and tasks she was capable of doing at all she did like a flash, so that when she called her aunts at five o'clock to pass judgment she had accomplished wonders. There were fresh towels on bureaus and washstands, the beds were fair and smooth, the pitchers were filled, and soap and matches were laid out; newspaper, kindling, and wood were in the boxes, and a large stick burned slowly in each air-tight stove. "I thought I'd better just take the chill off," she explained, "as they're right from Syria; and that reminds me I must look it up in the geography before they get here."

There was nothing to disapprove, so the two sisters went downstairs to make some slight changes in their dress. As they passed the parlour door Miranda thought she heard a crackle, and looked in. The shades were up; there was a cheerful blaze in the open stove in the front parlour, and a fire laid on the hearth in the back-room. Rebecca's own lamp, her second Christmas present from Mr. Aladdin, stood on a marble-topped table in the corner, the light that came softly through its rose-colored shade transforming the stiff and gloomy ugliness of the room into a place where one could sit and love one's neighbor.

"For massy's sake, Rebecca!" called Miss Miranda up the stairs, "did you think we'd better open the parlour?"

Rebecca came out on the landing braiding her hair.

"We did on Thanksgiving and Christmas, and I thought this was about as great an occasion," she said. "I moved the wax flowers off the mantelpiece so they wouldn't melt, and put the shells, the coral, and the green stuffed bird on top of the what-not, so the children wouldn't ask to play with them. Brother Milliken's coming over to see Mr. Burch about business, and I shouldn't wonder if Brother and Sister Cobb happened in. Don't go down cellar; I'll be there in a minute to do the running."

Miranda and Jane exchanged glances.

"Ain't she the beatin'est creetur that ever was born int' the world!" exclaimed Miranda; "but she can turn off work when she's got a mind to!"

At quarter-past five everything was ready, and the neighbors – those, at least, who were within sight of the brick house (a prominent object in the landscape when there were no leaves on the trees) – were curious almost to desperation. Shades up in both parlours! Shades up in the two south bedrooms! And fires – if human vision was to be relied on – fires in about every room. If it had not been for the kind offices of a lady who had been at the meeting, and who charitably called in at one or two houses and explained the reason of all this preparation, there would have been no sleep in many families.

The missionary party arrived promptly, and there were but two children, seven or eight having been left with the brethren in Portland to diminish travelling expenses. Jane escorted them all upstairs, while Miranda watched the cooking of the supper; but Rebecca promptly took the two little girls away from their mother, divested them of their wraps, smoothed their hair, and brought them down to the kitchen to smell the beans.

There was a bountiful supper, and the presence of the young people robbed it of all possible stiffness. Aunt Jane helped clear the table and put away the food, while Miranda entertained in the parlour; but Rebecca and the infant Burches washed the dishes and held high carnival in the kitchen, doing only trifling damage – breaking a cup and plate that had been cracked before, emptying a silver spoon with some dish-water out of the back-door (an act never permitted at the brick house), and putting coffee-grounds in the sink. All evidences of crime having been removed by Rebecca, and damages repaired in all possible cases, the three entered the parlour, where Mr. and Mrs. Cobb and Deacon and Mrs. Milliken had already appeared.

It was such a pleasant evening! Occasionally they left the heathen in his blindness bowing down to wood and stone, not for long, but just to give themselves (and him) time enough to breathe, and then the Burches told strange, beautiful, marvellous things. The two smaller children sang together, and Rebecca, at the urgent request of Mrs. Burch, seated herself at the tinkling old piano and gave "Wild roved an Indian girl, bright Alfarata," with considerable spirit and style.

At eight o'clock she crossed the room, handed a palm-leaf fan to her Aunt Miranda, ostensibly that she might shade her eyes from the lamplight; but it was a piece of strategy that gave her an opportunity to whisper, "How about cookies?"

"Do you think it's worth while?" sibilated Miss Miranda in answer.

"The Perkinses always do."

"All right. You know where they be."

Rebecca moved quietly towards the door, and the young Burches cataracted after her as if they could not bear a second's separation. In five minutes they returned, the little ones bearing plates of thin caraway wafers – hearts, diamonds, and circles daintily sugared, and flecked with caraway-seed raised in the garden behind the house. These were a specialty of Miss Jane's, and Rebecca carried a tray with six tiny crystal glasses filled with dandelion wine, for which Miss Miranda had been famous in years gone by. Old Deacon Israel had always had it passed, and he had bought the glasses himself in Boston. Miranda admired them greatly, not only for their beauty, but because they held so little. Before their advent the dandelion wine had been served in sherry glasses.

As soon as these refreshments – commonly called a "*colation*" in Riverboro – had been genteelly partaken of, Rebecca looked at the clock, rose from her chair in the children's corner, and said cheerfully: "Come, time for little missionaries to be in bed!"

Everybody laughed at this – the big missionaries most of all – as the young people shook hands and disappeared with Rebecca.

CHAPTER TWENTY

A CHANGE OF HEART

~

"That niece of yours is the most remarkable girl I have seen in years," said Mr. Burch when the door closed.

"She seems to be turnin' out smart enough lately; but she's consid'able heedless," answered Miranda, "an' most too lively."

"We must remember that it is deficient, not excessive, vitality that makes the greatest trouble in this world," returned Mr. Burch.

"She'd make a wonderful missionary," said Mrs. Burch, "with her voice, and her magnetism, and her gift of language."

"If I was to say which of the two she was best adapted for, I'd say she'd make a better heathen," remarked Miranda curtly.

"My sister don't believe in flattering children," hastily interpolated Jane, glancing toward Mrs. Burch, who seemed somewhat shocked, and was about to open her lips to ask if Rebecca was not a "professor."

Mrs. Cobb had been looking for this question all the evening, and dreaded some allusion to her favorite as gifted in prayer. She had taken an instantaneous and illogical dislike to the Rev. Mr. Burch in the afternoon because he called upon Rebecca to "lead." She had seen the pallor creep into the girl's face, the hunted look in her eyes, and the trembling of the lashes on her cheeks, and realized the ordeal through which she was passing. Her prejudice against the minister had relaxed under his genial talk and presence, but feeling that Mrs. Burch was about to tread on dangerous ground, she hastily asked her if one had to change cars many times going from Riverboro to Syria. She felt that it was not a particularly appropriate question, but it served her turn.

Deacon Milliken meantime said to Miss Sawyer: "Mirandy, do you know who Rebecky reminds me of?"

"I can guess pretty well," she replied.

"Then you've noticed it too. I thought at first, seein' she favored her father so on the outside, that she was the same all through; but she ain't: she's like your father, Israel Sawyer."

"I don't see how you make that out," said Miranda, thoroughly astonished.

"It struck me this afternoon when she got up to give your invitation in meetin'. It was kind o' cur'ous, but she set in the same seat he used to when he was leader o' the Sabbath-school. You know his old way of holdin' his chin up and throwin' his head back a leetle when he got up to say anything? Well, she done the very same thing; there was more 'n one spoke of it."

The callers left before nine, and at that hour (an impossibly dissipated one for the brick house) the family retired for the night. As Rebecca carried Mrs. Burch's candle upstairs, and found herself thus alone with her for a minute, she said shyly: "Will you, please, tell Mr. Burch that I'm not a member of the church? I didn't know what to do when he asked me to pray this afternoon. I hadn't the courage to say I had never done it out loud, and didn't know how. I couldn't think, and I was so frightened I wanted to sink into the floor. It seemed bold and wicked for me to pray before all those old church members, and make believe I was better than I really was. But then, again, wouldn't God think I was wicked not to be willing to pray when a minister asked me to?"

The candle-light fell on Rebecca's flushed, sensitive face. Mrs. Burch bent and kissed her goodnight. "Don't be troubled," she said. "I'll tell Mr. Burch, and I guess God will understand."

Rebecca waked before six the next morning so full of household cares that sleep was impossible. She went to the window and looked out: it was still dark, and a blustering, boisterous day.

"Aunt Jane told me she should get up at half-past six, and have breakfast at half-past seven" she thought. "But I dare say they are both sick with their colds, and Aunt Miranda will be fidgety with so many in the house. I believe I'll creep down and start things for a surprise."

She put on a wadded wrapper and slippers, and stole quietly down the tabooed front stairs, carefully closed the kitchen-door behind her so that no noise should awaken the rest of the household, busied herself for a half-hour with the early morning routine she knew so well, and then went back to her room to dress before calling the children.

Contrary to expectation, Miss Jane, who the evening before felt better than Miranda, grew worse in the night, and was wholly unable to leave her bed in the morning. Miranda grumbled without ceasing during the progress of her hasty toilet, blaming everybody in the universe for the afflictions she had borne and was to bear during the day; she even castigated the Missionary Board that had sent the Burches to Syria, and gave it as her unbiassed opinion that those who went to foreign lands for the purpose of saving heathen should stay there and save 'em, and not go gallivantin' all over the earth with a passel o' children, visitin' folks that didn't want 'em and never asked 'em.

Jane lay anxiously and restlessly in bed with a feverish headache, wondering how her sister could manage without her.

Miranda walked stiffly through the dining-room, tying a shawl over her head to keep the draughts away, intending to start the breakfast fire and then call Rebecca down, set her to work, and tell her, meanwhile, a few plain facts concerning the proper way of representing the family at a missionary meeting.

She opened the kitchen-door and stared vaguely about her, wondering whether she had strayed into the wrong house by mistake.

The shades were up, and there was a roaring fire in the stove; the tea-kettle was singing and bubbling as it sent out a cloud of steam, and pushed over its capacious nose was a half-sheet of note-paper with "Compliments of Rebecca" scrawled on it. The coffee-pot was scalding, the coffee was measured out in a bowl, and broken eggshells for the settling process were standing near. The cold potatoes and corned beef were in the wooden tray, and "Regards of Rebecca" stuck on the chopping-knife. The brown loaf was out, the white loaf was out, the toast-rack was out, the dough-nuts were out, the milk was skimmed, the butter had been brought from the dairy.

Miranda removed the shawl from her head and sank into the kitchen-rocker, ejaculating under her breath: "She is the beatin'est child! I declare she's all Sawyer!"

The day and the evening passed off with credit and honor to everybody concerned, even to Jane, who had the discretion to recover instead of growing worse and acting as a damper to the general enjoyment. The Burches left with lively regrets, and the little missionaries, bathed in tears, swore eternal friendship with Rebecca, who pressed into their hands at parting a poem composed before breakfast:

TO MARY AND MARTHA BURCH.

Born under Syrian skies,
'Neath hotter suns than ours,
The children grew and bloomed,
Like little tropic flowers.

When they first saw the light,
'Twas in a heathen land.
Not Greenland's icy mountains,
Nor India's coral strand,

But some mysterious country
Where men are nearly black,
And where of true religion
There is a painful lack.

Then let us haste in helping
The Missionary Board,
Seek dark-skinned unbelievers,
And teach them of their Lord.
REBECCA ROWENA RANDALL.

It can readily be seen that this visit of the returned missionaries to

Riverboro was not without somewhat far-reaching results. Mr. and Mrs. Burch themselves looked back upon it as one of the rarest pleasures of their half-year at home. The neighborhood extracted considerable eager conversation from it; argument, rebuttal, suspicion, certainty, retrospect, and prophecy. Deacon Milliken gave ten dollars towards the conversion of Syria to Congregationalism, and Mrs. Milliken had a spell of sickness over her husband's rash generosity.

It would be pleasant to state that Miranda Sawyer was an entirely changed woman afterwards, but that is not the fact. The tree that has been getting a twist for twenty years cannot be straightened in the twinkling of an eye. It is certain, however, that, although the difference to the outward eye was very small, it nevertheless existed, and she was less censorious in her treatment of Rebecca, less harsh in her judgments, more hopeful of final salvation for her. This had come about largely from her sudden vision that Rebecca, after all, inherited something from the Sawyer side of the house instead of belonging, mind, body, and soul, to the despised Randall stock. Everything that was interesting in Rebecca, and every evidence of power, capability, or talent afterwards displayed by her, Miranda ascribed to the brick-house training, and this gave her a feeling of honest pride – the pride of a master workman who has built success out of the most unpromising material; but never, to the very end, even when the waning of her bodily strength relaxed her iron grip and weakened her power of repression, never once did she show that pride or make a single demonstration of affection.

Poor misplaced, belittled Lorenzo de Medici Randall, thought ridiculous and good-for-naught by his associates because he resembled them in nothing! If Riverboro could have been suddenly emptied into a larger community, with different and more flexible opinions, he was, perhaps, the only personage in the entire population who would have attracted the smallest attention. It was fortunate for his daughter that she had been dowered with a little practical ability from her mother's family; but if Lorenzo had never done anything else in the world, he might have glorified himself that he had prevented Rebecca from being all Sawyer. Failure as he was, complete and entire, he had generously handed down to her all that was best in himself, and prudently retained all that was unworthy. Few fathers are capable of such delicate discrimination.

The brick house did not speedily become a sort of wayside inn, a place of innocent revelry and joyous welcome; but the missionary company was an entering wedge, and Miranda allowed one spare bed to be made up "in case anything should happen," while the crystal glasses were kept on the second from the top, instead of the top shelf, in the china closet. Rebecca had had to stand on a chair to reach them; now she could do it by stretching; and this is symbolic of the way in which she unconsciously scaled the walls of Miss Miranda's dogmatism and prejudice.

Miranda went so far as to say that she wouldn't mind if the Burches came every once in a while, but she was afraid he'd spread abroad the fact of his visit, and missionaries' families would be underfoot the whole continual time. As a case in point she gracefully cited the fact that if a tramp got a good meal at anybody's back-door 'twas said that he'd leave some kind of sign, so that other tramps would know where they were likely to receive the same treatment.

It is to be feared that there is some truth in this homely illustration, and Miss Miranda's dread as to her future responsibilities had some foundation, though not of the precise sort she had in mind. The soul grows into lovely habits as easily as into ugly ones, and the moment a life begins to blossom into beautiful words and deeds, that moment a new standard of conduct is established, and your eager neighbors look to you for a continuous manifestation of the good cheer, the sympathy, the ready wit, the comradeship, or the inspiration you once showed yourself capable of. Bear figs for a season or two, and the world outside the orchard is very unwilling you should bear thistles.

The effect of the Burches' visit on Rebecca is not easily described. Nevertheless, as she looked back upon it from the vantage-ground of after-years she felt that the moment when Mr. Burch asked her to "lead in prayer" marked an epoch in her life.

If you have ever observed how courteous and gracious and mannerly you feel when you don a beautiful new frock; if you have ever noticed the feeling of reverence stealing over you when you close your eyes, clasp your hands, and bow your head; if you have ever watched your sense of repulsion toward a fellow-creature melt a little under the exercise of daily politeness — you may understand how the adoption of the outward and visible sign has some strange influence in developing the inward and spiritual state of which it is the expression.

It is only when one has grown old and dull that the soul is heavy and refuses to rise. The young soul is ever wingèd; a breath stirs it to an upward flight. Rebecca was asked to bear witness to a state of mind or feeling of whose existence she had only the vaguest consciousness. She obeyed; and as she uttered words they became true in the uttering – as she voiced aspirations they settled into realities.

As "dove that to its window flies," her spirit soared towards a great light, dimly discovered at first, but brighter as she came closer to it. To become sensible of oneness with the Divine heart before any sense of separation has been felt, this is surely the most beautiful way for the child to find God.

CHAPTER TWENTY-ONE

THE SKY-LINE WIDENS

~

The time so long and eagerly waited for had come, and Rebecca was a student at Wareham. Persons who had enjoyed the social bewilderments and advantages of foreign courts, or had mingled freely in the intellectual circles of great universities, might not have looked upon Wareham as an extraordinary experience; but it was as much of an advance upon Riverboro as that village had been upon Sunnybrook Farm. Rebecca's intention was to complete the four years' course in three, as it was felt by all the parties concerned that, when she had attained the ripe age of seventeen, she must be ready to earn her own living, and help in the education of the younger children. While she was wondering how this could be successfully accomplished, some of the other girls were cogitating as to how they could meander through the four years, and come out at the end knowing no more than at the beginning. This would seem a difficult, well-nigh an impossible task; but it can be achieved, and has been, at other seats of learning than modest little Wareham.

Rebecca was to go to and fro on the cars daily from September to Christmas, and then board in Wareham during the three coldest months. Emma Jane's parents had always thought that a year or two in the Edgewood High School (three miles from Riverboro) would serve every purpose for their daughter, and send her into the world with as fine an intellectual polish as she could well sustain. Emma Jane had hitherto heartily concurred in this opinion, for, if there was any one thing that she detested, it was the learning of lessons. One book was as bad as another in her eyes, and she could have seen the libraries of the world sinking into ocean depths and have eaten her dinner cheerfully the while; but matters assumed a different complexion when she was sent to Edgewood and Rebecca to Wareham. She bore it for a week — seven endless days of absence from the beloved object, whom she could see only in the evenings when both were busy with their lessons. Sunday offered an opportunity to put the matter before her father, who proved obdurate. He didn't believe in education, and thought she had full enough already. He never intended to keep up "blacksmithing" for good when he leased his farm and came into Riverboro, but proposed to go back to it presently, and by that time Emma Jane would have finished school, and would be ready to help her mother with the dairy work.

Another week passed. Emma Jane pined visibly and audibly. Her colour faded, and her appetite (at table) dwindled almost to nothing.

Her mother alluded plaintively to the fact that the Perkinses had a habit of going into declines; that she'd always feared that Emma Jane's complexion was too beautiful to be healthy; that some men would be proud of having an ambitious daughter, and be glad to give her the best advantages; that she feared the daily journeys to Edgewood were going to be too much for her own health, and Mr. Perkins would have to hire a boy to drive Emma Jane; and, finally, that when a girl had such a passion for learning as Emma Jane, it seemed almost like wickedness to cross her will.

Mr. Perkins bore this for several days, until his temper, digestion, and appetite were all sensibly affected; then he bowed his head to the inevitable, and Emma Jane flew, like a captive set free, to the loved one's bower. Neither did her courage flag, although it was put to terrific tests when she entered the academic groves of Wareham. She passed in only two subjects, but went cheerfully into the preparatory department with her five "conditions," intending to let the steam of education play gently over her mental surfaces, and not get any wetter than she could help. It is not possible to blink the truth that Emma Jane was dull; but a dogged, unswerving loyalty, and the gift of devoted, unselfish loving — these, after all, are talents of a sort, and may possibly be of as much value in the world as a sense of numbers or a faculty for languages.

Wareham was a pretty village with a broad main street shaded by great maples and elms. It had an apothecary, a blacksmith, a plumber, several shops of one sort and another, two churches, and many boarding-houses; but all its interests gathered about its seminary and its academy. These seats of learning were neither better nor worse than others of their kind, but differed much in efficiency, according as the principal who chanced to be at the head was a man of power and inspiration or the reverse. There were boys and girls gathered from all parts of the county and State, and they were of every kind and degree as to birth, position in the world, wealth or poverty. There was an opportunity for a deal of foolish and imprudent behaviour, but on the whole surprisingly little advantage was taken of it. Among the third and fourth year students there was a certain amount of going to and from the trains in couples; some carrying of heavy books up the hill by the sterner sex for their feminine schoolmates, and occasional bursts of silliness on the part of heedless and precocious girls, among whom was Huldah Meserve. She was friendly enough with Emma Jane and Rebecca, but grew less and less intimate as time went on. She was extremely pretty, with a profusion of auburn hair and a few very tiny freckles, to which she constantly alluded, as no one could possibly detect them without noting her porcelain skin and her curling lashes. She had merry eyes, a somewhat too plump figure for her years, and was popularly supposed to have a fascinating way with her. Riverboro being poorly furnished with beaux, she intended to have as good a time during her four years at Wareham as circumstances would permit. Her idea of pleasure was an ever-changing circle of admirers to fetch and carry for her, the more publicly the better; incessant chaff and laughter and vivacious conversation, made eloquent and effective by arch looks and telling glances. She had a habit of confiding her conquests to less fortunate girls and bewailing the incessant havoc and damage she was doing — a damage she avowed herself as innocent of, in intention, as any new-born lamb. It does not take much of this sort of thing to wreck an ordinary friendship, so before long Rebecca and Emma Jane sat in one end of the railway train in going to and from Riverboro, and Huldah occupied the other with her court. Sometimes this was brilliant beyond words, including a certain youthful Monte Cristo, who on Fridays expended thirty cents on a round trip ticket and travelled from Wareham to Riverboro merely to be near Huldah; sometimes, too, the circle was reduced to the popcorn-and-peanut boy of the train, who seemed to serve every purpose in default of better game.

Rebecca was in the normally unconscious state that belonged to her years; boys were good comrades, but no more; she liked reciting in the same class with them — everything seemed to move better; but from vulgar and precocious flirtations she was protected by her ideals. There was little in the lads she had met thus far to awaken her fancy, for it habitually fed on better meat. Huldah's school-girl romances, with their wealth of commonplace detail, were not the stuff her dreams were made of, when dreams did flutter across the sensitive plate of her mind.

Among the teachers at Wareham was one who influenced Rebecca profoundly, Miss Emily Maxwell, with whom she studied English literature and composition. Miss Maxwell, as the niece of one of Maine's ex-governors and the daughter of one of Bowdoin's professors, was the most remarkable personality in Wareham, and that her few years of teaching happened to be in Rebecca's time was the happiest of all chances. There was no indecision or delay in the establishment of their relations; Rebecca's heart flew like an arrow to its mark, and her mind, meeting its superior, settled at once into an abiding attitude of respectful homage.

It was rumored that Miss Maxwell "wrote," which word, when uttered in a certain tone, was understood to mean not that a person had command of penmanship, Spencerian or otherwise, but that she had appeared in print.

"You'll like her; she writes," whispered Huldah to Rebecca the first morning at prayers, where the faculty sat in an imposing row on the front seats. "She writes; and I call her stuck up."

Nobody seemed possessed of exact information with which to satisfy the hungry mind, but there was believed to be at least one person in existence who had seen, with his own eyes, an essay by Miss Maxwell in a magazine. This height of achievement made Rebecca somewhat shy of her, but she looked her admiration, something that most of the class could never do with the unsatisfactory organs of vision given them by Mother Nature. Miss Maxwell's glance was always meeting a pair of eager dark eyes; when she said anything particularly good, she looked for approval to the corner of the second bench, where every shade of feeling she wished to evoke was reflected on a certain sensitive young face.

One day, when the first essay of the class was under discussion, she asked each new pupil to bring her some composition written during the year before, that she might judge the work, and know precisely with what material she had to deal. Rebecca lingered after the others, and approached the desk shyly.

"I haven't any compositions here, Miss Maxwell, but I can find one when I go home on Friday. They are packed away in a box in the attic."

"Carefully tied with pink and blue ribbons?" asked Miss MAxwell, with a whimsical smile.

"No," answered Rebecca, shaking her head decidedly; "I wanted to use ribbons, because all the other girls did, and they looked so pretty, but I used to tie my essays with twine strings on purpose; and the one on 'Solitude' I fastened with an old shoe-lacing just to show it what I thought of it."

"'Solitude'!" laughed Miss Maxwell, raising her eyebrows. "Did you choose your own subject?"

"No; Miss Dearborn thought we were not old enough to find good ones."

"What were some of the others?"

"'Fireside Reveries,' 'Grant as a Soldier,' 'Reflections on the Life of P. T. Barnum,' 'Buried Cities'; I can't remember any more now. They were all bad, and I can't bear to show them; I can write poetry easier and better, Miss Maxwell."

"Poetry!" she exclaimed. "Did Miss Dearborn require you to do it?"

"Oh no; I always did it, even at the farm. Shall I bring all I have? It isn't much."

Rebecca took the blank-book in which she kept copies of her effusions and left it at Miss Maxwell's door, hoping that she might be asked in and thus obtain a private interview; but a servant answered her ring, and she could only walk away, disappointed.

A few days afterwards she saw the black-covered book on Miss Maxwell's desk, and knew that the dreaded moment of criticism had come, so she was not surprised to be asked to remain after class.

The room was quiet; the red leaves rustled in the breeze and flew in at the open window, bearing the first compliments of the season. Miss Maxwell came and sat by Rebecca's side on the bench.

"Did you think these were good?" she asked, giving her the verses.

"Not so very," confessed Rebecca; "but it's hard to tell all by yourself. The Perkinses and the Cobbs always said they were wonderful, but when Mrs. Cobb told me she thought they were better than Mr. Longfellow's I was worried, because I knew that couldn't be true."

This ingenuous remark confirmed Miss Maxwell's opinion of Rebecca as a girl who could hear the truth and profit by it.

"Well, my child," she said smilingly, "your friends were wrong and you were right; judged by the proper tests, they are pretty bad."

"Then I must give up all hope of ever being a writer!" sighed Rebecca, who was tasting the bitterness of hemlock and wondering if she could keep the tears back until the interview was over.

"Don't go so fast," interrupted Miss Maxwell. "Though they don't amount to anything as poetry, they show a good deal of promise in certain directions. You almost never make a mistake in rhyme or metre, and this shows you have a natural sense of what is right; a 'sense of form,' poets would call it. When you grow older, have a little more experience – in fact, when you have something to say, I think you may write very good verses. Poetry needs knowledge and vision, experience and imagination, Rebecca. You have not the first three yet, but I rather think you have a touch of the last."

"Must I never try any more poetry, not even to amuse myself?"

"Certainly you may; it will only help you to write better prose. Now for the first composition. I am going to ask all the new students to write a letter giving some description of the town and a hint of the school life."

"Shall I have to be myself?" asked Rebecca.

"What do you mean?"

"A letter from Rebecca Randall to her sister Hannah at Sunnybrook Farm, or to her aunt Jane at the brick house, Riverboro, is so dull and stupid, if it is a real letter; but if I could make believe I was a different girl altogether, and write to somebody who would be sure to understand everything I said, I could make it nicer."

"Very well; I think that's a delightful plan," said Miss Maxwell; "and whom will you suppose yourself to be?"

"I like heiresses very much," replied Rebecca contemplatively. "Of course I never saw one, but interesting things are always happening to heiresses, especially to the golden-haired kind. My heiress wouldn't be vain and haughty like the wicked sisters in Cinderella; she would be noble and generous. She would give up a grand school in Boston because she wanted to come here where her father lived when he was a boy, long before he made his fortune. The father is dead now, and she has a guardian, the best and kindest man in the world; he is rather old of course, and sometimes very quiet and grave, but sometimes when he is happy he is full of fun, and then Evelyn is not afraid of him. Yes, the girl shall be called Evelyn Abercombie, and her guardian's name shall be Mr. Adam Ladd."

"Do you know Mr. Ladd?" asked Miss Maxwell in surprise.

"Yes, he's my very best friend," cried Rebecca delightedly. "Do you know him, too?"

"Oh yes; he is a trustee of these schools, you know, and often comes here. But if I let you 'suppose' any more, you will tell me your whole letter, and then I shall lose a pleasant surprise."

What Rebecca thought of Miss Maxwell we already know; how the teacher regarded the pupil may be gathered from the following letter written two or three months later:

> "Wareham,
> "December I.

"My dear Father,

"As you well know, I have not always been an enthusiast on the subject of teaching. The task of cramming knowledge into these self-sufficient, inefficient youngsters of both sexes discourages me at times. The more stupid they are, the less they are aware of it. If my department were geography or mathematics, I believe I should feel that I was accomplishing something, for in those branches application and industry work wonders; but in English literature and composition one yearns for brains, for appreciation, for imagination. Month after month I toil on, opening oyster after oyster, but seldom finding a pearl. Fancy my joy this term when, without any violent effort at shell-splitting, I came upon a rare pearl — a black one, but of satin skin and beautiful lustre! Her name is Rebecca, and she looks not unlike Rebekah at the well in our family Bible, her hair and eyes being so dark as to suggest a strain of Italian or Spanish blood. She is nobody in particular. Man has done nothing for her. She has no family to speak of, no money, no education worthy the name, has had no advantages of any sort; but Dame Nature flung herself into the breach and said:

> *'This child I to myself will take;*
> *She shall be mine, and I will make*
> *A Lady of my own.'*

Blessed Wordsworth! How he makes us understand! And the pearl never heard of him until now! Think of reading 'Lucy' to a class, and when you finish, seeing a fourteen-year-old pair of lips quivering with delight, and a pair of eyes brimming with comprehending tears!

"You poor darling! You, too, know the discouragement of sowing lovely seed in rocky earth, in sand, in water, and (it almost seems sometimes) in mud, knowing that if anything comes up at all it will be some poor starveling plant. Fancy the joy of finding a real mind – of dropping seed in a soil so warm, so fertile, that one knows there are sure to be foliage, blossoms, and fruit all in good time! I wish I were not so impatient and so greedy of results. I am not fit to be a teacher; no one is who is so scornful of stupidity as I am. . . . The pearl writes quaint, countrified little verses – doggerel they are; but somehow or other she always contrives to put in one line, one thought, one image, that shows you she is, quite unconsciously to herself, in possession of the secret. . . . Good-bye; I'll bring Rebecca home with me some Friday, and let you and mother see her for yourself.

"Your affectionate daughter,

"Emily."

CHAPTER TWENTY-TWO

CLOVER BLOSSOMS
AND SUNFLOWERS
~

"How d'ye do, girls?" said Huldah Meserve, peeping in at the door. "Can you stop studying a minute and show me your room? Say, I've just been down to the store and bought me these gloves, for I was bound I wouldn't wear mittens this winter; they're simply too countrified. It's your first year here, and you're younger than I am, so I s'pose you don't mind, but I simply suffer if I don't keep too 'cute for words! I don't believe any of the others can begin to compare with it! I don't know what gives it that simply gorgeous look – whether it's the full curtains, or that elegant screen, or Rebecca's lamp – but you certainly do have a faculty for fixing up. I like a pretty room, too, but I never have a minute to attend to mine; I'm always so busy on my clothes that half the time I don't get my bed made up till noon; and, after all, having no callers but the girls, it don't make much difference. When I graduate, I'm going to fix up our parlour at home so it'll be simply regal. I've learned decalcomania, and after I take up lustre-painting, I shall have it simply stiff with drapes and tidies and plaques and sofa-pillows, and make mother let me have a fire, and receive my friends there evenings. May I dry my feet at your register? I can't bear to wear rubbers unless the mud or the slush is simply knee-deep; they make your feet look so awfully big. I had such a fuss getting this pair of French-heeled boots that I don't intend to spoil the looks of them with rubbers any oftener than I can help. I believe boys notice feet quicker than anything. Elmer Webster stepped on one of mine yesterday, when I accidentally had it out in the aisle, and when he apologized after class, he said he wasn't so much to blame, for the foot was so little he really couldn't see it! Isn't he perfectly great? Of course, that's only his way of talking, for, after all, I only wear a number two; but these French heels and pointed toes do certainly make your foot look smaller, and it's always said a high instep helps, too. I used to think mine was almost a deformity, but they say it's a great beauty. Just put your feet beside mine, girls, and look at the difference; not that I care much, but just for fun."

"My feet are very comfortable where they are," responded Rebecca dryly. "I can't stop to measure insteps on algebra days. I've noticed your habit of keeping a foot in the aisle ever since you had those new shoes, so I don't wonder it was stepped on."

"Perhaps I am a little mite conscious of them, because they're not so very comfortable at first, till you get them broken in. Say, haven't you got a lot of new things?"

"Our Christmas presents, you mean," said Emma Jane. "The pillow-cases are from Mrs. Cobb, the rug from Cousin Mary in North Riverboro, the scrap-basket from Living and Dick. We gave each other the bureau and cushion covers, and the screen is mine from Mr. Ladd."

"Well, you were lucky when you met him! Gracious! I wish I could meet somebody like that. The way he keeps it up, too! It just hides your bed, doesn't it? And I always say that a bed takes the style off any room, specially when it's not made up, though you have an alcove, and it's the only one in the whole building. I don't see how you managed to get this good room when you're such new scholars," she finished discontentedly.

"We shouldn't have, except that Ruth Berry had to go away suddenly on account of her father's death. This room was empty, and Miss Maxwell asked if we might have it," returned Emma Jane.

"The great and only Max is more stiff and standoffish than ever this year," said Huldah, "I've simply given up trying to please her, for there's no justice in her; she is good to her favourites, but she doesn't pay the least attention to anybody else, except to make sarcastic speeches about things that are none of her business. I wanted to tell her yesterday it was her place to teach me Latin, not manners."

"I wish you wouldn't talk against Miss Maxwell to me," said Rebecca hotly. "You know how I feel."

"I know; but I can't understand how you can abide her."

"I not only abide her, I love her!" exclaimed Rebecca. "I wouldn't let the sun shine too hot on her, or the wind blow too cold. I'd like to put a marble platform in her class-room, and have her sit in a velvet chair behind a golden table."

"Well, don't have a fit, because she can sit where she likes for all of me. I've got something better to think of;" and Huldah tossed her head.

"Isn't this your study hour?" asked Emma Jane, to stop possible discussion.

"Yes; but I lost my Latin grammar yesterday. I left it in the hall half an hour while I was having a regular scene with Herbert Dunn. I haven't spoken to him for a week, and gave him back his class pin. He was simply furious. Then, when I came back to the hall, the book was gone. I had to go down town for my gloves, and to the principal's office to see if the grammar had been handed in, and that's the reason I'm so fine."

Huldah was wearing a woollen dress that had once been gray, but had been dyed a brilliant blue. She had added three rows of white braid and large white pearl buttons to her gray jacket in order to make it a little more "dressy." Her gray felt hat had a white feather on it, and a white tissue veil with large black dots made her delicate skin look brilliant. Rebecca thought how lovely the knot of red hair looked under the hat behind, and how the colour of the front had been dulled by incessant frizzing with curling-irons. Her open jacket disclosed a galaxy of souvenirs pinned to the background of bright blue – a small American flag, a button of the Wareham Rowing Club, and one or two society pins. These decorations proved her popularity in very much the same way as do the cotillion favors hanging on the bedroom walls of the fashionable belle. She had been pinning and unpinning, arranging and disarranging her veil, ever since she entered the room, in the hope that the girls would ask her whose ring she was wearing this week; but although both had noticed the new ornament instantly, wild horses could not have drawn the question from them, her desire to be asked was too obvious. With her gay plumage, her "nods and becks and wreathèd smiles," and her cheerful cackle, Huldah closely resembled the parrot in Wordsworth's poem:

> *"Arch, volatile, a sportive bird,*
> *By social glee inspired;*
> *Ambitious to be seen or heard,*
> *And pleased to be admired!"*

"Mr. Morrison thinks the grammar will be returned, and lent me another," Huldah continued. "He was rather snippy about my leaving a book in the hall. There was a perfectly elegant gentleman in the office, a stranger to me. I wish he was a new teacher, but there's no such luck. He was too young to be the father of any of the girls and too old to be a brother, but he was handsome as a picture, and had on an awful stylish suit of clothes. He looked at me about every minute I was in the room. It made me so embarrassed, I couldn't hardly answer Mr. Morrison's questions straight."

"You'll have to wear a mask pretty soon, if you're going to have any comfort, Huldah," said Rebecca. "Did he offer to lend you his class pin, or has it been so long since he graduated that he's left off wearing it? And tell us now whether the principal asked for a lock of your hair to put in his watch?"

This was all said merrily and laughingly, but there were times when Huldah could scarcely make up her mind whether Rebecca was trying to be witting or whether she was jealous; but she generally decided it was merely the latter feeling, rather natural in a girl who had little attention.

"He wore no jewellery but a cameo scarf-pin and a perfectly gorgeous ring — a queer kind of one that wound round and round his finger. Oh dear, I must run! Where has the hour gone? There's the study bell!"

Rebecca had pricked up her ears at Huldah's speech. She remembered a certain strange ring, and it belonged to the only person in the world (save Miss Maxwell) who appealed to her imagination, Mr. Aladdin. Her feeling for him and that of Emma Jane was a mixture of romantic and reverent admiration for the man himself, and the liveliest gratitude for his beautiful gifts. Since they first met him, not a Christmas had gone by without some remembrance for them both — remembrances chosen with the rarest taste and fore-thought. Emma Jane had seen him only twice, but he had called several times at the brick house, and Rebecca had learned to know him better. It was she, too, who always wrote the notes of acknowledgment and thanks, taking infinite pains to make Emma Jane's quite different from her own. Sometimes he had written from Boston and asked her the news of Riverboro, and she had sent him pages of quaint and childlike gossip, interspersed on two occasions with poetry, which he read and reread with infinite relish. If Huldah's stranger should be Mr. Aladdin, would he come to see her? and could she and Emma Jane show him their beautiful room with so many of his gifts in evidence?

When the girls had established themselves in Wareham as real boarding pupils, it seemed to them existence was as full of joy as it well could hold. This first winter was, in fact, the most tranquilly happy of Rebecca's school life — a winter long to be looked back upon. She and Emma Jane were room-mates, and had put their modest possessions together to make their surroundings pretty and homelike. The room had, to begin with, a cheerful red ingrain carpet and a set of maple furniture. As to the rest, Rebecca had furnished the ideas, and Emma Jane the materials and labor, a method of dividing responsibilities that seemed to suit the circumstances admirably. Mrs. Perkins' father had been a storekeeper, and on his death had left the goods of which he was possessed to his married daughter. The molasses, vinegar, and kerosene, had lasted the family for five years, and the Perkins' attic was still a treasurehouse of ginghams, cottons, and "Yankee notions." So at Rebecca's instigation Mrs. Perkins had made full curtains and lambrequins of unbleached muslin, which she had trimmed and looped back with bands of Turkey-red cotton. There were two table-covers to match, and each of the girls had her study corner. Rebecca, after much coaxing, had been allowed to bring over her precious lamp, which would have given a luxurious air to any apartment, and when Mr. Aladdin's last Christmas presents were added — the Japanese screen for Emma Jane and the little shelf of English poets for Rebecca — they declared that it was all quite as much fun as being married and going to house-keeping.

The day of Huldah's call was Friday, and on Fridays from three to half-past four Rebecca was free to take a pleasure to which she looked forward the entire week. She always ran down the snowy path through the pine-woods at the back of the seminary, and coming out on a quiet village street, went directly to the large white house where Miss Maxwell lived. The maid-of-all-work answered her knock; she took off her hat and cape and hung them in the hall, put her rubber shoes and umbrella carefully in the corner, and then opened the door of paradise. Miss Maxwell's sitting-room was lined on two sides with bookshelves, and Rebecca was allowed to sit before the fire and browse among the books to her heart's delight for an hour or more. Then Miss Maxwell would come back from her class, and there would be a precious half-hour of chat before Rebecca had to meet Emma Jane at the station and take the train for Riverboro, where her Saturdays and Sundays were spent, and where she was washed, ironed, mended, and examined, approved and reproved, warned and advised in quite sufficient quantity to last her the succeeding week.

On this Friday she buried her face in the blooming geraniums on Miss Maxwell's plant-stand, selected "Romola" from one of the bookcases, and sank into a seat by the window with a sigh of infinite content. She glanced at the clock now and then, remembering the day on which she had been so immersed in "David Copperfield" that the Riverboro train had no place in her mind. The distracted Emma Jane had refused to leave without her, and had run from the station to look for her at Miss Maxwell's. There was but one later train, and that went only to a place three miles the other side of Riverboro, so that the two girls appeared at their respective homes long after dark, having had a weary walk in the snow.

When she had read for half an hour she glanced out of the window and saw two figures issuing from the path through the woods. The knot of bright hair and the coquettish hat could belong to but one person; and her companion, as the couple approached, proved to be none other than Mr. Aladdin. Huldah was lifting her skirts daintily and picking safe stepping-places for the high-heeled shoes, her cheeks glowing, her eyes sparkling under the black and white veil.

Rebecca slipped from her post by the window to the rug before the bright fire and leaned her head on the seat of the great easy-chair. She was frightened at the storm in her heart, at the suddenness with which it had come on as well as at the strangeness of an entirely new sensation. She felt all at once as if she could not bear to give up her share of Mr. Aladdin's friendship to Huldah – Huldah so bright, saucy, and pretty; so gay and ready, and such good company. She had always joyfully admitted Emma Jane into the precious partnership, but perhaps unconsciously to herself she had realized that Emma Jane had never held anything but a secondary place in Mr. Aladdin's regard; yet who was she herself, after all, that she could hope to be first?

Suddenly the door opened softly and somebody looked in, somebody who said: "Miss Maxwell told me I should find Miss Rebecca Randall here."

Rebecca started at the sound and sprang to her feet, saying joyfully, "Mr. Aladdin! Oh! I knew you were in Wareham, and I was afraid you wouldn't have time to come and see us."

"Who is 'us'? The aunts are not here, are they? Oh, you mean the rich blacksmith's daughter, whose name I can never remember. Is she here?"

"Yes, and my room-mate," answered Rebecca, who thought her own knell of doom had sounded, if he had forgotten Emma Jane's name.

The light in the room grew softer, the fire crackled cheerily, and they talked of many things, until the old sweet sense of friendliness and familiarity crept back into Rebecca's heart. Adam had not seen her for several months, and there was much to be learned about school matters as viewed from her own standpoint; he had already inquired concerning her progress from Mr. Morrison.

"Well, little Miss Rebecca," he said, rousing himself at length, "I must be thinking of my drive to Portland. There is a meeting of railway directors there to-morrow, and I always take this opportunity of visiting the school and giving my valuable advice concerning its affairs educational and financial."

"It seems funny for you to be a school trustee," said Rebecca contemplatively. "I can't seem to make it fit."

"You are a remarkably wise young person, and I quite agree with you," he answered; "the fact is," he added soberly, "I accepted the trusteeship in memory of my poor little mother, whose last happy years were spent here."

"That was a long time ago!"

"Let me see, I am thirty-two – only thirty-two, despite an occasional gray hair. My mother was married a month after she graduated, and she lived only until I was ten; yes, it is a long way back to my mother's time here, though the school was fifteen or twenty years old then, I believe. Would you like to see my mother, Miss Rebecca?"

The girl took the leather case gently and opened it to find an innocent, pink-and-white daisy of a face, so confiding, so sensitive, that it went straight to the heart. It made Rebecca feel old, experienced, and maternal. She longed on the instant to comfort and strengthen such a tender young thing.

"Oh, what a sweet, sweet, flowery face!" she whispered softly.

"The flower had to bear all sorts of storms," said Adam gravely. "The bitter weather of the world bent its slender stalk, bowed its head, and dragged it to the earth. I was only a child, and could do nothing to protect and nourish it, and there was no one else to stand between it and trouble. Now I have success and money and power, all that would have kept her alive and happy, and it is too late. She died for lack of love and care, nursing and cherishing, and I can never forget it. All that has come to me seems now and then so useless, since I cannot share it with her!"

This was a new Mr. Aladdin, and Rebecca's heart gave a throb of sympathy and comprehension. This explained the tired look in his eyes, the look that peeped out now and then, under all his gay speech and laughter.

"I'm so glad I know," she said, "and so glad I could see her just as she was when she tied that white muslin hat under her chin and saw her yellow curls and her sky-blue eyes in the glass. Mustn't she have been happy! I wish she could have been kept so, and had lived to see you grow up strong and good. My mother is always sad and busy, but once when she looked at John I heard her say, 'He makes up for everything.' That's what your mother would have thought about you if she had lived, and perhaps she does as it is."

"You are a comforting little person, Rebecca," said Adam, rising from his chair.

As Rebecca rose, the tears still trembling on her lashes, he looked at her suddenly as with new vision.

"Good-bye!" he said, taking her slim brown hands in his, adding, as if he saw her for the first time, "Why, little Rose-Red-Snow-White is making way for a new girl! Burning the midnight oil and doing four years' work in three is supposed to dull the eye and blanch the cheek, yet Rebecca's eyes are bright, and she has a rosy color! Her long braids are looped one on the other so that they make a black letter U behind, and they are tied with grand bows at the top! She is so tall that she reaches almost to my shoulder. This will never do in the world! How will Mr. Aladdin get on without his comforting little friend? He doesn't like grown-up young ladies in long trains and wonderful fine clothes; they frighten and bore him!"

"Oh, Mr. Aladdin!" cried Rebecca eagerly, taking his jest quite seriously, "I am not fifteen yet, and it will be three years before I'm a young lady; please don't give me up until you have to!"

"I won't; I promise you that," said Adam. "Rebecca," he continued, after a moment's pause, "who is that young girl with a lot of pretty red hair and very citified manners? She escorted me down the hill; do you know whom I mean?"

"It must be Huldah Meserve; she is from Riverboro."

Adam put a finger under Rebecca's chin and looked into her eyes — eyes as soft, as clear, as unconscious and childlike as they had been when she was ten. He remembered the other pair of challenging blue eyes that had darted coquettish glances through half-dropped lids, shot arrowy beams from under archly-lifted brows, and said gravely: "Don't form yourself on her, Rebecca. Clover blossoms that grow in the fields beside Sunnybrook mustn't be tied in the same bouquet with gaudy sunflowers; they are too sweet and fragrant and wholesome."

CHAPTER TWENTY-THREE

THE HILL DIFFICULTY

~

The first happy year at Wareham, with its widened sky-line, its larger vision, its greater opportunity, was over and gone. Rebecca had studied during the summer vacation, and had passed, on her return in the autumn, certain examinations which would enable her, if she carried out the same programme the next season, to complete the course in three instead of four years. She came off with no flying colors – that would have been impossible in consideration of her inadequate training; but she did wonderfully well in some of the required subjects, and so brilliantly in others that the average was respectable. She would never have been a remarkable scholar under any circumstances, perhaps, and she was easily outstripped in mathematics and the natural sciences by a dozen girls, but in some inexplicable way she became, as the months went on, the foremost figure in the school. When she had entirely forgotten the facts which would enable her to answer a question fully and conclusively, she commonly had some original theory to expound; it was not always correct, but it was generally unique and sometimes amusing. She was only fair in Latin or French grammar, but when it came to translation, her freedom, her choice of words, and her sympathetic understanding of the spirit of the text made her the delight of her teachers and the despair of her rivals.

"She can be perfectly ignorant of a subject," said Miss Maxwell to Adam Ladd, "but entirely intelligent the moment she has a clue. Most of the other girls are full of information and as stupid as sheep."

Rebecca's gifts had not been discovered, save by the few, during the first year, when she was adjusting herself quietly to the situation. She was distinctly one of the poorer girls; she had no fine dresses to attract attention, no visitors, no friends in the town. She had more study hours, and less time, therefore, for the companionship of other girls, gladly as she would have welcomed the gaiety of that side of school life. Still, water will find its own level in some way, and by the spring of the second year she had naturally settled into the same sort of leadership which had been hers in the smaller community of Riverboro. She was unanimously elected assistant editor of the *Wareham School Pilot*, being the first girl to assume that enviable though somewhat arduous and thankless position, and when her maiden number went to the Cobbs, Uncle Jerry and Aunt Sarah could hardly eat or sleep for pride.

"She'll always get votes," said Huldah Meserve when discussing the election, "for whether she knows anything or not, she looks as if she did, and whether she's capable of filling an office or not, she looks as if she was. I only wish I was tall and dark, and had the gift of making people believe I was great things, like Rebecca Randall. There's one thing; though the boys call her handsome, you notice they don't trouble her with much attention."

It was a fact that Rebecca's attitude towards the opposite sex was still somewhat indifferent and oblivious, even for fifteen and a half! No one could look at her and doubt that she had potentialities of attraction latent within her somewhere, but that side of her nature was happily biding its time. A human being is capable only of a certain amount of activity at a given moment, and it will inevitably satisfy first its most pressing needs, its most ardent desires, its chief ambitions. Rebecca was full of small anxieties and fears, for matters were not going well at the brick house, and were anything but hopeful at the home farm. She was overbusy and overtaxed, and her thoughts were naturally drawn towards the difficult problems of daily living.

It had seemed to her during the autumn and winter of that year as if her Aunt Miranda had never been, save at the very first, so censorious and so fault-finding. One Saturday Rebecca ran upstairs, and, bursting into a flood of tears, exclaimed: "Aunt Jane, it seems as if I never could stand her continual scoldings. Nothing I can do suits Aunt Miranda. She's just said it will take me my whole life to get the Randall out of me, and I'm not convinced that I want it all out, so there we are!"

Aunt Jane, never demonstrative, cried with Rebecca as she attempted to soothe her.

"You must be patient," she said, wiping first her own eyes and then Rebecca's. "I haven't told you, for it isn't fair you should be troubled when you're studying so hard, but your Aunt Miranda isn't well. One Monday morning about a month ago she had a kind of faint spell; it wasn't bad, but the doctor is afraid it was a shock, and if so, it's the beginning of the end. Seems to me she's failing right along, and that's what makes her so fretful and easy vexed. She has other troubles, too, that you don't know anything about, and if you're not kind to your Aunt Miranda now, child, you'll be dreadful sorry some time."

All the temper faded from Rebecca's face, and she stopped crying to say penitently: "Oh, the poor, dear thing! I won't mind a bit what she says now. She's just asked me for some milk-toast, and I was dreading to take it to her, but this will make everything different. Don't worry yet, Aunt Jane, for perhaps it won't be as bad as you think."

So when she carried the toast to her aunt a little later it was in the best gilt-edged china bowl, with a fringed napkin on the tray, and a sprig of geranium lying across the salt-cellar.

"Now, Aunt Miranda," she said cheerily, "I expect you to smack your lips and say this is good. It's not Randall, but Sawyer, milk-toast."

"You've tried all kinds on me one time an' another," Miranda answered. "This tastes real kind o' good; but I wish you hadn't wasted that nice geranium."

"You can't tell what's wasted," said Rebecca philosophically. "Perhaps that geranium has been hoping this long time it could brighten somebody's supper, so don't disappoint it by making believe you don't like it. I've seen geraniums cry — in the very early morning."

The mysterious trouble to which Jane had alluded was a very real one, but it was held in profound secrecy. Twenty-five hundred dollars of the small Sawyer property had been invested in the business of a friend of their father's, and had returned them a regular annual income of a hundred dollars. The family friend had been dead for some five years, but his son had succeeded to his interests, and all went on as formerly. Suddenly there came a letter saying that the firm had gone into bankruptcy, that the business had been completely wrecked, and that the Sawyer money had been swept away with everything else.

The loss of one hundred dollars a year is a very trifling matter, but it made all the difference between comfort and self-denial to the two old spinsters. Their manner of life had been so rigid and careful that it was difficult to economize any further, and the blow had fallen just when it was most inconvenient, for Rebecca's school and boarding expenses, small as they were, had to be paid promptly and in cash.

"Can we possibly go on doing it? Shan't we have to give up and tell her why?" asked Jane tearfully of the elder sister.

"We have put our hand to the plough, and we can't turn back," answered Miranda in her grimmest tone. "We've taken her away from her mother and offered her an education, and we've got to keep our word. She's Aurelia's only hope for years to come, to my way o' thinkin'. Hannah's beau takes all her time 'n' thought, and when she gits a husband her mother 'll be out o' sight and out o' mind. John, instead of farmin', thinks he must be a doctor – as if folks wasn't gettin' unhealthy enough these days without turnin' out more young doctors to help 'em into their graves. No, Jane; we'll skimp 'n' do without, 'n' plan to git along on our interest money somehow, but we won't break into our principal, whatever happens."

"Breaking into the principal" was, in the minds of most thrifty New England women, a sin only second to arson, theft, or murder; and though the rule was occasionally carried too far for common-sense – as in this case, where two elderly women of sixty might reasonably have drawn something from their little hoard in time of special need – it doubtless wrought more of good than evil in the community.

Rebecca, who knew nothing of their business affairs, merely saw her aunts grow more and more saving, pinching here and there, cutting off this and that relentlessly. Less meat and fish were bought; the woman who had lately been coming two days a week for washing, ironing, and scrubbing was dismissed; the old bonnets of the season before were brushed up and retrimmed; there were no drives to Moderation or trips to Portland. Economy was carried to its very extreme; but though Miranda was well-nigh as gloomy and uncompromising in her manner and conversation as a woman could well be, she at least never twitted her niece of being a burden. So Rebecca's share of the Sawyers' misfortunes consisted only in wearing her old dresses, hats, and jackets, without any apparent hope of a change.

There was, however, no concealing the state of things at Sunnybrook, where chapters of accidents had unfolded themselves in a sort of serial story that had run through the year. The potato crop had failed; there were no apples to speak of; the hay had been poor; Aurelia had turns of dizziness in her head; Mark had broken his ankle. As this was his fourth offence, Miranda inquired how many bones there were in the human body "so 't they'd know when Mark got through breakin' 'em." The time for paying the interest on the mortgage, that incubus that had crushed all the joy out of the Randall household, had come and gone, and there was no possibility, for the first time in fourteen years, of paying the required forty-eight dollars. The only bright spot in the horizon was Hannah's engagement to Will Melville, a young farmer whose land joined Sunnybrook, who had a good house, was alone in the world, and his own master. Hannah was so satisfied with her own unexpectedly radiant prospects that she hardly realized her mother's anxieties; for there are natures which flourish in adversity and deteriorate when exposed to sudden prosperity. She had made a visit of a week at the brick house; and Miranda's impression, conveyed in privacy to Jane, was that Hannah was close as the bark of a tree, and consid'able selfish too; that when she'd clim' as fur as she could in the world, she'd kick the ladder out from under her, everlastin' quick; that, on being sounded as to her ability to be of use to the younger children in the future, she said she guessed she'd done her share a'ready, and she wasn't goin' to burden Will with her poor relations. "She's Susan Randall through and through!" ejaculated Miranda. "I was glad to see her face turned towards Temperance. If that mortgage is ever cleared from the farm, 'twon't be Hannah that'll do it: it'll be Rebecca or me!"

Then there was the sleigh ride, during which she found her tongue, and chattered like any magpie. (Chapter Seventeen.)

"Then I must give up all hope of ever being a writer!"
sighed Rebecca. (Chapter Twenty-One.)

A haycart had been decked with green vines and bunches of long-stemmed field daisies.
(Chapter Twenty-Seven.)

"I look like a drudge," said Rebecca mysteriously, with laughing eyes, "but I really am a princess."
(Chapter Twenty-Nine.)

CHAPTER TWENTY-FOUR

ALADDIN RUBS HIS LAMP

~

"Your esteemed contribution entitled 'Wareham Wildflowers' has been accepted for the *Pilot*, Miss Perkins," said Rebecca, entering the room where Emma Jane was darning the firm's stockings. "I stayed to tea with Miss Maxwell, but came home early to tell you."

"You are joking, Becky!" faltered Emma Jane, looking up from her work.

"Not a bit; the senior editor read it and thought it highly instructive. It appears in the next issue."

"Not in the same number with your poem about the golden gates that close behind us when we leave school?" — and Emma Jane held her breath as she awaited the reply.

"Even so, Miss Perkins."

"Rebecca," said Emma Jane, with the nearest approach to tragedy that her nature would permit, "I don't know as I shall be able to bear it; and if anything happens to me, I ask you solemnly to bury that number of the *Pilot* with me."

Rebecca did not seem to think this the expression of an exaggerated state of feeling, inasmuch as she replied, "I know; that's just the way it seemed to me at first, and even now, whenever I'm alone and take out the *Pilot* back numbers to read over my contributions, I almost burst with pleasure; and it's not that they are good either, for they look worse to me every time I read them."

"If you would only live with me in some little house when we get older," mused Emma Jane, as, with her darning-needle poised in air, she regarded the opposite wall dreamily, "I would do the housework and cooking, and copy all your poems and stories, and take them to the post-office, and you needn't do anything but write. It would be perfectly elergant!"

"I'd like nothing better, if I hadn't promised to keep house for John," replied Rebecca.

"He won't have a house for a good many years, will he?"

"No," sighed Rebecca ruefully, flinging herself down by the table and resting her head on her hand. "Not unless we can contrive to pay off that detestable mortgage. The day grows farther off instead of nearer, now that we haven't paid the interest this year."

She pulled a piece of paper towards her, and scribbling idly on it, read aloud in a moment or two:

> *"Will you pay a little faster?" said the mortgage to the farm;*
> *"I confess I'm very tired of this place."*
> *"The weariness is mutual," Rebecca Randall cried;*
> *"I would I'd never gazed upon your face!"*

"A note has a 'face'," observed Emma Jane, who was gifted in arithmetic; "I didn't know that a mortgage had."

"Our mortgage has," said Rebecca revengefully. "I should know him if I met him in the dark. Wait, and I'll draw him for you. It will be good for you to know how he looks, and then when you have a husband and seven children you won't allow him to come anywhere within a mile of your farm."

The sketch when completed was of a sort to be shunned by a timid person on the verge of slumber. There was a tiny house on the right, and a weeping family gathered in front of it. The mortgage was depicted as a cross between a fiend and an ogre, and held an axe uplifted in his red right hand. A figure with streaming black locks was staying the blow, and this, Rebecca explained complacently, was intended as a likeness of herself, though she was rather vague as to the method she should use in attaining her end.

"He's terrible," said Emma Jane, "but awfully wizened and small."

"It's only a twelve hundred dollar mortgage," said Rebecca, "and that's called a small one. John saw a man once that was mortgaged for twelve thousand.'

"Shall you be a writer or an editor?" asked Emma Jane presently, as if one had only to choose and the thing were done.

"I shall have to do what turns up first, I suppose."

"Why not go out as a missionary to Syria, as the Burches are always coaxing you to? The Board would pay your expenses."

"I can't make up my mind to be a missionary," Rebecca answered. "I'm not good enough in the first place, and I don't 'feel a call,' as Mr. Burch says you must. I would like to do something for somebody, and make things move, somewhere; but I don't want to go thousands of miles away teaching people how to live when I haven't learned myself. It isn't as if the heathen really needed me; I'm sure they'll come out all right in the end."

"I can't see how, if all the people who ought to go out to save them stay at home as we do," argued Emma Jane.

"Why, whatever God is, and wherever he is, He must always be there, ready and waiting. He can't move about and miss people. It may take the heathen a little longer to find Him, but God will make allowances, of course. He knows if they live in such hot climates it must make them lazy and slow; and the parrots and tigers and snakes and bread-fruit trees distract their minds; and having no books, they can't think as well; but they'll find God somehow, some time."

"What if they die first?" asked Emma Jane.

"Oh, well, they can't be blamed for that; they don't die on purpose," said Rebecca, with a comfortable theology.

In these days Adam Ladd sometimes went to Temperance on business connected with the proposed branch of the railroad familiarly known as the "York and Yank 'em,' and while there he gained an inkling of Sunnybrook affairs. The building of the new road was not yet a certainty, and there was a difference of opinion as to the best route from Temperance to Plumville. In one event the way would lead directly through Sunnybrook, from corner to corner, and Mrs. Randall would be compensated; in the other, her interests would not be affected either for good or ill, save as all land in the immediate neighborhood might rise a little in value.

Coming from Temperance to Wareham one day, Adam had a long walk and talk with Rebecca, whom he thought looking pale and thin, though she was holding bravely to her self-imposed hours of work. She was wearing a black cashmere dress that had been her Aunt Jane's second-best. We are familiar with the heroine of romance whose foot is so exquisitely shaped that the coarsest shoe cannot conceal its perfections, and one always cherishes a doubt of the statement; yet it is true that Rebecca's peculiar and individual charm seemed wholly independent of accessories. The lines of her figure, the rare colouring of skin and hair and eyes, triumphed over shabby clothing, though, had the advantage of artistic apparel been given her, the little world of Wareham would probably at once have dubbed her a beauty. The long black braids were now disposed after a quaint fashion of her own. They were crossed behind, carried up to the front, and crossed again, the tapering ends finally brought down and hidden in the thicker part at the neck. Then a purely feminine touch was given to the hair that waved back from the face – a touch that rescued little crests and wavelets from bondage and set them free to take a new colour in the sun.

Adam Ladd looked at her in a way that made her put her hands over her face and laugh through them shyly as she said: "I know what you are thinking, Mr. Aladdin – that my dress is an inch longer than last year, and my hair different; but I'm not nearly a young lady yet – truly I'm not. Sixteen is a month off still, and you promised not to give me up till my dress trails. If you don't like me to grow old, why don't you grow young? Then we can meet in the halfway house and have nice times. Now that I think about it," she continued, "that's just what you've been doing all along. When you bought the soap, I thought you were Grandfather Sawyer's age; when you danced with me at the flag-raising, you seemed like my father; but when you showed me your mother's picture, I felt as if you were my John, because I was so sorry for you."

"That will do very well," smiled Adam – "unless you go so swiftly that you become my grandmother before I really need one. You are studying too hard, Miss Rebecca Rowena!"

"Just a little," she confessed. "But vacation comes soon, you know."

"And are you going to have a good rest and try to recover your dimples? They are really worth preserving."

A shadow crept over Rebecca's face and her eyes suffused. "Don't be kind, Mr. Aladdin; I can't bear it; it's – it's not one of my dimply days!" and she ran in at the seminary gate, and disappeared with a farewell wave of her hand.

Adam Ladd wended his way to the principal's office in a thoughtful mood. He had come to Wareham to unfold a plan that he had been considering for several days. This year was the fiftieth anniversary of the founding of the Wareham schools, and he meant to tell Mr. Morrison that, in addition to his gift of a hundred volumes to the reference library, he intended to celebrate it by offering prizes in English composition, a subject in which he was much interested. He wished the boys and girls of the two upper classes to compete; the award to be made to the writers of the two best essays. As to the nature of the prizes, he had not quite made up his mind, but they would be substantial ones, either of money or of books.

This interview accomplished, he called upon Miss Maxwell, thinking as he took the path through the woods: "Rose-Red-Snow-White needs the help; and since there is no way of my giving it to her without causing remark, she must earn it, poor little soul! I wonder if my money is always to be useless where most I wish to spend it."

He had scarcely greeted his hostess, when he said: "Miss Maxwell, doesn't it strike you that our friend Rebecca looks wretchedly tired?"

"She does indeed; and I am considering whether I can take her away with me. I always go South for the spring vacation, travelling by sea to Old Point Comfort, and rusticating in some quiet spot near by. I should like nothing better than to have Rebecca for a companion."

"The very thing!" assented Adam heartily. "But why should you take the whole responsibility? Why not let me help? I am greatly interested in the child, and have been for some years."

"You needn't pretend you discovered her," interrupted Miss Maxwell warmly, "for I did that myself."

"She was an intimate friend of mine long before you ever came to Wareham," laughed Adam; and he told Miss Maxwell the circumstances of his first meeting with Rebecca. "From the beginning I've tried to think of a way I could be useful in her development, but no reasonable solution seemed to offer itself."

"Luckily, she attends to her own development," answered Miss Maxwell. "In a sense she is independent of everything and everybody; she follows her saint without being conscious of it. But she needs a hundred practical things that money would buy for her, and, alas! I have a slender purse."

"Take mine, I beg; and let me act through you," pleaded Adam. "I could not bear to see even a young tree trying its best to grow without light or air – how much less a gifted child! I interviewed her aunts a year ago, hoping I might be permitted to give her a musical education. I assured them it was a most ordinary occurrence, and that I was willing to be repaid later on if they insisted; but it was no use. The elder Miss Sawyer remarked that no member of her family ever had lived on charity, and she guessed they wouldn't begin at this late day."

"I rather like that uncompromising New England grit," exclaimed Miss Maxwell; "and so far I don't regret one burden that Rebecca has borne or one sorrow that she has shared. Necessity has only made her brave; poverty has only made her daring and self-reliant. As to her present needs, there are certain things only a woman ought to do for a girl, and I should not like to have you do them for Rebecca; I should feel that I was wounding her pride and self-respect, even though she were ignorant. But there is no reason why I may not do them if necessary, and let you pay her travelling expenses. I would accept those for her without the sightest embarrassment, but I agree that the matter would better be kept private between us."

"You are a real fairy godmother!" exclaimed Adam, shaking her hand warmly. "Would it be less trouble for you to invite her room-mate, too – the pink-and-white inseparable?"

"No, thank you; I prefer to have Rebecca all to myself," said Miss Maxwell.

"I can understand that," replied Adam absent-mindedly. "I mean, of course, that one child is less trouble than two. There she is now."

Here Rebecca appeared in sight, walking down the quiet street with a lad of sixteen. They were in animated conversation, and were apparently reading something aloud to each other, for the black head and the curly brown one were both bent over a sheet of letter paper. Rebecca kept glancing up at her companion, her eyes sparkling with appreciation.

"Miss Maxwell," said Adam, "I am a trustee of this institution; but, upon my word, I don't believe in coeducation!"

"I have my own occasional hours of doubt," she answered; "but surely its disadvantages are reduced to a minimum with – children. That is a very impressive sight which you are privileged to witness, Mr. Ladd. The folk in Cambridge often gloated on the spectacle of Longfellow and Lowell arm-in-arm. The little school world of Wareham palpitates with excitement when it sees the senior and the junior editors of the *Pilot* walking together."

CHAPTER TWENTY-FIVE

ROSES OF JOY

~

The day before Rebecca started for the South with Miss Maxwell she was in the library with Emma Jane and Huldah, consulting dictionaries and encyclopædias. As they were leaving they passed the locked cases containing the library of fiction, open to the teachers and townspeople, but forbidden to the students.

They looked longingly through the glass, getting some little comfort from the titles of the volumes, as hungry children imbibe emotional nourishment from the pies and tarts inside a confectioner's window. Rebecca's eyes fell upon a new book in the corner, and she read the name aloud with delight: "'The Rose of Joy.' Listen, girls! isn't that lovely? 'The Rose of Joy.' It looks beautiful, and it sounds beautiful. What does it mean, I wonder?"

"I guess everybody has a different rose," said Huldah shrewdly. "I know what mine would be, and I'm not ashamed to own it. I'd like a year in a city, with just as much money as I wanted to spend, horses and splendid clothes, and amusements every minute of the day; and I'd like, above everything, to live with people that wear low necks." (Poor Huldah never took off her dress without bewailing the fact that her lot was cast in Riverboro, where her pretty white shoulders could never be seen.)

"That would be fun – for a while, anyway," Emma Jane remarked. "But wouldn't that be pleasure more than joy? Oh, I've got an idea!"

"Don't shriek so!" said the startled Huldah. "I thought it was a mouse."

"I don't have them very often," apologized Emma Jane – "ideas, I mean. This one shook me like a stroke of lightning. Rebecca, couldn't it be success?"

"That's good," mused Rebecca. "I can see that success would be a joy, but it doesn't seem to me like a rose, somehow. I was wondering if it could be love."

"I wish we could have a peep at the book; it must be perfectly elergant," said Emma Jane. "But now you say it is love, I think that's the best guess yet."

All day long the four words haunted and possessed Rebecca; she said them over to herself continually. Even the prosaic Emma Jane was affected by them, for in the evening she said: "I don't expect you to believe it, but I have another idea; that's two in one day. I had it while I was putting cologne on your head. The rose of joy might be helpfulness."

"If it is, then it is always blooming in your dear little heart, you darlingest, kind Emmie, taking such good care of your troublesome Becky!"

"Don't dare to call yourself troublesome! You're – you're – you're my rose of joy, that's what you are!" And the two girls hugged each other affectionately.

In the middle of the night Rebecca touched Emma Jane on the shoulder softly. "Are you very fast asleep, Emmie?" she whispered.

"Not so very," answered Emma Jane drowsily.

"I've thought of something new. If you sang, or painted, or wrote – not a little, but beautifully, you know – wouldn't the doing of it just as much as you wanted give you the rose of joy?"

"It might if it was a real talent," answered Emma Jane, "though I don't like it so well as love. If you have another thought, Becky, keep it till morning."

"I did have one more inspiration," said Rebecca when they were dressing next morning, "but I didn't wake you. I wondered if the rose of joy could be sacrifice. But I think sacrifice would be a lily, not a rose, don't you?"

The journey southward, the first glimpse of the ocean, the strange new scenes, the ease and delicious freedom, the intimacy with Miss Maxwell, almost intoxicated Rebecca. In three days she was not only herself again, she was another self, thrilling with delight, anticipation, and realization. She had always had such eager hunger for knowledge, such thirst for love, such passionate longing for the music, the beauty, the poetry of existence. She had always been straining to make the outward world conform to her inward dreams, and now life had grown all at once rich and sweet, wide and full. She was using all her natural, God-given outlets, and Emily Maxwell marvelled daily at the inexhaustible way in which the girl poured out and gathered in the treasures of thought and experience that belonged to her. She was a life-giver, altering the whole scheme of any picture she made a part of by contributing new values. Have you never seen the dull blues and greens of a room changed, transfigured by a burst of sunshine? That seemed to Miss Maxwell the effect of Rebecca on the groups of people with whom they now and then mingled; but they were commonly alone, reading to each other and having quiet talks. The prize essay was very much on Rebecca's mind. Secretly she thought she could never be happy unless she won it. She cared nothing for the value of it, and in this case almost nothing for the honour. She wanted to please Mr. Aladdin, and justify his belief in her.

"If I ever succeed in choosing a subject, I must ask if you think I can write well on it; and then I suppose I must work in silence and secret, never even reading the essay to you, nor talking about it."

Miss Maxwell and Rebecca were sitting by a little brook on a sunny spring day. They had been in a stretch of wood by the sea since breakfast, going every now and then for a bask on the warm white sand, and returning to their shady solitude when tired of the sun's glare.

"The subject is very important," said Miss Maxwell, "but I do not dare choose for you. Have you decided on anything yet?"

"No," Rebecca answered; "I plan a new essay every night. I've begun one on 'What is Failure?' and another on 'He and She.' That would be a dialogue between a boy and girl just as they were leaving school, and would tell their ideals of life. Then, do you remember you said to me one day, 'Follow your Saint'? I'd love to write about that. I didn't have a single thought in Wareham, and now I have a new one every minute, so I must try and write the essay here – think it out, at any rate, while I am so happy and free and rested. Look at the pebbles in the bottom of the pool, Miss Emily, so round and smooth and shining."

"Yes, but where did they get that beautiful polish, that satin skin, that lovely shape, Rebecca? Not in the still pool lying on the sands. It was never there that their angles were rubbed off and their rough surfaces polished, but in the strife and warfare of running waters. They have jostled against other pebbles, dashed against sharp rocks, and now we look at them and call them beautiful."

> *"If Fate had not made somebody a teacher,*
> *She might have been, oh! such a splendid preacher!"*

rhymed Rebecca. "Oh, if I could only think and speak as you do!" she sighed. "I am so afraid I shall never get education enough to make a good writer."

"You could worry about plenty of other things to better advantage," said Miss Maxwell a little scornfully. "Be afraid, for instance, that you won't understand human nature; that you won't realize the beauty of the outer world; that you may lack sympathy, and thus never be able to read a heart; that your faculty of expression may not keep pace with your ideas – a thousand things, every one of them more important to the writer than the knowledge that is found in books. Æsop was a Greek slave who could not even write down his wonderful fables, yet all the world reads them."

"I didn't know that," said Rebecca, with a half-sob. "I didn't know anything until I met you!"

"You will only have had a high-school course, but the most famous universities do not always succeed in making men and women. When I long to go abroad and study I always remember that there were three great schools in Athens and two in Jerusalem, but the Teacher of all teachers came out of Nazareth, a little village hidden away from the bigger, busier world."

"Mr. Ladd says that you are almost wasted on Wareham," said Rebecca thoughtfully.

"He is wrong; my talent is not a great one, but no talent is wholly wasted unless its owner chooses to hide it in a napkin. Remember that of your own gifts, Rebecca; they may not be praised of men, but they may cheer, console, inspire, perhaps, when and where you least expect. The brimming glass that overflows its own rim moistens the earth about it."

"Did you ever hear of 'The Rose of Joy'?" asked Rebecca after a long silence.

'Yes, of course; where did you see it?"

"On the outside of a book in the library."

"I saw it on the inside of a book in the library," smiled Miss Maxwell. "It is from Emerson, but I'm afraid you haven't quite grown up to it, Rebecca, and it is one of the things impossible to explain."

"Oh, try me, dear Miss Maxwell!" pleaded Rebecca. "Perhaps by thinking hard I can guess a little bit what it means."

"'In the actual – this painful kingdom of time and chance – are Care, Canker, and Sorrow; with thought, with the Ideal, is immortal hilarity – the Rose of Joy; round it all the Muses sing,'" quoted Miss Maxwell.

Rebecca repeated it over and over again until she had learned it by heart; then she said, "I don't want to be conceited, but I almost believe I do understand it, Miss Maxwell. Not altogether, perhaps, because it is puzzling and difficult; but a little, enough to go on with. It's as if a splendid shape galloped past you on horseback; you are so surprised, and your eyes move so slowly you cannot half see it, but you just catch a glimpse as it whisks by, and you know it is beautiful. It's all settled: my essay is going to be called 'The Rose of Joy.' I've just decided. It hasn't any beginning, nor any middle, but there will be a thrilling ending, something like this – let me see: joy, boy, toy, ahoy, decoy, alloy:

> *"Then come what will of weal or woe*
> *(Since all gold hath alloy)*
> *Thou'lt bloom unwithered in this heart,*
> *My Rose of Joy!*

Now I'm going to tuck you up in the shawl and give you the fir pillow, and while you sleep I am going down on the shore and write a fairy story for you. It's one of our 'supposing' kind; it flies far, far into the future, and makes beautiful things happen that may never really all come to pass; but some of them will, you'll see; and then you'll take out the little fairy story from your desk and remember Rebecca."

"I wonder why these young things always choose subjects that would tax the powers of a great esayist," thought Miss Maxwell, as she tried to sleep. "Are they dazzled, captivated, taken possession of, by the splendour of the theme, and do they fancy they can write up to it? Poor little innocents, hitching their toy waggons to the stars! How pretty this particular innocent looks under her new sunshade!"

Adam Ladd had been driving through Boston streets on a cold spring day, when nature and the fashion-mongers were holding out promises which seemed far from performance. Suddenly his vision was assailed by the sight of a rose-coloured parasol gaily unfurled in a shop window, signalling the passer-by and setting him to dream of summer sunshine. It reminded Adam of a New England apple-tree in full bloom, the outer covering of deep pink shining through the thin white lining, and a fluffy, fringe-like edge of mingled rose and cream dropping over the green handle. All at once he remembered one of Rebecca's early confidences – the little pink sunshade that had given her the only peep into the gay world of fashion that her childhood had ever known; her adoration of the flimsy bit of finery, and its tragic and sacrificial end. He entered the shop, bought the extravagant bauble, and expressed it to Wareham at once, not a single doubt of its appropriateness crossing the darkness of his masculine mind. He thought only of the joy in Rebecca's eyes; of the poise of her head under the apple-blossom canopy. It was a trifle embarrassing to return an hour later and buy a blue parasol for Emma Jane Perkins, but it seemed increasingly difficult, as the years went on, to remember her existence at all the proper times and seasons.

This is Rebecca's fairy story, copied the next day, and given to Emily Maxwell just as she was going to her room for the night. She read it with tears in her eyes, and then sent it to Adam Ladd, thinking he had earned a share in it, and that he deserved a glimpse of the girl's budding imagination, as well as of her grateful young heart:

A FAIRY STORY

There was once a tired and rather poverty-stricken Princess who dwelt in a cottage on the great highway between two cities. She was not as unhappy as thousands of others; indeed, she had much to be grateful for; but the life she lived and the work she did were full hard for one who was fashioned slenderly.

Now the cottage stood by the edge of a great green forest where the wind was always singing in the branches and the sunshine filtering through the leaves.

And one day, when the Princess was sitting by the wayside quite spent by her labour in the fields, she saw a golden chariot rolling down the King's Highway, and in it a person who could be none other than somebody's Fairy Godmother on her way to the Court. The chariot halted at her door, and, though the Princess had read of such beneficent personages, she never dreamed for an instant that one of them could ever alight at her cottage.

"If you are tired, poor little Princess, why do you not go into the cool, green forest and rest?" asked the Fairy Godmother.

"Because I have no time," she answered. "I must go back to my plough."

"Is that your plough leaning by the tree? and is it not too heavy?"

"It is heavy," answered the Princess; "but I love to turn the hard earth into soft furrows, and know that I am making good soil wherein my seeds may grow. When I feel the weight too much, I try to think of the harvest."

The golden chariot passed on, and the two talked no more together that day; nevertheless, the King's messengers were busy, for they whispered one word into the ear of the Fairy Godmother and another into the ear of the Princess, though so faintly that neither of them realized that the King had spoken.

The next morning a strong man knocked at the cottage door, and, doffing his hat to the Princess, said: "A golden chariot passed me yesterday, and one within it flung me a purse of ducats, saying: 'Go out into the King's Highway, and search until you find a cottage and a heavy plough leaning against a tree near by. Enter, and say to the Princess whom you will find there: "I will guide the plough, and you must go and rest, or walk in the cool, green forest, for this is the command of your Fairy Godmother."'"

And the same thing happened every day, and every day the tired Princess walked in the green wood. Many *times* she caught the glitter of the chariot, and ran into the Highway to give thanks to the Fairy Godmother; but she was never fleet enough to reach the spot. She could only stand with eager eyes and longing heart as the chariot passed by. Yet she never failed to catch a smile; and sometimes a word or two floated back to her — words that sounded like: "I would not be thanked. We are all children of the same King, and I am only his messenger."

Now, as the Princess walked daily in the green forest, hearing the wind singing in the branches, and seeing the sunlight filter through the latticework of green leaves, there came unto her thoughts that had lain asleep in the stifling air of the cottage and the weariness of guiding the plough. And by-and-by she took a needle from her girdle and pricked the thoughts on the leaves of the trees, and sent them into the air to float hither and thither. And it came to pass that people began to pick them up, and, holding them against the sun, to read what was written on them; and this was because the simple little words on the leaves were only, after all, a part of one of the King's messages, such as the Fairy Godmother dropped continually from her golden chariot.

But the miracle of the story lies deeper than all this.

Whenever the Princess pricked the words upon the leaves she added a thought of her Fairy Godmother, and, folding it close within, sent the leaf out on the breeze to float hither and thither, and fall where it would. And many other little Princesses felt the same impulse and did the same thing. And as nothing is ever lost in the King's Dominion, so these thoughts and wishes and hopes, being full of love and gratitude, had no power to die, but took unto themselves other shapes, and lived on for ever. They cannot be seen, our vision is too weak; nor heard, our hearing is too dull; but they can sometimes be felt, and we know not what force is stirring our hearts to nobler aims.

The end of the story is not come, but it may be that some day, when the Fairy Godmother has a message to deliver in person straight to the King, he will say: "Your face I know, your voice, your thoughts, and your heart. I have heard the rumble of your chariot-wheels on the great Highway, and I knew that you were on the King's business. Here in my hand is a sheaf of messages from every quarter of my kingdom. They were delivered by weary and footsore travellers, who said that they could never have reached the gate in safety had it not been for your help and inspiration. Read them, that you may know when and where and how you sped the King's service."

And when the Fairy Godmother reads them, it may be that sweet odors will rise from the pages and half-forgotten memories will stir the air; but in the gladness of the moment nothing will be half so lovely as the voice of the King when he said: "Read, and know how you sped the King's service."

Rebecca Rowena Randall.

CHAPTER TWENTY-SIX

"OVER THE TEACUPS"

~

The summer term at Wareham had ended, and Huldah Meserve, Dick Carter, and Living Perkins had finished school, leaving Rebecca and Emma Jane to represent Riverboro in the year to come. Delia Weeks was at home from Lewiston on a brief visit, and Mrs. Robinson was celebrating the occasion by a small and select party, the particular day having been set because strawberries were ripe and there was a rooster that wanted killing. Mrs. Robinson explained this to her husband, and requested that he eat his dinner on the carpenter's bench in the shed, as the party was to be a ladies' affair.

"All right; it won't be any loss to me," said Mr. Robinson. "Give me beans; that's all I ask. When a rooster wants to be killed, I want somebody else to eat him, not me!"

Mrs. Robinson had company only once or twice a year, and was generally much prostrated for several days afterwards, the struggle between pride and parsimony being quite too great a strain upon her. It was necessary, in order to maintain her standing in the community, to furnish a good "set out"; yet the extravagance of the proceeding goaded her from the first moment she began to stir the marble cake to the moment when the feast appeared upon the table.

The rooster had been boiling steadily over a slow fire since morning, but such was his power of resistance that his shape was as firm and handsome in the pot as on the first moment when he was lowered into it.

"He ain't goin' to give up!" said Alice, peering nervously under the cover, "and he looks like a scarecrow."

"We'll see whether he gives up or not when I take a sharp knife to him," her mother answered; "and as to his looks, a platter full o' gravy makes a sight o' difference with old roosters, and I'll put dumplings round the aidge; they're turrible fillin', though they don't belong with boiled chicken."

The rooster did indeed make an impressive showing, lying in his border of dumplings, and the dish was much complimented when it was borne in by Alice. This was fortunate, as the chorus of admiration ceased abruptly when the ladies began to eat the fowl.

"I was glad you could git over to Huldy's graduation, Delia," said Mrs. Meserve, who sat at the foot of the table and helped the chicken while Mrs. Robinson poured coffee at the other end. She was a fit mother for Huldah, being much the most stylish person in Riverboro; ill-health and dress were, indeed, her two chief enjoyments in life. It was rumored that her elaborately curled "front-piece" had cost five dollars, and that it was sent into Portland twice a year to be dressed and frizzed; but it is extremely difficult to discover the precise facts in such cases, and a conscientious historian always prefers to warn a too credulous reader against imbibing as Gospel truth something that might be the basest perversion of it. As to Mrs. Meserve's appearance, have you ever, in earlier years, sought the comforting society of the cook and hung over the kitchen table while she rolled out sugar gingerbread? Perhaps then, in some unaccustomed moment of amiability, she made you a dough lady, cutting the outline deftly with her pastry-knife, and then, at last, placing the human stamp upon it by sticking in two black currants for eyes. Just call to mind the face of that sugar gingerbread lady, and you will have an exact portrait of Huldah's mother – Mis' Peter Meserve, she was generally called, there being several others.

"How 'd you like Huldy's dress, Delia?" she asked, snapping the elastic in her black jet bracelets after an irritating fashion she had.

"I thought it was about the handsomest of any," answered Delia; "and her composition was first-rate. It was the only real amusin' one there was, and she read it so loud and clear we didn't miss any of it; most o' the girls spoke as if they had hasty puddin' in their mouths."

"That was the composition she wrote for Adam Ladd's prize," explained Mrs. Meserve, "and they do say she'd 'a' come out first, 'stead o' fourth, if her subject had been dif'rent. There was three ministers and three deacons on the committee, and it was only natural they should choose a serious piece; hers was too lively to suit 'em."

Huldah's inspiring theme had been "Boys," and she certainly had a fund of knowledge and experience that fitted her to write most intelligently upon it. It was vastly popular with the audience, who enjoyed the rather cheap jokes and allusions with which it coruscated; but judged from a purely literary standpoint, it left much to be desired.

"Rebecca's piece wa'n't read out loud, but the one that took the boy's prize was; why was that?" asked Mrs. Robinson.

"Because she wa'n't graduatin'," explained Mrs. Cobb, "and couldn't take part in the exercises; it'll be printed, with Herbert Dunn's, in the school paper."

"I'm glad o' that, for I'll never believe it was better 'n Huldy's till I read it with my own eyes; it seems as if the prize ought to 'a' gone to one of the seniors."

"Well, no, Marthy, not if Ladd offered it to any of the two upper classes that wanted to try for it," argued Mrs. Robinson. "They say they asked him to give out the prizes, and he refused up and down. It seems odd, his bein' so rich and travellin' about all over the country, that he was too modest to git up on that platform."

"My Huldy could 'a' done it and not winked an eyelash," observed Mrs. Meserve complacently, a remark which there seemed no disposition on the part of any of the company to controvert.

"It was complete, though, the governor happening to be there to see his niece graduate," said Delia Weeks. "Land! he looked elegant! They say he's only six feet, but he might 'a' been sixteen, and he certainly did make a fine speech."

"Did you notice Rebecca, how white she was, and how she trembled when she and Herbert Dunn stood there while the governor was praisin' 'em? He'd read her composition, too, for he wrote the Sawyer girls a letter about it." This remark was from the sympathetic Mrs. Cobb.

"I thought 'twas kind o' foolish, his makin' so much of her when it wa'n't her graduation," objected Mrs. Meserve; "laying his hand on her head 'n' all that, as if he was a Pope pronouncin' benediction. But there! I'm glad the prize come to Riverboro, 't any rate, and a han'somer one never was give out from the Wareham platform. I guess there ain't no end of Adam Ladd's money. The fifty dollars would 'a' been good enough, but he must needs go and put it into those elegant purses."

"I set so fur back I couldn't see 'em fairly," complained Delia, "and now Rebecca has taken hers home to show her mother."

"It was kind of a gold net bag with a chain," said Mrs. Perkins, "and there was five ten-dollar gold pieces in it. Herbert Dunn's was put in a fine leather wallet."

"How long is Rebecca goin' to stay at the farm?" asked Delia.

"Till they get over Hannah's bin' married, and get the house to runnin' without her," answered Mrs. Perkins. "It seems as if Hannah might 'a' waited a little longer. Aurelia was set against her goin' away while Rebecca was at school, but she's obstinate as a mule, Hannah is, and she just took her own way in spite of her mother. She's been doin' her sewin' for a year; the awfullest coarse cotton-cloth she had, but she's nearly blinded herself with fine stitchin' and rufflin' and tuckin'. Did you hear about the quilt she made? It's white, and has a big bunch o' grapes in the centre, quilted by a thimble-top. Then there's a row of circle-borderin' round the grapes, and she done them the size of a spool. The next border was done with a sherry glass, and the last with a port glass, an' all outside o' that was solid stitchin' done in straight rows; she's goin' to exhibit it at the county fair."

"She'd better 'a' been takin' in sewin' and earnin' money, 'stead o' blindin' her eyes on such foolishness as quilted counterpanes," said Mrs. Cobb. "The next thing you know that mortgage will be foreclosed on Mis' Randall, and she and the children won't have a roof over their heads."

"Don't they say there's a good chance of the railroad goin' through her place?" asked Mrs. Robinson. "If it does, she'll git as much as the farm is worth, and more. Adam Ladd's one of the stock-holders, and everything is a success he takes holt of. They're fightin' it in Augusty, but I'd back Ladd agin any o' them legislaters if he thought he was in the right."

"Rebecca 'll have some new clothes now," said Delia, "and the land knows she needs 'em. Seems to me the Sawyer girls are gittin' turrible near!"

"Rebecca won't have any new clothes out o' the prize-money," remarked Mrs. Perkins, "for she sent it away the next day to pay the interest on that mortgage."

"Poor little girl!" exclaimed Delia Weeks.

"She might as well help along her folks as spend it on foolishness," affirmed Mrs. Robinson. "I think she was mighty lucky to get it to pay the interest with, but she's probably like all the Randalls; it was easy come, easy go, with them."

"That's more than could be said of the Sawyer stock" retorted Mrs. Perkins; "seems like they enjoyed savin' more 'n anything in the world, and it's gainin' on Mirandy sence her shock."

"I don't believe it was a shock; it stands to reason she'd never 'a' got up after it and been so smart as she is now. We had three o' the worst shocks in our family that there ever was on this river, and I know every symptom of 'em better 'n the doctors." And Mrs. Peter Meserve shook her head wisely.

"Mirandy's smart enough," said Mrs. Cobb, "but you notice she stays right to home, and she's more close-mouthed than ever she was; never took a mite o' pride in the prize, as I could see, though it pretty nigh drove Jeremiah out o' his senses. I thought I should 'a' died o' shame when he cried 'Hooray!' and swung his straw hat when the governor shook hands with Rebecca. It's lucky he couldn't get fur into the church and had to stand back by the door, for, as it was, he made a spectacle of himself. My suspicion is" – and here every lady stopped eating and sat up straight – "that the Sawyer girls have lost money. They don't know a thing about business, 'n' never did, and Mirandy's too secretive and contrairy to ask advice."

"The most o' what they've got is in gov'ment bonds, I always heard, and you can't lose money on them. Jane hed the timber land left her, an' Mirandy had the brick house. She probably took it awful hard that Rebecca's fifty dollars had to be swallowed up in a mortgage, 'stead of goin' towards school expenses. The more I think of it, the more I think Adam Ladd intended Rebecca should have that prize when he gave it." The mind of Huldah's mother ran towards the idea that her daughter's rights had been assailed.

"Land, Marthy, what foolishness you talk!" exclaimed Mrs. Perkins. "You don't suppose he could tell what composition the committee was going to choose; and why should he offer another fifty dollars for a boy's prize, if he wa'n't interested in helpin' along the school? He's give Emma Jane about the same present as Rebecca every Christmas for five years; that's the way he does."

"Some time he'll forget one of 'em and give to the other, or drop 'em both and give to some new girl," said Delia Weeks, with an experience born of fifty years of spinsterhood.

"Like as not," assented Mrs. Peter Meserve, "though it's easy to see he ain't the marryin' kind. There's men that would marry once a year if their wives would die fast enough, and there's men that seems to want to live alone."

"If Ladd was a Mormon, I guess he could have every woman in North Riverboro that's a suitable age, accordin' to what my cousins say," remarked Mrs. Perkins.

"'Tain't likely he could be ketched by any North Riverboro girl," demurred Mrs. Robinson;" "not when he prob'bly has had the pick o' Boston. I guess Marthy hit it when she said there's men that ain't the marryin' kind."

"I wouldn't trust any of 'em when Miss Right comes along!" laughed Mrs. Cobb genially. "You never can tell what 'n' who's goin' to please 'em. You know Jeremiah's contrairy horse, Buster? He won't let anybody put the bit into his mouth if he can help it. He'll fight Jerry, and fight me, till he has to give in. Rebecca didn't know nothin' about his tricks, and the other day she went int' the barn to hitch up. I followed right along, knowing she'd have trouble with the headstall, and I declare if she wa'n't pattin' Buster's nose and talkin' to him, and when she put her little fingers into his mouth he opened it so fur I thought he'd swaller her, for sure. He jest smacked his lips over the bit as if 'twas a lump o' sugar. 'Land! Rebecca,' I says, 'how'd you persuade him to take the bit?' 'I didn't,' she says; 'he seemed to want it; perhaps he's tired of his stall and wants to get out in the fresh air.'"

CHAPTER TWENTY-SEVEN

"THE VISION SPLENDID"

~

A year had elapsed since Adam Ladd's prize had been discussed over the teacups in Riverboro. The months had come and gone, and at length the great day had dawned for Rebecca — the day to which she had been looking forward for five years as the first goal to be reached on her little journey through the world. School-days were ended, and the mystic function known to the initiated as "graduation" was about to be celebrated; it was even now heralded by the sun dawning in the eastern sky. Rebecca stole softly out of bed, crept to the window, threw open the blinds, and welcomed the rosy light that meant a cloudless morning. Even the sun looked different somehow, larger, redder, more important than usual; and if it were really so, there was no member of the graduating class who would have thought it strange or unbecoming, in view of all the circumstances. Emma Jane stirred on her pillow, woke, and seeing Rebecca at the window, came and knelt on the floor beside her. "It's going to be pleasant!" she sighed gratefully. "If it wasn't wicked, I could thank the Lord, I'm so relieved in mind! Did you sleep?"

"Not much; the words of my class poem kept running through my head, and the accompaniments of the songs; and worse than anything, Mary Queen of Scots' prayer in Latin – it seemed as if

"'*Adoro, imploro,*
Ut liberes me!'

were burned into my brain."

No one who is unfamiliar with life in rural neighborhoods can imagine the gravity, the importance, the solemnity of this last day of school. In the matter of preparation, wealth of detail, and general excitement, it far surpasses a wedding; for that is commonly a simple affair in the country, sometimes even beginning and ending in a visit to the parsonage. Nothing quite equals graduation in the minds of the graduates themselves, their families, and the younger students, unless it be the inauguration of a governor at the State Capitol. Wareham, then, was shaken to its very centre on this day of days. Mothers and fathers of the scholars, as well as relatives to the remotest generation, had been coming on the train and driving into the town since breakfast-time; old pupils, both married and single, with and without families, streamed back to the dear old village. The two livery stables were crowded with vehicles of all sorts, and lines of buggies and waggons were drawn up along the sides of the shady roads, the horses switching their tails in luxurious idleness. The streets were filled with people wearing their best clothes, and the fashions included not only "the latest thing," but the well-preserved relic of a bygone day. There were all sorts and conditions of men and women, for there were sons and daughters of storekeepers, lawyers, butchers, doctors, shoemakers, professors, ministers, and farmers at the Wareham schools, either as boarders or day scholars. In the seminary building there was an excitement so deep and profound that it expressed itself in a kind of hushed silence, a transient suspension of life, as those most interested approached the crucial moment. The feminine graduates-to-be were seated in their own bedrooms, dressed with a completeness of detail to which all their past lives seemed to have been but a prelude. At least, this was the case with their bodies; but their heads, owing to the extreme heat of the day, were one and all ornamented with leads, or papers, or dozens of little braids, to issue later in every sort of curl known to the girl of that period. Rolling the hair on leads or papers was a favourite method of attaining the desired result, and though it often entailed a sleepless night, there were those who gladly paid the price. Others, in whose veins the blood of martyrs did not flow, substituted rags for leads and pretended that they made a more natural and less woolly curl. Heat, however, will melt the proudest head and reduce to fiddling-strings the finest product of the waving-pin; so anxious mothers were stationed over their offspring, waving palm-leaf fans, it having been decided that the supreme instant when the town clock struck ten should be the one chosen for releasing the prisoners from their self-imposed tortures.

Dotted or plain Swiss muslin was the favourite garb, though there were those who were steaming in white cashmere or alpaca, because in some cases such frocks were thought more useful afterwards. Blue and pink waist ribbons were lying over the backs of chairs, and the girl who had a Roman sash was praying that she might be kept from vanity and pride.

The way to any graduating dress at all had not seemed clear to Rebecca until a month before. Then, in company with Emma Jane, she visited the Perkins' attic, found piece after piece of white butter muslin or cheesecloth, and decided that, at a pinch, it would do. The "rich blacksmith's daughter" cast the thought of dotted Swiss behind her, and elected to follow Rebecca in cheesecloth as she had in higher matters, straightway devising costumes that included such drawing of threads, such hemstitching and pin-tucking, such insertions of fine thread tatting, that, in order to be finished, Rebecca's dress was given out in sections — the sash to Hannah, waist and sleeves to Mrs. Cobb, and skirt to Aunt Jane. The stitches that went into the despised material, worth only three or four pennies a yard, made the dresses altogether lovely, and as for the folds and lines into which they fell, they could have given points to satins and brocades.

The two girls were waiting in their room alone, Emma Jane in rather a tearful state of mind. She kept thinking that it was the last day that they would be together in this altogether sweet and close intimacy. The beginning of the end seemed to have dawned, for two positions had been offered Rebecca by Mr. Morrison the day before: one in which she would play for singing and calisthenics, and superintend the piano practice of the younger girls in a boarding-school; the other an assistant's place in the

Edgewood High School. Both were very modest as to salary, but the former included educational advantages that Miss Maxwell thought might be valuable.

Rebecca's mood had passed from that of excitement into a sort of exaltation, and when the first bell rang through the corridors announcing that in five minutes the class would proceed in a body to the church for the exercises, she stood motionless and speechless at the window with her hand on her heart.

"It is coming, Emmie," she said presently; "do you remember, in 'The Mill on the Floss,' when Maggie Tulliver closed the golden gates of childhood behind her? I can almost see them swing, almost hear them clang; and I can't tell whether I am glad or sorry."

"I shouldn't care how they swung or clanged," said Emma Jane, "if only you and I were on the same side of the gate; but we shan't be, I know we shan't!"

"Emmie, don't dare to cry, for I'm just on the brink myself. If only you were graduating with me! that's my only sorrow. There, I hear the rumble of the wheels! People will be seeing our grand surprise now. Hug me once for luck, dear Emmie; a careful hug, remembering our butter-muslin frailty."

Ten minutes later Adam Ladd, who had just arrived from Portland, and was wending his way to the church, came suddenly into the main street and stopped short under a tree by the wayside, riveted to the spot by a scene of picturesque loveliness such as his eyes had seldom witnessed before. The class of which Rebecca was president was not likely to follow accepted customs. Instead of marching two by two from the seminary to the church, they had elected to proceed thither by royal chariot. A haycart had been decked with green vines and bunches of long-stemmed field daisies, those gay darlings of New England meadows. Every inch of the rail, the body, even the spokes, all were twined with yellow and green and white. There were two white horses, flower-trimmed reins, and in the floral bower, seated on maple boughs, were the twelve girls of the class, while the ten boys marched on either side of the vehicle, wearing buttonhole bouquets of daisies, the class flower.

Rebecca drove, seated on a green-covered bench that looked not unlike a throne. No girl clad in white muslin, no happy girl of seventeen, is plain;

and the twelve little country maids, from the vantage-ground of their setting, looked beautiful as the June sunlight filtered down on their uncovered heads, showing their bright eyes, their fresh cheeks, their smiles, and their dimples.

Rebecca, Adam thought, as he took off his hat and saluted the pretty panorama – Rebecca, with her tall slenderness, her thoughtful brow, the fire of young joy in her face, her fillet of dark braided hair, might have been a young Muse or Sybil; and the flowery hayrack, with its freight of blooming girlhood, might have been painted as an allegorical picture of "The Morning of Life." It all passed him, as he stood under the elms in the old village street where his mother had walked half a century ago, and he was turning with the crowd towards the church when he heard a little sob. Behind a hedge in the garden near where he was standing was a forlorn person in white, whose neat nose, chestnut hair, and blue eyes he seemed to know. He stepped inside the gate and said: "What's wrong, Miss Emma?"

"Oh, is it you, Mr. Ladd? Rebecca wouldn't let me cry for fear of spoiling my looks, but I must have just one chance before I go in. I can be as homely as I like, after all, for I only have to sing with the school. I'm not graduating; I'm just leaving. Not that I mind that; it's only being separated from Rebecca that I never can stand."

The two walked along together, Adam comforting the disconsolate Emma Jane, until they reached the old meeting-house where the commencement exercises were always held. The interior, with its decorations of yellow, green, and white, was crowded, the air hot and breathless, the essays and songs and recitations precisely like all others that have been since the world began. One always fears that the platform may sink under the weight of youthful platitudes uttered on such occasions; yet one can never be properly critical, because the sight of the boys and girls themselves – those young and hopeful makers of to-morrow – disarms one's scorn. We yawn desperately at the essays, but our hearts go out to the essayists, all the same, for "the vision splendid" is shining in their eyes, and there is no fear of "th' inevitable yoke" that the years are so surely bringing them.

Rebecca saw Hannah and her husband in the audience; dear old John and Cousin Ann also, and felt a pang at the absence of her mother, though she had known there was no possibility of seeing her; for poor Aurelia was kept at Sunnybrook by cares of children and farm, and lack of money either for the journey or for suitable dress. The Cobbs she saw too. No one, indeed, could fail to see Uncle Jerry, for he shed tears more than once, and in the intervals between the essays descanted to his neighbours concerning the marvellous gifts of one of the graduating class whom he had known ever since she was a child; in fact, had driven her from Maplewood to Riverboro when she left her home, and he had told mother that same night that there wa'n't nary rung on the ladder o' fame that that child wouldn't mount before she got through with it.

The Cobbs, then, had come, and there were other Riverboro faces, but where was Aunt Jane in her black silk made-over especially for this occasion? Aunt Miranda had not intended to come, she knew; but where, on this day of days, was her beloved Aunt Jane! However, this thought, like all others, came and went in a flash, for the whole morning was like a series of magic-lantern pictures crossing and recrossing her field of vision. She played, she sang, she recited Queen Mary's Latin prayer like one in a dream, only brought to consciousness by meeting Mr. Aladdin's eyes as she spoke the last line. Then at the end of the programme came her class poem, "Makers of To-morrow"; and there, as on many a former occasion, her personality played so great a part that she seemed to be uttering Miltonic sentiments instead of school-girl verse. Her voice, her eyes, her body breathed conviction, earnestness, emotion; and when she left the platform the audience felt that they had listened to a masterpiece. Most of her hearers knew little of Carlyle or Emerson, or they might have remembered that the one said, "We are all poets when we read a poem well," and the other, "'Tis the good reader makes the good book."

It was over! the diplomas had been presented, and each girl, after giving furtive touches to her hair, sly tweaks to her muslin skirts, and caressing pats to her sash, had gone forward to receive the roll of parchment with a bow that had been the subject of anxious thought for weeks. Rounds of applause greeted each graduate at this thrilling moment, and Jeremiah Cobb's behavior when Rebecca came forward was the talk of Wareham and Riverboro for days. Old Mrs. Webb avowed that he, in the space of two hours, had worn out her pew more — the carpet, the cushions, and wood-work — than she had by sitting in it forty years. Yes, it was over, and after the crowd had thinned a little Adam Ladd made his way to the platform.

Rebecca turned from speaking to some strangers and met him in the aisle. "Oh, Mr. Aladdin, I am so glad you could come! Tell me" — and she looked at him half shyly, for his approval was dearer to her, and more difficult to win, than that of the others — "tell me, Mr. Aladdin, were you satisfied?"

"More than satisfied!" he said. "Glad I met the child, proud I know the girl, longing to meet the woman!"

CHAPTER TWENTY-EIGHT

"TH' INEVITABLE YOKE"

~

Rebecca's heart beat high at this sweet praise from her hero's lips, but before she had found words to thank him, Mr. and Mrs. Cobb, who had been modestly biding their time in a corner, approached her, and she introduced them to Mr. Ladd.

"Where, where is Aunt Jane?" she cried, holding Aunt Sarah's hand on one side and Uncle Jerry's on the other.

"I'm sorry, lovey, but we've got bad news for you."

"Is Aunt Miranda worse? She is; I can see it by your looks;" and Rebecca's color faded.

"She had a second stroke yesterday morning jest when she was helpin' Jane lay out her things to come here to-day. Jane said you wa'n't to know anything about it till the exercises were all over, and we promised to keep it secret till then."

"I will go right home with you, Aunt Sarah. I must just run to tell Miss Maxwell, for after I had packed up to-morrow I was going to Brunswick with her. Poor Aunt Miranda! And I have been so gay and happy all day, except that I was longing for mother and Aunt Jane."

"There ain't no harm in bein' gay, lovey; that's what Jane wanted you to be. And Miranda's got her speech back, for your aunt has just sent a letter sayin' she's better; and I'm goin' to set up to-night, so you can stay here and have a good sleep, and get your things together comfortably to-morrow."

"I'll pack your trunk for you, Becky dear, and attend to all our room things," said Emma Jane, who had come towards the group and heard the sorrowful news from the brick house.

They moved into one of the quiet side-pews, where Hannah and her husband and John joined them. From time to time some straggling acquaintance or old schoolmate would come up to congratulate Rebecca and ask why she had hidden herself in a corner. Then some member of the class would call to her excitedly, reminding her not to be late at the picnic luncheon, or begging her to be early at the class party in the evening. All this had an air of unreality to Rebecca. In the midst of the happy excitement of the last two days, when "blushing honours" had been falling thick upon her, and behind the delicious exaltation of the morning, had been the feeling that the condition was a transient one, and that the burden, the struggle, the anxiety, would soon loom again on the horizon. She longed to steal away into the woods with dear old John, grown so manly and handsome, and get some comfort from him.

Meantime Adam Ladd and Mr. Cobb had been having an animated conversation.

"I s'pose up to Boston girls like that one are as thick as blackb'ries?" Uncle Jerry said, jerking his head interrogatively in Rebecca's direction.

"They may be," smiled Adam, taking in the old man's mood; "only I don't happen to know one."

"My eyesight bein' poor 's the reason she looked han'somest of any girl on the platform, I s'pose."

"There's no failure in my eyes," responded Adam; "but that was how the thing seemed to me."

"What did you think of her voice? Anything extry about it?"

"Made the others sound poor and thin, I thought."

"Well, I'm glad to hear your opinion, you bein' a travelled man, for mother says I'm foolish 'bout Rebecky, and hev been sence the fust. Mother scolds me for spoilin' her, but I notice mother ain't fur behind when it comes to spoilin'. Land! it made me sick, thinkin' o' them parents travellin' miles to see their young ones graduate, and then when they got here hevin' to compare 'em with Rebecky. Good-bye, Mr. Ladd. Drop in some day when you come to Riverboro."

"I will," said Adam, shaking the old man's hand cordially; "perhaps to-morrow, if I drive Rebecca home, as I shall offer to do. Do you think Miss Sawyer's condition is serious?"

"Well, the doctor don't seem to know; but, anyhow, she's paralyzed, and she'll never walk fur again, poor soul! She ain't lost her speech; that'll be a comfort to her."

Adam left the church, and in crossing the common came upon Miss Maxwell doing the honors of the institution as she passed from group to group of strangers and guests. Knowing that she was deeply interested in all Rebecca's plans, he told her, as he drew her aside, that the girl would have to leave Wareham for Riverboro the next day.

"That is almost more than I can bear!" exclaimed Miss Maxwell, sitting down on a bench and stabbing the greensward with her parasol. "It seems to me Rebecca never has any respite. I had so many plans for her this next month in fitting her for her position, and now she will settle down to housework again, and to the nursing of that poor, sick, cross old aunt."

"If it had not been for the cross old aunt, Rebecca would still have been at Sunnybrook; and from the standpoint of educational advantages, or, indeed, advantages of any sort, she might as well have been in the backwoods," returned Adam.

"That is true. I was vexed when I spoke, for I thought an easier and happier day was dawning for my prodigy and pearl."

"Our prodigy and pearl," corrected Adam.

"Oh yes!" she laughed. "I always forget that it pleases you to pretend you discovered Rebecca."

"I believe, though, that happier days are dawning for her," continued Adam. "It must be a secret for the present, but Mrs. Randall's farm will be bought by the new railroad. We must have right-of-way through the land, and the station will be built on her property. She will receive six thousand dollars, which, though not a fortune, will yield her three or four hundred dollars a year if she will allow me to invest it for her. There is a mortgage on the land; that paid, and Rebecca self-supporting, the mother ought to push the education of the oldest boy, who is a fine, ambitious fellow. He should be taken away from farm work and settled at his studies."

"We might form ourselves into a Randall Protective Agency, Limited," mused Miss Maxwell. "I confess I want Rebecca to have a career."

"I don't," said Adam promptly.

"Of course you don't. Men have no interest in the careers of women. But I know Rebecca better than you."

"You understand her mind better, but not necessarily her heart. You are considering her for the moment as prodigy; I am thinking of her more as pearl."

"Well," sighed Miss Maxwell whimsically, "prodigy or pearl, the Randall Protective Agency may pull Rebecca in opposite directions, but, nevertheless, she will follow her saint."

"That will content me," said Adam gravely.

"Particularly if the saint beckons your way." And Miss Maxwell looked up and smiled provokingly.

Rebecca did not see her Aunt Miranda till she had been at the brick house for several days. Miranda steadily refused to have anyone but Jane in the room until her face had regained its natural look, but her door was always ajar, and Jane fancied she liked to hear Rebecca's quick, light step. Her mind was perfectly clear now, and, save that she could not move, she was most of the time quite free from pain, and alert in every nerve to all that was going on within or without the house. "Were the windfall apples being picked up for sauce? Were the potatoes thick in the hills? Was the corn tosselin' out? Were they cuttin' the upper field? Were they keepin' fly-paper laid out everywheres? Were there any ants in the dairy? Was the kindlin' wood holdin' out? Had the bank sent the cowpons?"

Poor Miranda Sawyer! Hovering on the verge of the great beyond – her body "struck," and no longer under control of her iron will – no divine visions floated across her tired brain; nothing but petty cares and sordid anxieties. Not all at once can the soul talk with God, be He ever so near. If the heavenly language never has been learned, quick as is the spiritual sense in seizing the facts it needs, then the poor soul must use the words and phrases it has lived on and grown into day by day. Poor Miss Miranda! — held fast within the prison walls of her own nature, blind in the presence of revelation because she had never used the spiritual eye, deaf to angelic voices because she had not used the spiritual ear.

There came a morning when she asked for Rebecca. The door was opened into the dim sickroom, and Rebecca stood there with the sunlight behind her, her hands full of sweet-peas. Miranda's pale, sharp face, framed in its nightcap, looked haggard on the pillow, and her body was pitifully still under the counterpane.

"Come in," she said; "I ain't dead yet. Don't mess up the bed with them flowers, will ye?"

"Oh no! they're going in a glass pitcher," said Rebecca, turning to the washstand as she tried to control her voice and stop the tears that sprang to her eyes.

"Let me look at ye; come closer! What dress are ye wearin'?" said the old aunt in her cracked, weak voice.

"My blue calico."

"Is your cashmere holdin' its color?"

"Yes, Aunt Miranda."

"Do you keep it in a dark closet hung on the wrong side, as I told ye?"

"Always."

"Has your mother made her jelly?"

"She hasn't said."

"She always had the knack o' writin' letters with nothin' in 'em. What's Mark broke sence I've been sick?"

"Nothing at all, Aunt Miranda."

"Why, what's the matter with him? Gittin' lazy, ain't he? How's John turnin' out?"

"He's going to be the best of us all."

"I hope you don't slight things in the kitchen because I ain't there. Do you scald the coffee-pot and turn it upside down on the winder-sill?"

"Yes, Aunt Miranda."

"It's always 'Yes' with you, and 'Yes' with Jane," groaned Miranda, trying to move her stiffened body; "but all the time I lay here knowin' there's things done the way I don't like 'em."

There was a long pause, during which Rebecca sat down by the bedside and timidly touched her aunt's hand, her heart swelling with tender pity at the gaunt face and closed eyes.

"I was dreadful ashamed to have you graduate in cheesecloth, Rebecca, but I couldn't help it nohow. You'll hear the reason some time, and know I tried to make it up to ye. I'm afraid you was a laughing-stock!"

"No," Rebecca answered. "Ever so many people said our dresses were the very prettiest; they looked like soft lace. You're not to be anxious about anything. Here I am, all grown up and graduated — number three in a class of twenty-two, Aunt Miranda — and good positions offered me already. Look at me! big and strong and young, all ready to go into the world and show what you and Aunt Jane have done for me. If you want me near, I'll take the Edgewood school, so that I can be here nights and Sundays to help; and if you get better, then I'll go to Augusta, for that's a hundred dollars more, with music lessons and other things beside."

"You listen to me," said Miranda quaveringly: "take the best place, regardless o' my sickness. I'd like to live long enough to know you'd paid off that mortgage, but I guess I shan't."

Here she ceased abruptly, having talked more than she had for weeks; and Rebecca stole out of the room, to cry by herself and wonder if old age must be so grim, so hard, so unchastened and unsweetened, as it slipped into the valley of the shadow.

The days went on, and Miranda grew stronger and stronger. Her will seemed unsassailable, and before long she could be moved into a chair by the window, her dominant thought being to arrive at such a condition of improvement that the doctor need not call more than once a week, instead of daily, thereby diminishing the bill that was mounting to such a terrifying sum that it haunted her thoughts by day and dreams by night.

Little by little hope stole back into Rebecca's young heart. Aunt Jane began to "clear starch" her handkerchiefs and collars and purple muslin dress, so that she might be ready to go to Brunswick at any moment when the doctor pronounced Miranda well on the road to recovery. Everything beautiful was to happen in Brunswick if she could be there by August, everything that heart could wish or imagination conceive, for she was to be Miss Emily's very own visitor, and sit at table with college professors and other great men.

At length the day dawned when the few clean, simple dresses were packed in the hair-trunk, together with her beloved coral necklace, her cheesecloth graduating dress, her class pin, Aunt Jane's lace cape, and the one new hat, which she tried on every night before going to bed. It was of white chip with a wreath of cheap white roses and green leaves, and cost between two and three dollars, an unprecedented sum in Rebecca's experience. The effect of its glories when worn with her nightdress was dazzling enough, but if ever it appeared in conjunction with the cheese-cloth gown Rebecca felt that even reverend professors might regard it with respect. It is probable, indeed, that any professorial gaze lucky enough to meet a pair of dark eyes shining under that white rose garland would never have stopped at respect!

Then, when all was ready and Abijah Flagg at the door, came a telegram from Hannah: "Come at once. Mother has had bad accident."

In less than an hour Rebecca was started on her way to Sunnybrook, her heart palpitating with fear as to what might be awaiting her at her journey's end.

Death, at all events, was not there to meet her, but something that looked at first only too much like it. Her mother had been standing on the haymow superintending some changes in the barn, had been seized with giddiness, they thought, and slipped. The right knee was fractured and the back strained and hurt, but she was conscious and in no immediate danger, so Rebecca wrote when she had a moment to send Aunt Jane the particulars.

"I don' know how 'tis," grumbled Miranda, who was not able to sit up that day; "but from a child I could never lay abed without Aurelia's gettin' sick too. I don' know's she could help fallin', though it ain't any place for a woman — a haymow; but if it hadn't been that, 'twould 'a' been somethin' else. Aurelia was born unfortunate. Now she'll probably be a cripple, and Rebecca 'll have to nurse her instead of earning a good income somewheres else."

"Her first duty's to her mother," said Aunt Jane; "I hope she'll always remember that."

"Nobody remembers anything they'd ought to — at seventeen," responded Miranda. "Now that I'm strong again, there's things I want to consider with you, Jane — things that are on my mind night and day. We've talked 'em over before; now we'll settle 'em. When I'm laid away, do you want to take Aurelia and the children down here to the brick house? There's an awful passel of 'em — Aurelia, Jenny, and Fanny; but I won't have Mark. Hannah can take him; I won't have a great boy stompin' out the carpets and ruinin' the furniture, though I know when I'm dead I can't hinder ye, if you make up your mind to do anything."

"I shouldn't like to go against your feelings, especially in laying out your money, Miranda," said Jane.

"Don't tell Rebecca I've willed her the brick house. She won't git it till I'm gone, and I want to take my time 'bout dyin' and not be hurried off by them that's goin' to profit by it; nor I don't want to be thanked, neither. I s'pose she'll use the front stairs as common as the back, and like as not have water brought into the kitchen; but mebbe when I've been dead a few years I shan't mind. She sets such store by you, she'll want you to have your home here as long 's you live; but any way, I've wrote it down that way. Though Lawyer Burns's wills don't hold more 'n half the time, he's cheaper, but I guess it comes out jest the same in the end. I wa'n't goin' to have the fust man Rebecca picks up for a husband turnin' you ou'doors."

There was a long pause, during which Jane knit silently, wiping the tears from her eyes from time to time, as she looked at the pitiful figure lying weakly on the pillows. Suddenly Miranda said slowly and feebly:

"I don' know, after all, but you might as well take Mark; I s'pose there's tame boys as well as wild ones. There ain't a mite o' sense in havin' so many children, but it's a turrible risk splittin' up families and farmin' 'em out here 'n' there; they'd never come to no good, an' everybody would keep rememberin' their mother was a Sawyer. Now, if you'll draw the curtin, I'll try to sleep."

CHAPTER TWENTY-NINE

MOTHER AND DAUGHTER

~

Two months had gone by — two months of steady, fagging work: of cooking, washing, ironing; of mending and caring for the three children, although Jenny was fast becoming a notable little housewife — quick, ready, and capable. They were months in which there had been many a weary night of watching by Aurelia's bedside, of soothing and bandaging and rubbing, of reading and nursing, even of feeding and bathing. The ceaseless care was growing less now, and the family breathed more freely, for the mother's sigh of pain no longer came from the stifling bedroom, where during a hot and humid August Aurelia had lain, suffering with every breath she drew. There would be no question of walking for many a month to come; but blessings seemed to multiply when the blinds could be opened and the bed drawn near the window, when mother, with pillows behind her, could at least sit and watch the work going on, could smile at the past agony, and forget the weary hours that had led to her present comparative ease and comfort.

No girl of seventeen can pass through such an ordeal and come out unchanged; no girl of Rebecca's temperament could go through it without some inward repining and rebellion. She was doing tasks in which she could not be fully happy – heavy and trying tasks, which perhaps she could never do with complete success or satisfaction, and, like promise of nectar to thirsty lips, was the vision of joys she had had to put aside for the performance of dull daily duty. How brief, how fleeting, had been those splendid visions when the universe seemed open for her young strength to battle and triumph in! How soon they had faded into the light of common day! At first sympathy and grief were so keen she thought of nothing but her mother's pain. No consciousness of self interposed between her and her filial service. Then, as the weeks passed, little blighted hopes began to stir and ache in her breast, defeated ambitions raised their heads as if to sting her, unattainable delights teased her by their very nearness – by the narrow line of separation that lay between her and their realization. It is easy for the moment to tread the narrow way, looking neither to the right nor left, upborne by the sense of right-doing; but that first joy of self-denial – the joy that is like fire in the blood – dies away, the path seems drearier, and the footsteps falter. Such a time came to Rebecca, and her bright spirit flagged when the letter was received saying that her position in Augusta had been filled. There was a mutinous leap of the heart then, a beating of wings against the door of the cage, a longing for the freedom of the big world outside. It was the stirring of the powers within her, though she called it by no such grand name. She felt as if the wind of destiny were blowing her flame hither and thither, burning, consuming her, but kindling nothing. All this meant one stormy night in her little room at Sunnybrook; but the clouds blew over, the sun shone again, a rainbow stretched across the sky, while "hope clad in April green" smiled into her upturned face and beckoned her on, saying:

> *"Grow old along with me;*
> *The best is yet to be."*

Threads of joy ran in and out of the gray tangled web of daily living. There was the attempt at odd moments to make the bare little house less bare by bringing in out-of-doors, taking a leaf from Nature's book, and noting how she conceals ugliness wherever she finds it. Then there was the satisfaction of being mistress of the poor domain; of planning, governing, deciding; of bringing order out of chaos; of implanting gaiety in the place of inert resignation to the inevitable. Another element of comfort was the children's love, for they turned to her as flowers to the sun, drawing confidently on her fund of stories, serene in the conviction that there was no limit to Rebecca's power of make-believe. In this and in yet greater things, little as she realized it, the law of compensation was working in her behalf, for in those anxious days mother and daughter found and knew each other as never before. A new sense was born in Rebecca as she hung over her mother's bed of pain and unrest – a sense that comes only of ministering, a sense that grows only when the strong bend toward the weak. As for Aurelia, words could never have expressed her dumb happiness when the real revelation of motherhood was vouchsafed her. In all the earlier years, when her babies were young, carking cares and anxieties darkened the fireside with their brooding wings. Then Rebecca had gone away, and in the long months of absence her mind and soul had grown out of her mother's knowledge, so that now, when Aurelia had time and strength to study her child, she was like some enchanting changeling. Aurelia and Hannah had gone on in the dull round and the common task growing duller and duller; but now, on a certain stage of life's journey, who should appear but this bewildering being, who gave wings to thoughts that had only crept before, who brought color and grace and harmony into the dun-brown texture of existence.

You might harness Rebecca to the heaviest plough, and while she had youth on her side she would always remember the green earth under her feet and the blue sky over her head. Her physical eye saw the cake she was stirring and the loaf she was kneading; her physical ear heard the kitchen fire crackling and the tea-kettle singing, but ever and anon her fancy mounted on pinions, rested itself, renewed its strength in the upper air. The bare little farmhouse was a fixed fact, but she had many a palace into which she now and then withdrew – palaces peopled with stirring and gallant figures belonging to the world of romance; palaces not without their heavenly apparitions, too, breathing celestial counsel. Every time she retired to her citadel of dreams she came forth radiant and refreshed, as one who has seen the evening star, or heard sweet music, or smelled the Rose of Joy.

Aurelia could have understood the feeling of a narrow-minded and conventional hen who has brought a strange, intrepid duckling into the world; but her situation was still more wonderful, for she could only compare her sensations to those of some quiet, brown Dorking who has brooded an ordinary egg and hatched a bird of paradise. Such an idea had crossed her mind more than once during the past fortnight, and it flashed to and fro this mellow October morning when Rebecca came into the room with her arms full of golden-rod and flaming autumn leaves.

"Just a hint of the fall styles, mother," she said, slipping the stem of a gorgeous red and yellow sapling between the mattress and the foot of the bed. "This was leaning over the pool, and I was afraid it would be vain if I left it there too long looking at its beautiful reflection, so I took it away from danger. Isn't it wonderful? How I wish I could carry one to poor Aunt Miranda to-day! There's never a flower in the brick house when I'm away."

It was a marvellous morning. The sun had climbed into a world that held in remembrance only a succession of golden days and starlit nights. The air was fragrant with ripening fruit, and there was a mad little bird on a tree outside the door nearly bursting his throat with joy of living. He had forgotten that summer was over, that winter must ever come; and who could think of cold winds, bare boughs, or frozen streams on such a day? A painted moth came in at the open window and settled on the tuft of brilliant leaves. Aurelia heard the bird, and looked from the beauty of the glowing bush to her tall, splendid daughter, standing like young Spring with golden Autumn in her arms.

Then suddenly she covered her eyes and cried, "I can't bear it! Here I lie chained to this bed, interfering with everything you want to do. It's all wasted — all my saving and doing without, all your hard study, all Miranda's outlay — everything that we thought was going to be the making of you!"

"Mother, mother, don't talk so — don't think so!" exclaimed Rebecca, sitting down impetuously on the floor by the bed, and dropping the golden-rod by her side. "Why, mother, I'm only a little past seventeen! This person in a purple calico apron, with flour on her nose, is only the beginnings of me. Do you remember the young tree that John transplanted? We had a dry summer and a cold winter, and it didn't grow a bit, nor show anything of all we did for it; then there was a good year, and it made up for lost time. This is just my little 'rooting season,' mother; but don't go and believe my day is over, because it hasn't begun! The old maple by the well that's in its hundredth year had new leaves this summer, so there must be hope for me at seventeen!"

"You can put a brave face on it," sobbed Aurelia, "but you can't deceive me. You've lost your place; you'll never see your friends here, and you're nothing but a drudge!"

"I look like a drudge," said Rebecca mysteriously, with laughing eyes, "but I really am a princess. You mustn't tell, but this is only a disguise; I wear it for reasons of state. The king and queen who are at present occupying my throne are very old and tottering, and are going to abdicate shortly in my favor. It's rather a small kingdom, I suppose, as kingdoms go, so there isn't much struggle for it in royal circles; and you mustn't expect to see a golden throne set with jewels. It will probably be only of ivory, with a nice screen of peacock feathers for a background. But you shall have a comfortable chair very near it, with quantities of slaves to do what they call in novels your 'lightest bidding.'"

Aurelia smiled in spite of herself, and though not perhaps wholly deceived, she was comforted.

"I only hope you won't have to wait too long for your thrones and your kingdoms, Rebecca," she said, "and that I shall have a sight of them before I die. But life looks very hard and rough to me, what with your Aunt Miranda a cripple at the brick house, me another here at the farm, you tied hand and foot, first with one and then with the other, to say nothing of Jenny and Fanny and Mark. You've got something of your father's happy disposition, or it would weigh on you as it does on me."

"Why, mother," cried Rebecca, clasping her knees with her hands — "why, mother, it's enough joy just to be here in the world on a day like this — to have the chance of seeing, feeling, doing, becoming! When you were seventeen, mother, wasn't it good just to be alive? You haven't forgotten?"

"No," said Aurelia, "but I wasn't so much alive as you are, never in the world."

"I often think," Rebecca continued, walking to the window and looking out at the trees — "I often think how dreadful it would be if I were not here at all. If Hannah had come, and then, instead of me, John; John and Jenny and Fanny and the others, but no Rebecca — never any Rebecca! To be alive makes up for everything. There ought to be fears in my heart, but there aren't; something stronger sweeps them out – something like a wind. Oh, see! there is Will driving up the lane, mother, and he ought to have a letter from the brick house."

CHAPTER THIRTY

GOOD-BYE, SUNNYBROOK!

~

Will Melville drove up to the window, and, tossing a letter into Rebecca's lap, went off to the barn on an errand.

"Sister's no worse, then" sighed Aurelia gratefully, "or Jane would have telegraphed. See what she says."

Rebecca opened the envelope, and read in one flash of an eye the whole brief page:

"Your Aunt Miranda passed away an hour ago. Come at once if your mother is out of danger. I shall not have the funeral till you are here. She died very suddenly and without any pain. Oh, Rebecca, I long for you so!

"Aunt Jane."

The force of habit was too strong: and even in the hour of death Jane had remembered that a telegram was twenty-five cents, and that Aurelia would have to pay half a dollar for its delivery.

Rebecca burst into a passion of tears as she cried: "Poor, poor Aunt Miranda! She is gone without taking a bit of comfort in life, and I couldn't say good-bye to her! Poor lonely Aunt Jane! What can I do, mother? I feel torn in two between you and the brick house."

"You must go this very instant," said Aurelia, starting from her pillows. "If I was to die while you were away, I would say the very same thing. Your aunts have done everything in the world for you — more than I've ever been able to do — and it is your turn to pay back some o' their kindness and show your gratitude. The doctor says I've turned the corner, and I feel I have. Jenny can make out somehow, if Hannah 'll come over once a day."

"But, mother, I can't go! Who'll turn you in bed?" exclaimed Rebecca, walking the floor and wringing her hands distractedly.

"It don't make any difference if I don't get turned," replied Aurelia stoically. "If a woman of my age and the mother of a family hasn't got sense enough not to slip off haymows, she'd ought to suffer. Go put on your black dress and pack your bag. I'd give a good deal if I was able to go to my sister's funeral, and prove that I've forgotten and forgiven all she said when I was married. Her acts were softer 'n her words, Mirandy's were, and she's made up to you for all she ever sinned against me 'n' your father. And oh, Rebecca!" she continued with quivering voice, "I remember so well when we were little girls together, and she took such pride in curling my hair; and another time, when we were grown up, she lent me her best blue muslin. It was when your father had asked me to lead the grand march with him at the Christmas dance; and I found out afterwards she thought he'd intended to ask her."

Here Aurelia broke down and wept bitterly, for the recollection of the past had softened her heart, and brought the comforting tears even more effectually than the news of her sister's death.

There was only an hour for preparation. Will would drive Rebecca to Temperance and send Jenny back from school. He volunteered also to engage a woman to sleep at the farm in case Mrs. Randall should be worse at any time in the night.

Rebecca flew down over the hill to get a last pail of spring water; and as she lifted the bucket from the crystal depths, and looked out over the glowing beauty of the autumn landscape, she saw a company of surveyors with their instruments making calculations, and laying lines that apparently crossed Sunnybrook at the favourite spot where Mirror Pool lay clear and placid, the yellow leaves on its surface no yellower than its sparkling sands.

She caught her breath. "The time has come," she thought. "I am saying good-bye to Sunnybrook, and the golden gates that almost swung together that last day in Wareham will close for ever now. Good-bye, dear brook and hills and meadows; you are going to see life, too, so we must be hopeful, and say to one another:

"Grow old along with me;
The best is yet to be."

Will Melville had seen the surveyors too, and had heard in the Temperance post-office that morning the probable sum that Mrs. Randall would receive from the railway company. He was in good spirits at his own improved prospects, for his farm was so placed that its value could be only increased by the new road; he was also relieved in mind that his wife's family would no longer be in dire poverty directly at his doorstep, so to speak. John could now be hurried forward, and forced into the position of head of the family several years sooner than had been anticipated, so Hannah's husband was obliged to exercise great self-control, or he would have whistled while he was driving Rebecca to the Temperance station. He could not understand her sad face or the tears that rolled silently down her cheeks from time to time, for Hannah had always represented her aunt Miranda as an irascible, parsimonious old woman, who would be no loss to the world whenever she should elect to disappear from it.

"Cheer up, Becky!" he said, as he left her at the depot. "You'll find your mother sitting up when you come back; and the next thing you know the whole family 'll be moving to some nice little house wherever your work is. Things will never be so bad again as they have been this last year; that's what Hannah and I think." And he drove away to tell his wife the news.

Adam Ladd was in the station and came up to Rebecca instantly, as she entered the door looking very unlike her bright self.

"The Princess is sad this morning," he said, taking her hand. "Aladdin must rub the magic lamp; then the slave will appear, and these tears be dried in a trice."

He spoke lightly, for he thought her trouble was something connected with affairs at Sunnybrook, and that he could soon bring the smiles by telling her that the farm was sold and that her mother was to receive a handsome price in return. He meant to remind her, too, that though she must leave the home of her youth, it was too remote a place to be a proper dwelling either for herself or for her lonely mother and the three younger children. He could hear her say, as plainly as if it were yesterday, "I don't think one ever forgets the spot where one lived as a child." He could see the quaint little figure sitting on the piazza at North Riverboro and watch it disappear in the lilac-bushes when he gave the memorable order for three hundred cakes of Rose-Red and Snow-White soap.

A word or two soon told him that her grief was of another sort, and her mood was so absent, so sensitive and tearful, that he could only assure her of his sympathy and beg that he might come soon to the brick house to see with his own eyes how she was faring.

Adam thought, when he had put her on the train and taken his leave, that Rebecca was, in her sad dignity and gravity, more beautiful than he had ever seen her — all-beautiful and all-womanly. But in that moment's speech with her he had looked into her eyes, and they were still those of a child; there was no knowledge of the world in their shining depths, no experience of men or women, no passion nor comprehension of it. He turned from the little country station to walk in the woods by the wayside until his own train should be leaving, and from time to time he threw himself under a tree to think and dream and look at the glory of the foliage. He had brought a new copy of "The Arabian Nights" for Rebecca, wishing to replace the well-worn old one that had been the delight of her girlhood; but meeting her at such an inauspicious time, he had absently carried it away with him. He turned the pages idly until he came to the story of "Aladdin and the Wonderful Lamp," and presently, in spite of his thirty-four years, the old tale held him spell-bound as it did in the days when he first read it as a boy. But there were cerain paragraphs that especially caught his eye and arrested his attention, paragraphs that he read and reread, finding in them he knew not what secret delight and significance. These were the quaintly-turned phrases describing the effect on the once poor Aladdin of his wonderful riches, and those descanting upon the beauty and charm of the Sultan's daughter, the Princess Badroulboudour:

Not only those who knew Aladdin when he played in the streets like a vagabond did not know him again; those who had seen him but a little while before hardly knew him, so much were his features altered; such were the effects of the lamp, as to procure by degrees to those who possessed it perfections agreeable to the rank the right use of it advanced them to.

The Princess was the most beautiful brunette in the world; her eyes were large, lively, and sparkling; her looks sweet and modest; her nose was of a just proportion and without a fault; her mouth small, her lips of a vermilion red, and charmingly agreeable symmetry; in a word, all the features of her face were perfectly regular. It is not, therefore, surprising that Aladdin, who had never seen, and was a stranger to, so many charms, was dazzled. With all these perfections the Princess had so delicate a shape, so majestic an air, that the sight of her was sufficient to inspire respect.

"Adorable Princess," said Aladdin to her, accosting her, and saluting her respectfully, "if I have the misfortune to have displeased you by my boldness in aspiring to the possession of so lovely a creature, I must tell you that you ought to blame your bright eyes and charms, not me."

"Prince," answered the Princess, "it is enough for me to have seen you, to tell you that I obey without reluctance."

CHAPTER THIRTY-ONE

AUNT MIRANDA'S APOLOGY

~

When Rebecca alighted from the train at Maplewood and hurried to the post-office where the stage was standing, what was her joy to see uncle Jerry Cobb holding the horses' heads!

"The reg'lar driver's sick," he explained, "and when they sent for me, thinks I to myself, my drivin' days is over; but Rebecky won't let the grass grow under her feet when she gits her Aunt Jane's letter, and like as not I'll ketch her to-day; or, if she gits delayed, to-morrow for certain. So here I be jest as I was more 'n six years ago. Will you be a real lady passenger, or will ye sit up in front with me?"

Emotions of various sorts were all struggling together in the old man's face, and the two or three bystanders were astounded when they saw the handsome, stately girl fling herself on Mr. Cobb's dusty shoulder crying like a child. "Oh, Uncle Jerry!" she sobbed – "dear Uncle Jerry! It's all so long ago, and so much has happened, and we've grown so old, and so much is going to happen, that I'm fairly frightened."

"There, there, lovey!" the old man whispered comfortably; "we'll be all alone on the stage, and we'll talk things over 's we go along the road, an' mebbe they won't look so bad."

Every mile of the way was as familiar to Rebecca as to Uncle Jerry; every watering-trough, grindstone, red barn, weather-vane, duck-pond, and sandy brook. And all the time she was looking backward to the day, seemingly so long ago, when she sat on the box-seat for the first time, her legs dangling in the air, too short to reach the footboard. She could smell the big bouquet of lilacs, see the pink-flounced parasol, feel the stiffness of the starched buff calico and the hated prick of the black and yellow porcupine quills.

The drive was taken almost in silence, but it was a sweet, comforting silence to both Uncle Jerry and the girl.

Then came the sight of Abijah Flagg shelling beans in the barn, and then the Perkins' attic windows with a white cloth fluttering from them. She could spell Emma Jane's loving thought and welcome in that little waving flag – a word and a message sent to her just at the first moment when Riverboro chimneys rose into view – something to warm her heart till they could meet.

The brick house came next, looking just as of yore, though it seemed to Rebecca as if death should have cast some mysterious spell over it. There were the rolling meadows, the stately elms, all yellow and brown now; the glowing maples, the garden-beds bright with asters, and the hollyhocks rising tall against the parlour window; only in place of the cheerful pinks and reds of the nodding stalks, with their gay rosettes of bloom, was a crape scarf holding the blinds together, and another on the sitting-room side, and another on the brass knocker of the brown-painted door.

"Stop, Uncle Jerry! Don't turn in at the side. Hand me my satchel, please. Drop me in the road, and let me run up the path by myself; then drive away quickly."

At the noise and rumble of the approaching stage the house door opened from within just as Rebecca closed the gate behind her. Aunt Jane came down the stone steps, a changed woman, frail and broken and white. Rebecca held out her arms, and the old aunt crept into them feebly, as she did on that day when she opened the grave of her buried love and showed the dead face, just for an instant, to a child. Warmth and strength and life flowed into the aged frame from the young one.

"Rebecca," she said, raising her head, "before you go in to look at her, do you feel any bitterness over anything she ever said to you?"

Rebecca's eyes blazed reproach, almost anger, as she said chokingly: "Oh, Aunt Jane! could you believe it of me? I am going in with a heart brimful of gratitude!"

"She was a good woman, Rebecca; she had a quick temper and a sharp tongue, but she wanted to do right, and she did it as near as she could. She never said so, but I'm sure she was sorry for every hard word she spoke to you; she didn't take 'em back in life, but she acted so 't you'd know her feeling when she was gone."

"I told her before I left that she'd been the making of me, just as mother says," sobbed Rebecca.

"She wasn't that," said Jane. "God made you in the first place, and you've done considerable yourself to help Him along; but she gave you the wherewithal to work with, and that ain't to be despised, specially when anybody gives up her own luxuries and pleasures to do it. Now let me tell you something, Rebecca. Your aunt Mirandy's willed all this to you – the brick house and buildings and furniture, and the land all round the house, as far 's you can see."

Rebecca threw off her hat and put her hand to her heart, as she always did in moments of intense excitement. After a moment's silence she said: "Let me go in alone; I want to talk to her; I want to thank her; I feel as if I could make her hear and feel and understand!"

Jane went back into the kitchen to the inexorable tasks that death has no power, even for a day, to blot from existence. He can stalk through dwelling after dwelling, leaving despair and desolation behind him, but the table must be laid, the dishes washed, the beds made, by somebody.

Ten minutes later Rebecca came out from the Great Presence looking white and spent, but chastened and glorified. She sat in the quiet doorway, shaded from the little Riverboro world by the overhanging elms. A wide sense of thankfulness and peace possessed her, as she looked at the autumn landscape, listened to the rumble of a waggon on the bridge, and heard the call of the river as it dashed to the sea. She put up her hand softly and touched first the shining brass knocker and then the red bricks, glowing in the October sun.

It was home: her roof, her garden, her green acres, her dear trees; it was shelter for the little family at Sunnybrook; her mother would have once more the companionship of her sister and the friends of her girlhood; the children would have teachers and playmates.

And she? Her own future was close-folded still — folded and hidden in beautiful mists; but she leaned her head against the sun-warmed door, and closing her eyes, whispered, just as if she had been a child saying her prayers: "God bless Aunt Miranda! God bless the brick house that was! God bless the brick house that is to be!"

Classic Library Titles

Alice's Adventures in Wonderland
Through the Looking-Glass
by Lewis Carroll
Illustrated by John Tenniel

Black Beauty
by Anna Sewell
Illustrated by Cecil Aldin and Glenn Steward
Rebecca of Sunnybrook Farm
by Kate Douglas Wiggin
Illustrated by Glenn Steward

Little Women
Little Men
by Louisa May Alcott
Illustrated by Clara M. Burd

The Secret Garden
by Frances Hodgson Burnett
Illustrated by Jan Burridge
A Little Princess
by Frances Hodgson Burnett
Illustrated by Louise Hill

The Water Babies
by Charles Kingsley
Illustrated by Jessie Willcox Smith
Peter Pan
by J.M. Barrie
Illustrated by Mabel Lucie Attwell

Treasure Island
by R.L. Stevenson
Illustrated by Eleanor Plaisted Abbott and Wal Paget
Kidnapped
by R.L. Stevenson
Illustrated by David Price

Pride and Prejudice
Sense and Sensibility
by Jane Austen
Illustrated

Andersen's Fairy Tales
by Hans Christian Andersen
Illustrated by E.H. Wehnert and W. Thomas
Grimm's Folk Tales
by The Brothers Grimm
Illustrated by E.H. Wehnert